John Conroy Hutcheson

Crown and Anchor

John Conroy Hutcheson

Crown and Anchor

ISBN/EAN: 9783337267728

Printed in Europe, USA, Canada, Australia, Japan

Cover: Foto ©Andreas Hilbeck / pixelio.de

More available books at **www.hansebooks.com**

CROWN AND ANCHOR

OR

Under the Pen'ant

BY

JOHN C. HUTCHESON

AUTHOR OF 'THE WRECK OF THE NANCY BELL,' ETC., ETC., ETC.

ILLUSTRATED BY JOHN B. GREENE

LONDON

F. V. WHITE & CO.

14 BEDFORD STREET, STRAND, W.C.

1896

CONTENTS

vi

CONTENTS

 CONTENTS

CHAPTER XXVIII

ILLUSTRATIONS

CROWN AND ANCHOR

Upright and Downright.   P 65.

J.B.GREENE

"Not d'id at all."

"Caged Birds."

" Harmony in the Gunroom."

Crown and Anchor

AN OLD SEA-LION

'HULLO, Dad!' I cried out, stopping abruptly in front of the red granite coloured Reform Club, down the marble steps of which a queer-looking old gentleman was slowly descending. 'Who is that funny old fellow there? He's just like that "old clo'" man we saw at the corner of the street this morning, only that he hasn't got three hats on, one on top of another, the same as the other chap had!'

We were walking along Pall Mall on our way from Piccadilly to Whitehall, where my father intended calling in at the Admiralty to put in a sort of official appearance on his return to England after a long period of foreign service ; and Dad was taking advantage of the opportunity to show me a few of the sights of London that came within our ken, everything being strange to me, for I had never set foot in the metropolis before the previous evening, when mother and I had come up by a late train from the little Hampshire village where we lived, to meet father on his arrival and welcome him home.

Under these circumstances, therefore, as might

reasonably have been expected, our halts had been already frequent and oft to satisfy the cravings of my wondering fancy ; and Dad must have been tired of answering my innumerable questions and inquiries ere half our journey had been accomplished.

He was very good-tempered and obliging, however, and bore with me patiently, giving me all the information in his power concerning the various persons and objects that attracted my attention, and never 'turning nasty' at my insatiable curiosity.

So now, as heretofore, obedient to my bidding, he turned to look in the direction to which I pointed.

'Where's your friend, the funny old fellow you spoke of, my boy?' he said kindly, though half-quizzingly. 'I don't see him, Jack.'

'Why, there he is, right opposite to us, Dad!' I exclaimed. 'He's coming down the steps from that doorway there, and is quite close to us now!'

'Oh! that's your friend, Jack, eh?' said father, glancing in his turn at the old gentleman who had caught my eye. 'Let me see if I can make him out for you.'

The old fellow was not one whom an ordinary observer would style a grand personage, or think worthy of notice in any way, very probably; and yet, there was something about him which irresistibly attracted my attention making me wonder who he was and want to know all about him. Boy though I was, and new to London and London life, I was certain, I'm sure I can't tell why, that he must be 'somebody.'

A short broad-shouldered man was he, with iron-grey hair, and a very prominent nose that was too strongly curved to be called aquiline, and which, with his angular face, equally tanned to a brick-dust hue from exposure to wind and weather, gave him a sort of eagle-like look, an impression that was supported

by his erect bearing and air of command; albeit,
sixty odd years or more must have rolled over his
head, and his great width of chest, as he moved
downwards throwing out his long arms, made his
thick-set figure seem stumpier than it actually was,
though, like most sailors of the old school, there was
no denying the fact, as Dad said subsequently, that
he was 'broad in the beam and Dutch built over
all!'

Nature had, undoubtedly, done much for the old
gentleman, but art little, so far as his personal appearance was concerned; for nothing could have
been more quaint and out of keeping with Pall Mall
and its fashionable surroundings than his eccentric
costume.

The upper part of his person was habited in a
rough shooting-jacket, considerably the worse for
wear, such as a farmer or gamekeeper might have
donned in the country, away from the busy haunts
of men, when out in the coverts or engaged thinning
the preserves; while his lower extremities rejoiced in
a yet shabbier pair of trousers, whose shortness for
their wearer did not tend to enhance their artistic
effect.

To complete the picture, his bushy head of iron-
grey hair was surmounted by an old beaver hat that
had once been white, but which inexorable Time
had mellowed in tone, and whose nap, having been
brushed up the wrong way, against the grain, frizzed
out around its circumference like a furze bush, making it resemble the 'fretful porcupine' spoken of by the
immortal Shakespeare.

His whole appearance was altogether unique for a
West-end thoroughfare in the height of the season;
and, the more especially, too, at that time of day, when
dandies of the first water were sauntering listlessly
along the shady side of the pavement ogling the

gorgeously - attired ladies who rolled by in their stately barouches drawn by prancing horses that must have cost fortunes, and on whose boxes sat stately coachmen and immaculate footmen clad in liveries beyond price, ' Solomon in all his glory ' not approaching their radiant magnficence !

Emerging as he did, however, from the Reform Club, the old gentleman's inconventional ' rig-out ' bore testimony to the incontrovertible fact that, no matter how ' advanced ' his principles may have become from the teachings of Cobden, and the example of Peel, he had not allowed his political convictions to revolutionise his original ideas on the subject of dress.

Nor was this the only peculiarity noticeable about the queer-looking old fellow.

He was coming down the steps of the club-house, while Dad and I looked at him, so slowly that his dilatory rate of progression conveyed the impression that he was either a martyr to corns or suffering from a recent attack of the gout ; feeling his way carefully with one foot first before bringing along its fellow, prior to adventuring the next step, just as my baby sister, a little toddlekin of six, used to go up and downstairs.

This, of course, was not so remarkable in itself, but as he descended thus, crab-fashion, to the level of the pavement where Dad and I stood observing him, my eyes grew wide with wonder at the enormous handfuls of snuff he took—not pinches, such as I had seen snuff-takers sniff up from the backs of their hands many a time before, without bestowing a thought on the action.

Oh, no, nothing of the sort !

They were actual handfuls that he extracted from his waistcoat pocket, as I could not help noticing, on account of his roomy shooting-jacket being wide open and thrown back ; the old prodigal scooping up the fragrant dust in his palm, and then doubling his fist and shoving it up his nostrils with a violent snort of inhalement, after which he proceeded to blow his red nose with another loud report, like that of a blunderbuss going off. This was accompanied by the flourish of a brightly coloured pocket-handkerchief, whose vivid hue approximated closely to the general tint of his cheeks and eagle-like beak, and which he held loosely, ready for action, in his disengaged left hand; for, his right was ever at work oscillating between the magazine of snuff in his deep waistcoat pocket and the nasal promontory that consumed it with almost rhythmical regularity, sniff and snort and resonant trumpet blast of satisfaction succeeding each other in systematic sequence, as the veteran came down the stairway leisurely, step by step.

It all appeared to me very comical; but, I did not laugh at the old man as another youngster might very pardonably have done, without any thought of mocking or making fun of him.

To tell the truth, he seemed to me to be so out of place there that I was actually pained on his account, believing, in my innocent ignorance, that he had unhappily made a mistake in going up to the members' entrance of the grand-looking club-house; and that the fat hall porter in scarlet, who now stood without the swinging glass doors of the portal, had warned him thence, ordering him, so it struck my fancy, to go down below by way of the area steps, to the basement of the establishment, where his business would probably rather lie with the lower menials of the mansion than with such an august personage as he, one who acted solely as the janitor to the great ones of the earth possessing the password of the club!

Yes, this was the thought uppermost in my mind; and, as the queer-looking old gentleman continued to hobble downwards I began to wonder whether the

scullions in the kitchen, whom I could dimly discern
beneath the street level and behind a screen of iron
railings, would not, likewise, turn up their noses at the
sight of such a seedy individual, telling him they had
no rags or bones or bottles for him to-day.

'Poor old fellow!' I said to Dad, uttering my
reflections aloud. 'What could have made him act so
foolishly as to go up there only to be turned away by
that bumptious porter? How very shabby he is,
Dad; and with such a noble face, too! May I give
him that shilling you made me a present of this
morning to buy himself some more snuff? He must
have exhausted all he had in his waistcoat pocket by
now; he does use it so extravagantly!'

'Hush, Jack, he may hear you!' whispered my
father, dropping his voice to a lower key than mine,
while the amused expression on his face changed
to one of pleased recognition. 'Why, it's the old
Admiral! I see he's as great a snuff-taker as ever,
and he seems to be even less careful than he used to
be about his clothes; though, I must say, he never
was a dandy at the best of times!'

At the moment Dad spoke, the old gentleman set
his right foot gingerly on the pavement in front of us,
his left following a second later, when the veteran
signalised his reaching a sound anchorage with a final
blast from his nasal trumpet and a fine flourish of his
bandana, which nearly knocked out my nearest eye
and set me sneezing from the loose particles of snuff
disseminated into the surrounding air.

This gave my father the opportunity he wanted.

'How do you do, Admiral?' said he, drawing himself up and raising his hat in salute, while still holding
me by the hand. 'I don't know if you remember me,
sir, but I cannot forget you and your kindness to me
of old, especially in getting me my last appointment.
I'm glad to see you looking so well, sir!'

The old fellow stared at Dad with his gimlet grey eyes, looking him through and through, knitting his brows, and sniffing and snorting at a fine rate.

'Eh—what, who the deuce are you?' he ejaculated in short, jerky accents after a pause, evidently puzzled for the nonce, and, in his agitation, another fistful of snuff got arrested half-way between his waistcoat pocket and expectant nose, the consequence of which was that more than half was spilt on the front of his shirt, and already snuff-stained coat collar. 'Eh, what? I think I know your face, but I'm hanged if I can recollect your name, sir!'

Dad smiled, and, whether this supplied a missing link to memory's aid or no, the next instant a gleam of intelligence flashed across the veteran's weather-beaten face making him look so animated that he seemed a different person.

Shoving out his horny fist, forgetful of the balance of snuff contained therein, and thus causing me to sneeze again, as well as nearly blinding me for a second time, the rough old sailor caught hold of my father's disengaged hand with a grip of iron, shouting a welcome in his hearty, loud voice which could have been heard across Pall Mall; for it was as breezy as the sea, echoing in ringing accents whose cordial tones I can almost fancy I now hear, like the surf of breakers breaking in the distance on some rock-bound shore.

'Bless my soul, Vernon! Is that you, my lad, hey?' he roared out, making a dandified exquisite, who was just then lounging past us, jump into the gutter and soil his polished patent leathers in nervous alarm. 'Glad to see me, you said? Stuff and nonsense, you rascal—you're not half so pleased as I am to clap my eyes on you again! Gad, you young scamp, why, it seems only the other day when I sent you to the mast-head, you remember, when you were a middy with me in the *Neptune?*   It was for cutting off the tail of my dog Ponto, and you said—though that was all moonshine, of course—you did it to cure him of fits!   By George! what a terrible young scapegrace you were, to be sure, Vernon, always in mischief from sunrise to gunfire, and always at loggerheads with my first-lieutenant and the master, poor old Cosine!'

CHAPTER II

THE ADMIRAL SPEAKS HIS MIND

I HAD been fidgeting all the time the old gentleman was speaking, squeezing Dad's hand in order to attract his attention and make him tell me who his old friend was; but, for the moment, he was too much taken up with the veteran's hearty greeting to give ear to me.

At last, however, in response to another squeeze of my hand, he bent down towards me, expecting, no doubt, some such inquiry.

'Who is it, Dad?' I whispered, dying with curiosity. 'Who is it?'

'Admiral Sir Charles Napier, Jack,' he replied, under his breath, 'late commander-in-chief of the Baltic Fleet.'

I doffed my cap at once, for I had often heard my father mention the name of the gallant old sailor before, though I hardly expected to see him in such a guise.

'Hullo, who've we got here?' cried the Admiral, noticing my action and patting my head in recognition of the salute with his snuffy palm. 'Your son, Vernon, eh?'

'Yes, Admiral,' said Dad, 'this is my boy, Jack.'

'Ha! humph! He's a smart - looking youngster, Vernon, and the very image of what you were at his age! How old is he?'

'Nearly fourteen now, sir,' answered my father. 'I'm afraid, though, Master Jack is rather a small boy for his years, being short and thick set.'

'Not a serious fault that, Vernon. He'll be able to go aloft more nimbly than any of those lamp-post sort of chaps with long legs, who always trip themselves up in the ratlines. Look at me, youngster, I'm not a big man, and yet I've not been the worse sailor on that account, I think!'

'True, Sir Charles,' replied Dad with a sly twinkle in his eye, 'but we're not all of the same tough stock and "ready — aye, ready" on all occasions when wanted, though we might be willing enough, to do our duty.'

'Gammon, Vernon, none of your blarney!' growled out the old sea-lion, pretending to be angry, albeit he looked pleased at Dad's covert allusion to the Napier motto, which he had always endeavoured to act up to. 'I'm sick of false compliments, old shipmate. I've had plenty of them and to spare from those mealy-mouthed, false-hearted, longshore lubbers in there!'

'What!' exclaimed my father, as the Admiral jerked his head with an expression of contempt in the direction of the club-house he had just left—'you don't mean to say, sir—'

'Ay! but I do mean to say they're a lot of confounded hypocrites, by George!' roared out the old sailor, his face flushing to almost a purple hue, while he snatched at another handful of snuff from his waistcoat pocket, and sniffed and snorted like a grampus. 'Why, you'll hardly believe it, Vernon! But, only a couple of years ago, when I was starting for the Baltic, and in high favour with the ministry, cnose miserable time-servers in there gave a public dinner in my honour in that very club; and now, by George! because things did not go all right, and I wasn't able to smash up the Russian fleet as everybody expected I would do, and so I would have done, too, by George! if I'd been allowed my own way, the mean-spirited parasites almost cut me to a man—to a man, by George!'

'It's a rascally shame, sir,' said my father, getting hot with righteous indignation in sympathy at this scurvy treatment of one whom he had served under, and looked upon as an honoured chief; while I felt so angry myself, that I should have liked to have gone up the steps of the club-house there and then, and dragged down from his proud post the fat, red-liveried porter who was looking down on the veteran from the top of the stairway, regarding that pampered menial as the cause and occasion of the slight of which he complained. 'Never mind, though, Admiral! you can well afford to treat their mean conduct with the contempt it deserves; for everybody whose opinion is worth anything knows that Sir Charles Napier won his laurels as a brave and skilful commander long before the Reform Club was founded or the Crimean war thought of. Believe me, sir, history will yet do you justice.'

'Ay! when I've gone to my last muster,' growled out the old fellow huskily, in a sad tone, which sent a responsive chill to my heart. 'But, that won't be your fault, Vernon. Thank you, my lad, I know you're not talking soft solder, so as to get to wind-'ard of me, like those fellows in there. Longshore lubbers like those never recollect what a man may have done for his country in times gone by. They live only in the present; and, if a chap chances to make a mistake, as the best of us will sometimes, they fall on him like a pack of curs on a rat, and worry him to death, by George!'

'The idle gossip of the clubs need not affect you, sir,' replied my father consolingly. 'Not a man in

England of any sense is ignorant of the fact that it is none of your fault that the Baltic Fleet was sent out on a wild-goose chase and failed to capture Cronstadt and annihilate the Russian ships inside that stronghold ; though, I believe, you would have astonished old Nick if you had been allowed a free hand !'

'Humph ! I don't know about that, Vernon, but I'd have tried to,' said the Admiral, smiling. The next minute, however, he knit his shaggy eyebrows and looked so fierce that the thought occurred to me that I would not have liked just then to be in the position of defaulter brought up before him on his quarter-deck and awaiting condign punishment ; for, he went on growling away angrily, as the recollections of the past surged up in his mind. 'By George ! it makes my blood boil, Vernon, as I think of it now. How could I succeed out there when those nincompoops at home in the Ministry did not want me to do anything but play their miserable shilly-shally game of drifting with the tide and doing nothing ! I was told I wasn't to do this and I wasn't to do that, while all the time that cute old fox the Czar Nicholas was completing his preparations. Why, would you believe it, Vernon, there wasn't a single long-winded despatch sent out to me by the Cabinet that did not countermand the one that came before?'

Dad laughed cheerily, trying to make the old sailor forget his wrongs.

'Even the immortal Nelson would have been unable to do anything under such conditions, Sir Charles,' he said, as the Admiral paused to take breath, sniffing up another handful of snuff with an angry snort. 'Those jacks in office at home are always interfering with things they know nothing about. How can they possibly have the means at their command like the man on the scene of action, one whom they themselves have selected for his supposed capacity? But, they will interfere, sir. They have always done so; and always will, I suppose!'

'Gad, you put it better than I could, Vernon. I didn't think you such a smart sea lawyer,' said the old Admiral, rather grimly, not overpleased, I think, at Dad's taking up the burthen of his grievances. 'Know nothing, you say? Of course they know nothing, the government, hang it! was a cabinet of nincompoops, I tell you—Aberdeen, Graham and the whole lot of 'em! If they could have mustered a single statesman amongst 'em who had pluck enough to tell Russia at the outset that if she laid hands on Turkey we should have considered it an ultimatum, there would never have been any war at all—the Emperor Nicholas confessed as much on his death-bed. It was all want of backbone that did it—not of the English nation, thank God! but of the government or ministry of the time. Some governments we've had, ay, and since then, too, Vernon, have been the curse of our country!'

'Ay, Admiral,' responded my father, heartily, 'I know that well!'

'Yes, they were all shilly-shally from first to last,' continued the old sailor, warming up to his theme. 'Why, when the Russians actually fired on our flag— the Union Jack of England, sir, that had never previously been insulted with impunity—they actually blamed me for returning the fire, and recalled me for it! I tell you what it is, Vernon, they were all a pack of pusilanimous time-servers, frightened at their own shadows; and, between you and me and the bedpost, that chap, Jimmy Graham, our precious late First Lord of the Admiralty, knew as much about a ship as a Tom cat does of logarithms, by George!'

Dad smiled at his vehemence, and I chuckled audibly; the Admiral's simile seeming very funny to me.

The old sailor patted me on the head approvingly.

'Ay, you may well laugh, youngster,' said he, looking very fierce with his knitted eyebrows, though speaking to me good-naturedly enough. 'The whole business would make a cat laugh were it not so humiliating, by George! But, avast there! let us drop it; for we've had enough of it by now and to spare. Things, though, were very different, Vernon, when you and I sailed together. I tell you what it is, my lad, the service is going to the devil, that's what it is!'

'By Jove! your right, sir, I quite agree with you there,' chorused Dad with much effusion, speaking evidently from the bottom of his heart. 'Everything is changed, Admiral, to what we were accustomed to in the good old times when I had the luck to serve under you; and, I'm afraid, sir, we'll never see such times again. There's no chance for a poor fellow like me nowadays at the Admiralty as I know to my cost! No one has an opening given him unless he's acquainted with some bigwig with a handle to his name, or knows the Secretary's niece, or the chief messenger's aunt. Otherwise, he may as well whistle for the moon as ask for a ship!'

'That's true enough, Vernon, by George!' said the Admiral, with equal heat. 'Interest with the Board is everything in these times, and personal merit nothing! You may be the smartest sailor that ever trod a quarter-deck and they will look askance at you at Whitehall; but, only get some Lord Tom Noddy to back up your claims on an ungrateful country or show those Admiralty chaps that you know a Member of Parliament or two, and can control a division in the House of Commons, then, by George! it is wonderful, Vernon, how suddenly the great Mister Secretary of the Board will recognise your previously unknown abilities and other good qualities to which he has hitherto been blind, and how anxious the

First Lord will be to promote you—eh, Vernon, you rascal? Ho! ho! ho!'

Dad joined in the hearty roar of laughter, with which the Admiral ended his sarcastic comments, the recital of which had apparently eased his mind and banished the last lingering recollections of the ill-treatment he had received at the hands of the government; for the old sailor now dismissed the subject, going on to talk about old shipmates and other matters as they sauntered onwards along Pall Mall, the Admiral hobbling on one side of Dad and I on the other, holding his hand, listening eagerly all the while to their animated conversation and taking in every word of it. I confess, however, I could not understand all their allusions to old times and byegone events afloat and ashore, many of the names and incidents mentioned in their talk being altogether unfamiliar to my ears.

'Where are you off to now, Vernon?' inquired Admiral Napier, stopping to take snuff again when we arrived at the last lamp-post at the corner abutting on Waterloo Place. 'If you're not otherwise engaged, come back with me and have lunch at the club, you and the youngster.'

'Thank you very much, Admiral,' returned Dad, 'I would be only to glad, but, to tell the truth, I'm bound for the Admiralty.'

'Ah! you want to see Mister Secretary just after he has finished *his* lunch!' said the knowing old fellow, giving Dad a dig in the ribs. 'Sly dog! I suppose you think you'll have a better chance of working to win'ard of him then?'

'That's it, Admiral,' said my father, laughing. 'There's no good in a fellow trying to bamboozle you, sir.'

'No, by George!' chuckled the old fellow, mightily pleased at this tribute to his 'cuteness,' 'you'd have

to get up precious early in the morning to take me
in as you know from old experience of me, Vernon !
But, what the deuce are you going to Whitehall to
kick your heels there for? They'll only keep you
waiting an hour in that infernal waiting-room, and
then tell you the Secretary's gone for the day, or some
other bouncer, just to get rid of you. I know their
dirty tricks—hang 'em ! What d'you want, eh ? '

'Well, sir, I thought I might get something in one
of the dockyards,' answered Dad, frankly. 'I heard
last night of there being an appointment vacant at
Devonport, and I was going to apply for it.'

'Any interest, eh ? '

'Not a scrap, Admiral,' replied my father. 'All my
friends are dead or out of favour with the powers
that be, I'm afraid now.'

'Then you might as well apply for a piece of the
moon,' said the Admiral in his curt, dogmatic way ;
'and if that's all, Vernon, that is taking you to
Whitehall, you had far better save your shoe leather
and come back with me to the club.'

'Thank you very much, Admiral, but I must really
say "no" again,' rejoined Dad, touched by his kindly
pertinacity. 'I confess, sir, though, that the object
of my journey to the Admiralty is not altogether on
my own account personally, for I wished to introduce
this youngster of mine here to the Secretary, and
thought it a good thing to kill the two birds with one
stone.'

'Humph !' growled the old Admiral. 'D'you think
he never saw a boy before, eh, Vernon? I'm sure
there's a lump too many of the young rascals knocking about already ! '

Dad smiled at the quizzical look and sly wink
with which this inquiry was accompanied, the Admiral
twisting his head on one side as he spoke and looking
just like a crested cockatoo !

' No, Sir Charles, not exactly,' he replied, putting his arm round my neck caressingly. ' However, for all that, even so great a man as Mr Secretary might not know as good a boy as my son, Jack, here !'

I tell you what, I did feel proud when Dad said that, though I could not help flushing up like a girl, and had to hold down my head to hide it.

' Yes, yes, quite right, Vernon, quite right, the sentiment does you honour, and him. I'm sure, though, I meant no offence to the little chap,' said the rough, old sea-dog hastily, afraid of having hurt our feelings. ' But, all the same, I don't see what you want to show him to that Jack-in-office for ? By George, the sight of his ugly phiz can't do any good to the youngster !'

' No, sir, possibly not, though I'm told he isn't such a bad-looking fellow,' answered Dad, laughing again at the Admiral's determination to get to the bottom of the matter. ' The truth, sir, is I want to get this youngster nominated for a naval cadetship before he oversteps the age limit. The boy is dying to follow in my footsteps ; but, though I have tried to dissuade him from it as much as I can, and the idea of his going to sea makes his poor mother shudder, still, seeing that he seems bent upon it, neither she nor I wish to thwart his inclination.

' Whee-ugh !' whistled the other through his teeth as he proceeded to take three or four enormous pinches of snuff in rapid succession from his waistcoat pocket and losing half of each pinch ere it reached his nose, the Admiral generously scattering it over the lapels of his coat and shirt front on the way. ' Why the deuce didn't you tell me all that before, my dear Vernon, instead of backing and filling like a Dutch galliot beating to win'ard ?'

' I—I—' hesitated my father, who had refrained from telling him before because he hated asking a favour of anyone whom he regarded in the light of a friend. 'I—I—didn't like to trouble you, sir.'

'Bosh, Vernon! You know well enough it's never a trouble to me to do anything for an old shipmate,' said the old fellow, heartily, and, putting his hand on my shoulder, he wheeled me round so as to look me in the face as I lifted up my head and gazed at him admiringly on his addressing me directly, 'so, my young shaver, you want to be a sailor, eh?'

'Yes, sir,' I replied, 'I love the sea, and I wouldn't be anything else for the world!'

'Ha, humph!' growled the veteran, who, I believe, was as fond of his profession at heart, in spite of his grumbles, as anyone who ever went afloat. 'You'd better be a tinker or a tailor, my boy, than go to sea! It's a bad trade nowadays! What put it into your head, eh?'

'It comes naturally to him,' said Dad, seeing me puzzled how to answer the question. 'I suppose it must run in the blood, sir.'

'Humph, like my gout!' jerked out Sir Charles, sharply, as if he just then felt a twinge of his old complaint, and, turning to me again, he asked as abruptly, 'D'ye think you can pass for cadet, youngster—know your three R's—readin', 'ritin' and 'rithmetic, eh?'

'Yes, sir, I think so,' said I grinning, having heard this old joke before from Dad many a time, 'I shall try my best, sir. I can't say more than that, sir, can I?'

'No, by George, no, youngster, that answer shows me, my boy, that you are your father's son!' cried the Admiral heartily, clapping me on the back as if I were a man, and making me sneeze with the loose snuff which he shook off from his coat as he did so. 'I said you were a chip of the old block the moment I first clapped eyes on you, and now I'm certain of it! Vernon, you shall have a nomination for the youngster. I think I've got sufficient interest at the Admiralty left to promise you that, at all events!'

'Oh, thank you, Admiral,' replied Dad, while I looked my gratitude, not being able to speak, 'thank you for your great kindness to me and the boy.'

'Pooh, pooh, stuff and nonsense, my lad! It's little enough to do for an old shipmate and brother officer,' muttered the good-hearted old fellow, quite overcome with confusion at our thanks, as Dad wrung one of his hands and I caught hold of the other. 'I've got an appointment to meet the First Lord this very afternoon, as luck would have it, so I'll mention the matter to him, and I've no doubt the youngster'll get his nomination in a day or two, at the outside. By-the-bye where are you stopping in London? You haven't told me that yet.'

My father, thereupon, gave him our address.

'All right, Vernon,' said the veteran, shoving Dad's card along with the snuff in his waistcoat pocket, 'I'll see to the matter without fail. Good-bye, now, Vernon, good-bye, young shaver, I hope you'll make as good a sailor and smart an officer as your father before you!'

With these parting words and a kindly nod to me the old Admiral toddled off across Waterloo Place to the Senior United Service Club opposite, to which, I presume, he intended transferring his patronage now that the Reform had given him the cold shoulder, while Dad and I returned to our temporary lodgings in Piccadilly to tell mother of our unexpected meeting and its happy result. I may here add that I was never fortunate enough to see the gallant old veteran again, though I heard of him often afterwards from my father, who told me he always asked how I was getting on. Circumstances prevented my meeting him when I was yet in England, and I was out in

China when he died, some four years subsequently to my making his acquaintance in Pall Mall that morning.

Strange to say, however, the other day, when engaged planning out this very yarn of my adventures afloat, I chanced to see an advertisement in one of the Portsmouth papers of an auction about to be held at Merchiston Hall, near Horndean, where I was informed the Admiral had resided for many years, and where he spent most of his time farming when not at sea, before he got mixed up in politics and Parliamentary matters, as he was in his later days after he was 'put on the shelf,' and hauled down his flag for aye!

Here, the very bed was pointed out to me in which the gallant old sailor died; a plain, old-fashioned piece of furniture, without any gilding or meretricious adornment, and honest and substantial like himself.

The house, too, was similarly unpretentious, being a low, one - storied, verandah - fronted structure, with plenty of room about it, but little 'style' or ornament. It was, though, picturesquely situated in the centre of a well-timbered little park and homestead and snugly sheltered by tall fir trees and a thick shrubbery from all north'ard and easterly winds, amid the prettiest scenery of Hampshire—wooded heights and pleasant dales, with coppice and hedgerow, and here and there a red-roofed old farmhouse peeping out from the greenery forming its immediate surroundings.

'Poor old Charley Napier!' as he was affectionately entitled by those who served under his flag—officers and men alike, the latter especially almost idolising him for he was ever a good friend to them.

He now sleeps his last sleep in the churchyard of Catherington, where he lies safe at anchor, hard by the dwelling where he lived when in the flesh.

Here his tomb may be seen by the curious under

the shelter of the early Norman church, dedicated to St Catherine, from which circumstance the village takes its name.

It is a fine old building, this church, dating back to the time of the Crusades, when heroes as gallant as Admiral Sir Charles Napier besieged Sidon and captured Acre—like as he himself did some eight centuries later, long prior to his unsuccessful mission to the Baltic, the somewhat inglorious termination of which, unfortunately, clouded his naval reputation and ended his career afloat !

CHAPTER III

I GET NOMINATED FOR A NAVAL CADETSHIP

'"Sharp's the word and quick the motion," eh, Jack?' said my father, using his favourite phrase, when the post next morning brought him a letter from the Admiralty in an oblong blue envelope, inscribed 'On Her Majesty's Service,' in big letters, stating that I had been nominated to a cadetship in the Royal Navy. 'I knew old Charley would be as good as his word!'

'Hurrah!' I shouted, throwing my cap in the air, and forgetting all about a long-promised visit to the Zoological Gardens for which we were just starting. 'Now I shall be able to go to sea at last!'

Dad seemed to share my enthusiasm; but my mother, I recollect well, ay, as if it had occurred but yesterday, put her arms round me and cried as if her heart would break.

Presently, when she had somewhat regained her composure, Dad, comforting her with the assurance that she was not going to lose me all at once, it not being probable that I would be drowned or slain or otherwise immolated on the altar of my country immediately on entering the navy, which appeared to be her first conviction, we all began talking the matter over; and then Dad proceeded to read over again the official communication he had received, commenting on the same as he went over it.

'Hullo, Jack!' he observed, on reaching the end

of the formal document, 'those red-tape chaps a'
Whitehall haven't given you much time to prepare
for your examination!'

The mention of this damped my ardour a bit, I can
tell you!

'Oh, I quite forgot that!' I exclaimed lugubriously.
'When have I got to go up for exam., Dad?'

'The "first Wednesday in August," my boy—so
says this letter at all events.'

'Good gracious me!' ejaculated my mother, again
breaking into our conversation after a brief pause,
during which she must have gone through an abstract
mental calculation. 'Why, that will be barely a month
from now, my dear!'

'Precisely, this being the third of July,' replied Dad
drily. 'So Master Jack will have to stir his stumps
if he hopes to pass, for I'm afraid he's rather shaky in
his Euclid.'

'Dear, dear!' said mother, throwing up her arms
in consternation, 'he is very backward in his history,
too! Would you believe it, he couldn't recollect when
Magna Charta was signed on my asking him the date
yesterday.'

'Really?' cried Dad, leaning back in his chair, and
bursting into a hearty laugh at my mother's serious
face, 'I'm sure, my dear, I could not tell you the
date off-hand myself at the present moment, not if
I were even going to be hanged in default! Jack
knows, though, I'd wager, when the glorious battle
of Trafalgar was fought; and that concerns a British
sailor boy more, I think, than any other event in the
whole history of our plucky little island, save perhaps
the defeat of the grand Armada. What say you,
my boy?'

'Of course, I know the date of the battle of
Trafalgar, Dad,' I answered glibly enough, having
heard it mentioned too often to have forgotten it in

a hurry; and, besides, I knew Southey's *Life of Nelson* almost by heart, it being one of my favourite books and ranking in my estimation next to *Robinson Crusoe*. 'It was fought, Dad, on the 21st October 1805.'

'There, mother, just hear that!' cried Dad, chaffingly. 'Are you not proud of your boy in blue? By Jove, he'll set the Thames on fire if he goes on at that rate!'

'I *am* proud of him; but I do not wish him to fail,' replied mother, who took things generally *au serieux*; and, turning to me, she said in her earnest way,— 'Dear Jack, I'm afraid you are too confident and do not attend to your lessons now as you used to do. Pray, work hard, my dear boy, for my sake!'

'I will, mother dear, I promise you that,' said I, kissing her. 'I won't get plucked if I can help it.'

'That's right, my brave boy, you cannot say more than that,' chimed in Dad, with a pat of approval on my head, as my mother drew me towards her in mute caress. 'By the way, I tell you what I'll do, Jack. I was asking my old friend Captain Gifford the other day about a good naval tutor for you, and you shall have the assistance of the same "crammer" he had for his boys if I can get hold of him.'

Prior to the year 1858, I may here explain, on a youngster being nominated to a naval cadetship he was appointed to a sea-going ship at once, going afloat there and then without any preliminary examination and the roundabout routine subsequently enjoined, wisely or not, by 'My Lords' when the 'competition wallah' system came in vogue. Unwittingly I was, thus, one of the first to suffer from the change, the order for cadets having to pass in certain specified subjects on board the *Excellent* before receiving their appointments having been issued within a comparatively recent period of my getting my nomination.

This proviso, too, I may add, was saddled with the condition that all cadets in future would have to go through a probationary period of three months' instruction in seamanship in a training-ship, which was set apart for the purpose ere they were supposed to have officially joined 'the service,' and become liable to be sent to sea.

These regulations, to make an end of my explanations, continue in force to the present day with very little alteration, the only difference, so far as I can learn, being that youngsters now have to pass a slightly 'stiffer' examination than I did on entry, and that they have to remain for two years on probation aboard the *Britannia* instead of the three months period which was esteemed sufficient for the 'sucking Nelsons' of my time in the old *Illustrious*. She was the predecessor of the more modern training-ship for naval cadets, which turns them out now *au fin de siècle*, all ready-made, full-blown officers, so to speak; though it is questionable whether they are any the better sailors than Nelson himself, Collingwood amongst the older sea captains, or Hornby and Tryon of a later day. None of these went through a like course of study, and yet they knew how to handle ships and manœuvre fleets without any such " great advantages " of training !

My moral reflections, though, have little to do with my story, to which I will now return.

The date of the examination being so perilously near, and my studies having become somewhat neglected during the long holiday I had spent in sight-seeing in London, my father thought the surer way to secure my passing would be, as he had said, to procure the aid of a good tutor who might peradventure succeed in tuning me up to concert pitch in the short interval allowed me by the patent process of 'cramming,' which had come into fashion with the competition craze, more speedily than by any ordinary mode of imparting instruction.

So, in accordance with his promise, Dad called on his friend Captain Gifford the same afternoon in quest of the experienced 'coach' or coachman, whom that gentleman had previously recommended, warranted to possess the ability to drive knowledge into my head at a sufficient rate to ensure my 'weathering,' the examiners when I went before them ; and, ere the close of this memorable week in which I was introduced to Admiral Sir Charles Napier and got my nomination, I was in as high a state of 'cram' as any Strasbourg goose destined to contribute his quota to a *paté* of fat livers.

'Dear, dear, my poor boy!' as mother said to me, 'what a lot you have to learn, to be sure!'

My mother was right you will say when you hear all. I was 'a poor boy,' indeed, and no mistake.

Latin, French, Arithmetic and Algebra, not forgetting my old enemy Euclid and his compromising propositions, with a synopsis of English History, and the physical and political geography of the globe, besides a lot of lesser 'ologies,' of no interest to anyone save my coach and myself, but all of which were included in the list of subjects laid down by the Admiralty as incumbent for every would-be naval cadet to acquire, were forced into my unfortunate cranium day and night without the slightest cessation.

The only let off I had were a few hours allowed me for sleep and refreshment, my hard task-master, the aforesaid coach, an old Cambridge wrangler, never giving me a moment's respite, insisting, on the contrary, that he would give *me* up instead altogether if I once stopped work!

For the time being I lived in a world of facts and figures, breathing nothing but dates and exuding mathematical and other data at almost every pore ;

so that, by the end of the month I felt myself trans-formed into a sort of portable human cyclopædia, containing a heterogeneous mass of information of all kinds, as superficial as it was varied.

The knowledge I acquired in this way, however, was only skin deep, so to to speak, exemplifying the truth of the old adage 'lightly come, lightly go'; for albeit this hot-bed process of imparting learning served its turn in enabling me to pass the crucial ordeal to which I was subjected, I verily believe that I could not have answered satisfactorily one tithe of the questions a fortnight after the dreaded examination was over that I then grappled successfully.

But this is anticipating matters.

Hot July sweltered to its close ere my tutor was satisfied with the progress I had made under his care and declared me fit for the fray.

This was on the very last day of the month, and on the following Tuesday, the 3rd of August, I remember, for it was the very day before the fateful Wednesday fixed for examination on board the *Excellent*, my mother, in company with Dad and myself, bade adieu to the sultry metropolis, of whose stagnant air and blistering pavements, and red-baked bricks and mortar we were all three heartily tired, journey-ing down to Portsmouth by some out-of-the-way route, all round the south coast, past Brighton and Worthing and Shoreham, which I never afterwards essayed.

Since then, though I have travelled, more often than I care to count now, from London to the famous old seaport which is veritably the nursery of our navy, and whence the immortal Nelson sailed, ninety odd years ago, to thrash the combined French and Spanish fleets at Trafalgar and establish England's supremacy afloat while ridding the world of the tyranny of Napoleon Buonaparte, not a single incident connected with my first trip thither has escaped my memory.

Yes, I recollect every detail of the journey, from the time of our leaving Waterloo station to our arrival at the terminus at Landport, just without the old fortifications that shut in Portsea and the dockyard, with all its belongings, within a rampart of greenery. The noble elms on the summit of the glacis, are now, alas! all cut down and demolished, but they once afforded a shady walk for miles, making the dirty moats and squalid houses in their rear, which are now also numbered, more happily, amongst the things of the past, look positively picturesque.

I could not forget anything that happened that day; for, then it was that I saw that dear old sea again which I had loved from the time my baby eyes first gazed on it, and which I had not now seen for months.

On reaching 'ye ancient and loyale toune,' as Portsmouth was quaintly designated by Queen Bess of virginal memory on the occasion of her visiting the place, our little party, I can well call to mind, put up at the 'Keppel's Head' on the Hard.

This was a hostelry which Dad had been accustomed to patronise when at the naval college in the dockyard learning all about the new principle of steam just then introduced into the service before I was 'thought of,' as he said, and, no doubt, the place is as well known to young fellows and old 'under the pennant' in these prosaic days of 'floating flat-irons and gimcrack fighting machines,' as the 'Fountain Inn' in High Street and the 'Blue Posts' at Point were to Peter Simple and Mr Midshipman Easy in the early part of the century, when, to quote dear old Dad again, 'a ship was a ship, and sailors were seamen and not all stokers and engineers!'

There was no harbour station then, as now,

fronting and affronting Hardway ; no trace of the hideous railway viaduct shutting out all the fore-shore, both of which at present exist in all their respective native uglinesses !

No ; for the upper windows of the old hotel commanded a splendid view of the whole of the harbour and the roadstead of Spithead beyond, and I seem to see myself a boy again that August afternoon, looking out over the picturesque scene in glad surprise.

After our early dinner, Dad pointed out to me the various objects of interest ; the old *Victory*, flagship then as she is now again after an interval of thirty years or more, during which time she was supplanted by the *Duke of Wellington*, which she has in time supplanted once more ; the *Illustrious*, the training-ship for naval cadets, near the mouth of the harbour, where the *St Vincent* is now moored ; and the long line of battered old hulks stretching away in the distance up the stream to Fareham Creek, the last examples extant of those ' wooden walls of old England ' which Dibdin sang and British sailors manned and fought for and defended to the death, sacrificing their lives for ' the honour of the flag ! '

Yes, I remember the name of every ship that Dad then pointed out to me. I can picture, too, the whole scene, with the tide at the flood and the sunshine shimmering on the water and the old *Victory* belching out a salute in sharp, rasping reports from the guns of her main-deck battery, that darted out their fiery tongues, each in the midst of a round puff ball of smoke in quick succession, first on the port and then on the starboard side, until the proper number of rounds had been fired and a proportionate expenditure of powder effected to satisfy the requirements of naval etiquette for the occasion, when the saluting ceased, as suddenly as it began.

The afternoon wore on apace after this, the sun sinking in the west over Gosport, beyond Priddy's Hard, amid a wealth of crimson and gold that nearly stretched up to the zenith, lighting up the spars of the ships and making their hulls glow again with a ruddy radiance while touching up the brass-work and metal about them with sparks of flame.

Still, I did not tire of standing there at the window of the old 'Keppel's Head,' looking out on the harbour in front, with the wherries plying to and fro and men-of-war's boats going off at intervals with belated officers to their respective ships.

Until, by-and-by the Warner lightship, afar out at sea beyond Spithead, and the Nab light beyond her again, could be seen twinkling in the distance, while the moon presently rose in the eastern sky right over Fort Cumberland ; and then, all at once, there was a sudden flash, which, coming right in front of me, dazzled my eyes like lightning.

This was followed by a single but very startling 'Bang!' that thundered out from the flagship, which, swinging round with the outgoing ebb tide, was now lying almost athwart stream, with her high, square stern gallery overhanging the sloping shore below the hotel, looking as if the old craft had taken the ground and fired the gun that had startled us as a signal of distress—so, at least, with the vivid imagination of boyhood, thought I !

'Goodness gracious me !' exclaimed my mother, almost jumping out of her chair at the unexpected report and making me jump, too, by her hurried movement towards the window where I stood, 'what is the matter, Jack ?'

'Nothing to be alarmed about, my dear,' said Dad soothingly to her. 'It is only the admiral tumbled down the hatchway.'

'Dear, dear,' replied poor mother in a voice full of

the deepest sympathy, 'I hope the old gentleman has not hurt himself much. He must have fallen rather heavily!'

Dad roared with laughter at her innocent mistake.

'You'll kill me some day, I think, my dear,' said he when he was able to speak, after having his laugh out. 'I only used an old nautical expression which you must have heard before, I'm sure. We always say that on board ship when the nine-o'clock gun is fired!'

'Oh!' rejoined mother, a little bit crossly at being made fun of. 'I do wish, Frank, you would explain what you mean next time beforehand, instead of puzzling people with your old sailor talk, which nobody can understand!'

'Humph!' said Dad; but, presently, I saw mother put out her hand and tenderly touch him on the shoulder, as if to tell him that her temporary tiff had been dispelled, like the smoke from the discharge of the *Victory's* last gun, whereat I could hear him whisper under his breath as he kissed her cheek softly, 'All's well that ends well, my dear!'

CHAPTER IV

DOWN AT PORTSMOUTH

NEXT morning, ere I seemed to have been asleep five minutes, it came upon my dreams so suddenly, I was awakened by a terrible din of drumming and bugling from the adjacent barracks close to the line of fortifications which at that time enclosed Portsmouth—but whose moats and ramparts were pulled to pieces, as I have already said, some few years ago to make room for the officers' and men's recreation grounds and gymnasium, with other modern improvements.

Then, I could hear the heavy tramp of men marching, followed by the hoarse sound of words of command in the distance, ' Halt! Front! Dress!'

I assure you, I really thought for the moment that the long-talked-of French invasion, about which I had been recently reading in my historical researches, had actually come at last and that the garrison had been hurriedly called to arms to resist some unexpected attack on the town.

This reminiscence of my cramming experiences, mixed up in hotch-potch fashion with the martial echoes that caught my ear from the banging drum and brazen bugle, at once recalled the gruesome fact that this was the eventful day fixed for my examination on board the *Excellent ;* so, dreading lest I should be late, I incontinently jumped out of bed in a jiffy, proceeding; albeit unconsciously, to obey the last gruff order of the sergeant of the guard, relieving the sentries.

This, as Dad subsequently explained, was the reason for all the commotion, the sergeant parading his men as he came up to each 'post' in turn, with the usual stereotyped formula, 'Halt! Front! Dress!'

Dear me! I did 'dress;' though in rather a different sense to that implied by the sergeant's mandate, huddling on my clothes in my haste so carelessly that I broke the button off my shirt collar and put on my jacket the wrong way!

All my hurry, too, was to very little purpose; for, when I reached the coffee-room of the hotel below, after getting confused and losing my proper course amongst the many intricate passages and curving corkscrew staircases that led downwards from the little dormitory I had occupied right under the tiles at the back of the building, I found that neither Dad nor mother had yet put in an appearance for breakfast.

I was in such good time, indeed, that old St Thomas's clock in High Street was only just chiming Eight; while the ships' bells over the water were repeating the same piece of information in various tones and the shrill steam whistle from the dockyard workshops hard by screeching its confirmation of the story.

There was no fear of my being late, therefore; so, consoling myself with this satisfactory reflection, I was making my way to the nearest window of the coffee-room to look out on the harbour beyond as I had done the evening before when, like as then, a big bouncing 'Bang!' came from the *Victory*, making me jump back and feel almost as nervous as poor mother was on the previous occasion.

'Yezsir, court-martial gun, sir, aboard the flagship, sir,' said the wiry little cock-eyed head waiter, who was hopping about the room 'like a parched pea on a griddle,' as dad expressed it, stopping to flick the dust from the mantelpiece with his napkin as he replied to the mute inquiry he could read in my glance. 'Look, sir! They've h'isted the Jack at the peak, sir, yezsir.'

'Oh, yes, I see,' said I, as if I had not observed this before and was perfectly familiar with the signal. 'I did not notice it at first.'

'No, sir? W'y, in course not, sir, or else ye'd ha' known wot it were,' answered the sly old fellow, ascribing to me a knowledge of naval matters which he knew as well as myself I did not possess, thus pandering, with the ulterior view, no doubt, of a sub-stantial tip, to a common weakness of human nature to which most of us, man and boy alike, are prone—that of wishing to appear wiser than we really are!

'But, as I was a-saying only last night to Jim Marksby, the hall-porter, sir,' he continued, 'court-martials, sir, isn't wot they used to was. Lordsakes! sir, I remembers, as if it were yesterday, in old Sir Titus Fitzblazes's time, sir, when they was as plentiful as the blackberries on Browndown!

'W'y, sir, b'lieve me or not if yer likes, but there wasn't a mornin'—barring Sundays in course—as yer wouldn't hear that theer blessed gun a-firin' for a court-martial, sir, jest the same as ye heerd jest now, sir, yezsir! Ah, them was fine times, they was, for the water-men on Hardway; for they usest to make a rare harvest a-taking off witnesses and prisoners' "friends," as they calls 'em, and lawyers and noospaper chaps to the flag-ship, they did. The old chaps called the signal gun "old Fitzblazes's Eight o'clock Gun," sir. They did so, sir, yezsir!'

'Indeed, waiter?' said I, feeling quite proud of his thus speaking to me as if I were a grown-up person. 'But who was this gentleman, old Fitz—what did you call him?'

'Old Sir Titus Fitblazes, sir,' glibly replied the coffee-room factotum, flicking off a fly as he spoke from the table-cloth whereon he had just arranged all the paraphernalia of our breakfast. 'Lordsakes, sir, yer doesn't mean for to say, sir, as a well-growed young gen'leman like yerself, sir, as is a naval gent, sir, as I can see with arf an eye, haven't heard tell o' he? Well, sir, he were port admiral here, sir, a matter of eight or ten year ago, sir, yezsir; and, wot's more, sir, he were the tautest old sea porkypine ye'd fetch across "in a blue moon," as sailor folk say!

'Yezsir, I've heerd when he were commodore on the West Coast, he used for to turn up the hands every mornin' regular and give 'em four dozen apiece for breakfast, sir!'

'Good gracious me, waiter!' I exclaimed, aghast at this statement. 'Four dozen lashes?'

'Yezsir. Lor'! four dozen lashings was nothink to old Sir Titus, for he were pertickeler partial to floggin', he were, and took it out of the men like steam, he did!

'The ossifers, in course, he couldn't sarve out in the same way, not being allowed for to do so by the laws of the service, sir; but he'd court-martial 'em, sir, as many on 'em as would give him arf a chance, and the court-martial gun used for to fire in his time here as reg'lar as clock-work every mornin' at eight, winter and summer alike, jest the same as when the flag's h'isted at sunrise, yezsir!'

'What an old martinet he must have been!' I said in response to this. 'Perhaps, though, the poor old admiral suffered from bad health, and that made him cross and easily put out?'

'Bad health, sir? Not a bit of it!' exclaimed my friend, the waiter, repudiating such an excuse with scorn. 'It were bad temper as were *his* complaint.

'Lordsakes, though, sir, he were bad all over, was Sir Titus; ay, that he were, from the crown of his head to the sole of his foot. As bad as they makes 'em!

' W'y, he 'ad the temper, sir, of old Nick hisself, ay, that he had!

' I don't mean the Czar of Roosia, sir. Don't you run away with that there notion! No, sir, I means the rale old gent as ye've heerd tell on, wot hangs out down below when he's at home and allers dresses in black to look genteel-like. Wears topboots for to hide his cloven feet, sir, and carries a fine tail under his arm with a fluke at the end of it, same as that on a sheet anchor—ah, yer knows the gent I means, sir!

' Well, yezsir, old Sir Titus wer him all over and must ha' been his twin-brother; barring the tail, the admiral being shaky about the feet, too, and his boots a'most as big as the dinghy of that sloop. They wos like as two peas, sir, old Nick and he!

' Lordsakes, though, yer must have heerd tell of him, sir, a young and gallant naval ossifer like yerself, 'specially that yarn consarnin' him and the washer-woman as was going into the dockyard one mornin' when he were a-spyin' round the gates?'

' No, waiter, I never heard the old gentleman's name before you told it me,' I replied, curious to learn some further disclosures concerning so celebrated a character. ' What was this story?'

' W'y, sir, it's enuff a'most for to make a cat laugh, sir,' he said with a snigger, which he immediately flicked away, as it were, with his napkin, resuming his whilom solemn demeanour. ' It happen'd, if yer must know, sir, in this way, sir, yezsir.

' Old Blazes—that wer the name he allers went by in the yard—was a-hangin' round the main gate a-lookin' out for to see who comes along, w'en all of a sudding he spies this good woman as was a-takin' in the clothes from the wash for Admirality House.

' That were where, yer knows, sir, he himself lived with Lady Fitz, close by the College and jest to the right as yer goes in the yard?

'Lordsakes, sir! The old admiral thinks he'd made a fine haul and that the woman were a-smuggling in sperrits or somethin' "contraband," as they calls it, for the sailors who is allers stationed round the commander-in-chief's office; and so, he orders her for to turn out her big baskets there in the gateway afore all the grinning policemen and men who was jest a-comin' into the yard.

'Ye never see such a show, sir in all yer born days ; and the beauty on it were that as he was in the middle of it sir, overhaulin' all the things from the wash, and a-pokin' 'em about with his gold-headed stick and turnin' over the ladies' fal-de-rals and all sorts of women's gear that they don't like men for to see, sir, up comes Lady Fitzblazes herself, a-going out for a walk.

'Seein' what he were after, she axes him wot he means by treating her clothes like that there.

'Lordsakes, sir, if he were old Nick, she had a temper, too, and were as fiery as a she-tiger cat, she were ; and, wot between the two, there was then— Breakfast, sir? Yezsir, comin', sir!'

The wiry little cock-eyed waiter rushed off, with his napkin over his shoulder, as he uttered the last words ; and, wondering what had caused him to break off so unexpectedly in the middle of his yarn, apparently just when he was approaching the most interesting part of it, I turned my head and saw mother and Dad were within the coffee-room, having entered the doorway just behind me.

'Hullo, Jack !' said my father, 'what was that waiter chap yarning about? You seemed very much taken up with what he was saying.'

I thereupon told him as much as I had heard of the old port admiral.

'Pooh, nonsense, the rascal has only been "pulling your leg" with a cock-and-a-bull story, Jack,' said dad in a contemptuous tone when I had finished— for he was an officer of the old school and always believed in the obligations of discipline, invariably "sticking up" for those superior to him in rank in the service—' I knew old Admiral Fitzblazes myself very well, and a better officer and gentleman never wore the Queen's uniform!'

While he was speaking to this effect, the 'cock-eyed rascal,' as Dad called him, came in with our breakfast, giving me a sly wink with his sound eye behind Dad's back as he passed him; so, sitting down, we hurried through the meal without any further conversation, I feeling more and more nervous the nearer the hour fixed for the examination approached, and mother and Dad both keeping silent, in sympathy with me.

Breakfast accomplished, Dad accompanied me to the dockyard, and saw me off to the *Excellent;* where, on getting on board, with my certificate of birth and moral character in my pocket and my heart in my mouth, I was ushered into the wardroom, with some twenty other aspirants for naval honours like myself.

All of us, of course, were mostly of the same age, but, naturally, of various builds and size; some tall, some short; some thin, some fat; some ugly, some handsome.

One little chap whom I noticed was much smaller than I was, although Dad had expressly drawn Admiral Napier's attention to the fact of my being rather short for my age.

This youngster had a bright merry face and smiled in a friendly way to me; but the others looked at me generally as a collection of strange dogs appear to regard any new comer suddenly brought amongst them, eyeing and sniffing him suspiciously before they can make up their minds whether to treat him as friend or foe—though, generally, preferring, as a rule, the latter footing!

On entering the wardroom, which had a sort of

scholastic look mingled with its ordinary nautical surroundings, we were summoned in turn to the further end of the apartment.

Here, on a raised portion of the deck abutting on the stern gallery, three gentlemen in clerical garb were seated behind a semi-circular green baize table, in front of which we stood, respectively, like so many prisoners on trial, while answering various questions appertaining to our Christian and surnames, age and so on.

We also handed in at the same time our baptismal and medical and character certificates, all of which were duly inspected, docketed and filed, in regular official style.

These preliminaries gone through, we were then directed to take our seats on either side of a long table that ran fore and aft the cabin, whose normal purpose was for the messing of the officers of the ship, but which on the present occasion was supplied with folios of foolscap paper and bundles of quill pens and bottles of ink, systematically distributed along its length, instead of the more palatable viands it more generally and generously displayed.

We were immediately under the eyes of the senior chaplain of the trio forming the board of examiners, a gentleman whose position at the centre of the cross table at the top of the room enabled him to command a full view of the double line of boys and detect at once any attempt at cribbing or unfair assistance given by one to the other ; and our ordeal began punctually on the ship's bell striking Ten o'clock, dictation being the first subject set us ' to test our spelling and handwriting,' as my Lords of the Admiralty were good enough to inform us.

Thanks to my mother's persistency in keeping me up to the mark with regard to my lessons, long before I had recourse to the crammer, this introductory stage of the examination presented no difficulties to me ;

and I was able not only to keep pace with the gentleman who dictated a portion of one of Macaulay's Essays to us, but also found time to look round me occasionally to see how my companions fared with the big words, the faces of some of them presenting quite a study when a portentous polysyllable was given them to spell.

The little chap with the curly hair who had smiled at me on coming in, I observed, did not smile now.

His whilom merry countenance, on the contrary, was all puckered up in the most comical way; while his brows were knit as he chewed the feather end of his quill pen trying to get inspiration from that source how to properly write some long word—I think it was ' Mesopotamia '!

Poor little fellow! he had a fearful struggle over it ; but, although I should have dearly liked to have helped him, it was against the rules, so I could only watch his growing despair with a mute sympathy that was mingled with amusement at the funny faces he made over the, to him, serious business.

A little later on, however, if this victim of the stiff dictation paper had looked at me when ruthless old Euclid, my former antagonist, came on the scene, he would in like fashion have pitied me ; for I was quite fogged by an easy proposition that I had thought I knew by heart the night before, but now found I had not the slightest glimmering of, although I answered most of the other questions.

Thus the examination proceeded, until the hour came for us to hand in our papers ; the lot of us then filing before the presiding genii seated behind the green baize table at the end of the wardroom, and each giving up his roll of spoilt foolscap in turn as he came up abreast of the reverend trio.

I was nearly the last of the file ; and, as I approached the table, the chaplain occupying the middle seat looked up.

He had a jolly, round, benevolent sort of face, which wore at the moment such a good-humoured expression that, I suppose, it became reflected on mine causing me to smile.

'Hullo, my boy!' said he, smiling, too. 'You seem in a very happy frame of mind, I'm sure. Answered all your questions right, eh?'

'I'm afraid not all, sir,' I replied diffidently; 'but I hope for the best.'

'That's right, youngster! There's no good to be got by despairing over things, and remember, you can have another try, you know, if you fail now,' said he encouragingly. '"Never say die," you know, as an old friend of mine used always to say, "care once killed a cat!"'

'Why, sir,' I exclaimed at this, 'that's what my father always tells me. It's his favourite expression when any difficulty arises. He never gives in, sir!'

'Indeed!' said the fat gentleman, while the others on either side of him looked interested. 'Who is your father, my boy, if you'll excuse my asking you the question?'

'Francis Vernon,' I answered promptly. 'A captain in the Royal Navy, now on half-pay, sir.'

The fat clergyman laughed at my laconic reply.

'Vernon, ha!' he repeated after me. 'I wonder if he is the Frank Vernon I once knew?'

'Can't say, sir,' said I, cautiously. 'My mother, though, always calls him "Frank."'

My new friend laughed again.

'Ah, I'm sure he is the same, if only from your manner, which is just like what I remember in the Frank Vernon who was in the *Pelican* with me,' said he, looking at me all over with his twinkling round eyes. 'Was your father ever up the Mediterranean with old Charley Napier, my boy?'

'Oh yes, sir,' I replied, glib enough now. 'It was

Admiral Napier who gave me my nomination the other day, sir.'

'Really, you don't say so?'

'I do, though, sir,' I said sturdily, thinking he doubted my assertion. 'Dad and I met him in Pall Mall, and I got my nomination from the Admiralty, sir, the very next morning as he promised!'

'All right, my boy, all right,' he observed in an absent way, turning to whisper to the two other gentlemen something, I think, about "old Charley," and "must be passed for my old shipmate's sake."— 'I quite believe what you say: I do not doubt your word for an instant; for Frank Vernon's son, I am sure, could not but always speak the truth. Did your father come down with you for your examination?'

'Yes, sir,' I answered. 'He and my mother came with me; and we're all staying at the old 'Keppel's Head Hotel,' on Hardway, sir.'

'Humph! I think I know the place you mention, youngster,' said he, with a significant twinkle in his eye which made the other two chaplains grin, I could see, at some joke they had between them. 'I'll try and call on your father, if I can find time before he leaves Portsmouth. Tell him when you get back, that old Tangent asked after him, please.'

'I'll make a point of doing so, sir,' I replied, with a bow, repeating the name after him to make certain. 'I will tell him, sir, about Old Tangent.'

'Old Tangent, indeed!' cried the old fellow, shaking his fat sides, while the other two examiners roared outright. 'You've a pretty good stock of impudence of your own, I'm sure! Be off with you, you young rascal, or I'll pluck you as certain as I'm that Old Tangent with whom you dare to be so familiar!'

His jovial face, however, belied the threat, so it did not occasion me any alarm; and, bowing again politely to the three clerical gentlemen collectively, I bent my steps, on the grin all the way, to the door of the wardroom, which was opened and shut behind me by a marine standing without.

I was Last of the Mohicans, all the other fellows having taken their departure and gone ashore long before I got my own happy dismissal.

'By Jove, Jack, I think you may put yourself down as passed!' said my father when I subsequently detailed the incidents of my examination, drawing a good augury from my description of what had occurred on board the gunnery ship. 'He was always a knowing hand was Old Tangent; and such a remark from him to his brother examiners, would be as efficacious as a whisper in ear of the First Lord's Secretary on your behalf, my boy!'

'Do you remember him, Frank? I mean the gentleman who spoke to Jack.'

'Oh, yes, my dear,' replied Dad to this question of my mother's, 'I recollect Old Tangent quite well. He was always a good-natured fellow and a capital shipmate. Why, he sang the best song of any of us in the mess on board the old *Pelican*.'

'What!' exclaimed my mother, holding up her hands in pious horror at the mention of such an unclerical characteristic. 'A clergyman sing songs?'

'Yes, why not?' retorted Dad, who was in his jolliest mood at the prospect of my having passed my examination successfully. 'They were spiritual songs of course, my dear, I assure you!'

'No doubt,' said mother, drily. 'I think, my dear, you can "tell that yarn to the marines," as you say in your favourite sea slang. *I* know what sort of spirits you refer to!'

At which observation they both laughed; and, naturally, I laughed too.

CHAPTER V

IN WHICH I REALLY 'JOIN THE SERVICE'

'LETTER for yer, sir, yezsir,' said my friend the cock-eyed waiter a week or two later, while we were at luncheon, bringing in a long, official-looking document on a salver, which he proceeded to hand me with a smirk and a squint from his cock-eye, that seemed to roam all over the apartment, taking in everything and everyone present in one comprehensive glance. 'It's jest come in, sir. It were brought by a messenger, sir, from the commander-in-chief's h'office, sir; and I thinks as 'ow it's a horder for yer sir, for to jine yer ship, sir, yezsir!'

'All right my man, that'll do,' interposed my father, who from his service-training had a rooted objection to anything approaching to familiarity from servants and other subordinates, besides which he particularly disliked the waiter's 'vulgar curiosity' as he styled it, saying he was always prying and poking his nose into other people's affairs; although, I honestly believe my worthy old cock-eyed friend only took a laudable interest in my welfare, as indeed he did in the business of everybody who patronised the hotel. 'You can leave the letter, waiter, and likewise the room!'

'For me?' said I, taking up the missive, which was inscribed on the outside in large printed characters 'on Her Majesty's Service,' similarly to the one which had brought my nomination from the Admiralty. 'I wonder Dad, what it contains! I suppose, it will tell whether I have passed my examination or not?'

'Open it, Jack,' said Dad, as soon as the waiter had left the room, flicking his napkin viciously over the sideboard which he passed on his way to the door as if he was considerably huffed at not being admitted to our confidence. Let us hear the news at once, good or bad. Suspense, you know, my boy, is worse than hanging.'

'No, I can't, Dad, I feel too nervous,' I replied, not laughing at his joke, as I might have done another time, although the pun was a regular old stager, passing the yet unopened letter across the table. 'You read it, mother, please.'

'You need not be alarmed Jack,' said she, smiling, and pointing to the superscription. 'See, the direction on it is to " John Vernon, Esquire, R. N."'

'Which means, Master Jack, that you have passed!' cried Dad, anticipating her explanation, and jumping up at once from his seat in great excitement, the contagion of which the next instant spread to me. 'You've passed, my boy, there's no doubt about that from this address; and, now, you really belong to Her Majesty's service, hurrah!'

Mother, though, did not say anything, and her hands trembled as she fumbled with the letter, trying to open the envelope without tearing it.

'My boy, my boy!' she exclaimed presently, her eyes filling with tears as she glanced at the contents of the enclosure, which she could only dimly see ; albeit, she learnt enough to know that I had passed for cadet and was directed to join the *Illustrious* training-ship, then stationed at Portsmouth, like as her successor the *Britannia* was for a long while prior to her removal to Dartmouth. 'It is as we thought, and as you hoped, Jack. You are going to have your wish at last and leave your father and me for your new home on the sea.'

The cock-eyed waiter broke the rather melancholy silence that ensued.

'Them's outfitters' cards, sir, yezsir,' he said, bringing

in his salver again presently, piled up with circulars and square pieces of pasteboard which he placed before Dad. 'Parties 'as heerd tell young gents 'as passed and wants fer to get the horder for his h'uniforms, sir, yezsir!'

Having thus eased his mind, my old friend bustled out of the room as quickly as he had entered, no doubt afraid of my father giving him another 'dressing-down.'

Dad, however, was not thinking of the waiter or his cheeky manner for the moment.

'By Jove, Jack!' he cried, 'you're getting quite an important personage. Why, we'll have all the trades-men of Portsea struggling for your lordly custom if we stop here much longer! Do they say anything about the boy's outfit in that letter, my dear?'

'Oh, yes,' replied my mother, taking up the missive, which she had dropped on her knee, and going on to read it over to herself again. 'There's a long list of things that he is ordered to get.'

'Then, the sooner we see about getting them the better,' said Dad, looking over the letter, too. 'We'll go round to Richardson's this afternoon if you like, my dear. I think he's the best man to rig out Jack, and, besides, I've had dealings with him before.'

'Very well, I'll go and put on my bonnet at once,' said mother, rising from the table as she spoke. 'You must tell the man, Frank, to have the poor boy's things ready as quickly as possible, for I must mark them all before he goes to sea. Ah! there'll be nobody to look after his clothes there!'

'No, my dear, no one but his messmates in the midshipmen's berth,' said Dad, jokingly, with a wink to me, wishing to get mother out of her sorrowful mood. '*They* will take precious good care of his wardrobe for him, I wager; that is, unless he keeps his weather eye open and a sharp look-out and never leaves his sea-chest unlocked. All the marking in the world won't save his gear if he does that, I can tell you and him!'

Mother was not to be put off her purpose, however, despite Dad's chaff.

So, when the outfitter sent home my elaborate kit, quite complete in every detail, within a couple of days after our visit to his shop, she carefully marked every article with my name in full, adding some numerical hieroglyph of her own that denoted how many of each description of garment I possessed.

Poor thing! She was firmly convinced in her innocent mind that I would be able to trace, by this means, anything missing from my stock of wearing apparel!

But, notwithstanding all her elaborate precautions, Dad proved a true prophet; for, on my return home from my first commission, I do not believe I had any two of a set out of the dozens of shirts and collars and handkerchiefs I was originally supplied with and which she had so neatly marked.

On the contrary, the scanty contents of my battered old donkey of a chest, whilom gorgeously painted in blue and gold, consisted but of a scant lot of half-worn-out items of clothing, not one of which matched the other, and the owners whereof, judging by the different inscribed initials thereon were as various as their respective conditions of wear!

On the same evening my things came from the out-fitter's, and even while my poor mother was engaged on the fruitless task she had imposed on herself of ensuring my continual possession, as she vainly thought of the same, I stole away from the dinner-table and retired for a brief space to the little bed-room I still occupied at the top of the hotel, with the way to and from which I was now better acquainted than on the morning after I first slept 'under the tiles.'

'Ain't we grand!' sang out Dad, chaffingly, when

I presently reappeared below in all the glory of my new uniform as a naval cadet.

This was the same then as now :—blue trousers and jacket with crown and anchor buttons and a cunningly-shaped little collar, that had a white facing to the lapel and the buttonholes of the turnback worked with twisted cord of the same colour in proper regulation fashion ; not to speak of my cap with its golden badge, and the formidable-looking carving-knife of a dirk, twenty inches long in its black scabbard, which I wore at my belt !

'Why, Master Jack, you'll be "topping the officer" over me now in your war paint,' added Dad, after turning me round twice to inspect me. 'You are rigged out smart, and no mistake !'

'Don't tease the poor boy, my dear,' said my mother, looking at me with fond admiration as most mothers would do, propably, under similiar circumstances. 'He looks very nice—very nice, indeed. I'm sure he is the very image of what you were when I first saw you, Frank !'

'Thanks, my dear, for the compliment,' replied Dad, bowing to her half-jocularly, half-seriously, while he heaved a deep sigh. 'I'm not making fun of Jack at all. I really was thinking how long ago it is since I donned the same uniform like him for the first time. Ah me, thirty years and more have passed since then ; and I'm an old fogey, while he's just beginning life ! I hope, my dear Jack, you'll never do anything to make you ashamed of having put on the Queen's livery !'

'That I won't, Dad,' said I emphatically ; and I meant it ! 'I'll try to follow your example, and always recollect I am your son.'

'You cannot do better, my dear Jack,' said mother, putting one of her arms round my neck caressingly, and stretching out her other hand to take Dad's. 'Your father was always known in the service as a gallant officer and an honourable gentleman ; and if you follow his example, my boy, you will neither disgrace the name you bear nor do discredit to Her Majesty's uniform ! I look forwards, Jack, to your being a credit, not only to us, but to your country and profession !'

I uttered no reply to my mother's little speech, though it made a deep impression on me, for she was seldom given to expressing herself at such length, her words being generally few and to the point ; but, I formed there and then a resolve, which I have endeavoured to adhere to all my life, that I would never do anything to make her ashamed of me, nor cause pain to her and Dad, the latter of whom remained silent like myself.

He was thinking, I felt sure, of the approaching parting between us, when I should be beyond his care and only have to trust to the training he had given me.

He knew, however, that I would still be under the watchful eye of another Father, who guards and guides the sailor afloat amidst the stormy waters of the deep as well as the landsman ashore, and whose love and forethought are more to be trusted even than that of our earthly parents, prize us as dearly as they will.

On the following morning, to make a long story short, I bade adieu to Dad and mother, both of them accompanying me to the landing steps at the foot of Hardway to see me off in the waterman's wherry that Dad hailed for the conveyance of myself and sea-chest to the *Illustrious.*

She was lying in the stream near the mouth of the harbour, as I mentioned I believe before when speaking of my first view of Portsmouth ; and as the tide was then at the ebb and running out fast, we were very soon alongside the training-ship, whose huge, black hull glistened in the bright sunshine.

There was a little chap standing by the marine sentry at the entry port on the main-deck, where I noticed as I went up the accommodation ladder a little chap only about my own age, but looking as 'cocksy' as you please.

He was dressed in a similarly smart new uniform to my own, and his face, somehow or other, seemed familiar to me. I could see, too, that he looked as if he recognised me in some sort of way, or was anxious to make my acquaintance.

'Hullo!' he cried, as I gained the deck and re-turned, with much conscious dignity, the marine's salute, 'why, you're the fellow who nearly got stranded in Euclid!'

This remark of his brought back to my mind in an instant the scene in the examination room on board the gunnery ship, and I identified him in an instant, giving him a 'Roland' for his 'Oliver.'

'Oh, you're the little chap who was so awfully stumped in spelling at dictation eh, old fellow?' I retorted, making the marine sentry grin as the ship's corporal on duty hailed my waterman to pull forward under the main yard for my chest to be hoisted inboard. 'How did you manage to scramble through, eh?'

'Only by the skin of my teeth,' he answered, smiling all over his face in such a good-humoured way that I could not help taking a liking to him. 'Just the same as you did, I suppose, Mr Sharp!'

'That isn't my name,' said I, laughing, 'but we won't quarrel about that. Let us make friends instead.'

'Agreed,' said he, laughing too. 'I liked the cut of your jib when I first saw you in that awful place the other day. I was so sorry I couldn't help you with your Euclid.'

'Really? Well, I was sorry I couldn't help you with your spelling, you looked so woe-begone over the big words,' I replied, giving him another dig for his unkind reminiscence of my old nightmare. 'I think it was "Mesopotamia" that finally finished you, wasn't it?'

'Pax!' cried he, beseechingly. 'You're a bit too sharp for me, I see, to try chaffing with. Let us be chums, as you suggest, old boy. My name is Tom Mills.'

'All right, old chap,' I rejoined, gripping the hand he stretched out to me as cordially as he had offered this gage of friendship. 'I am Jack Vernon. That's *my* name!'

'Well, Jack,' said he, addressing me as familiarly as if we had known each other for years. 'You seem a jolly sort of fellow, and I think I shall like you.'

'Ditto, Master Tom,' said I, much amused at his hearty frankness of speech, for I had never come across such a free and easy fellow before. 'You're another—that's all I can say, old chap!'

This set us off both laughing again; and, in the midst of our glee, up came a tall man in a long frock-coat with a black sword belt, but no epaulets or other distinguishing ornaments, whom I afterwards learnt was the master-at-arms. He asked me my name; and, informing me that I was to report myself to the commanding officer, he led the way up the main hatch to the quarter-deck above.

This interview having been satisfactorily got through, I was then escorted to the quarters of the naval instructor, who received me most graciously, telling me the hours of study and drill, and coaching me generally in the routine of my duties.

He catechised me all the while, I noticed, in a sly way in respect of my knowledge of mathematics, putting a series of innocent questions that I saw were meant to test my acquirements.

He did this, however, in such an insidious manner as to disarm me at the outset, preventing my feeling that I was being examined and 'turned inside out,' so to speak.

He was a nice fat old fellow like Mr Tangent.

Indeed, the majority of naval chaplains I have come

across in my time in the service have as a rule been fat, the sea air apparently exercising as beneficial an effect on the clerical constitution as a snug living ashore.

This gentleman now, after telling me he thought I should do very well, excused me from any lessons that day, it being the first I was on board. He then dismissed me to join my messmates, whom, he said, I would probably find below in the gunroom, as it was 'close on the luncheon hour!'

This reflection seemed to give him some inward satisfaction; for, he patted his waistcoat with a sort of pleasurable anticipation as I left him, asking the wardroom steward, who just then entered the cabin, whether there wasn't a veal and ham pie, I recollect.

When I got down to the lower deck I had no need to inquire as to the whereabouts of the gunroom.

Such a din and babel of voices proceeded from the after part of the ship that I was certain, from what Dad had let out to me of his former experiences at sea, the noise could only have been made by a batch of middies and naval cadets in their moments of relaxation from the stern discipline of the quarter-deck, when they were allowed to give their superabundance of animal spirits full play.

I was positive I must be in the near vicinity of the gunroom, the 'happy hunting ground' of my messmates.

Luncheon was evidently either over or not yet begun; for, a crowd of youngsters, amongst whom I at once perceived my friend Tom Mills, were grouped together on the open deck in front of the gunroom, where, as I afterwards heard, their hammocks were slung at night.

The lot were amusing themselves at some game I was not as yet acquainted with, but which evidently was one of the most boisterous character, a 'rough and tumble' fight being nothing to it.

'Hullo, Jack, here you are at last!' shouted out

Tom Mills, on seeing me. 'Come and join us, old fellow. We're playing at "piling the sacks."'

'Piling the sacks?' I repeated. 'What game is that?'

'Come along,' cried he, 'you'll soon learn it. Here's a new hand, Master Miller. Sacks to the mill! sacks to the mill!'

Thereupon he and a couple of other fellows seized me by my arms and legs and put me on top of a pile of other johnnies, who were scrambling and struggling and yelling on the deck in a confused mass, like an animated roly-poly pudding just turned out of the pot!

Another chap was then tossed on above me, and then another and another, till I was well-nigh suffocated; and then, when the pile had reached the top of the hatchway, the 'Master Miller' toppled the lot of us over.

On this, we all scrambled to our feet again, laughing and shouting in high glee; with collars torn and shirts crushed and the buttons wrenched off our jackets by the dozen, only to begin the game again as before—until, finally, the master-at-arms made his appearance below with the compliments of the first lieutenant to the 'young gentlemen,' and a polite request for them to 'make less noise.'

It was a jolly game, though, I can tell you!

The next day, we all commenced in earnest our studies in navigation and seamanship, the naval instructor with his assistants working us up in our mathematics and imparting to us the elements of plane and spherical trigonometry; while the boatswain and his mates gave us practical lessons in the setting up of rigging and making of knots, so that there should be no chance of our mistaking a 'sheepshank' for a 'cat's paw,' or a 'Flemish eye' for a 'grommet!'

Here I at once gained the good opinion of the boatswain by making a 'Matthew Walker' knot which, I may mention for the benefit of the uninitiated, is used generally on ship board for the standing part of the lanyards of lower rigging.

This I managed to achieve successfully at my first attempt, thanks to Dad's previous instruction; and I not only 'got to win'ard' of the old seaman by the knowledge I thus displayed, but added to my laurels by showing that I knew something also of the somewhat intricate arts of 'worming' and 'parcelling' and 'serving' ropes when occasion arose for dealing with them in such fashion, repeating aloud, to the great satisfaction of my teacher, the distich which guides the tyro and tells him how to do his work properly :—

> ' *Worm* and *parcel* with the lay,
> And *serve* the rope the other way !'

With my mathematical studies, too, I made equal progress, in spite of my original dislike to friend Euclid and his vexatious propositions.

I also learnt how to find my latitude, by 'bringing down the sun' with the sextant; and was taught the bearings and deviation of the compass, as well as the mastery of the logline and other similar little niceties of navigation.

These preliminaries achieved, I was reported by the naval instructor to the captain of the training ship as 'efficient' long before my probationary period of three months had expired.

The captain of the training-ship, in due course, reported me to the Admiralty; and, one fine morning I received official notice from the Secretary informing me that I was to go to sea, being appointed to the *Candahar*, line-of-battle ship, just commissioned for service on the China station; where, it was reported, matters were getting a little ticklish at the time, our government being at loggerheads with that of the emperor of the sun, moon and stars, and war imminent between the two countries.

It was certainly a splendid opening for me!

'By jingo! you're a lucky johnny,' said little Tom Mills when I told him the news, my chum heaving a sigh of disappointment at this early severance of our friendship.   He was, I could see, also a little jealous of my going to sea before him.   'I'll write to my father and see if he cannot get me appointed to the same ship!'

'I hope you will, Tom,' cried I, as I wrung his hand at the gangway, parting company at the same time with the rest of my old messmates, who had not yet passed through the course of the training-ship, all of whom gathered round to see the last of me. 'I promise you, old chap, I sha'n't have any other chum if you don't come with me!'

With these words, I ran down the ladderway; and, the next moment, was seated with three other cadets, who were leaving like myself to go afloat, in the sternsheets of the second cutter.

This last had been detailed by the commander to take us off to the *Candahar;* then lying alongside the old *Blake* hulk and moored in the stream, about midway between the Sheer Jetty and the King's Stairs, where she was 'fitting out for sea' as speedily as possible, the authorities having urged the utmost haste in her preparation.

'Shove off!' sang out the coxswain; and, impelled by her twelve oars, that were manned by as many pairs of stalwart arms, the boat sprang through the water.

The last sound I heard, beyond the wash of the tide against the side of the cutter and the subdued breathing of the men pulling, was little Tom Mills' voice in the distance shouting until I got out of earshot, 'Good-bye, Jack, old fellow, good-bye!'

CHAPTER VI

ON BOARD THE OLD 'CANDAHAR'

'IN bows!' cried the coxswain of the cutter as we neared the starboard side of the old hulk to which the *Candahar* was lashed ; and, the next minute, when close up to the foot of the accommodation ladder, the same functionary shouted the usual orders on approaching to board a ship. 'Way enough.   Oars!'

The oars were at once tossed, while the bowman gripped a projecting ringbolt in the side of the hulk with his boathook to hold on by; and the other cadets and myself, jumping out on to the ladderway, made our way nimbly enough up to the deck of the mastless *Blake*, passing over her by a gangway to the *Candahar* that lay on her further side.

Here all was apparent confusion, stores of all sorts being hoisted in by a derrick amidships from the dockyard lighters alongside and struck down the main hatchway, while ropes and tackle of every description lumbered the upper deck fore and aft.

Groups of men, clad in dirty overalls, were busy setting up the rigging and getting the yards into position ; and hoarse orders were shouted ever and anon, followed by the shrill pipe of the boatswain's whistle and the steady tramp of the hands as they walked round with the capstan and swayed the heavy spars aloft, or hauled away at the gantlines and steadying guys and purchase falls and other tackle.

The commander, the presiding spirit of the scene, if

a smart officer, has never a better opportunity for showing his smartness than when a ship is fitting for sea ; all the burthen of the work then falls upon his shoulders, for he has to be here and there and everywhere, directing a hundred different jobs at one and the same time.

As I went aft, and approached the hallowed ground of the quarter-deck, I saw him standing under the break of the poop.

He was a fine, big, broad-shouldered west-countryman with the voice of a stentor ; and, although he was dressed in a somewhat shabby old uniform coat and had his trousers tucked into his boots, he looked every inch a gentleman, as he was, indeed, not only by birth, but by breeding.

'Come on board, sir,' said I touching my cap, when a slight lull occurred in the general din caused by the creaking blocks and groaning tackle as the heavy spars were swayed aloft, and the continual tramp of men along the deck 'walking up the capstan' or hoisting at the whips leading down into the hold. ' I've just come on board, sir,'

'Oh, you've come on board, youngster, eh ?' he repeated questioningly, slewing round in his tracks and bringing his piercing black eyes to bear on my small person; when he looked me through and through, 'taking my measure' at a glance. 'Ah, I see, you're one of our new cadets from the *Illustrious* come to report yourself, eh ?'

'Yes, sir,' I replied, smiling in response to the pleasant look on his face. 'I've come to join the *Candahar*, sir.'

'What's your name, young gentleman ?'

I told him.

'Ah, you're the little shaver Mr Tangent spoke of to me the other night when I dined with the Admiral ! He said he knew your father, and thought you would turn out a smart officer ; so, I hope you'll support the good character he gave you. Belay there, bosun's mate, you'll let that cask down by the run if you don't look out !' he cried out suddenly to a stout petty officer who was superintending a gang of men who were taking in provisions from one of the lighters alongside, and lowering the same into the after hold. ' Steady, you may carry on, now ; that's better !'

' Now, my little friend,' he continued, resuming his conversation with me. ' We'll see how smart you can be. Run forruds and tell the bosun I want the sail burton brought aft, and an up and down tackle fitted to the mainyard, if you are able to recollect all that ?'

'Oh, yes, sir,' I replied, touching my cap again, ' I know what a sail burton is, sir.'

' And an up and down tackle, too ?'

' Yes, sir ; it is used for setting up the lower rigging.'

' Bravo, youngster ! You'll be a man before your mother if you go on at that rate !' said he, with a hearty laugh at my assurance, which seemed to frighten the other cadets who came with me, for they looked as meek as mice.

But, as I trotted away at a sign of dismissal from him to seek the boatswain on the forecastle, where I knew his especial domain lay, I heard Commander Nesbitt say in an undertone to one of the lieutenants who just then stepped down from the poop to join him, ' That's a sharp lad, Cheffinch, and one who'll make his mark, if I'm not mistaken. He's quite a contrast to the sucking Nelsons they generally send us from the training-ship, who don't, as a rule, know a goose from a gridiron !'

What the lieutenant said in reply to this complimentary allusion to my whilom comrades of the *Illustrious*, and the system of instruction pursued on board that vessel, I cannot tell, for I was out of earshot, hastening forward as speedily as I could, so as to deserve the good opinion the commander seemed to have already formed of me.

This, I may here add, I succeeded in doing ; for, I made my reappearance on the quarter-deck in a brace of shakes, with the boatswain in person and a party of topmen bringing aft the respective 'purchases' the commander had specified—blocks and strops and running gear of all sorts, all ready for instant service.

'Mr Hawser,' said Commander Nesbitt to the boatswain as we got near, giving me a kindly nod to express his approval of my having carried out his orders so promptly, 'I must have that maintops'l yard up before you pipe to dinner.'

'Very good, sir,' replied the warrant officer, touching his cap again, as he had done when approaching the sacred precincts of the quarter-deck. 'The spar, sir, 's fitted all right for going up ; but, sir, it's getting on now for Seven Bells.'

'I don't care what the time is, bosun ; it's got to be done, and that's the long and the short of it,' retorted the commander sharply, flashing his eyes in a way that showed he was not to be put off when he had once made up his mind. 'Maintop, there!'

'Ay, ay, sir,' answered the captain of the top, looking over the rail instantly and leaving off the work of fitting the upper standing rigging, on which he and his men were engaged when this vigorous hail reached the top, thundered out with all the power of the commander's lungs. 'Want me down, sir?'

'Down? No, my man ; but lower a whip at once for the sail burton, and you can lower the tops'l tye as well. I'm going to send up the yard at once!'

'Ay, ay, sir.'

Promptitude begets like promptness.

Before you could say 'Jack Robinson,' the whip was down and the purchase in the top; then, the standing part of the tackle was made fast to the yard pendant and the spar swayed up, as the men walked away with the fall, which was rove through a snatch-block hooked on to a ringbolt fixed in the deck and led to the capstan.

Ere a quarter-of-an-hour had elapsed, the yard was slung and firmly secured, with the halliards and braces rigged in proper fashion.

In the middle of the operation, however, the atten·tion of the hard-worked commander was called in another direction.

A fat, heavy, seafaring-looking man in a short pilot jacket came up to him as he was uttering rapid commands to the sailors aloft in stentorian accents from the poop-rail.

'Beg pardon, sir,' said this gentleman, whom I presently learnt was Mr Quadrant, the master, or navigating officer of the ship; one who used in the old days to have charge of all the material on board a man-of-war, just as the commander looks after the crew. 'None of those stores, sir, have come off from the dockyard that were promised this morning, and all my hands are idle below. What am I to do, sir?'

'Send a boat at once to the storekeeper, to lodge a complaint.'

'Yes, sir. But, there's only the jollyboat left, sir, now, besides the dinghy. All the others are ashore.'

'Well, send the jollyboat; and, I say, Mr Quadrant,' added Commander Nesbitt as the master was waddling off down the companionway, 'tell the midshipman who goes with the boat that if the things are not sent aboard at once, he is to make application at the Admiral's office, complaining of the delay. P'raps, though, you'd better go yourself, eh?'

'I will if you like, sir,' sighed the master, who had already had too much exercise between decks and up and down the hatchways to feel enamoured of a walk ashore over the rough cobblestones of the dock-yard. 'But, I don't think they'll hurry any the more for me than they would for a middy, sir. He would be able, too, sir, to check the yard people all the better, sir.'

'Just as you please, Mr Quadrant,' returned the commander in a decided tone. I should prefer, how-ever, your going yourself to sending any other officer.'

This was equivalent to an order; and the master with a deep groan disappeared, only to make room for Mr Nipper, the purser.

This gentleman came across the gangway from the hulk—on board of which we were all berthed while our own ship was fitting out. He seemed in a great heat, as if something had put him out very much indeed, looking worried beyond endurance.

'Captain Nesbitt, sir,' said he to the commander, touching his cap like the others, 'what am I to do, sir?'

'I'm sure I can't say, Mr Nipper,' rejoined the commander in an offhand way, for he had just given the order to sway the yard aloft, and was watching whether the spar cleared the top and keeping a wary eye that it did not get foul of the mainstay, or some-thing else aloft. 'What's the matter?'

'Those people at the victualling yard haven't sent our fresh beef yet aboard, sir,' answered the purser, a thin, fussy little man, in a whining way, as if he were going to cry, 'and there's nothing to serve out for the men's dinners—at least, not enough for all.'

'That's too bad!' cried the commander, indignantly; 'why did you not tell me of this before?'

'I was expecting the boat would come with the meat every minute, sir.'

'Is there no beef at all on board?'

'Only the wardroom and gunroom supply.'

'Then serve that out at once to the men—they sha'n't go without their dinner if I can help it.'

'But, sir, what will the officers do?'

'Ah, you must settle that as best as you can with the wardroom steward, sir! Let this, Mr Nipper, be a lesson to you in future not to put off things until the last moment! You may take the dinghy, if you like, by-and-by and go to Clarence yard yourself, to see what can be done for getting some more beef for the wardroom and gunroom mess; but, I cannot spare another officer or man. We're much too short-handed already!'

This was true enough, for we had only about a couple of hundred men of our crew, including the seamen, gunners and petty officers, as yet aboard.

In those days only the marines and boys were drafted to ships when first commissioned, the compliment having to be made up as hands volunteered to join in response to the bills inviting enrolment that were stuck up in some selected public-house or tavern ashore, which, as the master-at-arms told me, was called the 'Randy-woo!'

The continuous service system now in vogue was not adopted until within a comparatively recent period, say some thirty years ago at the outside; prior to this all bluejackets on their discharge from a ship when she was paid off, instead of being merely granted leave according to the present custom, became absolutely free men and having the right to quit the service, if they so wished, for good and all.

Although, should they change their minds after their money was all spent and come forward to join another ship about to be commissioned, the different periods they might have previously served afloat counted towards the time required to qualify them for a pension.

When, therefore, the *Candahar* was ordered to hoist the pennant and her captain and other officers appointed, she only received a certain percentage of trained gunnery hands from the *Excellent*, with a few boys and marines.

She had to go into the open market, as it were, for the rest of her crew, like any ordinary ship about to sail on a trading voyage.

Such being the case, following the usual practice at the time, the 'Earl St Vincent,' a tavern on Common Hard, was chosen for our rallying-place, or 'rendezvous.'

A large broadsheet was exposed in the window of this tavern inviting ablebodied seamen and artificers to join the battleship ; one of our lieutenants attending each day for a certain number of hours at the little shipping office which was established in the bar parlour of the tavern to inspect the discharge notices and certificates of any sailors or landsmen who might wish to join.

The officer relegated to this duty took care to satisfy himself that any candidates he selected should pass muster with the commander before sending them on board.

He knew well enough that if the men had previously served in the navy and their characters were marked 'very good,' or even 'good,' there was little doubt of their acceptance.

Up to the date of my going on board the ship, though, our recruiting agency had not been very successful.

Not half our required number of men, had, indeed, as yet volunteered for the *Candahar* ; for, most of the old hands worth their salt fought shy of the station she was reported to be going to, on account less of its unhealthiness, which to Jack is of small account, than to the absence of any prize money or extra pay, such as might be gained even on the deadly West Coast, with its malarial fever and pestiferous man-grove swamps that form the white man's grave.

But, all of a sudden, public opinion, so far as the sailor world was concerned, veered round in our favour.

It had leaked out that there was a prospect of our having a scrimmage with the mandarins.

In this case, of course, there would be dollars and other sorts of 'loot' knocking about.

So, that very day, volunteers began to come off to the ship; not by threes and fours as they had done before, but by twenties and more at a stretch.

Of these the launch brought off a large cargo alongside immediately after the commander's interview with the purser; and I thus had the opportunity of seeing how the men were scrutinised and sorted for the 'watch bill,' which the chief of our executive made out himself—as indeed he seemed to do everything, looking after everybody else all the while.

The coxswain of the launch, with a touch of his forelock, handed over the discharge notes and certificates of such of the motley group that came up the side that had these documents, which the second lieutenant, a knowing fellow, who was in charge of our shipping office that morning, had pocketed when he engaged the men; doing this as a sort of preventative to their backing out of the bargain afterwards.

These greasy papers, which he did not open, were then passed on to the midshipman on duty on the quarter-deck, with orders to take them to the purser s office; and the commander then proceeded to muster the lot abaft the mainmast bitts.

'What were you aboard your last ship?' asked he of a smart-looking seaman on the right of the line as they stood across the deck facing him, who appeared neater and nattier than the rest. 'What rating did you take up?'

'Cap'en of the foretop, sir.'

'All right, you're the very man I want!' said the commander. 'You may go and do the duty, and if you are diligent and active you shall have the rate.'

The next chap stated he had been an able seamen in his previous ship, so he was sent on to the forecastle to add to the long roll already there.

So was another and another, till Commander Nesbitt lighted on a man who said he had been a shipwright in the dockyard, whom he marked down to join the carpenter's crew.

Several ordinary seamen followed, until the fag end of the lot was reached, consisting of a number of greenhorns who had never been to sea previously; and these, on declaring their willingness to serve Her Gracious Majesty, were sent down into the steerage to join the afterguard.

'What are you?' inquired the commander of a sooty sort of gentleman, who, with another more morose personage, stood at the extreme rear of this group. 'I mean, what did you do ashore for a livelihood, my man?'

'Wot hev h'I been a-doin' of fur a lively-hood, sir?' repeated the sooty gentleman, who evidently was a wag, speaking, albeit with a comical expression on his countenance, with a native dignity that would have won the praise of Lord Chesterfield. 'W'y, sir, h'I'm a h' "upright," sir, that's wot I h' am!'

'An "upright"!' exclaimed Commander Nesbitt, with a smile. 'I've heard of wheelwrights, and millwrights and shipwrights, of course, but never of such a calling as an "upright"—what's that, eh?'

'I thought as 'ow I'd puzzle you, sir,' replied the man with a grin. 'I'm a chimbly-sweeper by trade.'

'Oh, a chimney-sweeper? Then you ought to be good at climbing, and I cannot do better than send you aloft. You can go forrud now.'

Saying this, the commander turned to the last man the morose one, questioning him in like fashion.

'And what have you been?'

'I'm a "downright," sir,' said he, as grave as a judge. 'Wot they calls a "downright," sir.'

'Now, don't you try on any of your jokes with me, my man, or you'll find yourself in the wrong box, which is the strong box on board ship, and vulgarly called chokey!'

'I ain't a-joking,' replied the other, speaking as gravely as before and without even the shadow of a smile on his face. 'I'm a "downright," that's what I am.'

'Pray, what profession is that,' asked the commander, sarcastically. 'I would not like to hurt your feelings by calling your avocation a trade!'

'You're right, sir,' returned the other, as calmly as possible, without turning a hair; 'I'm a grave-digger.'

This fairly made the commander collapse.

'You may muster with the afterguard,' was the only reply he made, but we all could see that he had hard work to keep his gravity, as he turned towards the boatswain's mate and ordered him to pipe the men to dinner in a sharp tone; and he said to Mr Cheffinch, the gunnery lieutenant, when he crossed over the deck to go on board the old *Blake* to lunch, 'He had me nicely there, like that other joker the chimney-sweeper. It must have been a planned thing between the two rascals!'

CHAPTER VII

WE GO OUT TO SPITHEAD

PASSING across the gangway with Commander Nesbitt to the hulk, which served as a sort of floating hotel for all of us while the *Candahar* was preparing for sea, officers and men alike sleeping and messing in her and only going on board our own ship during working hours between meals, as long as daylight lasted, I found Dr Nettleby, the chief of our medical staff, with one of his assistants, busily engaged in the sick bay on the main deck.

They were examining all the new hands who had just joined, to see whether any of them were suffering from organic disease, or some other physical infirmity that might incapacitate them for service afloat, none but the able-bodied being accepted.

The curtained door of the sick bay being open and the cabin itself close to the main-hatchway, which I had necessarily to pass in going below to the gunroom, I could not help overhearing something of what was proceeding in the medical sanctum, the more especially from the fact of Dr Nettleby, the presiding genius, having a short temper and a snappy manner of expressing himself peculiarly his own.

He was a good-hearted man at the bottom, however, and as tender as a woman in cases of real suffering; though woe to the malingerer or shammer of illness who incautiously ventured within reach of his caustic tongue!

A couple of the cadets who had come on board with me that morning were standing by the doorway of the sick bay, in company with one of the older midshipmen and some others; and, seeing these all grinning, as if enjoying themselves mightily at what was going on within, I joined the group—the lot of us sheltering ourselves from observation behind a tall canvas screen that was rigged across the deck amidships, shutting out the draught from the port holes fore and aft, besides serving also as an ante-room to the doctor's cabin and surgery. From this inner apartment would emerge ever and anon some culprit marine or shamefaced seaman, trying to walk steady, who, having perhaps been a trifle too jolly overnight and pleading indisposition as an excuse for his inability to attend to his duties, had been brought before the doctor for treatment—only, alas! to receive a dose of pungent satire, in lieu of the soothing medicine they craved to banish the effects of their drunken spree. Meanwhile, the new hands who were awaiting their medical examination were drawn up on the other side of the gangway, 'marking time' until these regular, or rather irregular, patients were disposed of in turn, no doubt enjoying the fun like ourselves.

'Listen,' whispered Larkyns, the senior midshipman, nudging the fellow next him and winking to me as I came up. 'That's Macan, our corporal of marines, who's getting it now. By Jove, the doctor is giving it him hot!'

He certainly was, judging from what reached my ears, at least.

'Stuff and nonsense, corporal!' I heard Dr Nettleby rasp out snappishly, his voice sounding from within the cabin just like a terrier dog barking, for I could hear him plainly enough. 'You can't gammon me, my man, though you might take in the first lieutenant! It's "rumatism," not rheumatism you're suffering from, you scoundrel! You've been drinking, that's what's the matter with you; and if I report you to the cap'en, as I ought, you'll not only lose your stripes before sunset, but get four dozen as well, and serve you right, too!'

'Faith, yer honour, I haven't tasted a dhrop of anythin' barrin tay since yesterday noon at Eight Bells. May I die this minnit if I have, sor,' boldly asserted the accused in a rich Irish brogue that was as distinct as the doctor's voice. 'It's the rheumaticks, sure! I've got 'em in the legs bad this toime and can't hould mesilf up at all, nor walk more than a choild!'

'MacGilpin, just diagnose this case for me,' cried the doctor to his assistant. 'What does he smell of?'

'Whuskey,' replied the assistant-surgeon, a raw-boned expert from Edinburgh, who had only recently donned Her Majesty's uniform and brought his north-country accent with him when he came southwards. 'There's nae doot aboot that. He smells o' whuskey, and bad whuskey, tae!'

'Begorrah, yer nose is wrong, sor, and the doctor's roight, as he always is, sor, beggin' yer pardon,' said the culprit, confessing his offence in his anxiety to stand up for the medical insight of the chief, with whom he had served before and whose professional pride he knew how to work upon. 'It was rhum, sure enough.'

'You rascal!' shouted out Dr Nettleby. 'Why, not a moment ago you swore you hadn't tasted a drop of anything but tea alone since yesterday.'

'Faith, yer honner, I didn't know it wor rhum till too late, sor. I sware, sor, I droonk it out av a taypot.'

'Out of a teapot, man?'

'Yis, sor, I'll till yer honner how it wor, sure,' explained the wily fellow, who could tell from the doctor's change of tone that his offence was condoned and that he need fear no worse consequences now than one of his usual lectures, which only went in at one ear and out at the other, as Dr Nettleby himself said. 'I wint over to the rendywoo last noight be the cap'en's orders, sor, fur to say if there wor any more hands a-waitin' to jine. Faith an' there I mates me wife's first cousin, Bridget O'Halloran, as is merried now be the same token to Sargint Lintstock.'

'Sergeant Lintstock?'

'Ay, sor, that same, which makes him, sure, me second cousin once removed, though, faith, he's me soupayrior orfiser! But, as I were a-tellin' ye, sor, in comes Bridget whilst I were talkin' to the jintleman behoind the bar at the rendywoo. I were jist axin' what the cap'en tells me to ax him ; an' "Mike," says she, cordial like, "have a partin' glass wid me fur the sake of the ould country as ye're abut to lave." "Faith an' that's more nor I dare, Bridget," says I. "I promist the docthor, sure, I wouldn't touch another dhrop o' sperrits for the nixt four-an'-twenty hours, as I'm a livin' sinner!" "But I don't want ye to dhrink sperrits," says she. "Me an' me frind Mistress Wilkins here is jist havin' a cup of tay, sure ; an' axes ye to jine us, that's all!" "Faith I'm not the bhoy fur to disobleege the ladies," says I, "ye can give us a cup, if that's all ye wants me fur to do." Wid that, Bridget ups with the taypot, a little brown one it wor, sure, by the same token, an' pours me out a cupful in a mug that lay handy sure on the counther, which I drinks to the hilth of her an' Missis Wilkins as wor standin' by. It wor right-down beautiful tay ; so I has another one to the hilth of Bridget's husband the sarjint, an' thin another, that wor a little one faith! to the hilth of the babby ; an,' begorrah, sor, I rimimbers no more till this mornin' whin I fales so bad wid the rheumatics as I couldn't lift me hid out of me hammock. The sarjint says I wor droonk, but I worn't, sor; though somehows or t'other I thinks it must have been rhum I wor drinkin' at the rendywoo an' not tay as Bridget telled me at the toime, sayin' it wor good fur the stummick an' wud kape the cowld out!'

'I don't believe a word of your story,' I heard the doctor answer to this long and circumstantial yarn. 'Why, Macan, you're drunk now!'

'Me droonk now, sor?' repeated the other in a tone of mingled sorrow and solemnity. 'Faith I'm as sobher as a jidge this very minnit, as I'm a livin' sinner!'

'Don't tell me any more of your lies!' cried out the doctor irascibly at this juncture, interrupting what further asservation the corporal might have made in support of his unblushing assertion. 'You can go forrud now and thank your stars I don't report you, as I had more than half a mind to at first. If I did, you'd be put into the black list and lose your stripes to a dead certainty.'

'May the saints presarve yer honner,' exclaimed Macan with effusion as he was thus dismissed, but he was still not satisfied apparently at his word being doubted; for, as he passed us, working his way forward by a series of short tacks, he kept on muttering half aloud, much to our amusement, 'It's all through that blissid Scoch sawbones wid his long "dog nose" as he calls it, sayin' it wor whisky. I'm as shober as a jidge, faith—as shober as a jidge!'

No more unfortunate circumstance, however, could have occurred for the corporal of marines, in spite of the doctor having let him off so easily, for, through our overhearing this dialogue between the two, the yarn he had told of meeting his "cousin Bridget" soon got round the ship, and the men could always put him in a rage whenever they liked by an allusion to the 'taypot' and his cousin's friend 'Missis Wilkins.'

We stopped a little longer listening outside the sick bay, but soon gave up the pastime, nothing occurring to interest us during the medical examination of the new hands, a fresh batch of whom came aft, by the way, at Four Bells; for all of them were quickly passed by the doctor and were detailed for duty aloft and below, where many jobs were at a standstill for want of men.

This enabled the commander to press on with the work of rigging the ship, the crossjack, or 'crochet' yard being sent up by the aid of the mizzen burton hooked on in front of the top ; after which the jack was slung and the trusses fixed on, the spar brought home to the mast, the lifts and braces having been fitted before swaying, as is the case with all the lower yards in men-of-war.

The mizzen-trysail mast, on which the spanker is set, was also got up by means of the same tackle ; and, what with hoisting in some of the maindeck guns and sails and other gear, the afternoon quickly passed.

I was not sorry when dinner-time came, Five Bells in the first dog-watch, for I was pretty well tired to death with this, my first day's experience on board the *Candahar*, in running up and down the decks fore and aft as Commander Nesbitt's special messenger

It was, however, a very good introduction to the life I should have to lead for the next few years of my career ; for, as a junior officer, I would be at the beck and call of everyone on the quarter-deck and 'hardly able to call my soul my own,'—as Dad had more than once warned me beforehand.

Still, I must say, notwithstanding certain drawbacks, which subsequent experience brought to light in due course, I liked it all, taking the rough side of

sea life with the smooth, and would not change
my lot if I had the opportunity of making my choice
over again, even knowing what I do now of the
service!

My captain I had not as yet seen much of; for,
although he came off every day to sign papers and
receive reports, as well as see how things were going
on generally, he lived on shore and did not interfere
at all with Commander Nesbitt, who carried on the
work as he pleased.

The latter being a good officer, who thoroughly
knew his duty and a sailor every inch of him, as
I have already described, Captain Farmer, as he
probably well understood, could not have done better
than thus leave matters to his second in command
while the ship was in harbour.

The Honourable Digby Lanyard, our first lieutenant, was a tall supercilious young man of five-
and-twenty or so who wore an eyeglass.

This was more for effect than from any defect of
vision, for he was as sharp as a needle ; and could see
a bit of spunyarn adrift or a rope out of place aloft even
quicker than the commander, keen-sighted as he was.

Amongst the men on the lower deck, who have,
as a rule, some pet nickname for most of their
officers, especially those whom they may chance to
like or dislike more than the rest, he always went
by the sobriquet of 'glass eye'; and it was wonderful
how this dandy chap who was so particular in his
dress and would mince his words in conversation
with his brother officers in the wardroom, speaking
with a lisp of affectation and a languid air as if it
were too much trouble to articulate distinctly, would,
when the occasion arose, roar out his orders in a
voice that could be heard from one end of the ship
to the other and make the men skip about, like the
young lambs mentioned by the Psalmist!

As for us youngsters, we dreaded his icy con-temptuous stare and his 'haw-haw' manner more than anything.

He seemed to have the power of freezing us with a look should he ever condescend to notice us at all; but this, fortunately, was very seldom, the lieutenant being wont to ignore our existence except when he had reason to call us to account for some neglect of duty, at which times we disliked more his disdainful glance, accompanied, as it invariably was, by some cold sarcastic allusion to our shortcomings, than the bullying and bad language of some of the other officers who were not so refined.

Such at all events was the opinion Dick Andrews and Teddy Allison and the other cadets had of him, as well as myself; though Fred Larkyns, the big senior midshipman, who patronised us and whom we all liked, he was such a jolly fellow and up to all sorts of fun, said we would find 'glass eye' not half a bad chap 'when we came to know him better.'

Subsequent events will tell how far Mr Larkyns proved to be right in this conclusion of his; albeit, we demurred to it at the time that he propounded it in his dogmatic way, rapping poor little Teddy Allison on the head with a parallel ruler, which he held in his hand at the moment, for daring to dispute his oracular assertion on the point and making us all laugh by a capital imitation of the haughty airs of our pet aversion and his cynical mode of speech, while in the same breath he took his part, generous lad that he was!

We were all too busy, however, to notice the various peculiarities and characteristics of our messmates beyond such as we were brought more immediately in contact with.

Indeed, we had not time even to settle down on board and know each other properly; for each day added to our company, increasing the number of strange faces around us, so that I began to wonder when we would at length get our requisite complement and finish our apparently endless task of fitting out.

'It is a long lane that has no turning,' though, as the old adage goes; and so, after three weeks more of enrolling volunteers at Corporal Macan's favourite 'rendywoo,' and the hoisting in of many guns and boats and stores and provisions of all sorts, until the *Candahar*, I thought, would never contain them all, we finally bent our sails, crossed royal yards and were declared 'ready for sea.'

Captain Farmer came on board with 'all his bag and baggage' on our ship's company 'turning over' from the old hulk *Blake*, to which we all bade a long and welcome adieu, all hands being then mustered by divisions to beat of drum along the upper and lower decks.

We were eight hundred strong, all told; officers and men; bluejackets of all ratings, and marines; boys and 'idlers,' as some of the hardest-worked fellows aboard are somewhat inappropriately designated in the watch bill, according to nautical etiquette; as motley a collection at the first start, and yet as fine a set of fellows as you could pick out in a year's cruise!

These preliminaries being all arranged, we cast off from the hulk late one November afternoon; and, the dockyard tug *Puffing Billy* taking us in tow, proceeded to Spithead, where we anchored in eleven fathoms, letting out some six shackels of cable, so that we could swing comfortably with the tide as it flowed in and out of the roadstead.

CHAPTER VIII

A LITTLE SURPRISE

'I SUPPOSE,' said I, after we had cast anchor, to
Larkyns, who had kindly noticed me the first day I
came aboard and had been very friendly with me
since, patronising me in the way the elder boys of
the sixth form sometimes do the younger fellows at
school, 'we'll sail to morrow, eh?'

'Sail to-morrow? Your grandmother!' he answered
with his usual grin. I believe that chap would have
grinned if you had told him his father was dead, for
he looked on everything from a humorous point of
view and could not help laughing even when the
captain spoke to him, which often got him in for an
extra mast-heading. 'Why, we haven't got in our
lower deck guns yet, booby, let alone our powder
and ammunition; besides all sorts of stores we could
not ship in harbour!'

'Oh!' I exclaimed, somewhat crestfallen at his
'snub,' 'I didn't think of that.'

'I suppose not,' replied he, mimicking me, 'but
you have a good deal to learn yet, let me tell you.
Hullo, though, Master Squaretoes, what do you mean
by coming on the quarter-deck with nails in your
boots? You'll have the first lieutenant after you,
my joker, if he notices it, and there'll be the dickens
to pay, I can tell you!'

'What do you mean?' I retorted indignantly. 'I have not got any nails in my boots at all.'

'Haven't you, young shaver?' said he, grinning again and looking down with mock pity at the pumps I wore, which were guiltless of even the smallest tack, being all sewn, as I held up the soles for his inspection. 'Then, all I can say is I'm sorry for you! I really didn't think you were deformed—and such a young and promising chap, too!'

I got alarmed at this.

'Deformed!' I repeated. 'What do you mean?'

'Why, if you haven't any nails in your boots, or shoes—it doesn't matter which, but we'll say boots for argument's sake,' said my tormentor quizzingly—'it follows, naturally and logically, that you have none on your toes! In which case, my poor young friend, you must be suffering from a malformation of the feet; or, in other words, you are deformed, according to Euclid, *quid demonstrandum est*, twiggy vous?'

'Oh, yes, I see,' said I, feeling rather nettled, I confess, at his thus taking a rise out of me. 'You think that funny, I suppose; but, I call it both silly and vulgar!'

'"Silly!" "vulgar!" You very small fragment of impudence,' rejoined Larkyns, highly delighted at being thus successful in 'pulling my leg' and making me angry, 'I'll have you keelhauled for speaking so disrespectfully to your superior officer, sir. Beg my pardon instantly, or—'

What he would have done, however, in case of my non-compliance with his imperative request remains a mystery to the present day; for, as at that moment, the commander, who had been surveying the maintop from the poop-rail above us, hearing my funny gentleman's voice, which he had raised in speaking to me, called out to him,—

'Below there,' he cried—'Mr Larkyns!'

'Yes, sir,' answered my 'superior officer' humbly

enough, touching his cap and looking up at Commander Nesbitt. 'Want me, sir?'

'Yes,' said the other, 'There's something wrong with the bunt of that tops'l, I think. It does not appear to me quite ship-shape somehow or other, Mr Larkyns. Go up to the maintop and see what's the matter with it at once.'

'Ay, ay, sir,' replied my tormentor, springing nimbly into the rigging and shinning up the ratlines almost as soon as the words were out of the commander's mouth, 'I'll see, sir.'

I looked up at the moment, and, catching Commander Nesbitt's eye I'm sure he gave a sort of sly wink, the which impressed on my mind the conviction that he must have overheard our conversation and, wishing to give Master Larkyns some employment for his spare time, had sent him aloft on a wild-goose chase.

The topsail was stowed snugly enough, so, my friend the middy's missive was set-off to his chaff at my expense.

This conviction was confirmed when the commander immediately afterwards ordered me to go forwards and tell the boatswain to get the fish tackle clear for hoisting in the lower deck guns as soon as they came alongside next morning in the dockyard lighters.

The old *Candahar*, you must know, although she was described in the 'Navy List' of that day as a 'two-decker,' had really four decks—the upper deck, main deck, lower deck and orlop deck.

The distinction of the designation lay in the fact that she carried guns on two decks besides her upper one, the armament of which, as well as that of her main deck had been got on board easily enough when she was in harbour; but, as she was then lashed alongside the hulk and the lower tier of guns had to be taken in through the ports, this operation could not be very well managed until her broadside was clear of the hull of the other ship, so that the cannon could be lifted out of the lighters and swung inboard, without any intervening obstacle blocking the way and possibly fouling the hoisting tackle and steadying gear, which was not the case until we reached Spithead.

Even then, it was no trifling task swaying the heavy guns out of the holds of the two lighters that brought them out to us early in the morning from the gunwharf, one of these craft coming under our main-yard on either side ; for, the guns were long thirty-two pounders, weighing fifty-six hundredweight, or nearly three tons apiece, and, even after they were hoisted up in mid air from the lighters they had then to be hauled through one of the midship ports, mounted on their carriages and run along the lower deck to their proper position, when the breechings and side tackle had to be fitted before the job was completed.

It was accomplished in good time, however, much to our commander's satisfaction ; and, by the aid of the fish davit with its tackle and another purchase, it did not take more than a couple of hours to ship the whole thirty of these guns that comprised our lower-deck armament.

What formidable weapons I thought them ! But, they were only babies to the big rifled breechloaders now in vogue ; albeit they did tidy enough work in the destructive line in their day, as the annals of our navy can tell, and other nations have experienced to their cost both on land and sea !

'Pretty little barkers, ain't they?' observed Mr Triggs, the gunner, noticing me looking at these 'long thirty-twos,' as they were styled, and wondering at the light and airy fashion in which the men handled them, tossing them about like shuttlecocks, so it seemed to me. 'They can do more than bark ; though, they can bite too, I tell ye !'

'Oh, yes, I quite believe that, Mr Triggs,' said I, taking advantage of the opportunity of giving a 'snop' to Larkyns, who was also standing by and, of course, grinning as usual. 'Not all smoke and noise, like some fellows' talk.'

'No, that they ain't, except, in course, when saluting,' replied the gunner, who was a plain matter-of-fact man and did not see the drift of my observation. 'But, with a ten-pound charge, now, they'd make a pretty fair hole in a six-inch plank, I tell ye.'

'How many of them, Mr Triggs,' I asked, 'have we got on board?'

'Of these long 'uns?' he said, patting one affectionately on the breech as he spoke. 'Well, we've jist fifteen here a-port and fifteen a-starboard, which makes thirty in all on this deck. A power o' metal, I tell ye!'

'Oh, I know that,' said I. 'But I mean how many of the same sort.'

'There ain't any more of the same sort, I tell ye, but what you sees,' rejoined the gunner a bit crossly. 'The guns as is on the main deck and upper deck are all short thirty-two's; and, they're thirty too, o' them on the main, and twenty-two on the upper deck. They all of 'em carries the same weight of shot, though not such heavy guns as these, being only forty-five hundredweight each.'

'There, young Vernon, you can put that in your pipe and smoke it!' chimed in Larkyns, at this juncture, making a face behind the gunner's back, which, had he seen it, might have altered the opinion that worthy presently expressed of the speaker. 'That's "the long and the short of it," as Mr Triggs has so eloquently explained!'

'Thank you, Mr Larkyns, for the compliment,' said the gunner, taking the remark as a tribute to his conversational ability. 'I allers tries to explain myself as well as I can. Is there anything more you'd like to know, Master Vernon? I'm allers pleased to instruct any of you young gentlemen when you asks civilly!'

'You spoke just now of a ten-pound charge,' I answered. 'I suppose you mean of powder without the shot?'

'That's not *charged*,' put in Larkyns, grinning. 'The shot is given in "free, gratis, for nothing," as Paddy said.'

'Yes, Master Vernon,' replied the gunner, taking no notice this time of Larkyns or his interpolation. 'These here guns take a full charge of ten pounds of powder for long range, and redooced charges of six and eight pounds; whilst the charges of them on the main and upper deck are either six or eight pounds, as the case might be, according to the service required.'

'It must take an awful lot of powder for all the eighty-four guns, besides the shot and shell!'

'You can bet on that,' replied Mr Triggs, moving towards the side and looking through the port in the direction of the harbour. 'We carries about a hundred rounds of each charge for every gun; or, something like ninety tons for our whole armament. That's what it takes.'

'Ninety tons of gunpowder!' I exclaimed in astonishment. 'Do you mean that we've got to take such a quantity as that on board?'

'Of course I do; I always says what I means and means what I says,' rejoined Mr Triggs, somewhat snappishly again, as if tired of the long string of puzzling questions with which I was now bothering him, like I used to do my dear old Dad. 'By Jingo! I'm blessed if there it ain't a-coming off now, I tell ye!'

'Coming off,' I repeated. 'Where?'

'There, booby,' said Larkyns, slewing me round and shoving my head right out of the port.

'Can't you see the powder hoy, there to your right,
passing .Blockhouse Fort, at the mouth of the harbour?'

'That one flying the red flag, eh?'

'Yes, my dear Squaretoes; but we don't call a
burgee a flag aboardships.'

'I wish you would not call me Squaretoes, Larkyns,'
said I, peevishly, for he hurt me, squeezing my neck
in his tight grip, holding me out of the port as if I
were a kitten, so that I could not turn my head round.
'I hate nicknames. Do leave me alone, please!'

'Ah, would you, now!' he exclaimed in reply, as
I tried to wrench myself free. 'Don't cry, my little
pet, you haven't got your mammy here to molly-
coddle you!'

'Let me go, Larkyns, you're choking me,' I gasped
out, wriggling violently and kicking out behind.
'I'll hurt you if you don't loose me; I will, indeed!'

He wouldn't release me yet, however, seeing I was
out of temper; and, some of the other middies not on
duty gathering round, it being their watch below,
egged Larkyns on, suggesting that as I seemed to
think myself such a 'big gun,' I ought to be sponged
and loaded and run out.

This humorous advice was immediately acted upon,
a couple of the gang laying hold of my legs in spite
of my kicks, while another assisted Larkyns, my tor-
menter; and the mischievous lot swung me backwards and forwards in and out of the port, until
nearly all my clothes were pulled off my back and
I hadn't a sound button left to my jacket.

I felt hot all over; and was in a fine rage, 'I tell
you,' as the gunner used to say.

Mr Triggs, meanwhile, had gone up the hatchway
to see about getting on board his ammunition, the
vermilion-painted powder hoys I had observed in the
distance at the mouth of the harbour being now

nearly alongside the ship ; and, all of a sudden, as my reckless shipmates were pulling me almost to pieces between them in their mad prank, there came a cry from the deck above, 'Stand clear, below there !'

At the same instant, a coil of rope whizzed by the port-hole out of which my body projected, the bight of it narrowly escaping my head in its down-ward descent, wetting my face with the spray it threw up as it splashed into the water right under me.

I could not restrain a shriek of alarm ; and, wriggling more violently than before in the hands of those holding me as I tried to release myself, I managed somehow or other to jerk away from their grasp, send-ing them all sprawling backward on the deck inboard, while I shot out of the port like a catapult, tumbl-ing headlong into the sea as if taking a header after the rope !

CHAPTER IX

FORTUNATELY, though, as I fell, my outstretched hands, clutching wildly in the air, came in contact with the identical rope whose sudden descent from the gangway above had been the unwitting cause of the disaster, the tail end of the 'whip' Mr Triggs had ordered to be rigged up from the lee yard-arm, in readiness to hoist in the powder when the hoy bringing the same was made fast along-side.

This naturally yielded to my weight as I clung to it, on account of the other end, which passed through a block fastened to the yard, not being secured.

However, it let me down easy into the water, my unexpected immersion making no noise to speak of and hardly causing a ripple on the surface of the tide as it gurgled past the ship's counter and eddied away in ripples under her stem.

Not a soul on board, indeed, knew of my mishap save those merry messmates of mine, all of whom doubtless, I thought, as soon as I regained my composure after the fright and knew that I was comparatively safe, would be in a great funk, fearing the worst had happened.

Glancing upward, my head being just clear of the water, which I trod to keep myself in an erect position, holding on, though, all the while, 'like grim death,' to

the rope, of which I had taken a turn round my wrist,
I saw Larkyns, the ringleader of the frolic, leaning
out over the port sill as pale as a ghost.

He was looking downwards, in every direction but
the right one, seeking vainly to discover me; and
he evidently dreaded that I was drowned, his face
being the picture of misery and despair.

'Hist, old chap, don't call out,' I whispered in a low
voice, as he was about to give up the search and
rouse the ship. 'I'm all right, my boy.'

'My goodness Vernon, is that you? I thought
you were lost, old chap,' he hailed back in the same
key, the expression of his face changing instantly
to one of heartfelt relief. 'Thank God you're not
drowned! But, where are you, old fellow; I can't
see you?'

'Right under your very nose, you blind old mole!
I am bent on to a bight of the whip falls,' I answered,
with a chuckle. 'Keep the other end of the rope taut,
old chap, and I'll be able to climb up back into the
port without anybody being the wiser but ourselves,
my hearty, and so we'll all escape going into the report.'

He grasped the situation in an instant; and, likewise, saw the advisability of keeping the matter quiet
now that I was not in any imminent peril.

Master Larkyns knew as well as myself that if the
tragic result of their skylarking should get wind and
reach the ears of Captain Farmer, he and his brother
mids would have a rough time of it, and probably all
be had up on the quarter-deck.

'All serene, Vernon, I underconstubble,' he softly
whispered back to me, in our gunroom slang. 'Do
you think you can manage to climb up by yourself,
or shall I come down and help you?'

'Fiddlesticks, you duffer! I can get up right enough
on my own cheek,' I said with a titter, though my
mouth was full of the brackish water into which I had

plunged at first head and ears over, while my teeth were chattering with cold, the frosty November air being chilly. 'I shall fancy I'm climbing the greasy pole at a regatta and that you're the pig on the top, old fellow. How's that, umpire, for your "Square-toes," eh?'

'Ah, pax! You're a trump, Jack Vernon, and I promise never to call you by that name any more as it annoys you,' he replied, chuckling at my joke, though it was at his own expense. He then leant out of the port further so as to get a tight grip of the whip fall, the other fellows holding on to him in turn to prevent his toppling over and joining me below, singing out as soon as their preparations were completed, calling out to me, 'Are you ready?'

'Ready?' I repeated, quoting my favourite Napierian motto again. 'Aye ready!'

'Then, up you come, my joker! Put your feet in the bight and hold on to the slack of the rope above your head and we'll hoist you up in regular man-of-war fashion. Now, my lads, pull baker, pull devil!'

He spoke under his breath; and yet, I heard every word he said, not only to me, but to the others inboard, grouped behind him within the port.

Quick as lightning I followed out his directions, clinging to the lower end of the rope like an eel; and, as soon as I gave the word, Larkyns and the rest of the mids clapping on to the running part cf the whip falls, which ran through the block above, hoisted me up in a twinkling, as if I were a sack of flour, to the level of the port sill.

Once there, I was clutched by a dozen eager hands, and my whilom tormenters dragged me in, all dripping, and landed me on the deck beside them—'very like a fish,' according to the old adage; and bearing just then the most unmistakable evidence of having come 'out of water!'

After thus 'landing me,' the ends of the whip tackle were dropped again over the side in the same stealthy manner in which my rescue was effected, and as promptly.

My frolicsome friends were not an instant too soon ; for, even while they were congratulating me all round, and declaring I was the best of good fellows for behaving so bravely and not 'kicking up a row,' though I had gone overboard so suddenly, the big, broad-beamed powder hoy slewed up alongside and Mr Triggs bustled down the hatchway.

Immediately after him came Mr Cheffinch, our gunnery lieutenant, accompanied by a strong working party to ensure the rapid transhipment of the combustible material and its storage in the magazines ; and we could hear the boatswain piping all hands on the upper deck to man the whip falls of the hoists and lowering tackle.

I at once rushed away to my chest in the steerage, to change my wet clothes, hoping to return as quickly as I could to see what was going on, without my plight being seen or anyone knowing what had happened to get me into such a drenched condition ; but, unfortunately, Corporal Macan caught sight of me as I was struggling to open my chest, for my fingers were so numbed with the cold that the keys I held in my hand jingled like castanets.

'Begorrah an' it's a purty state ye're in, sor,' he said, eyeing me with much commiseration. 'Sure an' ye've got the aguey.'

'Nonsense, Macan,' I answered shortly, wishing to shut him up at once, for he was Dr Nettleby's factotum and if he got hold of the story it would soon be all over the ship. ' I've only been splashed with some water and want to shift my rig, that's all.'

'Sphlashed is it, sor?' he repeated with a broad grin that completely shut out the rest of his face. 'Faith, if ye was to axe me I'd tell ye, begorrah, ye looks loike a drowned rat, sor!'

'None of your impudence, corporal,' I said with dignity, not liking his easy familiarity; though, poor fellow, he did not mean any harm by it, as it was only his Irish way of speaking; 'I'll report you to the sergeant.'

'An' is it rayporting *me*, sor, you'd be afther, an' you thremblin' all over,' he rejoined, catching hold of me and helping to peel off my soaking garments. 'Faith, sor, I'll be afther rayportin' *you* to the docthor!'

'Hi, hullo, who's taking my name in vain?' at that moment exclaimed Dr Nettleby himself, emerging from the gunroom at this critical juncture, the worthy medico having been making his rounds, looking up some of those of his patients who were not actually on the sick list. 'I'm sure I heard that Irish blackguard Macan's voice somewhere. Ah, it is you, corporal, as I thought! Hi, hullo, what's the matter, youngster?'

'I—I'm all right, sir,' said I, trying to rise, but sinking back again on the lid of my chest, where I had been sitting down while the good-natured marine was endeavouring to pull off my wet boots. 'It is nothing, sir.'

'He's bin taking a dip in the say, sir, wid all his clothes on,' explained Macan; 'an' faith he's got a bit damp, sir.'

'Damp, you call it, corporal? Why, he's dripping wet and chilled to the bone!' cried the doctor, feeling my pulse. 'How did this come about, youngster?'

'It was an accident, sir,' I replied hesitatingly, not wishing to incriminate my messmates. 'I would rather not speak of it, doctor, if you'll excuse me.'

'Oh, I see, skylarking, eh? Well, well, you must go to bed at once, or you'll be in a high fever before sundown. Corporal Macan!'

' Yis, sor.'

' Take this young gentleman to the sick bay and put him into a clean cot with plenty of blankets round him. By the way, too, corporal, ask Dr M'Gilpin to let you have a stiff glass of hot grog.'

' For mesilf, sor ? '

' No, you rascal, confound your cheek ! Certainly not,' replied the doctor, amused by the question. ' This young gentleman is to take it as hot as he can drink it. It will throw him into a perspiration and make him sleep. Do you hear, youngster ? '

' Y—es, sir,' I stammered out as well as I could, for my teeth were chattering again and I was shaking all over. ' Bu-but I'd rather not go to the sick bay, sir, if you don't mind. I don't want anyone to hear of wha—what has hap-hap-happened.'

' Ah, yes, I see,' said Dr Nettleby. ' You're afraid of some of your nice messmates getting hauled over the coals ? I bet that madcap Larkyns is at the bottom of it ; I saw him with you close to one of the ports just now, as I passed by on my way down here, and I wondered what mischief you were up to ! Well, well, I respect you, my boy, for not telling tales out of school, as the old saying goes; so, I won't split on you. Carry the youngster to my cabin, Macan, and then nobody will know anything about the matter. See here, I will look after you myself, youngster and keep you a prisoner till you're all right again. What d'you think of that, now ? '

' Th-a-nk you, doctor,' said I, faintly, for I felt very weak and giddy, everything seeming to be whirling round me. ' I'll—'

' Yes, yes, I know ; all right, my boy, all right,' interrupted the kind-hearted, old fellow, stopping any further attempt to speak on my part; and the brawny corporal of marines at the same instant lifting me up in his arms as if I were a baby, I lost consciousness, the last thing I recollect hearing being the doctor's voice, sounding, though, far away as if a mile off, like a voice in a dream, saying to me in the soft, purring tone he always adopted when in a specially good temper, ' Here, drink this, my boy, and go to sleep ! '

' Faith an' sure ye're awake at last ! ' exclaimed Corporal Macan when I opened my eyes, a minute or so after this, as I thought. ' How d'ye fale now, sor ? '

' Hullo ! ' said I, raising my head and looking round me in astonishment. ' Where am I ? '

' In Dr Nittleby's own cabin, sure,' answered the Irishman, grinning; ' an' by the same token, sor, as he wor called away by the cap'en, he lift me here for to say, he tould me, whither ye wor di'd or aloive, sure, whin ye woke up.'

' I feel awfully hungry, Corporal Macan,' said I, after a pause to reflect on the situation. ' Have I been asleep long ? '

' Ivver since Siven Bells, sure, in the forenoon watch, sor.'

' And what's the time now ? '

' Close on Four Bells in the first dog watch, sor.'

' Good gracious me ! ' I exclaimed in consternation, tossing off a lot of blankets that lay on the top of me and jumping out of the big bunk that was like a sofa, where I had been sleeping, on to the deck of the cabin ; when I found I was attired only in a long garment, which must have been one of the doctor's nightshirts, for it reached down considerably below my feet, tripping me up on my trying to walk towards the door. ' Where are my clothes ? '

' Here, sor,' replied the corporal, equal to the occasion, taking up a bundle that was lying on one of the lockers and proceeding to spread out my uniform, jacket and trousers and other articles of wearing apparel seriatim, on the top of the bed-place ; Macan smoothing down each with the palm of his hand as if he were grooming a horse. 'I had 'em dried at the galley foire, sor, whilst ye wor a-slapin'.'

'Thank you, corporal,' I said, dressing as quickly as I could with his assistance ; the marine, like most of his class, being a handy, useful fellow and not a bad valet on a pinch. 'I must hurry up. I wonder if I can get any dinner in the gunroom.'

'Faith ye're too late for that, sor,' answered Macan with much concern. 'An' for tay, too, sor, as will. It's all cleared away this hour an' more.'

'Oh, dear, what shall I do?' I ejaculated as I dragged on my boots, which had not been improved by their dip in the sea and subsequent roasting on top of a hot iron stove, although I noticed they had been nicely polished by the corporal. 'I feel hungry enough to "eat a horse and chase the rider," as I heard a fellow say the other day !'

'Ye must fale betther, sor, if you're hoongry,' observed Macan on my completing my toilet and donning my cap again. 'That's a raal good sign whin ye're inclined fur to ate—at laste that's what the docther sez.'

'Providing you've got something to eat !' I rejoined ruefully, for I knew there wouldn't be much left if the gunroom fellows had cleared out. 'What did Doctor Nettleby say was the matter with me, eh ?'

'He s'id ye wor a comet, sor.'

'A comet ?' I repeated, laughing. 'You're making a mistake, corporal.'

'The divil a ha'porth, sor. He called ye that same.'

'Nonsense, man !' I said. 'The doctor made use of some medical term, probably, which you don't understand.'

'Mebbe, sor, for I'm no scholard, worse luck !' replied the corporal, unconvinced. 'The docther do sometime bring out one of them outlandish wurrds that nayther the divvil nor Father Murphy, more power to him! could make out at all at all; but, whin ye dhropped down this afthernoon on the dick alongside o' yer chist, an' I picked ye up, he says, sez he, ye was ayther a "comet," or in a "comet house," or somethin' loike that, I'll take me oath wid me dyin' breath, though what the divvil he manes, I'm sure I can't say, sor!'

'Oh, I see now!' I exclaimed, a light suddenly flashing on me as to his meaning. 'I must have fainted away and the doctor told you I was in a comatose state, eh?'

'An' isn't that, sure, a comet, sor, as I tould ye!' cried the Irishman, triumphantly. 'Hullo, here's Peters, the cap'en's stooard dodgin' about the gangway. I wondther what he's afther?'

I walked out of the cabin as he spoke, and the man he referred to came up to me at once.

'Beg pardon, sir,' said he, civilly, touching his forelock in salute. 'Mr Vernon, sir, I believe?'

'Yes,' I replied, rather anxious to learn what was wanted of me, 'that is my name.'

'Cap'en Farmer presents his compliments, sir, and requests the pleasure of your company to dinner this evening.'

'Give my compliments to the captain, and say that I shall be most happy to accept his kind invitation,' I answered, putting on my most dignified manner, as if it was quite an everyday occurrence for me to be asked to dinner by officers of the highest rank; though, I felt inclined to jump with joy at the prospect, especially under the circumstances of my famished condition. 'What time do you serve up dinner, steward?'

'We allers dines at Four Bells, sir,' said he, with equal dignity, conscious of his position apparently as captain's steward, and at the same time not oblivious of the fact that I was only a naval cadet. 'In ten minutes time, sir, dinner will be on the table.'

'All right, my man, I'll be there,' I replied in an offhand way, as he went on towards the wardroom, opposite to where we were standing; and I added aside to the corporal, 'I don't think there's any fear of my being late!'

'Faith, the divil doubt ye, sor,' said Macan in reply to this, breaking into a broad grin as he set to work methodically to put the doctor's cabin straight again, while I turned to go below to my proper quarters, with the intention of making myself smart for the forthcoming feast. 'Musha, I wudn't loike to be the dish foreninst ye, sor, if ye can ate a hoss, as ye s'id jist now!'

A few minutes later, attired in my best uniform, I was ushered by the marine sentry, who stood without the doorway, into the big after-cabin beneath the poop that served for Captain Farmer's reception-room.

This was a handsome apartment, hung round with pictures and decorated with choice hothouse flowers and evergreens, as unlike as possible anything one might expect to find on board ship.

The very gun-carriages on either side were concealed by drapery, as well as the windows at the further end which opened on to the stern gallery, that projected, like a balcony, over the shimmering sea beneath, whereon the lights from the ports played and danced on the rippling tide in a hundred broken reflections, the evening having closed in and it now being quite dark around.

I was received very kindly by Captain Farmer.

He was a short and rather stout man, so he looked uncommonly funny in his mess jacket, which, according to the custom of the service, was cut in the Eton fashion and gave him a striking resemblance to an over-grown schoolboy, as I thought ; but, I soon forgot his appearance, his manner was so charming, while his anxiety to set me at my ease seemed as great as if I had been an admiral at the least, instead of being only little Jack Vernon, naval cadet !

The doctor was talking to him when I came in ; and he spoke to me very cordially, too, feeling my pulse as he shook hands with me.

'Ha ! No fear of your kicking the bucket yet, my little friend,' he said in his dry way, as we all proceeded into the fore cabin, where dinner was laid, Captain Farmer leading the way as soon as his steward Peters intimated that everything was ready. 'No cold or fever after your sudden chill, thanks to my prescription ! But, I won't answer for consumption after your long fast. I can see from your eye, youngster, you'll have a bad attack of that presently, eh ? Ho, ho, ho !'

'Of course I grinned at this ; and, I may state at once, that, by the time the repast was concluded, I had fully justified the doctor's sapient prediction, being blessed with the healthiest of appetites and a good digestion, which my temporary indisposition had in nowise impaired.

Mr Cheffinch, our gunnery lieutenant, who was one of the other guests, sat beside me, and from a remark or two he made I discovered that not only did he know of my adventure, but that the captain was also cognizant with the circumstances of the case, although the facts had not been officially communicated to him and he was not supposed to be aware of what had happened.

'He thinks you behaved very pluckily, youngster, observed Mr Cheffinch in the most gracious way, when informing me of this. 'Ay and so do we all in the wardroom, let me tell you !'

'I'm sure I don't know what I have done to deserve your praise, sir,' said I, feeling quite abashed by all these compliments. 'It was all an accident.'

'It is not so much what you did as what you didn't do, youngster,' he replied, frankly enough. 'You didn't show any funk or make a fuss when you fell overboard, and you did not wish to get your mess-mates into a scrape when Dr Nettleby—he told us this himself in confidence—found out the state you were in and made inquiries. In so doing, you behaved like a true sailor and a gentleman, and we're all proud to have such a promising brother officer amongst us, young Vernon, I assure you. If you go on as you have begun, you'll be a credit to the service.'

Such a flattering eulogium made me blush like a peony, and I was very glad when the captain presently proposed the toast of 'The Queen,' which we drank, all standing.

This being satisfactorily done, taking that hint from the doctor that I had "better turn in early and have a good night's rest after all the exertions I had gone through," as a sort of reminder that they had seen enough of me for the occasion, I paid my adieux to the captain and company and went on deck, where I remained while the watch was being called at Eight Bells.

I need hardly add that, in this interval, I ruminated over the strange succession of events that had taken place within so short a period ; events which, possibly, might make, as they just as probably might have marred, my entire future career in the service—ay, and, perhaps, have ended it altogether, but for God's good providence !

CHAPTER X

FOR a couple of days longer, we were as busy as
bees, taking in our boats and spare spars and other
gear, besides filling up our stock of provisions and
water and completing with stores of all sorts; until
Saturday arrived, the last day of our stay at Spithead,
when all our preparations were finished and all hands,
likewise, paid their advance of two months' pay, prior
to our sailing for China.

No one was allowed on shore that afternoon, for
fear of desertion; but, to make amends for this
stoppage of all leave, the men were granted permission generally to receive their friends on board, so
as to get rid of all the loose cash they were debarred
from spending in more legitimate fashion on land.

The consequence of this licence was, that the ship
was crowded from stem to stern with strangers of
every description, shape and sex, from dinner-time
to dusk; Jew and Gentile, kinsman and creditor, each
and all alike in turn, having a final tug at poor Jack's
purse-strings, striving to ease him of his superfluous
wealth before departure.

As may readily be imagined, some queer customers
came aboard; and some curious scenes took place,
both of the sentimental and comic order.

One of these latter I especially noticed; for it

occurred under my very eyes, within earshot of where I was standing by the gangway.

'Downy,' as the men called him, the whilom digger of graves, who had so puzzled Commander Nesbitt on the first day of his joining, by giving his profession so peculiar a designation, had come on board without any sort of an outfit for the voyage.

So, at last not being able to go ashore to buy a stock of clothes on receiving his advance pay, the purser at that time not supplying the men, as is the custom nowadays, with what they required, the morose gentleman was obliged to have recourse to Poll Nash, one of the bumboat women, who had brought off a lot of 'slop' clothing for those requiring a rig-out, and was selling the same on her own terms to all comers as quickly as she could dispose of her stock.

To her, therefore, Master 'Downy' now applied, having nothing beyond the rather shabby suit of black in which he stood up, which was certainly somewhat unsuitable, to say the least, for a sailor's wear, particularly a man-o'-war's man, as the once gravedigger had been transformed into.

He had well-nigh fully invested, in this way, the entire amount he had just received from the purser, Mr Nipper, on account of his advance pay as an 'ordinary seaman,' that being his rating; when, I noticed, a dark-faced, long-nosed gentleman come up to him and speak.

The two then got into a violent altercation that speedily attracted everyone's attention, a small crowd gathering round the disputants just abaft the mainmast.

'I tell you I haven't a ha'penny left,' I heard 'Downy' say, after a lot of words passing between them the gist of which I could not catch. 'No, not a ha'penny left, I swear. I've paid it all to this good lady here for clothes!'

'You haven't paid me for the monkey jacket yet,' interposed Mrs Poll Nash, the bumboat woman, who was holding up the garment in question, waiting for the coin to be passed over before parting with it, the good lady having in her career learnt the wisdom of caution. 'That'll make three pun' seventeen-and-six in all. Now, look sharp, my joker, or I'll chuck the duds back into the wherry. I ain't a-going to wait all day for my money, I tell you!'

'I'll let you have it in a minute,' whined 'Downy,' who was apparently afraid to show what he had in his pocket, the dark gentleman's eye being upon him. 'Can't you give a fellow time? I ain't a-going to run away.'

'Ye vood, ye liar, presshus shoon if ye 'ad arf a shance, I bet, s'help me!' shouted out the other man, who, from his speech, was evidently a Hebrew and a creditor. 'Ye're von tam sheet, dat's vot ye vas, a bloomin' corpse swindler, vot sheets de living, s'help me, and rops ze dead! I shpit upon ye, I does!'

'Come, come, you fellows there, I can't allow such language on board this ship,' sang out from the poop Lieutenant Jellaby, the officer of the watch, when matters had come to this pass. 'Ship's corporal, bring those men here!'

In obedience to this command, the two disputants were both brought aft, Poll Nash following also, being an interested party, to get back her clothes or the money from 'Downy.'

The latter was at once recognised by Lieutenant Jellaby, a jolly fellow, in whose watch I was. He went by his Christian name of 'Joe' amongst us all, being very good-natured and always full of fun and chaff.

'Hullo!' he exclaimed. 'You're the gravedigger, ain't you?'

'Yes, sir,' replied "Downy" sedately, as his original

profession probably inculcated. 'That were my humble calling, sir.'

'Why did you give it up, eh?'

'Trade got slack, sir.'

'How was that?'

'Porchmouth's too healthy a place, sir,' answered the man, as grave as a judge. 'People won't die there fast enough, sir, for my trade; so I had to turn it up, 'cause I couldn't make a decent living out of 'em.'

'By burying them, I suppose?'

'Yes, sir,' answered the man, seriously. 'That is, when I were lucky enough to get a job.'

'Well, that's a rum start, a fellow complaining of not being able to make a living out of the dead!' said Joe Jellaby to me, smiling; and then, turning again to the man he continued, 'now, tell me what all this row is about?'

Here the Jew, who introduced himself as the keeper of a lodging-house in Portsea, put in his word.

'Dis shcoundrel vas owe me five blooming pounds,' he cried out excitedly. 'I vash keep him ven he vash shtarving; and now, ven he got money, he von't shettle. He's a shvindler and a tief, s'help me; and I shvear I'll have the law on him!'

'Why don't you pay this man if you owe him anything?' said the lieutenant, sharply, to 'Downy.' 'You've received your advance money from the pay-master, have you not?'

'Yes, sir; but I'd better tell you the whole story, sir,' said the ex-gravedigger. 'I acknowledge owing Mister Isaacs some money, though he's piled it on pretty thick, I must say; for I were four weeks out of work and had to board at his place.'

'Yes, s'help me, and ate and drank of the best, too. Oh, Father Moses, how he did eat!' interrupted his creditor. 'Look you, sir, it's only a mean shcoundrel that voud call a pound a week too much for good vittles.   I'll put it thick on him, I will !'

'Stop that, or I'll have you turned out of the ship at once,' said Mr Jellaby, as the Jew made a dart at 'Downy,' who dodged behind the marine sentry on the quarter-deck ; while he repeated his injunction to the defaulter.   'Pay the man his money and let him go.'

'I can't, sir.   I've expended all my money in buying clothes of this good lady here,' explained Downy, pointing to the fat, old bumboat woman.   'I hadn't a stitch to my back and had to get a rig-out for the voyage, sir.'

'Yes, sir, he's 'ad three shirts, as is twelve-and-six, and cheap at the price, too, sir,' corroborated Mistress Poll Nash, with a low curtsey to the lieutenant.   'Yes, sir, and two pair of trousers for thirty shillin', besides a hoilskin and a serge jumper ; and this monkey jacket here, sir, which makes three pun' seventeen-and-six, sir.'

'Well, well, I suppose the calculation is all right,' said Joe, laughing at her volubility and the queer way in which she bobbed a curtsey between each item of her catalogue.   Then, addressing poor 'Downy' he cried out curtly, 'Turn out your pockets !'

The ex-gravedigger sadly produced four sovereigns.

'Is that all the money you've got ?'

'Yes, sir,' replied 'Downy,' in a still more sepulchral tone.   'Every ha'penny !'

'Then, pay this woman here, for you must have a rig-out for the voyage,' said the lieutenant.   'I'm afraid, Mr Isaacs, you'll have to wait till your debtor returns from China for the settlement of your claim. Your friend, the gravedigger here, will then probably have lots of loot ; and, be better able to discharge his debt.'

'Ach, holy Moses !' cried the Jew, refusing with spluttering indignation the half-a-crown change

'Downy' received from Polly Nash, and which he handed to his other creditor with great gravity as an instalment of his claim. 'He vill nevaire gome back to bay me.'

'Oh yes he will,' said Joe Jellaby, chaffingly, 'and probably, he'll bury you, too, for joy at seeing your pleasant face again—all for love, my man.'

Mr Isaacs, however, got furious at this and used such abusive language both to 'Downy' and the lieutenant that the latter gave orders at last for him to be shown over the side.

This order was instantly carried out by the ship's corporal, with the assistance of the master-at-arms, who had now arrived on the scene, when the incident terminated; but we could hear the Jew still cursing and swearing, and calling on his patron saint, Father Moses, for a long while after, as he was being rowed ashore.

Shortly before evening quarters, all strangers were ordered also to go ashore; and, later on, the captain came off, bringing word that we were to sail early the following morning.

I heard him tell Commander Nesbitt that he had better begin shortening in cable at daylight, so that we might weigh anchor immediately after breakfast.

'Very good, sir,' the commander replied. 'But who is this with you, sir—another youngster?'

'Yes; he's Admiral Mills's son,' said Captain Farmer, much to my delight, for I had not noticed my old friend, Master Tom, who was the very last fellow I expected to see. 'I have taken him to oblige his father, though he hasn't quite completed his time on board the *Illustrious.*'

'Oh, he won't lose anything by that,' rejoined Commander Nesbitt, who did not have a very high opinion of my old training-ship, as I have already pointed out; and, just then, seeing me standing by, he said, 'Take this young gentleman down to the gunroom, Vernon, and make him comfortable. I suppose you are already acquainted, both of you coming from the same ship?'

'Oh yes, sir,' I answered glibly enough, overjoyed at having little Tommy Mills as a messmate once more. 'He and I are old chums, sir.'

'Indeed? Then there's no need for my introducing you,' said the commander, with his genial laugh, which it was quite a pleasure to hear sometimes, it put one so much at one's ease. 'Mind though, youngster, not too much skylarking when you get below. We don't want any more of that overboard business on board here, you know.'

Of course I sniggered at this, understanding the allusion ; but, naturally, Tom was not in the secret, and I had a good deal to tell him when I got him below.

The two of us took our seats on one of the lockers in a quiet corner of the gunroom and had such a very long chat, that we were only interrupted by Larkyns flinging a boot at us at Four Bells, calling out that it was high time for us to turn in to our hammocks.

He wanted to go to sleep he told us ; for he would have to go on deck to take the middle watch at midnight, which was as close-handy as the boot he had sent at our heads to remind us!

This set us both giggling, which brought the companion boot to our corner, where it thumped against the bulkhead, grazing little Tom's nose and making him sniff.

However, this second missile had the desired end of sending us off; and so we left Master Larkyns to enjoy his repose undisturbed any longer by our chatter.

CHAPTER XI

'SHORTENING IN CABLE'

'ROUSE out, port watch and idlers! Rouse out! rouse out!' hoarsely shouted out the boatswain's mates along the lower deck; and this call, mingled with the shrill piping wail of their whistles and the tramp of hurrying feet as the men straggled up the hatchway to stow their hammocks in the nettings above, awoke me from my slumbers next morning in the dreary semi-darkness of the so-called daylight.

I was so tired and sleepy that I was hardly half-roused even by all this uproar. Indeed, I was just dropping off again, when Dick Andrews, one of my fellow cadets from the training-ship, who had joined the *Candahar* the same time as myself and was rather a bumptious and overbearing sort of chap, shook me violently.

'Turn out, you lazy lubber, turn out,' he shouted. 'It's long past Eight Bells, and old Bitpin, who has taken Joe Jellaby's watch and is looking after the men scrubbing decks, has been asking for you. He's in a fine temper this morning, Master John Vernon, I can tell you; so, you'd better look sharp, my lad, or you'll "catch Tommy" when he sees you.'

'Oh, bother!' I cried, with a yawn that nearly dislocated my jaw, shoving a leg over the side of my hammock lazily enough, loth to leave my snug, warm nest for the cold, uncomfortable quarter-deck, where I knew there would be a lot of water sluicing about and the men holystoning, to make it more unpleasant. 'I wish you wouldn't call me names, Andrews! You're not so awfully smart at rousing out yourself, that you can afford to brag about it! Why, Larkyns had to drag you round the gunroom last night in your nightshirt before he could make you wake up.'

'Larkyns is a bully!' exclaimed Andrews, angrily. 'He's a mean, cowardly bully!'

'Is he, my joker?' said that identical individual, whose approach was unnoticed by either of us, catching his slanderer a crack on the head which sent him spinning. 'There, take that in proof of your statement! If I'm a bully, Mr Andrews, I must act as such, or you'll call me a liar next!'

'I was only joking,' snivelled Dick, picking himself up and rubbing his cheek ruefully. 'I didn't mean anything.'

'Neither did I,' replied Larkyns, drily, as he peeled off his jacket and the thick woollen comforter he had wrapped round his neck to keep out the chilly night air, and prepared to turn in after his watch on deck so as to have a nice snooze before breakfast. 'I only gave you a striking proof of my devoted friendship for you, old chappie, that's all!'

With which parting words, he dexterously jumped into his hammock, rolling himself up like a worm in the blankets within; and, such was the facility of habit, I declare he was snoring like a grampus ere I had completed my dressing, although I scrambled into my clothes as quickly as I could, and hurried out of the steerage.

I left Dick Andrews still rubbing his cheek disconsolately and muttering impotent threats against his now unconscious assailant; but, he didn't do this until he was certain Larkyns could not hear good wishes on his behalf!

On going up the hatchway, I found all hands busy scrubbing and washing down the decks, which were in a precious mess.

There was a fair division of labour in carrying out
the operation, the topmen and after-guard scouring
the planks with sand; after which the decks were
flushed fore and aft with floods of water pumped up
by the 'idlers.'

Those are really a most useful and industrious
class of misnamed men consisting of the carpenters,
sailmakers, coopers, blacksmiths and other artificers,
besides the cook's mates and yeomen of stores.

In our ship the lot numbered no less than some
seventy in all, who every morning assisted in this
praiseworthy task!

Creeping up as quietly as I could and trying to
avoid observation from the squinting eye of Mr
Bitpin, our fourth lieutenant, who was the oldest in
seniority although he occupied such a subordinate
position, I made my way to the side of Ned
Anstruther, the midshipman of the watch, who stood
on the weather side of the quarter-deck on a coil
of rope so as to keep his feet out of the way of the
water that was swishing round.

Ned nodded me a greeting; and, I fancied myself
safe, when in an instant my presence was noted by
the lieutenant, who turned on me.

'Hullo, youngster!' he called out, looking down
from the break of the poop, whence he had been
surveying operations, finding fault with the men
beneath in quick succession, according to his general
wont, and having a snap and a snarl at everyone.
His temper, never a good one originally, had been
soured by a bad digestion and ill luck in the way
of promotion, the poor beggar having been passed
over repeatedly by men younger than himself. 'How
is it you were not here when the watch was mustered?'

'I'm very sorry, sir,' said I, apologetically. 'I over-
slept myself, sir.'

'Oh, indeed? You'd better not be late again

when I'm officer of the watch, or I'll have you spread-eagled in the mizzen rigging as a warning to others, like they nail up crows against a barn door ashore. That'll make you sharper next time, my joker! Do you hear me, youngster?'

'Yes, sir,' said I, touching my cap. 'I hear you, sir.'

'Very well, then. Mind you heed as well as hear!' he replied snappishly, rather disappointed, I thought, at my making no further answer, or trying to argue the point with him. 'You can go down now to the wardroom steward and tell him to get me a cup of coffee as quickly as he can. Now, don't be a month of Sundays about it! Say it must be hot and strong, and not like that dish-water he brought me yesterday; or, I'll put him in the list and stop his grog! Do you hear me?'

'Yes, sir,' I said respectfully as before, giving no occasion for offence so as to come in for more grumbling on his part. 'I hear you, sir.'

'Confound that youngster, I can't catch him anyhow!' I heard him mutter to himself as if uttering his thoughts aloud, as I turned away with another touch of my cap and left the quarter-deck to fulfil my errand. 'He's like those monkeys at the Rock—too artful to speak. Keeps his tripping lines too taut for that!'

He was quite right; for, three weeks' association on board, though I had been brought little in contact with him, had taught me to know his character pretty well.

I had learnt that the best way to get on with Mr Bitpin was, to let him do all the talking and only to answer him when necessity required.

It was advisable also that the reply should be made in the fewest words possible, such a course giving him no ground for further complaint.

When I returned, some few minutes later, with the desired refreshment for the lieutenant, which I brought up myself, thus saving the wardroom steward, who was a very decent fellow, a probable wigging besides getting a cup of coffee myself as a bonus for performing the service, I found the decks swabbed and almost dry; the ropes, too, were all coiled and flemished down handsomely, and everything around looking as neat as a new pin.

Mr Bitpin, also, was in a better humour, a sip of the smoking coffee, which apparently was just to his taste, adding to his content at the scrubbing operations having been accomplished to his satisfaction.

'Thank you, my boy, for bringing this,' he said, with a smack of his lips as he took a good long gulp of the grateful fluid, giving an approving nod to me. 'That lazy steward would have taken half-an-hour at least if you had left it to him. When I'm as young as you are, I'll do as much for you.'

I grinned at this, as did Ned Anstruther, who likewise winked in a knowing way to me behind Mr Bitpin's broad back; but, before I could reply to the lieutenant's complimentary speech, Commander Nesbitt made his appearance on the poop, having come up the after-hatchway and gone into and out of the captain's cabin again, without either of us seeing him.

'Ah, good morning, Mr Bitpin,' he said, looking somewhat surprised at seeing that gentleman there. 'I thought Mr Jellaby had the morning watch to-day?'

'So he had, sir,' answered the lieutenant, hastily putting down his empty cup under the binnacle out of sight of the commander, who he knew disliked anything out of order on deck. 'But, sir, Mr Jellaby was late off last night from the admiral's ball, and he begged me to take the duty for him. It is a great nuisance; for, I only turned in at Two Bells in the middle watch, myself. Of course, though, I couldn't be disobliging, you know, sir.'

'Of course not, Mr Bitpin,' said Commander Nesbitt, amused at this unexpected piece of good nature from one who very seldom put himself out for anybody. 'It does not matter in the least; but, I told Jellaby I wished to shorten in cable as soon as the decks were washed down.'

'He didn't tell me anything about that, sir, when he came on board this morning; for, I met him at the gangway,' growled out the crusty lieutenant in his usual surly way. 'He was full of some Miss Thing-amy's dancing and made me sick by telling me at least twenty times over what a " chawming gurl " she was!'

'No doubt of that. He's a rare chap amongst the ladies, is our friend Jellaby!' said Commander Nesbitt laughing at Mr Bitpin's imitation of Joe's favourite ex-pression. 'We must see now, though, about shorten-ing in without any further delay, for time's getting on.'

'Very good, sir,' replied the lieutenant, dropping his unwonted jocularity and relapsing into his matter-of-fact official manner. 'I'd better go on the fo'c's'le and join Mr Morgan, the mate of the watch, who's already there.'

'Thank you, Mr Bitpin,' briefly said the commander by way of dismissal; and then, bending over the poop-rail, he called out, 'Bosun's mate! Pipe all hands to shorten cable!'

'Ay, ay, sir,' answered the petty officer addressed, putting his whistle to his mouth and blowing a shrill, ear-piercing call that echoed through the ship and was taken up by his brother mates below on the main and lower decks, whose voices could be heard, in every key, gruffly shouting out fore and aft, until the sound gradually died away in the distant recesses of the hold, 'All hands, shorten cable!'

Immediately, as if touched by an enchanter's wand, the quiet that had reigned on board since the decks had been washed down disappeared, and all was bustle and apparent confusion; although, it need hardly be said, order was paramount everywhere.

Such, indeed, is always on board a man-of-war, where each man knows his place and takes care to be in it as quickly as he can ; especially when 'all hands' are called as in the present instance.

In this case, as now, all the crew turn out and come on deck to their stations, whether it be their watch below or not.

Up, therefore, tumbled the men of the starboard watch, who had only been relieved from duty an hour before, at the same time I was first roused out by the obliging Dick Andrews.

After the men, but a little more leisurely, came the other officers not already on deck.

Amongst these were, the Hon. Digby Lanyard, our swell first lieutenant, eyeglass in eye as usual, and dressed as neatly as if going to divisions, although he had only such very short notice for his toilet ; Joe Jellaby, the proper officer of my watch, whose place Mr Bitpin had taken for the nonce, rubbing his eyes and only half awake from his dreams of 'that chawming gurl' at the admiral's ball ; Charley Gilham, our third lieutenant, a manly, blue-eyed sailor and fond of his profession, but no bookworm and bad at headwork ; Mr Cheffinch, or 'Gunnery Jack' as he was styled ; the three other mates ; and, all the middies and cadets, including Larkyns.

The latter was wroth at his anteprandial snooze being so suddenly cut short ; while Andrews, who followed in his rear, was savage at meeting his late antagonist so soon again, his friendly feelings towards whom were not increased by the foot of Larkyns giving him a 'lift' up the hatchway as the pair scrambled on deck together, the cadet, unfortunately for himself, being a trifle ahead of the midshipman.

The first lieutenant, or 'glass eye' as the men called him, went out at once on the forecastle, where a number of the hands, under the superintendence of Mr Hawser, the boatswain, were already engaged rigging the fish davit and overhauling the anchor gear, with Mr Bitpin and Morgan looking on to see that everything was done properly.

'Charley' Gilham, and 'Gunnery Jack,' stopped down on the main deck to look after the capstan, which was soon surrounded by a squad of 'jollies' under the command of one of the marine officers, Lieutenant Wagstaff, a fellow as tall as a maypole and with a headpiece of very similar material!

Mr Jellaby, however, not knowing where his deputy, Mr Bitpin, might be, came up on the quarter-deck; but he had no sooner appeared there than the commander despatched him to another station.

'Please go down at once to the lower deck, Mr Jellaby,' said he, on catching sight of him. 'I want you to attend to the working of the cables. See how smart you can be with those new hands we have from the foretop!'

'Very good, sir,' replied 'Joe,' all on the alert in an instant. 'I will go down directly.'

Away he accordingly went; whereupon, I, having nothing special to do, and seeing everyone else appointed to some station or other, was just scuttling down the hatchway after him when the Commander called me back.

'Stop here, Mr Vernon,' he cried. 'I want you to act as my messenger again. Try if you can be as useful as the one they have to bring in the cable with. I suppose you know what sort of " messenger " that is, eh?'

'Oh, yes, sir,' I replied glibly enough. 'It is a species of endless chain, passing round the base of the capstan amidships, and through a stationary block called a " controller " on the forepart of the lower deck, to which the cable is attached by nippers as it comes through the hawse-hole inboard; and, as the capstan is hove round, the messenger drags the cable up, the nippers being released and taken forward again to get a fresh grip, while the slack of the cable passes down the deck pipes into the cable lockers below, sir.'

'Very well answered, youngster,' said Commander Nesbitt, approvingly, when I had reeled off this long yarn. 'But, I think, it's about time for Mr Jellaby to give us the signal for heaving round now.'

He liked things done smartly, did the commander, for he knew how they should be done; and, being prompt and ready in his own actions, judged others by himself.

Barely five minutes had elapsed since 'all hands' had been piped, and in that interval the cable had to be unbitted and the 'slip' stopping it to the deck knocked off by the blacksmith.

In addition to this, the messenger had to be brought up to the unbitted end and the nippers gripped on before those working the capstan on the main deck above could commence heaving round in order to 'bring in the shekels, like unto the Israelites of old and the Hebrews of the present day,' as Master Larkyns explained to me later; and yet, the commander grew impatient at the delay, in spite of all this having to be done in such a short space of time.

But, at last, the signal was given.

'Heave round!' shouted Mr Jellaby from the extreme fore-end of the lower deck, where he had been bustling up the topmen and seeing to the messenger being properly attached to the cable.

'Heave round,' also cried Sylvester, one of the midshipmen with him.

'Heave round,' repeated the boatswain's mate further aft; while his fellow mates stationed along the hatchways above passed on the cry, till it reached the commander on the poop, who in his full-toned voice now transformed what was merely a signal that all was ready into an order.

This gave the required impetus to the working party on the main deck, who were waiting for this order, really to ' Heave round ! '

At once, the drummer and bugler, in attendance on the eager marines and after-guard, struck up with fife and drum the festive strains of ' Judy Calaghan,' which Corporal Macan said ' did his sowl good to hear, faith!'

Then, the bars having been previously shipped by Mr Cleete, the carpenter and his crew, round tramped the 'jollies,' round went the capstan ; and, with it, the messenger, the endless chain of which, revolving slowly, hauled the cable foot by foot in-board, the 'lengths' dropping down the deck pipes out of the way as the slack was released from the messenger, and the nippers passed forwards again ; and so on, over and over again !

I had ample opportunity for noticing this, the commander sending me on another errand down to the scene of operations almost as soon as the drumming and fifing began. This was much to my delight; for I enjoyed the strains of the jolly air played as much as Corporal Macan, as well as the steady tramp of the marines and after-guard round the capstan, the men stamping on the deck in time to the music, as if they would smash through the planking.

' Go and tell Mr Jellaby,' said he, ' to shorten in to two shakels.'

' Ay, ay, sir.'

With which response to Commander Nesbitt's order, I sprang down the after-hatchway on to the main deck, proceeding thence below to where old ' Joe ' and his topmen were working.

Of course I gave the lieutenant the mandate with which I had been charged ; but I remaining, boylike, to watch what was going on, the commander not having told me to return immediately, though I ought to have done so.

The capstan, however, was spun round so merrily by the marines while the nippers, in the hands of the active seamen, passed so freely; that, ere I knew how far the task had progressed, so as to be able to report to the commander the state of things, Mr Jellaby suddenly sang out 'Belay!'

Instantly, the word being passed by the boatswain s mates as before, so that the order reached the lieutenant in charge of the working party at the capstan above almost as soon as Mr Jellaby sang out from the lower deck forward, the music stopped suddenly, as if the drummer and fifer had both been shot on the spot.

With it, too, ceased the monotonous tramp, tramp, tramp of the men above our heads, which sounded through the thickness of the deck like a band of Ethiopian minstrels dancing a flap dance and marching 'round the mulberry bush' afterwards, to 'show their muscle,' as is the wont of these negro 'entertainers,' so-called!

'You may go up now to the commander,' said Mr Jellaby to me, as a polite hint to be off, 'and tell him that the second shakel's just inside our hawse.'

'Very good, sir,' I replied, moving away as the blacksmith went to put the slip on the cable to secure it from running out until we were ready to weigh anchor later on. 'I'll tell him at once, sir.'

'All right,' said Commander Nesbitt, when I reached the poop and repeated Mr Jellaby's message, the import of which he already knew from the stoppage of all movement below, and the report of the boatswain from the forecastle that the anchor was 'a short stay apeak'; when, advancing to the rail, he called out in a louder key, 'Bosun's mate, pipe the hands to breakfast!'

H

CHAPTER XII

BELOW IN THE GUNROOM

'WELL!' exclaimed little Tommy Mills, a little later, when he and I, with young Morgan, the mate and Ned Austhruther, on being relieved by the starboard watch, all went down to the gunroom and sat down to have our breakfast, 'I call this a beastly shame!'

'Hullo,' said Popplethorne, one of the other middies, looking up from the plate on which he was busily engaged; while several other fellows, similarly employed ceased operations likewise, staring at Tommy in astonishment. 'What's up?'

'Nothing's up, but everything seems down,' replied my little chum in an aggrieved tone. 'I don't see a crumb left for a poor, hungry chap; no bloaters, no marmalade, no nothing. When I was in the *Illustrious*, if they did grind a fellow a bit, one always had some-thing decent to eat, at all events!'

'First come, first served,' mumbled Phil Plumper, the senior mate of our watch, who had his mouth full and was tucking in some species of 'burgoo,' or porridge with much gusto. He was an awfully fat fellow and looked just like a boiled lobster bursting out of its shell, for the buttons of his jacket were continually carrying away at odd moments. 'If you don't look out for yourself on board ship you'll find nobody 'll look after you; and, you'll come off *minus*.'

'That'll never be your case,' retorted Tommy, with a snigger. 'Judging by appearances, I should say your condition represents a *plus* quantity!'

'Beg pardon, sir,' apologised Dobbs, the gunroom steward, who from his comical little screwed-up eyes and manner must have been first cousin to my old friend the waiter at the 'Keppel's Head,' noticing the disdainful expression with which Tommy Mills continued to glance round the empty table, seeking in vain something appetising in the way of food for his hungry eye to rest upon,—'Beg pardon, sir, but the bumboat woman didn't come off this morning. Sunday, you know, sir.'

'That's all gammon, steward,' said Master Tommy, still looking about here and there and finding nothing but a desert of empty dishes and dirty plates. 'You ought to have sent one of the ship's boats ashore if you didn't have enough on board for everybody in the mess. Our steward in the *Illustrious* always kept a good look out and sent himself for them when the things were not brought off in time. Why didn't you do the same?'

'I'm sure I'm werry sorry, sir,' answered Dobbs, humbly, awed by the way in which little Tommy spoke to him; for my old comrade, I noticed, had lost none of his cheek since our separation, and now put on the air of a post captain at the least. Begging y'r pardon, sir, but getting ashore from Spithead, with a northerly wind a-blowin', ain't quite so easy as landing from Point and you're moored over against Blockhouse Fort!'

'That may be, but it's none of my business,' said young Mills, loftily, waiving Dobbs's plea aside as a mere trivial matter. 'I want some breakfast. What have you at all fit for a christian to eat? I see nothing here, nothing at all.'

'Got some werry nice cold 'am, sir, in my pantry,' cried Dobbs, with effusion, at this opening, glad of having something he could offer. 'Shall I cut you a plate o' that, sir—just try a wee bit off the knuckle end, sir?'

'All right, if there is nothing else, but I suppose it will be all bone and gristle, or as hard as a cat block,' replied Tommy; heaving a most portentous sigh of disappointment, though winking slily to me to show that he was only 'putting all this on' to astonish the other fellows, who were gazing at him with open mouths in wonder at his assurance and grand seigneur manner. 'You may get me a couple of eggs, also, while you're about it, steward. Mind they're fresh and have no chickens in them; I don't like poultry in the morning so early!'

Of course there was a loud guffaw at this, the three purser's clerks, who were eating bread and butter at the lower end of the table, not daring to put in a word of objection to the fare, seeming to enjoy the joke mightily.

Not so, however, Dobbs.

'Werry sorry, sir, but there's no heggs,' he replied to this somewhat imperative order from Master Tommy, looking absolutely crestfallen at having thus to confess the shortcomings of his commissariat. 'The caterer of the mess, sir, forgot to horder 'em, sir.'

'No eggs!' cried Tommy, in the tone of tragic denunciation which Cicero might have used when exposing the iniquities of Cataline. 'This is really impardonable!'

'Never mind, sir,' hastily whispered Dobbs, holding out a gleam of hope, as he thought, 'we'll get some at Plymouth as soon as we anchor in the Sound, sir. You shall get some there, sir, never you fear, sir.'

'Plymouth? Why, I may lose the number of my mess myself long before I ever reach there!' said Tommy, contemptuously. 'A caterer who forgets to provide eggs for the mess ought to be keel-hauled! Who *is* the caterer, steward?'

'Mr Stormcock, sir.'

'Oh, indeed! Storm—cock, eh?' repeated little Mills, making me choke with suppressed laughter. 'Then you can tell Mister Storm—cock, with my compliments, that unless he looks after the mess catering better, he'll precious soon find himself in foul weather with me!'

'Highty, tighty, my young bantam!' cried out the gentleman in question, the master's mate, a thick-set, full-grown fellow, old enough to be Tommy's father, who happened to be stretched at full length on one of the lockers at the further end of the gunroom, and was roused from his nap on hearing his name mentioned. 'You seem to have a pretty considerable stock of impudence of your own for so young a shaver, and crow so loudly you must want to have your comb cut, I think!'

'Not to-day, thank you, sir, all the same,' answered Master Tommy, demurely, but with a grimace that made us all laugh. 'If I'm a shaver, of course I can cut it myself, can't I?'

'Hang me, but you *are* a cheeky young beggar, the cheekiest we have on board, I think, and that's saying a good deal!' ejaculated the other, utterly dumbfounded at his effrontery. 'What are you rowing the poor steward about, eh?'

'Nothing—only I thought we might have had a better spread for breakfast than I see on the table as we're not yet at sea, that's all!'

'Oh, that's all, is it, young gentleman?' cried the master's mate, not liking to hear his catering criticised so frankly. 'I'm sorry you didn't let us know we had a lord coming aboard; for, if we had heard in time, we'd have hired a French cook and laid in every delicacy you could desire. By jingo! when I was a youngster and joined my ship for the first time, I remember, I was glad enough to get a mouthful of salt junk and hard tack, without any of your bloaters and marmalade and foreign kickshaws—ay, and thought myself doocid lucky, I can tell you, if I didn't get a thrashing from one of the oldsters in the mess, if I grumbled, to make me relish my grub the better. Things are coming to a pretty pass nowadays for a young jackanapes to growl about his vittles and call his seniors to account!'

'Pardon me, sir, but my name is Tom Mills, not "Jack Napes,"' said my cheeky chum, with meek subservience; and, turning then to Dobbs, he called out, 'a cup of tea, please, steward, with plenty of milk in it.'

'Werry sorry, sir, but there ain't no milk,' replied Dobbs, still more apologetically, at this further demand which he was unable to supply, as if he grieved from his inmost heart thereat. 'Mr Jones 'as 'ad the werry last drop, sir.'

'We'll send ashore for a cow for you, Master Impudence,' put in Mr Stormcock, ironically, before Tom could say anything. 'Just wait a bit for your breakfast till we can get it off. Dobbs, you know the sort of cow the young gentleman wants—one with an iron tail!'

'Did I ever tell you that yarn about a cow we had on board the *Duke*, eh?' observed a tall gentleman with long whiskers, regular 'weepers' of the Dundreary type, who was seated on another locker at the after end of the gunroom, right opposite to the irascible master's mate. 'I mean the cow old Charley Napier took with him in his flagship when we went up the Baltic?'

'Good Lord! Jones, don't get your jaw tacks aboard now,' cried Mr Stormcock, as I pricked up my ears on hearing the name of Sir Charles Napier, Dad's old captain. 'We've heard that yarn of yours three times at least since we started fitting out; and, I'm hanged if it'll stand telling again!'

'Oh, very well, then,' said the whiskered gentleman in a displeased tone. He wore a plain undress sort of uniform, I noticed, and Dobbs, the steward, told me he was the paymaster's assistant and kept the ship's books; though, he messed in the gunroom with all the midshipmen and cadets, like the master's mate, both of them seeming to my mind far too old to associate on such a footing with a parcel of boys like ourselves. 'I may as well spare my breath to cool my porridge! I assure you, Mr Stormcock, I have no wish to bore you.'

'Do tell us about the cow, sir,' I interposed anxiously, afraid he would not continue his story. 'I have often heard Dad, I mean my father, speak about Admiral Napier; and, I saw him myself when I was in London last summer. It was he who got me my nomination for a cadetship.'

'Ah, then you know what a queer old customer he is?' went on Mr Jones, evidently mollified by the interest I took in his yarn. 'It isn't much of a story, as Mr Stormcock appears to think; but, if you care to hear it, I'll tell you all about it.'

'I do care, sir,' I replied, 'very much indeed, sir.'

'Well, then, youngster,' he proceeded, 'the Baltic fleet was lying at Spithead, where we mustered, you must know, before sailing up the North Sea; and one fine day, when we were about to weigh anchor for the Queen to review us as she passed us in the royal yacht, up comes the dockyard tug alongside, with "Sally," that was the admiral's daughter, bringing along with her the old ship's cow and pigeons and a lot of other stock he had ordered from his place t'other side of Portsdown Hill on the road to Petersfield, "Merchiston Hall," I think he called it, or some other Scotch name sounding like that.'

'Oh, yes,' put in Mr Stormcock, satirically—'I recollect it all quite well. Heave ahead, my hearty!'

The assistant-paymaster, however, took no notice whatever of the interruption, pursuing the even tenor of his narrative.

'The admiral had the cow and stock taken in; but just as his daughter Sally was coming across the gangway, he ordered her back, for the royal yacht was now coming up. "Stop where you are, Sally!" he shouted out from the poop. "Stop, Sally, stop!" bawling out the words so loudly that you could have heard him in Common Hard, for he had a powerful pair of lungs had Old Charley, and could raise his voice above a gale. Almost in the same breath, too, he sang out to the wives and friends of the sailors who had come out from Portsmouth to wish them good-bye, "Now, all you women and people there! go aboard the tug with my darter, and when Her Majesty has passed you may come back again." Of course, they all cleared out at once, the master-at-arms and his corporals assisting them over the side; but when they were all comfortably landed on board the tug, she steamed off right away for the harbour, with a long string of wherries and shore boats pulling like blue niggers after her, the men in them swearing like anything at being cheated of their fares. We all the while were getting up anchor and in another minute or two were under weigh. Captain Gordon, who was the admiral's flag captain, spoke to him about the poor watermen and bumboat women being robbed of their money by our starting so suddenly; but he could get no satisfaction from old Charley. "Bumboat women be hanged!" was all he said. "Let 'em take their payment out of the fore tops'l, and the main topgallant s'l shall be witness to the bargain!" With that, he orders the men, who were muttering to be piped down.'

'But the cow, sir,' said I, on the paymaster's assistant thus coming to a conclusion, without alluding to what I considered the principal point of his story. 'You haven't told us yet about that, sir.'

'Oh, yes, I forgot,' said he. 'It was a fine beast, I remember, one of the red Alderney breed. Well, this cow was first stowed away in a pen the admiral had rigged up for her on the starboard side of the main deck, forrud; but on the gunner objecting to the mess the animal made there, she was then shifted to the port side, in the middle of the mess deck of the foretopmen. Here, too, she was found such a nuisance that the hands in a very short time determined to get rid of her as quickly as they could, either by fair means or foul; and, of course, they managed this right enough. Let sailors alone for that!'

'But, how did they manage it, sir?' asked Tommy Mills, who appeared to take as much interest in the narrative as myself. 'Did they kill her, or chuck her overboard?'

'They did neither directly; but, indirectly, I may say they did both,' answered Mr Jones, enigmatically, smiling and pulling his long whiskers caressingly through his fingers, as if particularly proud of these hirsute adornments. 'The fact was, the unprincipled scoundrels gave her alternately buckets full of dry biscuit-dust and water which so inflated the poor beast that she became the size of a balloon in less than a week; and, if she had not through this been suffocated, she would of course have burst from the "abnormal expansion!" That is how our doctor, old Nettleby, the same we've got on board here now, described it to the admiral when he was sent to inspect the cow, when the butcher reported her dead.'

'What did the admiral say, sir, when he heard this?'

'Oh, he stormed and let fly a volley of picturesque language,' replied Mr Jones to this inquiry of mine; 'but what could he do? "Throw her out of the bow port," he said to the gunner, who pitched a yarn about it being the foretopmen who had done the fell deed. " I don't know whether its your foretopmen or maintopmen that are to be blamed for it, and I don't care; but, you've stopped my milk between you, and I'm hanged if I don't stop your grog!"'

'And did he, sir?' asked little Tom Mills. 'Did he stop their grog for it?'

'No,' replied Mr Jones. 'He was too good-natured an old chap for that.'

'More than you were half-an-hour ago,' observed Mr Stormcock, sarcastically, rising up from his recumbent position. 'You didn't think of the fellows coming down from their watch on deck, when you drained off the last remains of the milk, eh? Yes, my joker, you left this cheeky youngster here to go without any in his tea, making him think of home and his mammy! yes, all through your selfishness.'

'Now, really, Stormcock,' expostulated the paymaster, 'upon my word I didn't think of that, or I wouldn't have been so greedy. Really, now, upon my honour!'

Just then, the boatswain's call was heard ringing through the ship, and the drummers began beating to quarters, which made us all jump up.

'By jingo, I wonder what's in the wind now!' exclaimed Mr Stormcock, making a grab at his swordbelt, which he had unfastened for comfort after his breakfast, laying it alongside him on the locker while taking his snooze. 'It's always "All hands," or "Quarters," or the "Fire Bell," or something! I was just thinking of going into my cabin and having a fair lay off the land till noon, for there's nothing for me to do on deck; when here comes this hanged rattle of the drum, confound it, to upset my caulk. A fellow can't call his soul his own aboardship —a sailor's life's a dog's life, by jingo!'

CHAPTER XIII

THE CHAPLAIN MAKES A MISTAKE, AND WE MAKE SAIL

'Ah! my little friend, here you are, I see, in your proper place,' said Commander Nesbitt kindly to me, on my ranging myself by his side on the poop, where he was standing with the captain ; for, being his special messenger, or aide-de-camp, so to speak, although it was not really my watch on deck again till late in the afternoon, I thought on hearing the drummer beat to quarters that I ought to go to him at once. 'Every man to his station is the rule on board ship. That is only how order and discipline can be carried out with such a large company to deal with!'

I could see, too, that this rule was observed to the very letter, for the first lieutenant was already on the forecastle, eyeglass in eye, of course, as usual; while Mr Bitpin was on the quarter-deck, just below the break of the poop ; and 'Joe' Jellaby on the main deck, close to the hatchway, so as to be within easy hail.

Mr Cheffinch, the gunnery lieutenant, and Charley Gilham, in their turn, were on the lower deck, looking after things there, with all the mates and midshipmen and cadets, each at his allotted post and everyone equipped with sword or dirk buckled on ready for instant action.

Mr Triggs, the gunner, likewise had taken the keys of the magazine from their proper resting-place when not wanted for use, just without the door of the captain's cabin, where a sentry always stood guard over them; and was now prepared with all his staff of 'powder monkeys' to send up whatever ammunition might be required at a moment's notice.

The carpenter, too, stood by the pumps, and Dr Nettleby, with Mr Macgilpin and Mr Leech, the two assistant surgeons, had all the contents of their surgical cases—most murderous-looking instruments they were, too—spread out on the wardroom and gunroom tables, as well as plenty of lint and bandages for dressing; while Corporal Macan, with a working party of marines, were told off to act as stretcher bearers, and supply hospital aid to the imaginary wounded.

The remainder of the 'jollies' were drawn up in martial array on the after part of the poop, under the command of Captain Targetts and Lieutenants Wagstaff and Shunter of the same serviceable corps; all of the men spic and span in their full regimentals and appearing as smart as if on the parade ground at Forton; although, but a few minutes previously, most of the poor fellows had been washing plates and mess traps, and performing other menial duties below.

Young as I was, I could not help observing all this, and noting, as the commander had pointed out to me, how, thanks to a rigid discipline and the inexorable regularity, almost like that of a machine, with which the routine of duty is conducted on board a man-of-war, every officer and man, from the captain down to the smallest 'powder monkey,' was in his proper place and at his station before the rat-tat-tat of the drum had ceased reverberating fore and aft; albeit, most of the hands had only recently joined the ship, while some, indeed, had never before been to sea.

Of course, there was a good deal of scurrying to and fro and apparent confusion whilst the men were getting to their stations, the hasty trampling of feet along the decks and the scambling up of hatchways, some snatching their rifles from the arm racks and belting on their cutlasses as they hurried by, slinging their cartridge pouches over their shoulders at the run ; and, meanwhile, Commander Nesbitt, with my insignificant self by his side, remained at the end of the poop-rail, taking in everything that went on with his quick-glancing, watchful eye, waiting quietly till all the preparations were complete.

'Bosun's mate !' he sang out when all were ready. ' Pipe the hands to secure the guns for sea !'

This was a sad come down from all the grand things which some new to the game expected ; but, as we all learnt within a very short time of our novitiate, life at sea is a series of surprises, and, if the ruling maxim be ' To hear is to obey,' carried out with Draconian severity to the extreme letter of the law, the beauty of it lies in the fact that you never know what you *are* going to hear until you actually hear it.

The captain, is, it must be remembered, a sort of Delphic oracle of the marine genus, who invariably keeps his mystic intentions locked within the secret recesses of his own breast and only gives them utterance, when the occasion arrives for him to speak, through the lips of his chief augur, the commander.

None of ' the profane vulgar,' in the shape of the ship's company, know what will be the next move on the board until he gives the inspired word ; although, if unguessed until finally uttered, it is generally short, sharp and to the point !

That word being now given, needless to add, it was immediately acted upon.

The breechings of the guns on each deck were bowsed up and the side tackle falls hove taut and frapped, with preventer tackles rigged and secured round the brackets at the after part of the carriages and hooked to the ring-bolts in the ship's side ; all the guns' crews assisting in this task, and the marines and idlers tailing on to the falls and hauling away at the sound of the boatswain's pipe and only stopping pulling at the order being given 'Avast heaving!'

When passing round with the commander presently to see if all the guns had been properly made fast, so that there should be no chance of their 'taking charge' in a heavy seaway and running themselves out without leave or licence when we least expected it, I overheard 'Joe' Jellaby talking to Charley Gilham, who had now come up from the lower deck and was standing by the main hatchway.

'I say, Charley,' observed Mr Jellaby, 'have you seen our "sky pilot" yet?'

'No, "Joe,"' replied the other. 'He didn't come into the wardroom till after dinner, and I had to go on deck for the first watch, and so didn't see him.'

'Well, he's the greenest chaplain I ever saw on board ship before,' went on 'Joe,' with a chuckle of merriment. 'He's been dodging in and out of his cabin since One Bell sounded, with all his pulpit rig on, as if he didn't know what exactly to do with himself and was afraid to ask anyone.'

'Perhaps he thought the bell rang for church,' suggested Mr Gilham. 'One of the fellows told me the parson has never been to sea before; so, my boy, of course, he doesn't know he's got to wait till the cap'en gives the order for service to be held. Those shore Johnnies have got a lot to be knocked into them! He doesn't know Farmer as we do, or he'd fight shy of taking a liberty with him!'

'Fancy, though, his skylarking round, in all his war paint,' said 'Joe,' breaking into his jovial laugh, which always made me join in for sympathy. 'I shouldn't wonder if he belonged to what they call the church militant; and on hearing the drummer beat to quarters, he naturally thought he ought to be prepared with his spiritual weapons as we were buckling on our arms, eh? By Jove, there he is now coming out of the wardroom right up to us!   I say, Charley, stand by me, like a good chap.'

But, Mr Gilham, thought in this instance that 'discretion was the better part of valour,' for he gave poor 'Joe' the slip by incontinently bolting up the hatchway, leaving his comrade to encounter alone the chaplain, who the next moment, in full canonicals, surplice and hood and cassock and all, confronted him.

He was a slim, sandy-coloured gentleman, I noticed, with hair of the tint of tow.   He had also white eyelashes, and spoke in a thin, hesitating voice, with a timid manner, as if very nervous and uncertain of his footing.

'A—hem,' he began, with a slight affected cough of introduction.   'I be—believe I'm addressing Mr—'

'Jellaby is my name, sir,' said the lieutenant, filling up the hiatus in his speech and bowing politely. 'Joe Jellaby, at your service.   Is there anything I can do for you, Mr—?'

'Smythe, sir, is my name,' replied the other.   'I am the ah—chaplain.'

'So I see, sir,' said Joe, drily, glancing at his canonicals.   'Glad to have the pleasure of making your acquaintance, Mr Smith.'

'"Smythe," that is "Smith" with a final "e," if you please,' corrected the reverend gentleman in a plaintive tone.   'My name is not "Smith," Mr Jelly-boy.'

'Nor is mine Jellyboy, Mr Smythe,' retorted 'Joe,' laughing outright at the comical situation.   'We've both made a mistake, Mr Smythe; and I apologise for mine.   But, is there anything I can do for you, sir?'

'We-ll,' hesitated the other, 'I want, you know, to hold a service, you know—ah, and—'

'You'll have to ask the captain after divisions, sir,' put in 'Joe' anxious to close the interview, for the drums had begun to beat the Retreat for the men to return their arms.   'Excuse me, though, please, Mr Smythe, I've got to go on deck now.'

With that he vanished up the hatchway after Mr Gilham; and, thereupon the unhappy Mr Smythe found himself, with his 'final e,' in the midst of a seething mass of men racing along the deck to put their rifles and cutlasses back in the racks, being finally compelled to beat a retreat himself to the wardroom, while the boatswain and his mates were piping and shouting all over the ship for the hands to clean themselves and dress for 'Divisions.'

A quarter-of-an-hour later, both watches were mustered, all decently dressed, like 'Sally in our Alley,' in their Sunday best, according to their respective stations; the first and second divisions on the upper deck and forecastle, under the first lieutenant and Mr Jellaby; the third and fourth divisions on the main deck, with Mr Gilham and Mr Bitpin at the head of the men ; and the fifth and sixth on the lower deck, in charge of 'Gunnery Jack,' in lieu of one of the regular lieutenants, and the second mate, the fat Plumper, bursting out of his buttons as usual, who was at the head of the after-guard, among whom I recognised the ex-gravedigger, 'Downy.'

This worthy, I noticed, looked quite smart and seaman-like in the dungaree suit he had purchased from Mrs Poll Nash, the bumboat woman, which his messmates had taught him to rig up in proper man-o'-war fashion, the good-hearted chaps also supplying whatever other necessaries were required for his wardrobe, such as the black silk handkerchief, tied in a loose knot round his neck, and the knife and lanyard without which no bluejacket's toilet is complete.

The men were drawn up in line, two deep, in open order, ready for inspection, and the captain and commander were just about descending from the poop to go round the ranks ; when, up came the Reverend Mr Smythe on the quarter-deck in his complete clerical regalia, only now with his college cap on, which, when I had seen him before by the main hatchway, he had carried in his hand.

He now raised this in salute to the captain and then immediately replaced it, seeing that none of us were uncovered, all of us having our caps on of course, being in uniform.

Captain Farmer only gave the regulation touch to the peak of his in return for the chaplain's courtesy.

'Well, sir,' said Captain Farmer in his direct way, as Mr Smythe struggled to speak, feeling that the eyes of all hands were upon him, blushing a rosy red up to the roots of his sandy hair, 'what is it?'

'Am I—ah—to begin now, sir,' he stammered; 'or, wa—wa—wait till the bell rings again, sir?'

'Bell rings!' repeated the captain, abruptly. 'For what, sir?'

'For service, sir.'

'Service?' said Captain Farmer, in a questioning tone still. 'I've given no orders about any service to-day. There's no time for it now. We're going to weigh anchor in another minute or two.'

'Weigh the anchor, sir!' exclaimed Mr Smythe, in a voice of holy indignation, losing all his hesitancy and awkwardness of speech. 'Why, it is Sunday!'

'The better the day, the better the deed,' rejoined the captain, rather sternly, I thought. 'If you overhaul your Bible you'll find it was only the Pharisees who objected to any necessary work being done on the Sabbath, and I myself see nothing wrong in our sailing on this day if we have a fair wind, Sunday though it be; besides which, I am obeying the orders of my queen and country.'

'But, sir,' cried Mr Smythe, flushing up again, though now more from the heat of argument than from the feeling of bashfulness which at first oppressed him, 'it is my duty to celebrate divine service, and my bishop'—

'Mr Smythe, I'm bishop here; and, as commanding

officer, my word is law,' interrupted Captain Farmer. 'The next time you may desire to hold service on board this ship, please be good enough to ask my permission first ; for, remember, my rule is paramount here over matters spiritual as well as things temporal. No doubt you have erred through ignorance in trying to set your authority against mine, and I'll not dwell further on the matter. I am sorry there'll be no time to-day for you to hold any regular service, for I am now going to inspect the men at divisions ; but, after that, you may have a short prayer, if you like, before we make sail.'

The Rev. Mr Smythe, I was glad to notice, took this rebuke in dignified silence, standing aside on the quarter-deck while the captain and commander descended the poop-ladder and went their rounds.

He waited until they had passed forwards before he went down the after hatchway to the main deck ; where, on the completion of the inspection, all hands were mustered and he read the form of prayer enjoined by the rubric for those about to travel by sea, which was listened to more attentively perhaps than it is in any church ashore.

Sailors, however, watch as well as pray ; so, no sooner had the chaplain finished than his congregation dispersed instantly to their stations, the commander singing out from the poop, the moment he had reached that coign of vantage, the long-delayed but welcome order, for which we had all been waiting in expectancy since the morning.

' Hands, up anchor !' he cried in a brave shout, to which the boatswain on the forecastle gave a shrill response with his whistle, while his mates re-echoed the cry between decks, up and down the ship fore and aft, ' All hands, up anchor !'

The capstan was again manned below, and the marines and idlers heaved in the cable to the sound of the drum and fife, as before; although, this time, the tune was 'The Girl I Left Behind Me,' the tramp of their feet coming in every now and again as a sort of chorus to the music, while on the forecastle above, the boatswain overhauled the catfalls, and got up the up and down tackle, and the gunner's crew rigged out the fish davit with its gear.

'The cable's "up and down," sir,' presently reported the boatswain to 'glass eye,' our first lieutenant, who passed the word aft in the usual manner to the commander on the poop.   'Cable's up and down, sir!'

The merry sound of the drum and fife, and steady tramp of the men round the capstan on the main deck continued until, anon, the boatswain once again reported to the Hon. Digby Lanyard, as he stood surveying the progress made in heaving in from the knight heads, 'Anchor's weighed, sir.'

This implied that the heavy mass of metal, of some four tons weight, by which we had been moored, was now off the ground, a fact that increased the strain on the cable and messenger, taking a longer and a stronger pull out of those working the capstan, and making the nippers, too, pass a trifle less briskly than before.

'Anchor's in sight, sir, and a clear anchor, too!' was the next cry from the forecastle that went from hand to hand aft, causing 'The Girl I Left Behind Me' to come out stronger than previously and the tramping feet to hasten their measured tread; and, in another minute or so, the ring of the anchor was chock up to the hawse pipe at the bows, and the boatswain piped 'Belay!'

'Hands make sail!' next came from the commander aft, the midshipmen stationed in the tops jumping into the rigging and scrambling up the ratlines before he could shout 'Way aloft!'

In an instant, up started the topmen in pursuit, as it seemed, of the middies in a sort of 'follow my leader' chase; and ere the vibration of the commander's voice had ceased to tremble in the air, the active fellows were spread out along the footropes of the yards, loosing the lanyards of the gaskets and casting them off, while the deckmen let go the buntlines and clewlines and other running gear.

'All ready for letting fall, sir,' the middy stationed in the foretop was the first to sing out. This was Dick Popplethorne, a smart lad, who prompted the topmen under his charge to emulate his ready example, so as to get ahead of the others. Larkyns at the maintop was a good second, while Adams at the mizzen was the last; the officer of the watch, on hearing his hail, reporting 'All ready!'

'Let fall and sheet home!' thereupon shouted out Commander Nesbitt, with the captain standing behind, as it were, to 'back him up,' following this order with another warning hail—'Topsail halliards!'

Our topsails and courses were at once spread; and, then, the men on deck stood by the halliards, hoisting the yards up as soon as the word of command reached them from the commander with his next breath 'Hoist away!'

The wind was blowing steadily from the northward and westward as the yards were braced up, and the *Candahar* payed off handsomely on the port tack with the tide, making for the Warner Lightship to the eastwards; and, as we trimmed sails and bore away from our whilom anchorage in the roadstead, the breeze brought out to us the silvery chimes of the bells of old St Thomas', ringing the good people to church while we stood out to sea.

There was a clear blue sky overhead and the bright sun mellowed the frosty feel of the air, lighting up the blue water around us, as we ploughed our way through the dancing waveiets; our noble ship curveting and prancing along, similar to some gallant charger tossing its head and showing off its paces, throwing up the spray over her forecastle when she dipped deeper than usual and leaving a long wake behind her, like a lady's fan, all sprinkled over with pearls, stretching back to Spithead, now far away astern.

CHAPTER XIV

DOWN CHANNEL

MEANWHILE, the first lieutenant and boatswain were busy forward with the forecastle hands, seeing to the catting and fishing of the anchor ; and, as soon as our port bower was properly secured by the aid of the cathead stopper and shank painter, the courses, which were all ready to let fall, were dropped and sheeted home, topgallants and royals spread, and the jib and foretopmast staysail set, as well as the spanker aft, the old *Candahar* being presently under a cloud of canvas alow and aloft, and slowly but surely making an offing and reaching out to sea.

We continued on the same tack until we had weathered the Nab Lightship, some ten miles out, when, being favoured with a 'sojer's wind,' fair both ways, we trimmed sails again and braced the yards up, wearing ship and gradually altering course from a nearly due east direction to one 'west-half-south,' fetching a compass down Channel.

We passed on our starboard hand within easy cannon shot of the Isle of Wight, whose bold, projecting headlands and curving bays of white and yellow sand we opened in turn every minute, with their purple hills beyond and deep-shadowed valleys lit up ever and anon by a gleam of sunshine as we sailed gaily on; the blue sky above our heads seeming in the clear atmosphere to recede further and further back into the immensity of space as we proceeded while the blue water around us became bluer and, more intense in tone, except where here and there the crest of a breaking wave flecked it with foam.

At Seven Bells, when the watch was set, we had given the snub-nosed Dunose the go-by and were heading for St Catherine's Point, going about eight knots under all plain sail, the wind freshening as we drew away from under the lee of the land, and the ship getting livelier.

Just as I was looking over the side and noting this fact, while watching the gull's circling in our wake, uttering their plaintive screams at intervals that sounded like the ghost cries of drowned sailors buried beneath the sea, Mr Quadrant, the master, who was on the poop, sextant in hand, reported it was twelve o'clock; whereupon, the commander telling him to 'make it so,' Eight Bells was struck, the men being piped to dinner immediately afterwards in obedience to another order from headquarters aft.

Not being wanted any longer on deck, and the crisp, bracing sea air giving me a good appetite, I hurried down the hatchway to join my messmates in the gunroom, mindful by my morning's experiences of the disadvantage of being late for meals.

Quick as I was, I found the majority of the other fellows not on duty had already forestalled me, chief among these early birds being my chum, Tom Mills.

This young gentleman, all in his glory, was lording it over poor Dobb's, the long-suffering steward, at a fine rate, I noticed, making Mr Stormcock waxy with his remarks about the fare.

This, really, was not at all bad in quality nor scanty in quantity, as the irate master's mate asseverated with considerable heat.

It was much better, indeed, than most of us youngsters had probably been accustomed to when at school in our longshore days, no matter how we might growl and turn up our noses at it now; but, cocksy Master Tommy, of course, was incorrigible, treating such an innuendo as this, in spite of the loud voice and pointed manner of Mr Stormcock, with the contempt it deserved, the young rascal grinning and sticking his tongue in his cheek in so provocative a fashion that the master's mate instantly pitched a hot potato at him.

This caught Mr Fortescue Jones, the unoffending assistant-paymaster, in the eye, and made all the purser's clerks yell with laughter.

When I went on deck again, shortly after Three Bells, we were pretty well clear of the Isle of Wight, the Needles Rocks being off our weather quarter and some miles distant, with the Dorset coast looming ahead.

As I stood listening to the quartermaster instructing the helmsmen, one of whom was a young hand, telling them to keep the ship a couple of points free, until, as time went on, it came close to the next hour, two o'clock, or Four Bells; when, according to the routine of the service, Adams, who was midshipman of the watch, hove the log and reported that we were still only going eight knots, with the ebb tide in our favour.

At that moment, Captain Farmer came out of his cabin; and, hearing this, directed the officer of the watch, Mr Bitpin, whose rightful turn of duty it was, to set studding sails, not being satisfied, apparently, with the old *Candahar's* progress, although she was doing her best and surging along in grand style, as I thought.

'Bosun's mate!' thereupon sang out the lieutenant. 'Pipe watch to set starboard topmast and to'gallant stu'ns'ls!'

'Ay, ay, sir,' replied the boatswain's mate from

his post by the after hatchway; and, almost in the same breath, his piercing shrill whistle was heard, followed by his hoarse shout repeating Mr Bitpin's gruff command. 'Watch set starboard topmast and to'gallant stu'ns'ls!'

'Topmen aloft!'

'Jiggers at the tops'l lifts!'

'Clear away stu'ns'l gear!'

These successive orders were now jerked out in rapid rotation by Mr Bitpin, who stood at the poop-rail bellowing away like a wild bull, Captain Farmer remaining alongside him and surveying with critical eye all that was done as the hands scrambled up the rigging and bustled about the deck, casting off ropes and getting the booms prepared; until, anon, the captains of the fore and maintops and the captain of the forecastle, as well as the gunner's mate, whose task it was to see to the main topmast studding sail, reported 'All ready!'

Therefore the lieutenant, with a deeper bellow than before, shouted 'Sway away!'

In an instant, the watch on deck, bending on to the halliards with a will, hoisted the gleaming white sails aloft and sheeted them home; when, bellying out before the northerly breeze, they expanded their folds, making the yardarms creak again, and looking like the wings of some gigantic seabird, the ship herself bearing out the resemblance and swooping away in a heavy lurch to leeward, after apparently preening her pinions for a fresh flight, being now a perfect pyramid of canvas from truck to deck.

'Mr Adams,' called out Mr Bitpin presently from the poop, evidently in obedience to some quiet order given by the captain, to the midshipman, who of course stood immediately below his superior officer on the quarter-deck, 'heave the log again and tell me what she's going now!'

· 'Very good, sir,' replied Frank Adams ; and, after the necessary interval of heaving the log-ship over the side to leeward and counting the knots on the line while the fourteen-second glass held by the quartermaster was running out, he sang out 'She's going nearly ten, sir.'

'Ah !' muttered Captain Farmer, who had come down the poop-ladder and was waiting for the news before returning to his cabin, as he passed the marine sentry before disappearing within the sliding door, expressing his thoughts aloud, 'That's better, much better—I thought she could do it with this wind !'

It was a beautiful afternoon ; and, from its being Sunday, several of the wardroom officers came on deck after luncheon, having nothing especial to do below.

Amongst the lot were Dr Nettleby and Mr Nipper, the paymaster.

I also observed on the poop the Rev. Mr Smythe and 'Joe' Jellaby, who had contrived to secure sufficient snoozing, during the odd moments when he was off duty since the morning, to make up for the sleep he had lost by going to the admiral's ball and there meeting the witching houri of his dreams, 'that chawming gurl,' who had subsequently prevented him from taking his proper rest when he came aboard in the small hours of the middle watch.

The chaplain seemed to have taken a fancy to 'Joe,' for he stuck on to him as soon as he came up the hatchway, joining with some considerable difficulty in the lieutenant's constitutional 'quarter-deck walk.'

The reverend gentleman had not got his sea legs yet, and did not find it an easy matter to keep step, or indeed keep his footing sometimes.

This was more especially the case when the ship heeled over every now and again before the force of the wind and then righted herself on an even keel without warning, throwing Mr Smythe off his balance and causing him to clutch frantically at Joe's arm for support till he recovered his lost centre of gravity.

The lieutenant's courtesy was put to a severe test in making him preserve *his* gravity ; albeit, he had an itching inclination to burst out into his jovial laugh at the reverend gentleman's ridiculous contortions and praiseworthy attempts to sustain a sort of disjointed conversation between the pauses of his grotesque sprawls and restoration to a more dignified attitude.

As they were marching up and down the deck in this desultory way, describing the while a series of irregular ellipses, Six Bells was struck forwards, and the marine stationed by the taffrail at once shouted out in a high key, 'Life buoy!'

'Dear me!' exclaimed Mr Smythe in a shrill tone of alarm, which his squeaky voice was well calculated to express, bringing up suddenly against one of the quarter boats which was swung inboard from the davits ; and knocking his head violently against the bottom planking, through the ship lurching as he stopped.   'What has happened—is anyone lost overboard?'

'Oh, no,' replied ' Joe,' laughing as usual.   ' It's only the jolly in charge of the life buoy.   He has to sing out every time the bell is struck to show that he's at his post, just as the sojers ashore on sentry-go cry "All's well!" to tell their sergeant they're not napping, that's all.'

'Ah!' ejaculated the chaplain with a feeble smile, putting his hand to his head as if in great pain from the blow he had received, ' I see—ah, I see.'

'I hope you haven't hurt yourself,' said ' Joe,' seeing that the other kept his white cambric handkerchief still tightly pressed to his forehead.   ' That was a rather nasty knock you got !   Cut yourself, eh ? '

'I—I—don't quite know, you know,' answered the reverend gentleman, removing the handkerchief after some hesitation and proceeding to examine it carefully as if fearing the worst ; but, finding now no trace of blood on its snowy surface, he became reassured and said, in a more cheery tone, 'no, not cut, I think, only a severe contusion, thank you, Mr Jellaby. The pain has nearly gone now !'

'That's right ; I'm glad you've escaped so well,' said 'Joe,' taking Mr Smythe's arm again and wheeling him in line so as to resume their walk ; while I stood by, with my ears cocked, listening to the detached fragments of their talk. 'On board my last ship, the *Blanche*, we had a rum start one day with our life-buoy sentry. Would you like me to tell you the story ? '

'Thanks, much,' responded the chaplain ; 'I should be delighted.'

'Well, you see,' began the lieutenant, starting off with his yarn and quarter-deck walk again simultaneously, 'we had a lot of raw marine lads who had just enlisted sent us from Forton to complete our complement ; and, one of these green hands, as luck would have it, was placed as sentry on the poop by the sergeant of the guard, the first day he came aboard, though he'd probably never seen a ship in his life before. You see, eh ? '

'Ah !' ejaculated the chaplain as 'Joe' turned abruptly when close up to the taffrail and nearly twisted him off his legs. 'Yes, I—ah—see.'

'When the poor jolly was put on sentry,' continued the lieutenant, bolstering up Mr Smythe with his arm and just saving him in the nick of time from coming to grief again over a ringbolt on the deck, 'the sergeant told him he would have to call out when the bell was struck, thinking, of course, he knew all about it. The poor fellow, though, as you are aware, was quite ignorant of the custom ; so, as soon as the sergeant's back was turned, he asked one of the men of the starboard watch standing by, "What am I to call out when they strike the bell?"

'"Life buoy!" replied the other. "Life buoy!"

'"All right, chummy, I thank you kindly," said the young marine, full of gratitude; and so, when, by-and-by, Two Bells were struck, he called out in a voice that could be heard all over the ship, "Live boy!"'

'He—he—he!' chuckled the chaplain in his feeble way, he and Mr Jellaby coming to a stop, I was glad to see, close to where I stood. 'That was funny! Very, very funny!'

'Nothing to what's coming,' went on Mr Jellaby, pleased that his efforts at comic narrative under such difficulties had been so far successful, the chaplain not objecting to the secular amusement from any conscientious scruples. 'Well, as soon as the ignorant chawbacon chap yelled out this, which naturally made everyone who heard it laugh, although they put the mistake down to the poor fellow's provincial pronunciation, he turns to the man who had previously instructed him and asks in a proud sort of way, as if seeking praise for his performance, "Say, how did I sing out that, chum?"

'"Very well," replied the other, who, if he had advised him in good faith in the first instance, on now seeing the result of his teaching was anxious to take a rise out of the "stupid jolly," as he thought him. "But, chummy, you'll have to do different next time."

'"Oh!" exclaimed the marine. "What shall I have to sing out, then?"

'"You called 'Live boy' at Two Bells; and so it'll be 'Dead boy' when it strikes Three Bells. It's always turn and turn about aboard ship."

'"Yes, that's fair enough and I thank you kindly," answered the poor marine, sucking in the other's

gammon like milk, not perceiving for a moment
that the sailor was "pulling his leg"; and, the next
time the bell sounded, as sure as we both stand here,
if you'll believe me, Mr Smythe, the silly donkey
shouted out, even louder than he had done before, at
the very pitch of his voice, "Dead boy."'

'He, he, he!' cackled Mr Smythe again, while
Dick Popplethorne, who had joined me by the taffrail
and was intently listening like myself to 'Joe's' yarn,
burst out in a regular guffaw, which he had to choke
his fist into his mouth to suppress; for, any such
violent expression of merriment was totally at vari-
ance with the discipline of a man-of-war and had to
be checked at once for the good of the service!
'But, what—ah, happened, Mr Jellaby, to the poor
fellow, eh?'

'Why, the officer of the watch sent for the sergeant
of the guard with a file of marines, and put the man
under arrest for being drunk and mutinous!'

'You don't—ah, mean to say he was punished?'

'No,' replied 'Joe,' with a wink to us. 'He certainly
was brought up on the quarter-deck before the captain,
who had heard his queer shout, as everybody did,
indeed, who was on deck at the time; but, the bluejacket who had misled him came forward at the last
moment and got him released from chokey, our
captain, who was a good-tempered chap and enjoyed
a joke, letting them both off, although he read 'em a
lecture and had to bite his lip the while he spoke of
the heinousness of their joint offence, he being hardly
able to speak seriously!'

'Ah, I see,' said the Rev. Mr Smythe approvingly,
though in a very faint tone, walking off towards
the poop-ladder with the lieutenant's aid, having
evidently had enough of the ship's rolling. He
expressed a wish to seek the seclusion of his own
cabin, whereat I was not surprised, both Dick Popple-

thorne and myself having observed his face assume a greenish-yellowy-liver sort of look during the last few moments of 'Joe's' narrative; but he kept up his courage to the last, murmuring yet more faintly as he tottered below. 'Ve-wy good—ah! Ye-es, ve-wy good—ah, in-deed!'

'Funny, wasn't it?' said Dick Popplethorne to me as the two turned away, laughing again, only more quietly now. 'What a rum start for him to sing out, "dead boy!"'

I thought so, too—afterwards.

CHAPTER XV

OFF USHANT

AT Eight Bells, or four o'clock in the ordinary
parlance of landsmen, Mr Bitpin was relieved by the
first lieutenant, who then came on deck with the
rest of the starboard watch to take charge, while the
port watch went below at the same time.

This hour marked the beginning of the first dog
watch, which, it may be here mentioned for the benefit
of the uninitiated, only lasts two hours, from four
o'clock to six, when the second dog watch, of similar
duration, commences and continues until eight o'clock,
or 'Eight Bells,' again.

These subdivisions of time are necessary on board
ship in order to allow all to share alike 'the rough
with the smooth,' and give the officers and men a
change at regular intervals from day to night service,
and the reverse; for, if all the watches were of equal
length, there could not be any possible variation of
the hours during which the hands would be on and
off duty respectively, the one section of the crew in
such case coming on deck at precisely the same time
each day and going below in similar rotation.

By the system in vogue, however, of cutting one of
the watches into two parts, which is common to the
seamen of all countries in the mercantile marine and
is not merely limited to the routine of our men-of-
war, there is a constant change introduced; so that,
the men who take, say, the first watch to-night, from

eight o'clock till midnight, will have the middle watch to-morrow night, and so on in regular sequence until the time comes round again for them to 'return to their old love' again!

'Glass eye,' as the men called the first lieutenant, I noticed, was a much smarter hand than Mr Bitpin, in spite of his drawly way of speaking and lackadaisical airs below; and when he was officer of the watch there was no lolling about the deck or any of the talking that went on behind the boats and in odd corners, as was the case while 'old growler' had charge.

Everyone then, on the contrary, brightened up and kept to his station; while even the old quartermaster and helmsman drawing themselves up at 'attention' as soon as the Honourable Digby Lanyard's long, telescopic form appeared on the poop, just as if he were the commander, or Captain Farmer himself.

The Honourable was not long inactive, for the sun was already beginning to sink below the western horizon, lighting up St Alban's Head, abreast of which we were now speeding along, with a bright glare that displayed every detail of its steep escarpment and the rocky foreshore at its base; the glorious orb of day presently disappearing beneath the ocean, leaving a track of radiance behind him across the watery waste and flooding the heavens overhead with a harmony of vivid colouring in which every tint of the rainbow was represented—crimson and purple and gold, melting into rose, that paled again into the most delicate sea - green and finally became merged in the more neutral tones of night!

'Looks like a change coming, I think,' observed Mr Quadrant, the master, glancing at the sunset more with the eye of a meteorologist than that of an artist. 'Those northerly winds never last long in the Channel, especially at this time of year.'

K

'The evening's closing in, too,' said the 'first luff,' screwing his eyeglass more tightly into the corner of his eye and bending his lanky body over the poop-rail to see if everything was all right on the deck below, after taking a hurried squint aloft. 'I shall shorten sail at once. Bosun's mate!'

You should have heard him roar out this hail. Why, it made me jump off my feet as if a cannon had been fired, with a full charge, close to my head!

'Ay, ay, sir,' replied the boatswain's mate, coming under the break of the poop, so as to be nearer at hand; but there was certainly no necessity for his approaching in order to hear better, for the lieutenant's voice would have been audible a mile off, 'I'm here, sir.'

'Pipe the watch to shorten sail!'

'Ay, ay, sir.'

There was no need, though, of pipe or shout from the worthy petty officer addressed, notwithstanding that the lusty seaman could have piped and shouted with the best, should duty demand it of him; for, the lieutenant's order had already reached the ears of every man of the watch, and all were at their several stations, ready for the next command.

This was not long delayed.

'Topmen aloft! In royals and to'gallant stu'ns'ls!' he bellowed, in a tone that put that of poor Mr Bitpin completely into the shade; his voice sounding as if the wild bull which that gentleman had apparently imitated, according to the facetious Larkyns, had since been under the instruction of Signor Lablache or some other distinguished bass singer and had learnt to mellow his roar into a deeper tone. No sooner, too, had the hands jumped into the rigging and the studdingsail halliards and tacks been cast off by the watch on deck and the downhauls and sheets manned, than the 'first luff,' pitching his voice to yet a higher key, sang out in rapid sequence, 'Topmast stu'ns'l downhaul—haul taut—clew up—all down!'

'Bosun's mate,' he then cried, 'turn the hands up!'

This was the last order he gave on his own responsibility; for, while the men of the watch below were hurrying up on deck in obedience to the busy boatswain's mates' whistle and shout of 'all ha-a-nds,' which could still be heard ringing through the ship, Commander Nesbitt came up on the poop and took charge.

He thus superseded his subordinate, the lieutenant; it being the custom of the service for the commander to 'carry on' on such occasions and the officer of the watch, whoever he might be, to 'play second fiddle,' as the saying goes, which part the 'first luff,' took in the present instance, proceeding at once to his proper station on the forecastle.

No cessation occurred, however, in the task of shortening sail.

'Hands reef tops'ls!' shouted the commander almost on the instant he gained the poop, following this up by the command, 'Topmen aloft—take in one reef—way aloft!'

Of course Adams and Larkyns and Popplethorne had to scramble up to their posts in the mizzen and main and foretops, much to my admiration and envy; for, being only a cadet, I was not allowed to go aloft except for drill, and then only under special supervision, as I will presently tell.

While these lucky beggars, as I then thought them, were footing it up the ratlines, the commander sang out in rapid rotation, the orders necessary to make the way clear for taking in the reef required,—

'Weather topsail braces—round in—lower the tops'ls!'

'Trice up and lay out!'

By these being acted on, the wind was first 'spilled' out of the three topsails, which were then lowered on the caps ; and, the studdingsail booms being triced up to their usual place when not set, in the topmost rigging, the men were able to go out on the yards and commence reefing in earnest.

On the completion of this, the command was given to hoist away; whereupon the halliards were manned below and the topsails run up again.

'Trim sails!' sang out Commander Nesbitt as soon as he saw the middies and their men coming down from aloft. 'Lee braces—brace up the yards!'

During all this time, though, the wind had been shifting to the westward and ahead ; and, noticing the jib beginning to shiver and flap, the commander came to the fore again.

'Brace the mainyard sharp up!' he shouted; when, on the seamen at the bitts reporting that 'the mark' was 'down,' or, in other words, that the yard had been braced up as far as it would go, the other yards were trimmed parallel and the active commander cried, 'Belay the main brace!'

'By jingo, I think he might say "splice the main brace" now, after all this jollification!' growled Mr Stormcock, who had come up on the quarter-deck while the ship was thus being made snug for the night and left now under easy sail, consisting of the courses with reefed topsails and topgallants, as well as the jib and spanker and foretopmast staysail. 'The poor fellows must be precious dry with all that cutting about up and down the ratlines, and I wouldn't mind a glass of grog myself.'

'No, really, you don't mean that!' said Larkyns chaffingly. 'Wouldn't you prefer a cup of tea, now?'

'Cup of tea be hanged!' rejoined the master's mate, angrily. 'You youngsters of the present day are always thinking of your tea, like a lot of blessed old women! In my time, fellows at sea didn't go in for slops and mollycoddling, as all of you do now. By jingo, the gunroom might as well be turned into a nursery at once, with such a pack of children about!'

'At all events, we'd never be at a loss for a nurse, old chappie, with you aboard,' said Larkyns, sniggering. 'Indeed, you'd make even a better one than we could get ashore.'

'Hey!' exclaimed Mr Stormcock, a bit puzzled at this. 'What do you mean?'

'I don't mean a dry nurse, you know, old chappie, though you said, you were "dry" just now,' replied Larkyns, laughing at his own joke. 'Nor do I mean a wet 'un. No, old chappie, I mean a wetter-un, do you twig?'

'Phaugh!' ejaculated the master's mate, with a gesture of disgust, as he turned towards the binnacle to take the course the ship was steering, so as to lay it off on his chart and estimate the distance run and our probable position by dead reckoning. 'A beastly pun like that is enough a make a fellow sick!'

'All right, old chappie, I'd better get out of your way, if that's the case,' rejoined Larkyns, chuckling. 'I'll go below and finish my tea, which I would certainly not have left behind me, with you about, had it been grog!'

With which parting shot at what was generally believed to be Mr Stormcock's particular weakness, and one which had delayed his promotion, Larkyns hopped down the after hatchway on his way to the gunroom, I following after him, nothing loth to have some little refreshment after my long stay on deck, this having made me hungry again.

Things were pretty quiet below, I found, most of the noisier spirits of the mess having eaten their fill and departed; and, fortunately, the gunroom steward had not forgotten us late-comers, there being plenty of the 'water-bewitched' sort of beverage that goes by the name of 'tea' on board ship, albeit we had to be content with an extra allowance of sugar in lieu of milk.

To make up for this, however, the good-natured Dobbs had thoughtfully reserved for the delectation of Larkyns and myself a fragment of some very stale cake, which, from the important air he assumed when presenting it to our astonished gaze, he evidently considered a great treat; and, I was really sorry at Larkyns making some unkind remark or other about Noah and the Ark in connection with this venerable dainty that, I'm sure, must have hurt the feelings of the steward, who meant to do us a kindness, no doubt, and, at all events, did his best !

At Four Bells, or six o'clock, I went on deck again with Mr Jellaby and the port watch, remaining on duty until the end of the second dog watch.

By that time, we were passing the Bill of Portland, sailing close-hauled still down Channel on the starboard tack ; but, I was so tired out that I could hardly keep my eyes open, only knowing what the quartermaster kindly told me, so on getting below again soon after Eight Bells, I turned into my hammock without troubling much at undressing, and was 'as fast as a top' within less than a minute of reaching the steerage.

Next morning, on awakening, I was much surprised at everything being very quiet between decks, without any motion of the ship or rush of the water past her sides, and I wondered what had happened to cause this stillness.

On turning out, however, my wonder was soon allayed by discovering that we had made Plymouth during the small hours, and were now anchored in the Sound, midway between Mount Edgecombe and the breakwater.

I may add, that the mess table in the gunroom at breakfast clearly demonstrated our p oximity to this very hospitable port, by the lavish abundance of milk and eggs, not to speak of bloaters and marmalade, so that even Tom Mills was satisfied.

He did not have the heart to take another rise out of the irascible caterer, Mr Stormcock; while, as for Plumper, the senior mate, I never saw a chap eat in my life as he did.

An ostrich of the most enterprising digestion, or the boa-constrictor at the Zoological Gardens who recently swallowed its messmate in a weak moment, would neither of them have been a match for the fat little gourmand, who made even Dobbs stare at his efforts in the knife-and-fork line.

We stopped at Plymouth for some four-and-twenty hours, shipping supernumeraries and taking in surplus stores.

After which, weighing anchor again, we worked out of the Sound, having to tack twice before clearing the breakwater; and, resuming our passage we passed the Lizard the same afternoon, being some ten or twelve miles to the southward of the Bishop's Rock in the Sicilly Isles at midnight.

I noticed the bright, star-like light of the latter, low down on the horizon, away on our weather quarter, only just dimly discernible in the distance through the haze, when I came on deck for the middle watch, the lighthouse looking to me as if twinkling to us a last farewell from home and the land we had left, never, perhaps, to see again.

But, although we made fair enough progress, we were not able to preserve as straight a course as Captain Farmer and the master would have liked to have done.

The wind was continually on the shift and trying to head us, thus causing us to keep the ship away

and steer more to the southward; instead of making
all the westering we could when leaving the channel,
so as to give Cape Ushant, with its erratic currents
and treacherous indraught, as wide a berth as possible—the French coast being a bad lookout under
one's lee at any time!

However, we had to make the best we could of the
wind we had; and by noon next day, when Mr
Quadrant took the sun, having all of us round him
on the poop, cadets as well as midshipmen, on the
alert to watch for the dip and mark off the angle on
our sextants, we were found to be in latitude 48° 50'
North, and longitude 7° 35' West, showing that we
had run some two hundred miles or so since leaving
Plymouth Sound.

After observing the sun's altitude, we were supposed to work out the reckoning for ourselves inde-
pendently of each other; though, when the master
sent us down to the gunroom to do this, the lazy hands
amongst us, who were by a long way in the majority,
cribbed from those who were readier at figures, like
Larkyns and Ned Anstruther, both of whom arrived
at the same result as Mr Quadrant, ay even in a
shorter time, handing in their papers for inspection
before I had well nigh begun mine.

'Here, Vernon, take my log and copy it out,' cried
Larkyns, seeing me somewhat puzzled over the calculations I was making by the aid of a fat volume
of logarithm tables and Roper's 'Navigator'; 'you
look considerably fogged, old chappie, by the cut of
your jib.'

'No thank you,' I replied, all on my mettle, determined not to be beat. 'I want to try and make it out
by myself, so that I shall know how to do it next
time.'

'Bravo, youngster,' put in Mr Stormcock. 'That's
the only way to become a good navigator. Fudging

your reckoning will never teach you how to work out your altitudes; you stick to it, my boy, and do it on your own hook.'

Nor did the master's mate content himself with merely giving me this sound advice; for, sitting down by my side, he overhauled my figures and, being an expert mathematician, soon put me in the right road to arriving at a solution of my difficulties.

Really, he explained the various steps necessary in order to work out the reckoning in such a simple way that I understood it thoroughly; learning more in this one lesson from Mr Stormcock than I had done, I think, during the three months that I had studied navigation while on board the training ship *Illustrious*.

I learnt even yet more.

That was, not to judge by appearances and form hasty conclusions as to the character of my messmates; as, up to the moment of his coming thus to my aid, I had always considered Mr Stormcock an ill-tempered and soured man—whereas I now saw he was at bottom a good-natured fellow and one ready enough to help another when opportunity offered!

It was a lesson which, like the one he had just taught me in navigation, I never forgot.

Towards sunset that afternoon, when we were entering the Bay of Biscay, the lookout man on the foretopsail yard hailed the deck.

'Sail in sight, sir!' he sang out loudly. 'She's on our port bow, sir.'

'All right,' answered the officer of the watch, Mr Jellaby, who was up on the poop and I below on the quarter-deck at the time; and then, turning to the yeoman of signals, he cried, 'Signalman, a vessel's in sight on our port bow, go and look at her and see what she is.'

'Ay, ay, sir,' replied the seaman, putting his telescope to his eye; when, scanning in the direction pointed out to him, he soon made out the ship. 'She appears like a strange man-of-war, sir.'

'Very well,' said Mr Jellaby. 'Watch her till you can make her out perfectly.'

In another minute or two, the signalman made the result of his second scrutiny known.

'She's a French man-of-war and is making for Brest, I think, sir.'

'Ah!' exclaimed 'Joe,' having a look at her, too, with his binocular. 'Hoist the ensign!'

This was done; but, the stranger made no sign, until, gradually approaching each other all the while, she was about three miles off, when she displayed the gallant tricolour flag of France.

'Signalman,' sang out Mr Jellaby on seeing this, 'Dip the colours!'

Our ensign was thereupon raised and lowered from the peak three times in succession, according to the usual nautical etiquette observed on such occasions, the other ship returning the compliment in like fashion; and we were just passing each other, she crossing our bows and sailing away right before the wind on our starboard beam, when, all of a sudden, she brought up, backing her maintopsail and firing a gun at the same time to attract our attention.

'By Jove, she wants to speak us; something must be up!' said the commander who had come on deck in the meanwhile. 'Go below, Vernon, and tell the cap'en at once.'

CHAPTER XVI

'MAN OVERBOARD!'

'CONFOUND those mounseers,' I heard Mr Stormcock say to the master as I came out from Captain Farmer's cabin. 'I wonder what they want to stop us for now, just as we were getting clear of Ushant? It's sure to bring us bad luck!'

'By jingo, it is a nuisance bringing us up like this,' chorused Mr Quadrant, a fellow-grumbler of the same kidney. 'We might have carried on as we were standing, if those blessed Parlyvoos, had only let us alone; while now, when we do make a start again, the wind will most probably have headed us, and we'll then have to go about and bear away to the nor'ard on the port tack, losing all the southing we've made since yesterday!'

In spite of both their growls, however, we could not well avoid the interview, albeit it was none of our seeking ; and while I went down to summons the captain, Commander Nesbitt ordered the courses to be clewed up and the mainyard squared, so as to heave the ship to.

When I came up again the Frenchman and ourselves had both our heads to windward and were bobbing about abreast of each other, though still some distance apart; dipping deeply in the rough seaway and occasionally rolling broadside on, with the salt spray and spindrift coming in over our hammock nettings in sprinkles of foam.

'Hullo!' cried Larkyns, who was signal midship-man and was looking at the stranger with a diminutive telescope screwed up to his starboard eye. 'She's hoisted the answering pen'ant under her ensign.'

'That means she's going to use the International Code,' said the commander, overhearing him. 'Signalman, keep a sharp lookout on her, and have your book handy to read her signal as soon as it goes up!'

'Ay, ay, sir,' replied the man, who was, like Larkyns, squinting his best at the other ship, although with a much bigger glass. 'Something's going up now, sir.'

'Yes, I see,' said Commander Nesbitt, as a string of flags were run up to the French ship's main. 'Have our answering pen'ant ready to hoist as soon as you can make it out. Look sharp, signalman! What does she say?'

'It's "B D N," sir,' stammered out the man, who was rapidly turning over the pages of the signal book, seeking the meaning of the flags in that dictionary of the sign language of the sea, and missing what he sought to find in his hurry. 'I—I—can't find it, sir."

'Can't find your grandmother!' cried the Commander, impatiently, vexed at the delay. 'Here, give me the signal book!'

'The hoist means "I want to communicate," I think,' observed Captain Farmer, who had come up quietly on the poop meanwhile, and stood behind the commander. 'But the Frenchman might have saved himself the trouble of sending such a signal aloft; for, the mere fact of his already coming up to the wind and firing a gun, told us as much beforehand!'

'I should think so, sir; but it's just like those Johnny Crapauds — always gabbling a lot about nothing!' rejoined the commander, who, at last, had now found the right page of the signal book. 'Yes, sir, you're quite right, as usual! I wish I had your memory for signals! He "wants to communicate." Signalman, hoist our answering pen'ant!'

At this order, the red-and-white barred pennant, which had long since been bent ready to the signal halliards, was run up to our main truck.

From this point of vantage, it flew out fair above all our sails and tophamper, visible all round the compass and telling the French corvette, still curveting and prancing abreast of us and showing her bright copper sheathing as she rolled, that we had at last made out her signal and were waiting to learn what she had to say.

'I hope it's really important,' said Captain Farmer to the commander; while Larkyns and the head signalman kept their glasses fixed on the opposite ship, ready to take in her next signal. 'International courtesies are all very well in their way, but I don't like being stopped for a mere exchange of bunting and that sort of balderdash, Nesbitt.'

'Nor I, sir,' agreed the commander. 'Ha, they're sending up another hoist now, and we'll soon know all about it. What's that now, signalman?'

'"B L K," sir,' replied the yeoman of signals and Larkyns in one breath; and the former, running his fingers over the pages of the signal book, which Commander Nesbitt had returned to his custody, soon found that the interpretation of the flags thus clustered was, 'We have passed a wreck, but were unable to stand by to see if any survivors were aboard her.'

'Oh!' exclaimed the captain on this being read out aloud, as the signalman put it down on the slate for entry into the ship's log, according to the usual custom. 'This is getting interesting. Hoist "Q R S" after the answering pen'ant.'

'I say, Larkyns,' I asked, in an undertone of my friend the senior mid, as a string of square flags went up on our side—a yellow on top, a red square with a yellow cross in the middle, and a white flag with a blue centre the lowermost—'what does our signal mean, eh?'

'It means,' he whispered back, keeping his starboard eye still glued to his telescope, "whereabouts is that wreck you're speaking of?"'

Some considerable delay now occurred on board the corvette; the Frenchies, in spite of their taking the initiative in the matter, being not as handy as our man in the manipulation of their flags.

At last, however, they sent up two hoists in rather a slovenly fashion, one going up after the other.

'Ha, that's the latitude,' said Captain Farmer. '"F K S" and "G T V" Signalman, what does that make, eh?'

'Forty-seven degrees, and fifteen minutes north latitude, sir.'

'Good, my man,' returned the captain, approvingly. 'You've read that pretty smartly! Now, hoist the answering pennant; though, I suppose we'll have to wait another month of Sundays for their longitude. No, by Jove! Messieurs les Français are a trifle quicker this time. "F N J" and "G V L." How do you make them out, signalman? See if you can be as smart again as you were just now.'

'Ay, ay, sir,' returned the yeoman, all on his mettle and his eye the quicker to scan the alphabetical pages of his flag lexicon where the signals were catalogued in groups according to their subjects, this one being a numeral and, therefore, all the easier to read. 'Its longitude 9° 15' west, sir.'

'All right, put it down correctly, signalman,' said Captain Farmer; and, turning to the commander, he added, 'Why, Nesbitt, it's nearly in our direct course across the Bay, only we shall have a tighter squeeze, perhaps, in weathering Finisterre.'

'But, we can go a couple of points more free, sir,' observed Mr Quadrant, who had busied himself shaping a course on a chart by the binnacle as soon as he heard the latitude and longitude given. 'That'll be better than going about on the port tack, as I thought we should have to do, sir.'

'Yes—ha—humph! But I don't like going too near Finisterre, though, Mr Quadrant, with a westerly gale threatening,' said the captain. 'We cannot help ourselves, however, at present, for we must go after this wreck and see if there're any unfortunate people aboard; though, I think those Frenchmen might have overhauled her themselves, instead of leaving it for us to do! Hoist "H V L," signalman! That will serve, Nesbitt, to tell them we'll attend to the wreck. Let us fill and bear away again. We can't afford to waste any more time palavering with our friend over yonder, who keeps us bowing and scraping like a veritable Frenchman as he is! Run up the signal now, signalman; and, Nesbitt, give him a parting dip of the ensign, and then brace round the yards and bear up!'

'Very good, sir,' replied the commander; and, as soon as the Frenchmen had hoisted their answering pennant to show that our signal had been taken in and understood, he turned to the poop-rail and sang out, 'Bosun's mate, pipe the watch to trim sails!'

The braces were then manned and the main yard swung, while our helm put hard a-starboard; when, the upper sails now filling and drawing again, our courses were dropped and the tacks hauled aboard, the clew garnets rattling as they were brought aft, and the ship put on her course.

We bore away, though, a couple of points more to the southward than before, steering sou'-sou'-west, towards the position of the wreck, as pointed out to us by our communicative friends, the strange ship.

'By Jove, sir,' exclaimed the commander as we bade farewell to the Frenchman, who also filled at the same time and went about on his way, both of us dipping our ensigns once more in salute, 'we never thought of asking his name!'

'No more we did, Nesbitt,' said Captain Farmer; and the two stared at each other for a moment in silence, the captain ultimately breaking into a laugh. 'But, that need not trouble you; for, I should know that corvette anywhere, I think, from the way she tumbles home from her water line abaft the beam. She's the old *Sérieuse* for a thousand!'

'Indeed, sir?'

'Yes. She was one of the French fleet in the Black Sea when I was out there with old Dundas. I've been alongside her too often to forget her queer build!'

'But, I thought most of those French corvettes were wall-sided, sir?'

'Ay, true enough,' replied Captain Farmer, with a chuckle, as he came down the poop-ladder and turned to go into his cabin. 'But, not all of them, Nesbitt, not all of them, my boy. I tell you, I would know the old *Sérieuse* anywhere, for they haven't got another tub like her afloat.'

'The "old man's" right,' I heard the master say to Mr Stormcock when the captain had disappeared. 'The corvette was on the right of our line when we bombarded Odessa; and I recollect she missed stays when tacking, and pretty nearly came aboard us.'

'By jingo,' replied Mr Stormcock, enthusiastically, 'what an eye the old man has for a ship, and what a memory for signals! I never came across his equal.'

So thought I too; however, each day disclosed some fresh trait in our captain's character, which surprised us all the more from his being such a very reserved man.

He was in the habit of keeping himself to himself until occasion arose to bring out his latent qualities.

Time, and a longer acquaintance with him, only taught us this pregnant fact, amongst other things!

While all the signalling had been going on, the wind was gradually freshening and the sea getting up; and by the time we made sail again the waves had put on their white caps, while a heavy, rolling swell had set in.

This met us almost full butt as we lay on our course and broke over our weather bow in columns of spray, washing the forecastle fore and aft and tumbling into the waist in a cataract of foam.

The water was knee-deep on the lee side of the deck, whenever the ship heeled over to port under the pressure of her canvas, passing out of the scuppers like a mill-race on her rising again and righting on an even keel.

The more the gale blew, however, the better the old *Candahar* appeared to like it; racing along in grand style, and kicking up her heels to the Frenchman who was pretty soon hull down astern, the distance between us widening each instant all the more rapidly from the fact of our proceeding in opposite directions!

At Two Bells, when the log was hove, we were found to be going over nine knots but the ship began to plunge so much presently, that Commander Nesbitt, after one or two anxious glances aloft, ordered the boatswain's mate to call the hands to shorten sail, setting them to work the moment they came up from below, the topgallant sails and royals being taken in without delay and the royal yards sent down.

'I thought we were going to have bad luck,' observed Mr Stormcock, who had made his appearance again on the quarter-deck on hearing the boatswain's pipe for all hands. We haven't seen the worst of it yet, I'm afraid.'

L

'Shut up, you old croaker,' said Mr Jellaby. 'Why, you're a regular Jonah with your prophecies of evil!'

'I hope you won't chuck me overboard for it, though, as they did him!' replied Mr Stormcock, good-humouredly. 'Goodness knows, I don't wish any harm to the old ship, or anyone in her! It isn't likely I would; but, look at those clouds there away to win'ard and judge for yourself what sort of weather we're likely to have before nightfall!'

'Yes; no doubt you're right, Stormcock,' said 'Joe' in answer to this, squinting as he spoke over the side to the westward, where a heavy bank of cloud was rising up and nearly blotting out now the sun as it sank lower and lower towards the horizon. 'It does look squally, certainly; still, I can't see the use of anticipating the worst and trying to meet troubles half-way, as you do, old chap!'

'I would rather be prepared for them than be caught napping,' rejoined the master's mate, eyeing the quartermaster at the wheel, who was giving a helping hand to the two helmsmen, their task being by no means easy to make the ship keep her luff under the circumstances of wind and sea. 'I wonder the commander doesn't reef tops'ls? We can't carry on much longer like this!'

'I hope he won't,' whispered little Tommy Mills to me aside, my chum having come up with the rest from the gunroom at the general call. 'Ain't it jolly, spinning along like this, eh, Jack?'

Before I could reply, however, the commander seemed to have arrived at Mr Stormcock's opinion, that we were still carrying too much canvas, for he came to the break of the poop and shouted out to the boatswain's mate.

'Hands reef topsails!' he cried. 'Topmen aloft! Take in two reefs!'

'Not a bit too soon,' growled the master's

mate, under his breath. 'He ought to have given that order when the to'gallants were taken in !'

'Better late than never, say I,' said Mr Jellaby, laughing, as the topmen raced up the ratlines and the weather braces were rounded-in, preparatory to reefing. 'Really, Stormcock, you're the most inveterate growler I have come across in the service since first I went to sea, by Jove !'

Tom Mills and I chuckled at this; but, alas! our merriment was suddenly hushed by hearing a wild shriek come from aloft, that rose above the moaning of the wind as it whistled through the rigging and the melancholy wash of the waves, while, at the same instant, a dark body whizzed through the air and fell into the water alongside with a heavy plunge.

'Good heavens!' exclaimed Commander Nesbitt, as we all stared at one another with blanched faces. 'What is that?'

His question was answered in the moment of its utterance by a loud shout from forward that rang through the ship, sending a chill to every heart.

'Man overboard !'

CHAPTER XVII

A HOPELESS QUEST

'Sentry, let go the life buoy!' cried out Commander Nesbitt at once to the marine guard on duty on the poop, as the shout reached his ears; and then, facing round again forward, he said, 'Bosun's mate, call away the lifeboat crew!'

On the order being given, the marine had instantly pulled the trigger releasing the slip by which the patent buoy was suspended over the stern, whereupon it dropped into the sea below; the same mechanism igniting the port fire with which it was charged, although it was not yet dark, as the friction-tube had been put in a short while previously when the watch was relieved at Eight Bells, it being the rule on board for the gunner's mate to do this every day before sunset and take out the percussion-tube again in the morning at daybreak when the hands turned out to wash and scrub decks.

So, no sooner had the buoy touched the water than it floated away, flaming in our wake; the lurid blue light casting a spectral glare on the phosphorescent foam of the broken wave crests that contrasted wierdly with the last expiring gleams of the setting sun, now nearly hidden by the pall-like black cloud, which had gradually risen along the horizon and stretched itself across the whole western sky, creeping up steadily towards the zenith and shutting out little by little the last bit of blue.

At the sound of the boatswain's pipe, too, the cutter's crew had begun to muster on the poop, the leading hands unloosing the gripes with which the boat was secured and the coxswain attending to the tiller; while two or three of the men had already put on their cork jackets and taken their seats on the thwarts, ready for lowering away, the little craft being swung out from the davits to leeward.

Excitement there was, of course, amongst us all, everybody looking eager enough, as was natural; but I noticed that, while the commander's orders were executed with the utmost promptitude, there was no reckless hurry and confusion.

The most perfect order and discipline prevailed, everything being done systematically, although the accident had occurred so suddenly and unexpectedly; ay, and despite the fact that every soul on board, from Captain Farmer, who had come out of his cabin again immediately on hearing the lifeboat's crew called away, down to the youngest cadet and powder-monkey, was willing and anxious to do his best to save our unfortunate shipmate, without one of us knowing as yet who the poor fellow was whose life was thus imperilled.

No; nor, indeed, did we learn his name until after the topsails had been double-reefed and hoisted again and the ship hove-to with her maintopsail to the mast—which was accomplished in less time, I believe, than was ever known before, the operation not taking more than three minutes from first to last!

Then it was that we heard who had been lost overboard.

'It's poor Popplethorne,' said Charley Gilham, the third lieutenant, who had rushed up to the poop from amidships, where he had been stationed, to take command of the lifeboat. 'He fell from the upper rigging as he was climbing up into the foretop. The sail ballooned out; and then, slatting against the yard as the brace was hauled in, the clewline caught him unexpectedly, tripping him up and knocked him out of the rigging headlong into the sea!'

'Poor young fellow!' said Captain Farmer. 'Do you think he was hurt at all, or fell clear of the ship?'

'I'm afraid not, sir,' replied Mr Gilham, sorrowfully, as he grasped the after falls and sprang into the cutter. 'One of the foretopmen, who witnessed the accident, says that he appeared to cannon off something below, bounding out from the ship's side before striking the water, when he sank like a stone.'

'I'm afraid, then, there's no hope of picking him up,' said the captain. 'Are you all ready, Gilham?'

'All ready, sir.'

'Lower away, then,' cried Captain Farmer. 'We can but try to save him!'

With that, down went the boat into the water alongside, in such a speedy fashion that the after falls slipping too quickly through the lieutenant's fingers peeled off the skin from the palms of his hands; though Mr Gilham was quite unconscious of the injury he had received until he returned on board, his attention being absorbed in the attempt to save the unhappy midshipman by endeavouring to reach the spot where he had gone down, by this time half-a-mile or so astern.

Meanwhile, the commander had stationed lookout men on the crossjack yard and mizzen top, as well as in the weather rigging, to seek for any trace of the poor fellow.

The captain and a dozen of the officers or more were also on the alert, scanning the broken surface of the choppy sea surrounding us; but, alas, it was all in vain, no dark speck was to be seen anywhere in the distance resembling the head of the poor fellow trying to keep himself afloat, although the signal staff of the life buoy could be made out distinctly from the deck, without the assistance of its flaming fuse, which the shades of evening rendered all the more visible as daylight waned.

Beyond this and the boat, which was cruising about beyond the buoy, away to leeward, roving hither and thither on its vain quest, there was nothing in sight of us on board the ship, either from the hammock nettings or masthead.

No, nothing but the restless, rolling billows, tossing up their white caps in triumph over the victim who had fallen a sacrifice to Neptune; and the breaking waves, that seemed to chuckle with malicious glee while the remorseless deep below seemed to give vent every now and again to a hoarse roar of triumph!

'Signalman, hoist the cutter's recall,' said Captain Farmer, presently; after an age of waiting and looking out, as it appeared to me, during which not a word was spoken by anyone. 'There is no use searching any more now. If he were afloat, they would have found him long since!'

'Alas! I'm afraid there's no hope,' replied the commander. 'He will never be seen again, sir, I think, till the sea gives up its dead!'

'No, poor fellow. May he rest in peace!'

Captain Farmer raised his cap reverently as he said this; the commander doing the like and adding in his deep voice,—

'Amen to that, sir.'

The signalman had run up B flag for the cutter's return; but, as no notice was apparently taken of the signal, the captain ordered one of the bow guns to be fired.

Even then, however, the boat did not at once obey this imperative command, rowing off, indeed, in the opposite direction still, as if those in charge of her had noticed some object in the water, which we could not observe from the ship.

A minute or two later, we could see the cutter come to a stop; when, by the aid of the telescope, Larkyns, who was standing by the side of Captain Farmer, said he was sure he saw them pick up something and that they had now turned and were making for the ship.

All of us grew excited again on hearing this news, hoping for the best; and as the cutter came closer, the captain, who could not restrain his impatience, hailed her!

'Boat, ahoy!' he sang out. 'Have you got him?'

Charley Gilham, who was sitting in the sternsheets, with his head bent down, looked up on hearing the captain's call.

'No, sir,' he hailed back. 'Only his cap!'

The boat came alongside in silence, and the falls were hooked on; when, it was hoisted up to the davits slowly, the men hauling in a sort of spiritless way, as if saddened by the painful episode, while even the boatswain's pipe seemed to whistle in a subdued tone in the minor key!

On reaching the deck, the lieutenant came up to the captain with poor Popplethorne's cap, turning it over as he presented it to him to draw his attention to it.

It was torn and bloody on one side.

'The topman was right, sir, you see,' he said to Captain Farmer. 'He must have struck some part of the ship heavily when he fell from aloft before going overboard.'

'Yes,' replied the captain. 'I see.'

Just then, Mr Jellaby, who had gone forward in the meantime to see if there were any traces there of the accident, returned aft, looking more serious than I had ever seen him before.

His head struck against one of the flukes of the sheet-anchor, sir,' he reported to Captain Farmer who had sent him on the errand. 'The bill of it, just abaft the forerigging to port, is now spattered with the poor little chap's brains. I wonder nobody observed it before, sir.'

'He would, therefore, have been killed instantly and did not suffer any pain,' said the captain. 'Poor young fellow, poor young fellow! He was a most promising lad and always smart at his duty!'

'Trim sails!' cried out the commander at this juncture, in a voice husky with emotion; as if anxious to hide his feelings, now that the captain had pronounced his requiem to the memory of our late shipmate. 'Brace up the mainyard!'

At once our sails filled, when the ship was put upon her course again; and, the watch being then set, we all went below, the boatswain piping the hands down to supper, for it was nearly Three Bells and more than an hour after the usual time for that meal.

Naturally everybody in the gunroom was full of the accident, the fellows all thinking more of poor Dick Popplethorne when dead, for the moment at least, than they had ever done while he was living; and I, myself, could not help remembering the strange coincidence of his laughing over Mr Jellaby's yarn about the marine as we were sailing down Channel only a few days before and being especially merry over the young sentry's mistake in calling out 'Dead boy' when the bell struck.

Poor chap, he was a dead boy now, indeed; although, he had been alive and as hearty and jolly as any of us that very afternoon down there at dinner in the mess.

It was almost incredible to recollect this!

'I have just calculated,' observed Mr Stormcock amidst the general talk about our late messmate, as if stating a most important fact, 'that the youngster fell overboard in latitude 48° north, pretty nearly, and longtitude 8° 10' west—a trifle to the westward of where we met that confounded Frenchman.'

'I don't see how that information can be of any use to his friends, Stormcock,' said Mr Fortescue Jones, with a coarse laugh. 'We can't very well put up a tombstone over him in the Bay of Biscay.'

'For shame, sir!' exclaimed little Tom Mills, who was huddled up crying in a corner of the gunroom, Dick Popplethorne having been an old home friend. 'Don't make fun of the po—poor fellow now he's dead!'

'That's right, youngster,' put in Mr Stormcock. 'Stick up for your friend. I didn't mean anything against him for a moment, for I always found him a good sort of chap; though, I can't say I had very much to do with him.'

'Well, for my part, I won't say I'm sorry he has lost the number of his mess,' said that brute Andrews. 'He was as big a bully as Larkyns, and I don't owe him any good will, I can tell you.'

'You cowardly cur!' exclaimed Tom Mills, his face flaming up, though the tears were still coursing down his cheeks. 'You know you wouldn't say that if Larkyns were here now.'

'Wouldn't I, cry babby?'

Tom did not reply to this in words; but he sent a telescope, that lay at the end of one of the tables near him, flying across the gunroom, catching Andrews a crack on his uplifted arm.

This saved his head, fortunately for him, Tom's shot being a vicious one and well aimed!

'What do you mean by that?' said the ill-natured brute. 'Do you want to fight?'

'Not with you,' rejoined Tommy, whose anger had conquered his grief, speaking with much dignity. 'I only fight with gentlemen, and you're a snob! No gentleman would speak ill of those unable to defend themselves, or say a thing behind a fellow's back which he would not have the pluck to do when he was present. Andrews, you're a cad and a coward!'

'Stow that, youngster!' interposed Mr Stormcock, as little Tommy rose up and made towards the cad, who, however, showed no inclination to resent the insult offered him. 'I won't allow any quarrelling in the mess! If you want to fight, my boys, you must go into the steerage.'

Andrews, I noticed, did not offer to stir, however, in response to this suggestion of the master's mate, which he would certainly have done if he had been possessed of an ounce of courage in his nature.

Tom and I both agreed on this when talking over the matter subsequently ; so, seeing what a chicken-hearted fellow he was, my cocky little chum sat down again and began tucking into his tea, Andrews getting up presently and sneaking away when he thought the coast clear.

Mr Stormcock proved to be a false prophet with regard to the foul weather that evening ; for, when I went up on deck again to have a look round before turning in, although it was still blowing fresh from the westwards, the black cloud that had previously covered the sky had partly cleared away, leaving only a few fleecy flying masses in its stead.

Between them the moon fitfully shone occasionally and an odd star or two peeped out here and there ; while our good ship was bowling along under her topgallants, which had been set again by the commander over the double-reefed topsails, with her courses and jib and spanker, and the foretopmast staysail, continuing under the same canvas during the night, without hauling a sheet or tautening a brace, the wind hardly shifting half-a-point all the while.

We made such progress, too, towards the spot where the French ship reported having passed the wreck of which we were in search, that, at Six Bells in the morning watch, the lookout man forward, who had been specially ordered to keep a good watch to windward, hailed the deck.

'Sail in sight, sir!' he sang out, just as the hands were in the middle of their breakfast. 'She's hull down on the weather bow!'

CHAPTER XVIII

ON THE DECK OF THE DERELICT

'WHERE away, my man?' shouted Commander Nesbitt, who, at the same moment, came up on the poop and was scanning the horizon on his own account. 'How does she bear, eh?'

'Two points off the weather bow, sir,' replied the lookout from the foretopsail yard. 'We're rising her now, sir; and I can see one of her masts, though the rest of her spars seem to have gone by the board.'

'All right, my man, keep her in your eye,' sang back the commander, who then turned to the helmsman. 'Give her more lee helm, quartermaster; and see if you can't luff her up a couple of points! Watch, trim sails! Head lee braces! Brace up your head yards!'

With this, we hauled our wind; and, by bracing the yards sharp up and keeping her full and bye, we were able to bring the ship's head a bit more to the westward than we had been previously sailing, steering now south-west by south instead of sou'-sou'-west as before, which was as near as we could get her to proceed in the direction where the lookout man had reported the vessel.

By Eight Bells, we could make out the derelict clearly from the deck; and, shortly after breakfast when we had closed her within half-a-mile, we could see that somehow or other she had got terribly knocked about, her bulwarks having been carried away, as well as most of her spars and rigging, only the stump of her mainmast being left still standing, with the yard, which had parted at the slings, hanging down all a-cockbill.

There was a portion of the shrouds left, also, and the backstay; but, of everything else, as far as we could judge at that distance, a clean sweep had been made fore and aft and the vessel seemed to be a complete wreck.

The commander's keen eyes, however, caught sight of something, which at the first glance had escaped the notice of both lookout and signalman; not to speak of the many officers who stood around on the poop, scrutinising the dismantled vessel through their glasses, none of whom had observed this object until Commander Nesbitt pointed it out.

'Hullo!' he exclaimed abruptly. 'What is that lashed to the rigging on her port beam?'

Every glass was instantly directed to the point he had indicated.

'It's a man, sir,' said the signalman, noticing the object on its now being pointed out to him, very wise after the event, as most of us are disposed to be in everyday life. 'I think I can see him move, sir.'

'Yes, by Jove!' cried Mr Jellaby, who stood near, holding on to one of the davits, jumping up on the gunwale to have a better view. 'There he is waving one of his arms now!'

'I don't know about that, imagination sometimes goes a great way in these matters,' observed Commander Nesbitt, after carefully inspecting the battered hulk with the glass Mr Jellaby handed him; 'but, at all events, we'll send a boat aboard and see. Bosun's mate, pipe the watch to stand by to heave the ship to! Clew up the courses. Square the main yard!'

Larkyns, being, as I mentioned before, signal midshipman, had gone down to report the fact of our being close up with the wreck to Captain Farmer, who now appeared on the scene of action.

He at once gave an order for the first cutter to be lowered and preparations made for boarding the strange vessel, an order which was immediately carried into effect.

Mr Jellaby had better go in charge of the boat, sir, I should think,' suggested the commander. 'There's a bit of a sea running and I don't like sending a midshipman in such a case; for, you know, sir, we cannot expect old heads on young shoulders.'

'All right, Nesbitt,' replied the captain; 'do as you like.'

This was a great disappointment to Ned Anstruther, who had come on deck fully equipped for the expedition in his sea boots and monkey jacket.

He had hurriedly dressed himself on hearing the cutter piped away as he was her proper officer, it being the general custom on board a man-of-war for each of the ship's boats to be under the charge of one of the midshipmen, who invariably goes away in her under all circumstances of wind or weather for whatever duty she may be required.

There is little doubt that it is mainly owing to this practice of being early trained to exercise their judgment and discretion, and taught to command as well as to obey when young, that the officers of our service acquire that dash and readiness of action which is usually found lacking, it may be asserted without being accused of any insular prejudice or partiality, amongst those of other nations, who never have the same opportunities extended to them as a rule until they are almost too old to learn.

Boat service has been the school that brought forth the Nelsons and Rodneys of the past, as it has produced the Hornbys and Kanes and Beresfords of the navy of to-day, so to speak ; and, whether our sailors have to fight behind wooden walls or in armoured turrets, the practice will continue to teach self-reliance and the use of brains.

Ay, boat service will always stand our sailors, officers and men alike, in good stead; despite the fact that they go to sea now in 'floating factories' instead of on board ships such as our forefathers learnt their seamanship in, and that modern scientists, who treat everything on strictly theoretical principles, and, though have never smelt blue water, lay down laws for our guidance in the naval tactics of the future, dictating how we are to act and fight and manœuvre under any and every possible prearranged contingency !

It was an awful sell, therefore, for poor Ned Anstruther when Mr Jellaby was deputed to the charge of his boat and he was thus 'left out in the cold,' as the saying goes !

Nor was his mortification in any way lessened when the commander told him that the reason why he would not let him go, was because he could not swim properly ; for there might be danger in getting along-side the wreck, with the wind and sea that was on.

So, Ned did not appear at all pleased when the lieutenant stepped forward to take his place in the cutter, giving him an envious look when he took his seat in the sternsheets prior to her being lowered down.

I, too, cast an appealing glance at Mr Jellaby; and this, fortunately for me, Commander Nesbitt inter-cepted.

'I suppose you would like to go, youngster, eh?' he said to me. 'Well, you may, if you like. I know that you can keep yourself afloat, at anyrate if you get capsized, from what I learnt of your experiences the other day at Spithead ; and, perhaps, Mr Jellaby may find you of use. Jump in, my boy.'

It is hardly necessary to say how promptly I obeyed the order.

As my dear old Dad would have expressed it, 'Sharp was the word and quick the action.'

All the cutter's passengers, however, were not yet aboard.

'Hold on, there!' cried Captain Farmer, as the falls were slackened off and the boat slowly lowered down into the heaving water alongside, the waves coming half-way up the counter to meet her. 'I think the doctor had better go with you, Mr Jellaby. There may be some poor fellow on the wreck in need of immediate medical aid; and it will be a great saving of time, indeed, it may be the means of saving a life, if it be on the spot instead of your having to send back to the ship for it. Sentry, pass the word below for Dr Nettleby.'

We did not have to wait long; for, almost as soon as the captain's message could have reached the main deck, the doctor made his appearance on the poop, accompanied by my old friend, Corporal Macan, carrying a surgical case and a roll of bandages, while the neck of a suspicious-looking flask could be also seen peeping out from one of his pockets.

In another minute or so, Dr Nettleby and his factotum managed to slide down by the aid of the after life-line into the sternsheets of the boat; though, they took their seats in a rather hurried fashion beside the lieutenant and myself.

Then, watching our opportunity to lower away, we managed so to time it that the cutter lighted on the crest of one of the rollers.

This took us some yards away from the ship's side with the following swell of the sea; when our oars were dropped into the water at the word of command and we made for the wreck.

It was a stiff piece of work reaching her, for wind

and waves were both against us and rowing difficult;
the cutter at one moment being on the top of a
mountainous billow and the next plunged deep down
into a yawning valley of green water, the broken ridges
of which curled over our gunwales on either hand,
threatening to overwhelm us till we rose again beyond
their clutch.

But, the men 'putting their backs into it,' and the
coxswain steering judiciously so as to prevent the
boat from broaching to, we finally got alongside the
battered hulk.

We boarded her under the forechains to leeward,
as she was down by the head, with a considerable
list to port; and this seemed the safest point at
which to approach her.

Getting close up, the bowman at once threw a
grapnel that caught in some of the loose ropes hanging over the side; and, before we were well alongside, Mr Jellaby had scrambled up on to the forecastle of the ill-fated vessel.

Dr Nettleby and myself were not far behind him,
Corporal Macan and Bill Bates, the coxswain of the
cutter, following to render any assistance that might
be necessary; the boat meanwhile being veered away
to the end of the grapnel rope so as to be out of
harm's way and yet within easy reach of us as soon
as we might want to go on board her again.

On gaining the deck, the scene presented to our
gaze was piteous beyond all description, the ship
appearing to have been first run into by some other
craft and then left to drift about at the mercy of the
elements.

Her starboard bow had been cut right through
up to the head of the foremast, which had been
carried away completely, with all its spars and
rigging, as well as the bowsprit and maintopmast.

In addition to these, the mizzen and everything aft

had gone; not a stick being left standing in her save the stump of the mainmast, as our lookout man had reported soon after just sighting her, as well as part of the lower rigging amidships.

Besides this, a section of the mainyard that had snapped in two at the slings was still held aloft by the truss, the other end of the spar having brought up, against the chainplates, the brace being twisted round the shrouds and deadeyes in the most wonderful way!

Mr Jellaby, however, did not stop to notice these details, but made his way as well as he could through the maze of tangled cordage and heaps of wreckage that lay about in every direction towards the portion of the main rigging yet remaining intact, where, lashed to a fragment of the bulwarks that had not been washed away, was the figure of the man Commander Nesbitt had noticed.

There was no doubt now of his being alive; for, he was gesticulating violently and waving his arms about like those of a windmill.

The rolling of the ship and the clean breach which the sea made across the open deck amidships rendered the task of reaching the poor fellow all the harder; but, watching his chance between the lurches of the water-logged barque and clambering over the wreckage that filled the waist from the forecastle up to the main hatchway, Mr Jellaby was able at last to get near enough to hear the voice of the man, who was a most ragged and miserable-looking creature, and was yelling out wildly as if he were insane in the intervals of his frantic motions, when there was a lull in the noise of the waves.

'He's saying something, doctor,' he cried to Dr Nettleby, who had pluckily followed him up close, albeit so much older a man. 'See if you can make him out; I don't understand the lingo.'

The doctor listened for a moment and shook his head.

'It's no language that I can recognise,' he said after a pause, as if thinking over all the dialects he had ever come across in his wanderings. 'The poor chap has evidently gone mad and is jabbering some gibberish or other. Look how his eyes are rolling!'

By this time, however, I had managed to come up to where Mr Jellaby and the doctor were holding on to the backstay, and as the wind just then dropped for an instant and the deafening din of the clashing waters ceased, I caught a word or two out of a long sentence which the unfortunate man screamed out at the moment at the top of his voice.

'He's talking Spanish, sir!' I exclaimed, much to the surprise of my seniors. 'I can make out something that sounds like "por Dios," which means "for the love of God," sir.'

'Indeed!' said Mr Jellaby, gripping hold of one of the clewlines which hung down from the broken yard and swayed about in the wind, preparing to swing himself across the encumbered deck to the port shrouds beyond, where the man was lashed. 'I didn't know you were so good a linguist, young Vernon. By Jove, you'll be of more use than I thought you would be when the commander told me to take you with me.'

'Oh!' I cried, rather shamefaced at this, 'I only know a little of the language. I learnt it when I was in the West Indies with my father. We lived in one of the islands where there were a lot of Spaniards, and I heard their lingo spoken often enough.'

'Well, anyway, it's lucky that you know something about it now, for you can keep your ears cocked and hear what the poor beggar says, while we try to release him from his uncomfortable billet. Here, Bates, bear a hand!'

So saying, Mr Jellaby swung himself across the

frothing chasm that lay between him and the object of his pity, with the coxswain of the cutter after him, while Dr Nettleby and I remained by the mainmast bitts, Corporal Macan busying himself in getting the doctor's medical traps ready for immediate use.

I soon had to exercise my new office of interpreter, for the man began shouting again on seeing Mr Jellaby and the coxswain near him.

'Ah del buque!' he screamed out, holding up, as if to signal with it, one of his emaciated hands, the bony fingers of which looked like those of a skeleton. 'Como se llama el buque?'

'He says "ship ahoy!" sir,' I explained to the doctor. '"What ship is that?"'

'Tell him who we are, then,' replied Dr Nettleby. 'He is probably out of his mind, but it may quiet him.'

'Somos marineros Inglesas—we are English sailors,' I therefore cried in as shrill a key as I could to reach his ear, raking up the almost forgotten memories of my early years, and, I'm afraid, speaking very bad Spanish. 'Del buque de guerra el Candahar de la regna Ingleterra—we belong to Her Majesty's ship, *Candahar.*'

Bad Spanish or not, however, the poor fellow understood me.

'Gracias á Dios!' he said, his wild eyes brightening with a gleam of intelligence, as Mr Jellaby and Bill Bates, having unloosed him from the ropes by which he was seized up to the rigging, brought him across the deck to the doctor, who at once put a small quantity of brandy between his lips. 'Habran llegado á tiempo.'

'What is that, eh?'

'"Thanks be to God,"' I replied, translating what he had said. '"You've just come in time."'

'He never made a truer statement,' observed the

doctor, significantly, as he plied him gently from time to time with the spirit, keeping his hand on his pulse the while. 'In another half-hour he would have been a dead man; for, his circulation is down to nothing!'

Presently, the effects of the brandy told upon the poor fellow and he sprang suddenly to his feet by a sort of spasmodic effort, knocking Corporal Macan backwards into the water which was washing about the deck around us as he stood up.

'Ah los marineros cobardes!' he cried. 'Vamos printo, hascia abajo!'

'Hullo, Vernon,' said Mr Jellaby. 'What's he talking about now, eh?'

'I believe he's referring to the crew who deserted the ship and left him behind to his fate, sir,' I answered, 'for he has spoken of the "cowardly sailors," as he calls them. I think they must have been curs, sir, to have left him to die tied up like that, sir!'

'Anything else, eh?'

'He also says, "be quick and look below." I suppose he means for us to examine the vessel's hold.'

'Si si—yes, yes,' exclaimed the rescued man as I said this, seeming to understand what I suggested. 'Abajo—abajo—go below! go below!'

He nodded his head also as he spoke, looking towards the after part of the wreck and pointing downwards with his finger; while a shudder of horror passed over his corpse-like face, the dark hair surrounding which made it look all the paler.

'By Jove, I think there is something in what you say, my boy,' cried the lieutenant, moving away at once in the direction indicated as quickly as he could, telling the coxswain to follow him. 'I ought to have overhauled the cabin before. The sea is getting up again, I notice; and, we'll soon have to shove off from here if we wish to get back to our own ship again!'

The moment the Spaniard saw Mr Jellaby start off on this mission, he drew a deep breath of satisfaction.

'Buena, buena—good, good!' he murmured softly, as if talking to himself.   'Soy muy mal—I feel very ill!'

He then threw up his arms and dropped down as if he had been shot, Corporal Macan just catching him in time, crying out in a loud tone as he fell, louder indeed than he had yet spoken, as if giving a per-emptory order,—

'Fonde el ancla!'

'Begorrah, I can't say to his ankles!' said the Irishman, not understanding of course what he said, and mistaking the sound of the words.   'Till him they're all right, sor.   Faix it's all I can do to hould his arms, let alone his legs, sure!'

'Nonsense, Macan,' I cried, not able to keep from laughing.   'He didn't say anything about his ankles, or legs either.'

'Thin, what did he say, sor, if ye'll excuse me for axin?'

'"Fonde el ancla,"' I replied, 'means, you donkey, to "let go the anchor!"'

CHAPTER XIX

'Poor fellow!' said Dr Nettleby, on my thus translating the Spaniard's exclamation for Corporal Macan's benefit. 'I'm afraid he has dropped his anchor in real earnest.'

'Oh, doctor,' I cried, 'you don't mean that he is dead?'

'Not quite yet, but pretty nearly so,' he replied, feeling the man's pulse again and then putting his hand to his heart. 'I do wish Jellaby would come out of that cabin; for, I should like to take our patient to the ship at once and put him under treatment without further delay as he's in a very bad way. I can't think what's keeping the lieutenant so long!'

'Shall I go and see, sir?'

'I wish you would, my boy. Really, I don't like the look of the weather at all!'

'Faix, sor, naythor does I, sure,' I heard the corporal say as I turned to go in search of Mr Jellaby, who having made his way to the after part of the vessel, with the coxswain, had been out of our sight now for some time. 'It'll be blowin' great guns in a brace of shakes, or I'm a Dutchman, for the say is gettin' purty rough already, an', begorrah, it's wishin' I wor safe aboord the ould *Candahar* agen, I am; ay, an' alongside ov the cook's galley sure!'

I could not catch what the doctor said in reply to this, being too much occupied in looking after my own safety while trying to pick my steps towards the stern; for there was a lot of loose dunnage washing backwards and forwards as the hulk rolled sluggishly from side to side and tons of water continually came in as the waves broke over her, causing me to keep my weather eye open and clutch hold of every stray rope I could grip that was secured in anyway to prevent 'me from going overboard. The noise of the wind and sea and creaking and groaning of the poor ship's timbers, too, was something awful.

When I succeeded at last on getting aft, I found the entrance to the cabin from the deck was blocked by the wreck of the mizzenmast.

By means of this, I climbed up on to the poop, the proper ladder belonging to which had also been smashed by the fall of the spars from aloft, as well as the covering of the booby hatch and sky-light; a yawning chasm of splintered glass and broken framework only now representing the latter structure, while the former had disappeared entirely.

The companion way, however, seemed still firm enough, although nearly filled up with fragments of wood and odds-and-ends of all sorts, besides being about a foot or so of water over all at the bottom of the stairway; and, I was just on the point of adventuring down in my quest of the lieutenant, when the latter emerged from the passage that led into the cabin or saloon below, followed by Bill Bates.

Mr Jellaby's face was as pale as that of the man we had rescued.

So was the coxswain's; and both seemed to start on seeing me as if I had been a ghost.

'Good heavens, my boy!' exclaimed the lieutenant. 'How did you get here?'

'The doctor sent me, sir,' I answered glibly. 'He was getting anxious about you and thought something had happened.'

'By Jove, you gave me quite a turn after coming out of that infernel den there!' he said with a shudder, pointing over his shoulder. 'I never saw such a sight in my life. Did you, Bates?'

'No, sir,' replied the coxswain. 'I hopes to God, sir, I never shall again, sir!'

'What is it, sir?' I asked, all my curiosity aroused. 'May I come down and see the place, sir?'

'No, Vernon, it's not fit for a boy like you to look at such a horrible sight. Why, it would haunt your memory for months, as I'm sure it will mine!'

So saying, he began to mount the companion way towards me slowly, but had hardly ascended a couple of steps when he came to a halt, looking up for a moment as if undecided in his mind.

'Stay; I think you may come down, youngster, after all,' he said at length. 'Perhaps it might be as well that you should see with your own eyes what Bates and I have seen; for, then you will serve as an additional witness in the event of there being any future inquiry. I hope you have a good strong stomach, my boy, and are not squeamish?'

'Oh, no, sir,' I rejoined as I followed him down the steps again to the gangway below, 'I'm not squeamish.'

'Well, then,' he cried, throwing open the opposite door which gave entrance to the cabin directly under the broken skylight, 'look in there!'

It was fortunate that I had a steady nerve and was not easily frightened, for the sight that met my gaze would have startled most grown-up persons, let alone one of my age!

The place was in as great confusion as the open deck above, the sea having worked its ravages here as well as there and littered it with lumber of every description, which the water that had likewise gained admittance was washing about the floor, in company with the overturned tables and chairs.

Broken plates and dishes were mixed up with stray articles of clothing; while books and empty bottles, which, strangely whole, bobbed up and down amidst the general ruin, floated in and out between the heavier dunnage.

I noticed even a mandoline, with a blue riband attached to it cruising round the bottles; which seemed quite out of its latitude there!

But, this was not all.

There was a strange, sickly smell in the room; and what was that looking up at me from the rubbish-strewn deck close to where I stood by the cabin door?

I almost shrieked out as it caught my wandering glance, the eyes seeming to look right into mine, opened wide in one fixed stare.

It was the face of a dead woman, over whose marble-like features the water rippled as the ship lurched, tossing her long hair about as if playing with it and giving her the appearance of being alive.

'Poor thing!' I whispered to Mr Jellaby, who was near me and also gazing down at her, the presence of the dead making me drop my voice. 'She was drowned, I suppose?'

'Murdered!' he replied laconically, drawing my attention to a terrible cut across her neck, which I had not observed before, almost severing the head from the body. 'Look there—and there, Vernon!'

I followed the motions of his directing hand, and saw, first, a poor little dead baby floating about in the corner of the cabin; and then, behind the door by which we had entered, the corpse of a big, handsome man propped up against one of the lockers, in a kneeling position.

The man was only half-dressed, being in his

shirt and trousers, as if caught unawares, holding a cocked revolver yet in his rigid fingers, stretched out in steady aim ; while, at the further end of the cabin, where there was another doorway, communicating apparently with the main saloon, lay four ruffianly-looking fellows, all with long Spanish knives in their hands tightly clutched as if to strike.

These scoundrels had evidently killed the lady and little baby, and had then been shot by the poor chap on his knees, before he had himself fallen a victim to the cowardly stab from behind of a fifth scoundrel.

The latter he had got down, however, before he died ; for, he was kneeling on his chest, as the second lieutenant pointed out to me prior to our leaving this chamber of horrors, though the villain's dagger was still sticking in the brave fellow's back.

I could see this now for myself as a gleam of sunshine came down through the shattered skylight, showing up all the hideous details of the place, with the sides of the cabin and the bulkhead dividing it from the passage, as well as the deck beams overhead, all spattered with blood; albeit, the water sluicing about below had removed all traces of the sad tragedy from thence long since.

'Let us go now,' said Mr Jellaby, as soon as I had taken in all these sickening surroundings, leading the way out of the accursed place. 'We have stopped here long enough !'

'We have indeed, sir,' I replied, following him up the companion, with Bill Bates bringing up the rear in silence. 'But, what do you think has happened, sir ?'

'It's a case of mutiny first, most probably ; and then, murder,' said the second lieutenant, gravely, stepping over the coaming of the hatchway on to the deck of the poop as he emerged from the companion way.

'We'll never know the rights of it, however, unless
the doctor manages to bring round that poor chap
we released from the rigging, who must have been
tied up by the mutineers and thus escaped them
somehow or other! I couldn't find a log-book or
anything else in the cabin which would give us a
scrap of information about the vessel or those
belonging to her; and, all the rest of the wreck is
under water—indeed, I don't think she's far off
sinking.'

'Beg pardon, sir,' observed the coxswain, interrupting him. 'The ship's just sent up our recall, and she's
bearing away now to pick us up to leeward when we
cast off from here, sir.'

'Yes, my man, I see, and I notice, also, she has sent
down her topgallants and taken in another reef,'
returned Mr Jellaby, proceeding to work his way back
amidships to those we had left there, wading through
the water and wreckage and tophamper strewing the
waist. 'The old doctor, too, looks in a precious wax
and is carrying on at a grand rate about our keeping
him waiting, I bet. He's jawing away now to that
knowing hand of a marine of his; so the sooner we
see about getting him aboard our old barquey again
the better!'

He could not have came to a wiser conclusion, for
the wind had increased in force rapidly, even during
the short interval since I had left the deck, now blowing more than half a gale; while the sea was beginning to run high, breaking over the bows of the half-
submerged hulk, sending up columns of spray that
wetted us where we were and almost drenching
Doctor Nettleby and the corporal, who were
attending to the poor Spaniard amidships, just
under the lee of the mainmast.

'You're a nice fellow!' cried the doctor to Mr
Jellaby on our approaching near enough to hear

what he said. 'It won't be your fault if we're not all drowned here like rats in a hole and never reach the ship. As for the cutter, I believe she's swamped already!'

He was in a fine rage, certainly; but, the lieutenant, whose good temper was proof against any amount of irritability, soon calmed him down.

'I beg your pardon, doctor,' he said, as he hailed the bowman of the cutter, which was not swamped as yet, although making very bad weather of it, telling him to haul up alongside under the lee of the wreck. 'I really beg your pardon, doctor, but I could not be any quicker; for the captain ordered me to examine the vessel and see if I could find her papers.'

He thereupon described to Doctor Nettleby what the three of us had seen in the cabin; when that gentleman was as much shocked as we were.

'Can I do anything, Jellaby?' he asked. 'Are you sure they were all lifeless?'

'As dead as herrings, doctor.'

'Then there would be no use in my going down to see the poor creatures?'

'My dear sir, you couldn't do them an ounce of good, for they're long past the reach of all human aid!' replied the lieutenant, while he gave a helping hand to Corporal Macan to lift up the still unconscious Spaniard whom we had rescued, the sole survivor, so far as we knew, of all those who had perhaps started gaily enough on their disastrous voyage in the now dismantled and water-logged barque. 'Besides, my dear doctor, we haven't got the time. If we don't clear out of this pretty sharp, we'll all go below, I'm afraid! Steady there, Bates, with that grapnel rope! You'll have the boat coming broadside on against the wreck, if you don't take care and she'll be stove in. Be smart now and rig out that clewline there to the braceblock at the end of the yardarm. It will serve

to lower down this poor beggar into the boat, which
· you must all fend off. Let her just come under the
spar handsomely, without touching the side.'

These directions being carefully adhered to, we
contrived, by using great caution, though not without
considerable risk, to lower down the almost lifeless
man into the cutter; after which we descended ourselves, Mr Jellaby being the last to leave the hapless hulk, letting go the grapnel as he dropped into
the sternsheets.

The doctor and I caught him as he joined us,
everyone else having enough to do to keep the boat
steady with the oars; while Bates, of course, was busy
with the tiller, which he kept amidships.

As the boat drifted past the low rail of the vessel,
now almost level with the water, which partly sheltered
us from the full force of the wind and waves, I had
the opportunity, when we glided under the stern,
to read her name emblazoned thereon in large gilt
letters.

It was *La Bella Catarina.*

'Give way, men!' cried the lieutenant, on our getting out into the open sea the next moment beyond
the hull of the derelict, the coxswain heading the
cutter directly for our ship, which had run down to
leeward of the wreck so that we could fetch her more
easily. 'Pull all you can, my lads. Our lives depend
on it!'

We were about half-way towards the *Candahar,*
which had gone about on the port tack, beating to
windward and coming up to meet us, the crew of the
boat bending their backs and pulling their hardest till
the stout ash blades nearly doubled in two with the
strain, while the big, rolling sea raced after us, trying
to catch us up; when, all of a sudden, the man holding the stroke oar on the after thwart uttered an exclamation which made the lieutenant look behind.

' By Jove!' he cried, 'we've had a narrow shave.'

The doctor and I both turned round at this.

We were only just in time to see the ill-fated vessel, which we had so recently left, rear herself end on and sink beneath the waves, bow foremost!

CHAPTER XX

'A BIT OF A BLOW!'

THE doctor did not like the flippant way in which the lieutenant alluded to our providential escape.

'You ought to thank God, Mr Jellaby, with all your heart that you have not gone down in her,' he said in a grave and impressive tone, looking him full in the face. 'It is far too serious a matter for you to speak of so lightly. Just think, man, we've only been saved by a hair's-breadth from death!'

The lieutenant, however, was incorrigible.

'A miss is as good as a mile, doctor,' he rejoined with a laugh, which made all the boat's crew grin in sympathy, his devil-may-care philosophy appealing more strongly to their sailor nature than the doctor's moral reflections. 'Stand by, bows!'

On this, the bowmen unshipped their oars with great care, so as not to cause any rocking; and, laying them in dexterously, faced round at the same time, one holding a boathook ready and the other the grapnel with a coil of rope attached, prepared to fling it when we were near enough to the ship.

Our gallant vessel was plunging along athwart our course as if she meant to give us the go-by, the sea foaming up at her bows in a big wave that curled up in front of her forefoot and broke over her figure-head as she dipped, sending the surf high in the air in a sheet of foam over her forecastle.

Those on board, though, had no intention of

abandoning us, as we could quickly see, had we needed any assurance on the point.

Just as she was within half a cable's length of our starboard beam, we could hear the sound of the shrill boatswain's pipe above the splash of the sea; when she came up to the wind so close to the cutter that it looked as if she was going to run us down instanter.

But, we knew better than that.

'Way enough!' shouted Mr Jellaby; and, by an adroit turn of the tiller, the boat's nose shoved in under her lee to port into the slackwater made by her hull. 'Be ready with that grapnel there forrud!'

There was no necessity, however, for using this, for Commander Nesbitt had stationed a man in the chains to watch for us; and, immediately we rounded in under the counter the seaman payed out a long grass rope attached to a buoy, which, as it floated past the bowman was easily able to pick up with his boat-hook and make fast beneath the thwarts of the cutter forwards.

We were, by this means, hauled up alongside until we were right below the quarter, with the side of our noble vessel towering above us like a great wall, and swinging over our heads; the creaking boat falls, oscillating backwards and forwards as if they were a couple of pendulums, rendering it very difficult to hook on the cutter, especially as she was lifted up one moment by a wave passing under the keel to the main deck ports, and lowered the next down to the ship's bilge.

But, at last, the task was accomplished, and then at the pipe of the boatswain, which we could now hear more clearly than before, the cutter, with all her crew and passengers still in her, was run up to the davits and secured, the ship at once filling and bearing away on her course again, now close hauled on the starboard tack.

Captain Farmer was standing on the poop talking with the commander when we gained the deck ; and, as Mr Jellaby at once went up to them to make his report, while Dr Nettleby was busying himself with superintending the removal of the man we had rescued, who had not yet regained consciousness, down to the sick bay, a couple of other marines being called to help the corporal, I thought I might as well go below also and shift my uniform, which was pretty nearly soaked through, making me feel very cold and uncomfortable.

This was a day of surprises.

For, no sooner had I got down to my chest in the steerage and begun to peel off my wet clothes, than Ned Anstruther came up to me.

I thought at first he was going to congratulate me on having got off from the wreck before she foundered, all on board, having, of course, seen her sink.

But, greatly to my astonishment, my watchmate raised a rope's-end which he held in his outstretched hand and proceeded to lay it across my shoulders ; the beggar giving me several sharp cuts with the "colt" ere I realised what he was up to.

'That will teach you not to supplant me and go in my boat again, you young rascal !' he cried, pegging away merrily with the rope's-end on my bare back. 'I intend to give you one of the best thrashings you ever had in your life for doing it !'

'What do you mean ?' I exclaimed, trying to ward off the cuts with my arm. 'Anstruther, you're mad, I think ! I never wished to supplant you. It was the commander who would not let you go in the cutter, not I.'

'Oh, was it ?' said he, ironically, still laying on as hard as he could with the rope's end, which really stung me very much. 'Well, as I can't lick him, my joker, I shall lick you !'

'Will you?' I retorted; and, finding expostulation of no avail, I tried retaliation, commencing now to hit out with my fists in return. 'Two can play at that game, old fellow; and as you force me to do it, take that and that!'

My action followed suit to my words, as I gave him a smart 'one, two' with my left, which knocked him backwards against Mr Stormcock just as the latter was coming out of the gunroom.

'Hullo, what is this?' cried the master's mate, as Ned Anstruther, cannoned off his stomach, sending him flying across the deck from the ship lurching. 'Fighting again? By jingo, I never saw such a pack of young gamecocks in my life. There was, cheeky little Tom Mills wanting to peg into that swab Andrews last night, and now here are you two at it hammer and tongs. Why, I thought you were chums and both of you in the same watch, the very closest of friends.

'Of course we are,' said I, laughing at the comicality of the situation, which struck me all of a moment. 'Anstruther and I are very good friends. I'm sure I don't want to do him any harm.'

'So I should think,' replied Mr Stormcock, drily. 'It looks uncommonly like it, judging by the way you are slogging each other about! But come now, I won't have any more of this. Shake hands and make it up at once, do you hear, or I'll report you to the commander.'

'Why,' exclaimed my antagonist, rubbing his eye ruefully, 'Commander Nesbitt is the cause of it all!'

'Indeed!' said Mr Stormcock, with a whistle of surprise at this extraordinary assertion. 'How do you make that out?'

'Because he sent Jack Vernon in the first cutter in my place.'

'Oh, you ass! It was for that, then, that you were fighting this poor chap here, who I'm sure you ought to be grateful to for taking a very nasty job off your hands. See, he's not only wet to the skin, but narrowly escaped going to the bottom, as you know; and now, in return for this kindness, you try to wop him, and end in getting wopped instead yourself. Anstruther, you're an ass, and more than that, you're an ungrateful ass; and I've half a mind to thrash you myself for your conduct to Vernon!'

'I never thought of it in that light,' said Ned, holding out his fist to me in a different fashion to that in which I had presented mine to him shortly before. 'Let us be friends again, old chap. I'm very sorry I struck you, Jack; but I was so jealous of your going off in the cutter and angry at being left behind that I didn't think of what I was doing.'

'Well, I'm sorry I hit you, too, my dear Ned,' said I, shaking hands in a cordial grip. 'I hope I didn't hurt you much.'

'You've only given me a black eye, which will make me go on the sick list,' he replied with a grin. 'I can't very well appear on the quarter-deck with the "Blue Peter" hoisted; for, the cap'en would notice it in a minute and ask me how I came by it.'

'There would be no difficulty about that,' interposed Mr Stormcock; 'you could tell him the commander gave it to you, for you said just now he was the cause of all the row, you know.'

This made us both laugh, and dinner being now ready, Ned Anstruther and I went into the gunroom together as soon as I had completed my interrupted toilet.

Here, sitting side by side, the best of friends, and enjoying our pea soup, no one looking at us not in the secret would have readily imagined that any such 'little unpleasantness,' as I have described had just occurred between us two; though, I am happy to be able to state, this was our first and last quarrel, Ned and I remaining the closest chums ever after and never subsequently having even a word squabble.

During the afternoon, the wind veered to the north-west, blowing stronger after the sun passed the meridian and increasing hourly so much in force that, at Four Bells, we hauled down the jib and close-reefed the spanker, the mizzen topsail being also taken in at the same time.

There was every indication of our having a gale, the barometer having fallen considerably since the morning; while the sea got up more and more and the horizon ahead became banked with a mass of blue-black clouds as dark as night, patches of lighter vapour also scudding rapidly across the sky.

At Six Bells things began to look serious, the wind now shrieking as it tore through the rigging and the heavy rolling waves to break inboard, washing the decks fore and aft; so, the hands were turned up to furl the mainsail and take in the spanker.

This relieved the ship somewhat; but, as she still laboured very much, the topsails were close-reefed and a reef taken in the foresail, the men being almost blown off the yards when aloft while doing this and having hard work to get down safely on deck again when the job was done, the force of the gale being such that they were flattened against the rigging and had to hold on 'by the skin of their teeth,' as sailor folk say.

Even this amount of canvas, however, reduced though it was, presently proved too much for her; and the commander therefore gave the order to furl the foresail and haul down the foretopmast staysail, a storm staysail being set on the forestay to keep the vessel under steerage way as she tore through the tempest-tossed water like a maddened thing, rolling her gunwales under and pitching sometimes to that extent that she seemed about to dive into the deep never to rise again.

There were four men at the wheel; and yet, with all their exertion, it was impossible to preserve a straight course, for the ship yawed from side to side, as if seeking to escape the following seas that raced after her, rearing their threatening crests right over the taffrail.

So, fearing that we might get pooped, we now furled the foretopsail and lay-to under our close-reefed maintopsail and storm staysails; thus awaiting what might further be in store for us, although it did not then seem possible that anything could be worse!

We were all soon undeceived, however, on this point; although we had about half-an-hour's let off, during which interval the commander and gunnery lieutenant employed themselves in having the guns secured with double breechings and stout seven-inch hawsers triced up along the decks in their rear, a separate tackle being bent on into this and passing under the neck ring of each of the long thirty-two pounders, in order to prevent their taking charge and waltzing about amidships when the vessel rolled.

Ay, and she did roll, too!

The decks also were battened down to keep out the floods of water, which she was continually taking in over the bows, from passing too freely below, where a considerable quantity had already, indeed, gone, making us rather damp down in the steerage.

Lifelines were likewise rove on the poop and upper deck, where it was now impossible to move a step without having something to lay hold of.

This was not only on account of the heavy lurches the vessel gave from port to starboard and then back again to port; but, the planks were wet and slippery, and besides, as she plunged and pitched, head to sea, great green, rolling waves would break on the fore-castle and pour down into the waist, rushing aft like a river and sweeping anyone off his legs who was caught unprepared.

The wind itself was blowing so strongly that I couldn't stand upright, having to shelter myself under the lee of the bulwarks when I was on the poop.

But, this was nothing to what came later, old Boreas then putting a fresh hand to his bellows.

Hardly had the guns been properly secured and everything made snug and fast below and aloft, when the gale recommenced with tenfold violence; constant squalls bursting over the ship, accompanied by showers of hail that pattered on the planks like rifle bullets and took the skin off any fellow's face that was exposed to it without protection.

It made mine smart, I know!

In the midst of one of these sharp squalls, the maintopsail was blown to pieces with a report that sounded as if a gun had been fired off close to my ear; and, at the same moment, there was a loud crack heard from the top as if something had given way in addition to the sail.

Nothing, though, could be done about this for the moment, more pressing business being on hand; for, in consequence of the topsail giving, the ship's head payed off and getting into the hollow of the sea she precious nearly rolled her masts out her in less time than one could count.

'Down with that fore staysail,' shouted the commander through his speaking trumpet. 'Look alive man and set the topsail at once!'

His voice could not be distinguished beyond the length of the trumpet he roared through; but the boatswain's mates passed on the order from hand to hand until it reached the first lieutenant and the master, both of whom were stationed forwards, where it was instantly acted on and the ship's head brought back to the wind.

After this the storm staysail was rehoisted and we lay-to again in comparative safety.

Mr Cleete, the carpenter, then went up into the maintop to see what had happened to cause the loud crack we had heard.

He came back from his perilous journey with the unwelcome news that the topsail yard had been sprung and was in a very ticklish state, the carpenter adding that the spar ought to be fished as soon as possible or it might part company.

It had to remain as it was, however, for the present, the commander not wishing to peril the men's lives needlessly by sending them aloft unless it was absolutely necessary for the safety of the ship; for it was not any easy thing to shift such a big spar as the topsail yard in a gale of wind. 'If it chooses to go by the board before it could be seen to,' said he, 'why, well and good, go it must, that's all!'

So Commander Nesbitt evidently thought, I was sure, from the way in which he shrugged his shoulders and pointed in dumb show aloft and then to the sea, when the carpenter tried to press the claims of the topsail yard on his notice.

When the hands were sent down and the watch set at Eight Bells, to my inexperienced eyes the hurricane appeared to be at its height; the howling of the wind and angry roar of the clashing waves being absolutely awful to listen to, drowning as they did every other sound on board the ship on deck.

Nor was it any the better below, the groaning of the timbers there, as of a lost soul crying out in its last agony, with the rattling of crockery and other mess gear, adding to the tumult without, made a perfect pandemonium of the gunroom.

A fellow could not hear what another said, though

it were shouted in his ear as loudly as the speaker could bawl; albeit some of my messmates certainly had powerful lungs of their own—lungs which they were not chary of testing when occasion offered!

I turned in early; but, not being able to sleep for the racket that was going on, I returned to the deck, remaining there in the most sheltered corner I could find with Tom Mills, the two of us watching with spellbound attention until close on midnight the wonderful struggle between the spirits of the air and the demons of the deep—the pale-faced moon shining out occasionally from the dark vault of the heavens overhead, lighting up the stormy sea that served as the battle-ground of the storm fiends with her sickly gleams and making it seem like a field of snow, its vast expanse being covered with yeasty foam as far as the eye could reach.

The gale lasted all that night and the following day; when, late in the evening, the weather commenced to moderate, the wind calming down finally towards the close of the middle watch next morning.

It had then been blowing for thirty-six hours, during the whole of which time neither Captain Farmer nor the commander had left the deck; while most of the officers and men also had remained up on duty, it being a case almost of 'all hands' from the beginning of the tempest to its end!

CHAPTER XXI

THE SPANISH CAPTAIN'S STORY

WHEN I went up on deck that morning I could hardly believe my eyes, on seeing that the storm and all its wild surroundings had miraculously disappeared; for, the sun was shining brightly on a blue sea that seemed to ripple with laughter and the good old ship was speeding along under all plain sail, looking none the worse for the buffeting she had experienced only a few hours before!

'Rather a change from yesterday, ain't it, youngster?' observed Mr Gilham, who was officer of the watch, addressing me kindly, noticing the expression of astonishment on my face as I glanced up aloft and then over the side. 'Things look a little more shipshape than they were then.'

'Yes, sir,' I replied. 'But what a fearful gale it was!'

'Pooh, nonsense, Vernon!' cried he, with a laugh. 'Don't overlay your yarns like that. We've certainly had a bit of a blow, but I've seen it much worse crossing the bay!'

Of course, I could not contradict him; and, I may here mention that on narrating the circumstance to Dad on my return home some time afterwards, he said that he had never known a sailor acknowledge anything unusual about a storm at the immediate moment of its occurrence, or even shortly afterwards.

All those with whom he had ever been brought in contact, Dad told me, might possibly allow that the wind was 'freshening,' perhaps, or 'blowing stiffly,' or 'inclined to be rough'; but, a gale or a hurricane they would never admit, in spite of the fact of its 'blowing great guns and small arms'!

Should anyone, Dad also said, incautiously hazard some definite opinion on the state of the weather, any seaman thus spoken to would invarably recall a previous occasion within his own experience when it was really bad enough to speak about—it being the rule with all true sons of the sea to minimise danger and laugh at the perils they have escaped, instead of making mountains out of molehills in the manner natural to most landsmen!

Besides thus upsetting my ideas as to the terrible ordeal we had gone through, concerning which, however, I held to my own view in spite of his protest to be contrary, although, of course, I did not tell him so, Mr Gilham informed me that we had suffered no serious damage beyond the injury to the topsail yard.

This, he said, too, was much less than Mr Cleete, the carpenter, had made out, that worthy being one of the sort of men who always take a despondent view of everything.

The spar, however, was sent down and replaced by a spare yard which we carried; and everything was all right aloft now.

We had lost something in another way, though; for, when Mr Quadrant took the sun at noon, with all of us youngsters standing round him with our sextants, like a parcel of chickens gathered about an old hen, which indeed the master greatly resembled with his shock head of hair and fussy manner, the ship was found to be in latitude 44° 5' north and longitude 7° 50' west.

She had been driven to the south-east by the gale,

aided by the drift of the current setting in to the Bay of Biscay.

This was more than two hundred miles out of our proper track, and far too much to the eastward to be able to weather the northern extremity of the Spanish coast, which would soon be perilously near to us, running as we then were to the sou'-sou' west.

Fortunately for us, though, the wind had now veered to the southward; and, as we were sailing on the port tack, by giving the ship a good deal of weather helm and bracing round the yards, we were able to bear up to the westward out of the ill-omened bay, steering west by south until we were in longitude 11° 10′ west and well clear of Cape Finisterre, when we hauled our wind and shaped a course direct for Madeira.

This, however, was not until next day; and, I recollect, after we luffed up again and bore to the southward, a lot of talk went on in the gunroom at dinner-time about the probability of our stopping or not at that beautiful island, the gem of the Atlantic.

'I say, Jack Vernon,' sang out Larkyns to me, across the table, 'I suppose you know why it is called Madeira?'

'No,' I replied. 'Why?'

'Well,' he began, 'it is rather a romantic story—'

'Then, I shouldn't think it can be much in your line,' interrupted Mr Stormcock, who somehow or other was always down upon any chap for ever starting a yarn. 'You tell very practical ones; only, instead of the term "story" I would use a shorter and more expressive word.'

'Say "lie" if you like; I know you mean it,' rejoined Larkyns, in no way put out by the rude insinuation and continuing his narrative quite composedly. 'But, you're wrong in this case, old Stormy, for "faix it's no lie I'm telling you now," as the doctor's Irish marine would say. It's the plain, un-adulterated truth. I had the tale from a Portuguese monk at Funchal.'

'Funchal,' put in Mr Fortescue Jones, the assistant-paymaster, caressing his whiskers as usual and cocking his eye as if he were going to catch Larkyns tripping. 'When were you there?'

'In the *Majestic*, when I was a cadet,' promptly returned the mid, taking up the cudgels at once. 'It was in the same year you were tried by court-martial for breaking your leave!'

This was a 'settler' for poor Mr Jones.

'Go on, Larkyns,' I said, at this point, to change the conversation and cover the paymaster's confusion as he bent his head over his plate. 'I want to hear that yarn of yours about Madeira.'

'All right, Johnny,' he replied in his chaffy way; 'only, you don't pronounce the name right, my son. It should be called "My-deary," not "Madeir-ah." Hang it all, Stormcock, stow that!'

'Don't apologise,' said the master's mate, who just at that instant had thrown a biscuit at Larkyns, causing the violent interjection which he interpolated in his story. 'I thought I would supply the proper accentuation for you, that's all.'

'If you don't look out and leave me alone, I will pretty soon accentuate your nose, Stormy,' retorted the other, all good humour again, as he always was; for he took a joke, even of the most practical sort, as freely as he perpetrated one. 'Yes, Johnny Vernon, it should be called "My deary," and I'll tell you why. The island, so the monk told me, owes its origin, or rather discovery, to two lovers who fled thither in the year fourteen hundred and something. One of these lovyers, my young friend, was a Scotchman named Robert Matchim, and the other was a Miss Anna D'Arfet, a young lady residing at Lisbon, whose parents objected to Robert and refused to match her with Matchim.'

Mr Stormcock pitched another biscuit immediately at Larkyns, crying out at the same time,—

'That's for your bad pun!'

The wag, however, dodged it and proceeded with his yarn.

'Being a Scotchman, although poor, as few of the nation are,' proceeded he, aiming this retaliatory shot at the master's mate, who, he knew, hailed from the North and hadn't a spare bawbee to bless himself with, 'our friend, Robert Matchim, being as brave as he was bold, would not be done by a pitiful Portuguese laird. So, he pawned the title-deeds of his ancestral estates in Skye, where I forgot to mention he lived when at home; and, chartering a caravel, which happened luckily to be lying at anchor off the port at the time, smuggled his sweetheart on board and sailed away—with the intention of eloping to France, where her stern paryent would, he thought, be unable to follow him for certain political reasons.'

'Very good so far,' interposed Mr Stormcock again at this point, in an ironical tone. 'Pray go on; it is most interesting!'

'Glad you like it,' said Larkyns, coolly, without turning a hair. 'Well, then, to finish the story. Very unfortunately for these fond lovyers, a storm arose, like that bit of breeze we had t'other day. This blew them out of their course and they lost their reckoning, landing at this very island, of which we are speaking instead of at some French port as they expected. The spot they pitched on was called Machico Bay on the eastern side; and there they lived happy ever after, having the additional satisfaction after departing this life of being both buried in one grave. Their last resting-place was seen by a party of Spaniards who subsequently re - discovered the island; when these sentimental mariners, noting the names of the aforesaid lovyers on their joint tombstone, and the account there detailed of their strange adventures, very romantically and devoutly erected a chapel to their memory. This chapel exists to this very day and can be seen by you, Stormy, or any other unbeliever in the truthfulness of my yarn! It is for this reason, my worthy Johnny, that I insist that the island shall be properly styled "My deary"; for, as Robert loved Anna, he would naturally have addressed her as "My deary." Do you twig, young 'un, eh?'

'Oh, yes,' I answered with a snigger, 'I think, though, it's rather far-fetched.'

'So it is,' said he. 'It came from Madeira; and that's some six hundred miles, more or less, from where we now are.'

At that moment, Corporal Macan appeared at the door of the gunroom and walked up to where I was sitting.

'If you plaize, sor,' he said, pulling his forelock, 'the docthor would loike to say yez in the sick bay.'

'Indeed, Macan,' I cried. 'Do you know what he wants me for?'

'The jintleman we tuk off the wrack's rekivered his sinses, an' none ov us, sure, can underconstubble his furrin lingo barrin' yersilf, sor. So, the docther wants ye fur to say what he's jabberin' about.'

'All right,' said I, bolting as quickly as I could a piece of 'plum duff' which Dobbs had just brought me. 'Tell the doctor I'm coming.'

'By jingo, talk of the devil!' observed Larkyns. bursting into a laugh as Macan turned to go away. 'Why, I was only just talking of that blessed Irish marine a minute ago, and here he has come on the scene in person, with his rum brogue.'

'Hush!' I said. 'He'll hear you.'

'No matter if he does,' rejoined Larkyns. 'I suppose he knows he has got the Cork brogue strong enough to hang a catblock from. Besides, he won't mind what I say.'

'Faix, that's thrue for yez, sor,' muttered the corporal, who caught this remark as he was going out of the gunroom door, his ears being as sharp as those of a fox. 'Begorrah, it's moighty little onyone ivver does mind what ye says at all, at all!'

With which doubtful compliment, capable of a double construction, Corporal Macan marched on in front of me, holding his head very erect and with a broad grin on his face, as if conscious of carrying off the honours of the war, towards Dr Nettleby's sanctum on the main deck.

Here, on entering, I noticed the Spaniard sitting up in one of the doctor's easy chairs.

He was near an open port, looking very different to what he was the last time I had seen him, a healthy colour being now in his face; although this was still very much drawn and careworn, but his black hair and beard were tidily arranged, much improving his personal appearance.

He raised his eyes as I came into the cabin, and smiled faintly, seeming to recognise me somehow or other, though he was certainly off his head on board the wreck and could not have remembered what took place there.

'Hé, señor muchaco—so, young gentleman,' said he, on my approaching nearer to him. 'Ta hablas Española—you speak my language then?'

'Si, señor—yes, sir,' I replied. 'Un poco—a very little!

His face instantly brightened, and he poured out a flood of Spanish which I could hardly follow, he spoke so quickly; although, I could gather that he wanted to know where he was and how he had been rescued, inquiring as well what had become of the rest who were in the ship with him.

The doctor, to whom I tried to translate what he said, cautioned me to be very careful what I told him in reply; for, the man, he said, was still in a critical state and any sudden shock would retard his recovery.

I was, therefore, very guarded in my answers to his questions, letting out all he wished to learn only little by little, as he drew it from me by his interrogations.

He expressed the most fervent gratitude on my narrating how we had boarded his water-logged vessel and the difficulty Mr Jellaby had in releasing him from his dangerous position; and, he bowed his thanks to Doctor Nettleby, addressing him as 'Señor Medico—Mr Doctor,' for his kind care of him.

But, when I came to describe what the lieutenant and I had seen in the cabin, his manner changed at once; his eyes rolling with fury and his thin, nervous hands clenching in impotent rage and despair, and he tried to stand up, raising himself out of the chair.

'Ay la povera señora—oh, the poor lady!' he cried out, his eyes now filling and his mouth working with emotion, which he vainly tried to suppress as I told him of the poor dead lady and the little baby floating about on the floor, both of them murdered—'É la péquiña niña—and the little child, too!'

On my telling him next, in answer to another question, about the fine-looking fellow with the revolver in his hand, his feelings could no longer be suppressed.

'Mi hermano! Oh, my brother!' he exclaimed, bursting into tears. 'Muerto! muerto! dead, dead!'

Doctor Nettleby and I turned away, it being painful in the extreme to see a grown man such as he crying like a child; for his breast was heaving and his shoulders shaking with the sobs he endeavoured to conceal, and he hid his face in his hands as he leant back again in the chair.

After a bit, on his becoming more composed again, the doctor gave him a stimulant, which quieted his nerves.

Just then the captain came in, followed by Lieutenant Jellaby, to make inquiries, the doctor having reported his patient convalescent.

'El capitano—this is the Captain,' said I, to attract his attention to the new arrivals as they advanced up to his chair. 'El capitano del nostro buque—the captain of our ship!'

I also pointed out in like fashion Mr Jellaby, saying that he was the officer who had effected his rescue; and the Spaniard bowed silently to both.

Captain Farmer, however, did not need any introduction from me, for he spoke the other's language fluently, being a most accomplished linguist; so, he and the poor fellow were soon on the best of terms, the survivor from the wreck proceeding presently to tell the succinct history of the ill-fated vessel.

This we had all been longing to hear; and Captain Farmer now translated it word for word for the benefit of the doctor and Mr Jellaby, who, as I have already said, did not understand the original Spanish in which it was rendered.

The Spaniard said that his name was Don Ferdinando Olivarez and that he had been the captain and part owner of the barque, which was bound from Cadiz to Havana with a cargo of the wines of Xeres. She had on board, besides, a large quantity of specie, which the Spanish Government were sending out for the payment of the troops in Cuba.

'Your ship was named *La Bella Catarina*, señor,' said I, at this point, as he had not mentioned this fact, though I don't think Captain Farmer approved of my interruption, for he gave me a look which made me shut up at once, 'was she not sir?'

'Yes, young gentleman,' he replied. 'She was so-called after my poor sister-in-law, the murdered lady whose body you saw in the cabin which proved her tomb—Aye que hermosa esta—oh, how beautiful she was! She was the wife of my only brother, Don Pedro Olivarez, who died in defending her. Thus his corpse you also beheld. Oh, my friends, he was the noblest, best and bravest brother in the world. He had, alas, a joint share with me in that accursed vessel!'

He was overcome with emotion again when he had got so far; and Dr Nettleby, fearing the narration was too much for him in his present weak state, wanted him to leave off his story until he felt better.

But after resting a minute or two and taking another sip of the cordial the doctor handed him, the Spaniard insisted on going on with the painful recital.

His brother, he said, had charge of the specie sent out in their ship; and, as his wife had been recommended change of air, he determined to take her with him on the voyage to Cuba, thinking the trip out and home would do her good, as well as the poor little baby, who had been only born two months to the very day on which they sailed from Cadiz.

All went well with them until they were near the Azores, or Western Islands, where the ship sprang a leak and met with such baffling winds that she was driven back to the eastward, close in to the Portuguese coast; when the crew, who were tired out with keeping to the pumps, managed to broach the cargo and madden themselves with the liquor they found below.

'What happened next?' asked Captain Farmer, on

his pausing here to take breath and put the cordial to his lips. 'I suppose they got drunk on the sherry, my friend?'

'Ah, yes, los maladettos—the cursed devils!' replied the Spanish captain, his eyes flashing with anger. If the brutes had only got drunk, neither my brother nor I would have minded it much, although they might have done so at our expense, it being our wine which they wasted, the brutes!'

He then went on to state that the men became so violent and insubordinate, that when his brother and himself battened down the hatches to prevent their broaching any more of the casks, they broke into open mutiny.

The mate was the ringleader of the conspiracy.

It was this rascal, he said, who informed the crew that they had specie aboard, which the mutineers now demanded should be given up to them and they be allowed to leave the ship in one of her boats, the mate telling them that the vessel was almost in sight of Vigo—a fact which he, the captain, had only disclosed to him in confidence that very day within an hour or so of the outbreak, so that the mutiny appeared to be a planned thing.

'Well,' said Captain Farmer, 'what did you do then?'

'We refused their insolent demand, of course,' he answered, 'in spite of the mate and another scoundrel drawing their knives and making for us. My brother knocked down Gomez at once, and the sailor I kicked into the scuppers; the two of us then retreated to the cabin, where we kept them at bay for the whole of that night and all the following day, as we had with us all the firearms in the ship, and it was out of their power to dislodge us.'

'And how was it then you did not succeed in getting the upper hand of them in the end, instead of the affair turning out as it did?'

In reply to this question from our captain, the Spaniard's emotion again overcame him.

'Ay, it was all my fault, and I of all men am the most miserable!' he cried.' 'Yo, I it was who caused the death of those I loved best!'

'Carramba, Señor Capitano,' said Captain Farmer, trying to soothe him. 'You do yourself an injustice. I can't see where you were to blame!'

'Ah, but I do,' he answered doggedly, as if he had made up his mind on the point and no argument would persuade him to the contrary. 'I ought to have recollected that there was no water or provisions in the cabin, the steward, who had joined the mutineers, keeping these always in the fore part of the ship; and, there was the poor señora, who had her little baby to nurse, suffering from hunger and thirst, as we could see, my brother and I, although she never uttered a word of complaint!'

'Poor, brave lady,' observed the captain. 'She deserved a better fate!'

'Si, si, yes, yes,' said the other, 'She did not complain—no, never; but, how could we stand by and see her suffer? My brother Pedro, when it came on to nightfall on the close of the second day of our blockade in the cabin, said that he would adventure out in search of food and water, the mutineers then having drunk themselves to sleep. I, however, pointed out that he had a wife and child dependent on his life, while I had no claims on mine and insisted on my right to take the risk, the more especially from my being the master of the ship. Still, he would not give in; and, ultimately, we cast the dice to decide the matter and I won the cast.'

'You then left the cabin?'

'Yes, señor. My brother barricaded the door behind me and kept watch with his revolver, while I crept forwards stealthily. I reached the steward's pantry in the deckhouse amidships, without being seen and secured some polenta and a baraca of water; when, as I was creeping aft again and close to the poop, that villain of a mate caught hold of my arm, pointing a stiletto in my face at the same time, and threatening to stab me if I uttered a cry. But, before I could open my mouth, he shoved a gag in it and then proceeded to drag me to the side of the ship, lashing me to the spot whence your two officers released me some three days afterwards, if my calculation is correct.'

'Good heavens!' exclaimed the captain. 'What agony you must have suffered tied up like that, and without anything to eat or drink, I suppose, all the while?'

'Nothing, not a bite or drop, passed my lips from the time of the night of the mutiny until your brave officers and men, Señor Capitano, so nobly came to my assistance.'

'You must then have been quite five days without sustenance,' said Captain Farmer, astonished at his endurance. 'I wonder you lived through it, with all that exposure to the weather, too!'

'Ah, it was nothing. I did not think of myself,' replied the other. 'I was in torture for my brother and his poor wife and little child, for, as soon as I was gagged and bound, I saw Gomez and six of the villains all draw their knives and start towards the poop; and, presently, I heard the shriek of a woman's voice which I recognised as my sister's, the señora, and then four pistol-shots in rapid succession, after which I don't know what happened for a time. I must have lost my senses or fainted.'

'And then?'

'When I came to myself again,' continued the Spanish captain, as we all listened breathlessly to his narrative, 'it was near morning and the light of the coming dawn beginning to show in the eastern sky; so, hearing a lot of talking and quarrelling going on, I looked towards the forecastle, whence the sound seemed to proceed.'

'Well,' said Captain Farmer, who was as interested apparently as I was, 'what did you see?'

'I saw a lot of the crew sitting round a tub of brandy, some of which we had shipped along with the wine as part of our cargo, although it had escaped their observation at first, being stowed low down, under the casks of the sherry. However, they had discovered it now, and had evidenty been having an orgie, all of them being more than half drunk. They were swearing and fighting, playing cards by the dim light of one of the ship's lanterns, which was stuck up on the deck beside them. I noticed, too, that a heap of gold was piled up on top of an empty brandy tub, standing to the right of the man dealing the cards, which showed that they had managed to break open the treasure chest containing the government specie; and, I was in an agony of apprehension about my brother's fate, not to speak of his wife and child, when, with a wild shout, one of the villains threw down his cards and clutched at the pile of gold, scrambling up on his feet at the same time and making for the side of the ship where I was lashed against the bulwarks. It was that scoundrel Gomez.'

'The mate, eh?'

'Yes, Señor Capitano. He had a revolver, I saw, in his hand, which he must have got from the cabin after murdering my brother. This thought flashed through my mind instantly, and as it did so, the wretch advanced nearer to the break of the forecastle and fired at me, calling out at the same time, "Carramba, I've settled your dog of a brother and now I am going to finish you off!" The good God, however, defeated his purpose, for the bullet did not penetrate my brain as he intended. No, strange to say, it shot away the knot of the rope's-end that was passed across my mouth to gag me, relieving me at once from considerable pain.'

'Did he not fire again?'

'No,' replied the Spaniard, his countenance lighting up with a sort of ferocious joy that made me think for the moment he had gone suddenly mad at the recollection of his past sufferings. 'Before the villain could aim a second shot in my direction, the most wonderful thing happened that, I believe, could ever have occurred. Yes, Señor Capitano, I declare to you, it was the most wonderful thing, now that I recall it again in speaking to you, that I have ever heard of in all my life. Ay, so wonderful and providential, that it would seem incredible to me were I not certain by this very occurrence, which has brought it home to me, that there is a Power above which watches over us and preserves us from danger, no matter how imminent that danger may be, and when the help of man is of no avail; a Power, too, that as frequently punishes the wicked in the very act of their wickedness, as happened in this case.'

At that moment, the sentry who always stood on guard without the door of the sick bay entered the cabin, and saluting Captain Farmer, said the first lieutenant wished to speak to him; whereupon the captain, apologising for having to absent himself at such a critical point, at once withdrew, saying that he would not be long away.

CHAPTER XXII

'À DIOS!'

'I CAN quite believe you, señor,' said Captain Farmer
on his return after a very brief interval, resuming the
thread of the discourse as if no interruption had
occurred. 'Pray continue your story. I am dying
to know what happened to checkmate that scoundrel
of a mate as he was going to take another shot at you,
thus defeating the design of the murdering ruffian.'

'Without doubt, Señor Capitano, I will tell you,'
replied the Spaniard, drawing a long breath as he
recommenced his yarn. 'As the villain Gomez
cocked and raised the revolver again—for I could
see him plainly from the light of the ship's lantern
flashing on the barrel—Dios! I perceived under the
sheet of the foresail, which was flapping loosely
about, for we were becalmed and the vessel was
drifting aimlessly as she pleased, the mutineers taking no heed of anything but their accursed drink—
I perceived, I say, a steamer approaching, end on
and going apparently at full speed. I could have
shouted out to warn the men on the forecastle, for
the gag had been miraculously removed from my
mouth, as I have told you, only a minute or so.
But, Carramba, I would not have lifted my voice to
have saved them, had I possessed a hundred mouths;
for, I thought of my brother and his wife and child,
and I exulted at their coming fate—Dios! My heart
was throbbing with joy.'

'How awful,' said Captain Farmer, on the Spaniard's voice failing him at the terrible recollection of his experiences ; 'but, I can sympathise with you.'

'Es Verdad, it was awful—so awful, that my heart was nigh bursting and my brain seemed on fire,' replied the other in a calmer tone. 'However, I had not long to wait, the whole thing, from the first moment I observed the steamer to the collision, lasting barely a second of time, although to me it was an eternity ; for, as I saw the steamer, and heard the sound of her paddle-wheels, even as the villain Gomez aimed at me, the prow of the avenging vessel—which I regarded then, as now, as an instrument in the hand of God— came crashing into the bows of our ship, cutting through her hull and deck, and crumpling up the forecastle, señor, as if it had been a paper bag.'

'And the mutineers ?'

'Carramba !' cried the Spaniard, whose vindictiveness I thought appalling ; only, of course, one had to make allowances for what he had suffered and the crimes the men of whom he spoke had committed. 'They were all mangled and crushed in a moment, in the midst of their game of monté, as they were fighting and quarrelling over the stakes. The villain Gomez had his skull cracked like an eggshell by the foremast coming down on top of him, as it went by the board with all its yards and gear. The maintopmast, then fell also leaving *La Bella Catarina* the wreck you saw, Señor Lieutenant, and you, young gentleman, before she foundered.'

He bowed to Mr Jellaby, as well as to myself, on saying this, as if to emphasise his description.

'Did not the steamer stop ?'

'No, Señor Capitano,' replied he in answer to this qnestion of Captain Farmer's. 'Everybody must have been asleep aboard, I think, just before it happened, and they had no lookout man on the watch ; although

as it was in the early grey of the morning, and we
had no lights except that lantern on the forecastle,
which could not have been seen at any distance, and
was, of course, extinguished in the general smash-up
afterwards, it was perhaps not to be wondered that
they ran us down. The collision, though, appeared
to wake them up, for I saw a dark figure on the
paddlebox nearest to me as the steamer swung herself
clear of us and forged ahead again. She had a good
deal of way on, and by the time she stopped her
engines she was some distance away and lost to
sight in the darkness, there being a slight surface fog
on the water ; so, hearing nothing and seeing nothing
of us, her people must have come to the conclusion
that we had gone to the bottom, and so put her on
her course again.'

'Why,' inquired the captain, 'did not those
wretched scoundrels cry out when the steamer
came on them like that ?'

'How could they? It was all done in a moment,
as I have told you. One instant the devils were there,
gambling and drinking and swearing amongst themselves, and the next, cr-r-r-ash, and they were gone to
their patron saint below !'

'And then you were alone ?'

'Yes, so far as I knew ; but I was not quite certain
yet that the scoundrel Gomez had not lied merely to
sport with my misery, and that, perhaps, my poor
brother might be still alive. However as the hours
wore on without him ever making his appearance,
and the crash of the collision would have well nigh
wakened the dead, I gave up hope, beginning to
wonder then, as the sun rose up and the sea became
illumined with light, whether some passing vessel
might not sight the wreck and bear down to rescue me.
By-and-by, though, on morning melting into day, and,
later on, the afternoon waning on the approach of the

shades of night, without ever a distant sail coming in sight to banish my despair, this hope, too, fled.'

'You saw nothing, then?'

'Nothing but the seagulls, which swooped down over my head to see whether I were alive or dead; and it was fortunate my hands were free, or else they would have pecked out my eyes. Nothing but these and the boundless waste of the ocean, whose waters lapped the sides of the ship, which kept afloat, much to my surprise. Her buoyant cargo supported her, although her hold was full up to the main deck, and the sea washing in and out of her forwards; and, there was I, tied up there in the rigging like a dog, listening to the melancholy sound of the breaking waves. I was, you must recollect, utterly unable to help myself, for my arms were pinioned like my legs, although my hands were loose and I could move them about: but, otherwise, I was powerless and could not stir from the place where I was lashed, the ropes binding me being just secured beyond my reach by that villain Gomez, so as to make my agony all the greater.'

'It must have been fearful,' said Captain Farmer. 'I wonder your brain did not give way.'

'Thanks be to God, no! My reason was preserved throughout this terrible ordeal for some wise purpose or other; though, I must say, I prayed for death to release me from my sufferings, a maddening thirst now consuming me, to add to the torture that was prey-ing on my mind,' replied the other, shuddering at the recollection. 'At last, the wind began to blow more strongly and the sea to get up. This lessened my pangs of thirst; but, the waves, constantly breaking over the side, almost drowned me, so one evil took the place of another, and this was all the benefit I reaped from the change. It must have been the following day, I think, for I became so numbed with the cold and exposure, the circulation of my blood being

arrested by my cramped position, that I took no heed
how the time went, when a ship at length hove in
sight, and my heart began to beat again with re-
newed hope, in spite of my despairing thoughts and
misery. Oh, heavens! The ship came nearer and
nearer, so that I could see she was a vessel of war
belonging to the French nation, and my torturing
hope became a certainty. But, would you believe
it, señor, when she had closed the wreck so that I
could see the gunports on her upper deck, she luffed
up and bore away again, hoisting her tricolour flag,
which I shall always loathe the sight of now, as if in
mockery of my condition. Fancy, deserting a ship-
wrecked man like that!'

'The commander of this very ship stopped us to say
he had sighted the wreck of your vessel; but, unhappily, he was unable to lay-to to send a boat aboard,'
explained Captain Farmer, to excuse the French
captain's conduct. 'If he had not done this, perhaps
we would never have come across you and been able
to take you off, which I am heartily glad we were
fortunate enough to succeed in doing!'

'Gracias, señor,' rejoined the Spaniard, stretching
out his hand, which our captain gripped in cordial
interchange of friendship, 'but *you* did not tell another ship to go to my rescue, *you came yourself!*
The English are always brave and generous!'

'By Jove, he's right about that French ship,' observed Mr Jellaby to me, aside, when the captain had
translated this remark of the Spaniard, leaving out,
however, his personal compliment to himself and our
nation. 'It was a scurvy trick to sail off like that, without examining the wreck. But, it's just like those Johnny
Crapauds, youngster. They're deuced good fair-
weather friends but never stand by a fellow in distress!'

'I have not much more to tell you,' went on the
Spaniard after those little reciprocities between him

and the captain. 'It was one morning that the French vessel abandoned me and the next that yours came to my help. Dios, I could not believe I was in my senses when I heard the voices of your officers! I thought I was in a state of delirium and that the sight of your ship, especially after the disappointment of the preceding day, was only a mirage of my imagination, like the Fata Morgana!'

'But, you hailed us, sir,' I said here, on the captain motioning me to come forward. 'Why, you answered me when I spoke to you, sir!'

'I may have done so, my dear young gentleman,' he replied with a faint smile, patting me on the head in an affectionate sort of way, as if he were caressing a pet poodle, so at least Mr Jellaby said afterwards to the other fellows; 'but, I have no recollection of it, I assure you. Still, I must say that your voice seemed familiar to me just now, when you first came into the cabin here and addressed me. It seemed to me a voice that I had heard in a dream.'

He then proceeded to compliment me on my Spanish, saying, in true hidalgo fashion, that I spoke it better than himself, which, as Mr Jellaby remarked, had to be taken 'with a good deal of side on'!

Don Ferdinando Olivarez, to give him his rightful name, concluded his narrative by asking Captain Farmer to land him at Madeira, where he had friends who would supply all his needs, giving him the means to return home to Cadiz, to which port, he said, he must go back for business reasons; besides having to report the loss of his ship, though, as he added with a sigh, he no longer had a 'home' there, now that his poor brother was dead, for he was the last of his race!

Of course, the captain promised to comply with his request, explaining that, although he had not intended stopping at the island, we would in any case have passed pretty close to it in our passage to the Cape;

and that he would be only too glad to call in and put our passenger ashore, regretting, however, that he should have to lose the pleasure of his company so soon.

Dr Nettleby at this point interrupted any further exchange of civilities between the captain and the Spaniard, who was profuse in his thanks, declaring that his patient required rest, or he would not be able to go ashore either at Madeira or any other place on this planet.

The stern medico, who had been very much interested in Don Ferdinando's story, or he would never have permitted so much talking, then bundled us all incontinently out of the sick bay, Captain Farmer included.

Four days later we arrived off Funchal, passing, at the eastern extremity of the island, Machico Bay, where the lovers mentioned by Larkyns landed and lived and died, according to the legend. This, the Spanish captain said was quite true, for he had seen the grave himself and the little church erected to their memory, a statement that quite delighted our friend Larkyns, as he was able to throw it in the teeth of Mr Stormcock as soon as he heard it, in refutation of the base calumny of the latter in asserting that he had invented the yarn he told us at mess.

I was very sorry when Don Ferdinando left the ship, for his misfortunes and the fact of my having been in the boat that rescued him, made him seem like an old friend whom I had known for years, although we had only been such a short time acquainted.

He was very kind, too, in noticing me ; and, before he was rowed ashore in the captain's gig, he presented me with a real gold medallion with the image and superscription stamped thereon of St Nicholas, the protector of all sailors. The Spanish captain told me that this had originally belonged to the great navigator, Christopher Columbus, of whom he was a distant descendant, and that it had been in his family for generations. He had always worn it, he said, next his heart as a preservative against shipwreck, and he fervently believed it was owing to his having it on him that he had been so miraculously saved when everyone else who had been on board *La Bella Catarina* with him had perished.

His now giving it to me was the most practical proof of his friendship he could offer, as he valued it beyond anything he possessed, and I only took it for fear of hurting his feelings, for I did not like to deprive him of it. He was, in truth, a noble fellow, and showed that his gratitude did not merely lie in mere empty words and idle compliments.

No, 'out of sight out of mind' was not his guiding maxim, like it is of some people whom we all have met in the course of our lives; for, even after he had uttered his farewell as he rowed away from the ship in the captain's gig, wishing us with a graceful wave of the hand 'À Dios!' he did not forget us, sending back by the coxswain a splendid present of flowers and fruit and vegetables, almost loading the gig, indeed, for the acceptance of the wardroom and gunroom messes. He forwarded, as well, a case of valuable wine of some special vintage for Captain Farmer's own table.

No one in fact who had done him a kindness when on board passed out of his remembrance, apparently, on his leaving; for, to the doctor he sent a diamond ring, to Lieutenant Jellaby a lady's fan, which, judging by what he had heard of his partiality for the fair sex, I suppose he thought would please him most; and to Corporal Macan and Bill Bates, who had been especially prominent at his rescue, a box of cigars each, while he also sent to the captain a handsome sum of money for him to distribute amongst the crew as he thought best.

CHAPTER XXIII

'CAPE SMOKE!'

WE only stopped at Madeira long enough to get a few purser's stores to add to the supply with which the generosity of Don Ferdinando had already provided us. We also took in some water, for two of our tanks below had been 'started' during our bucketting about in the bay, and Captain Farmer feared we might run short when we reached the warm latitudes ; as, in the event of our falling across the usual calms prevalent in the neighbourhood of the Equator, we might be rolling about a week or two, roasting, in the Doldrums !

But, luckily, we were blessed with favouring winds and made a good passage, picking up the North-East Trades shortly after we said 'good-bye' to Funchal, with its pretty white villas nestling on the hillside amid a background of greenery ; and then, meeting with strong westerly breezes instead of calms, on getting further south into the Tropics, we crossed the Line on Christmas Day, when all the good people at home, I thought at the time, would be shivering with cold and saying, as they snuggled up to the fire, gazing perhaps on a snow-covered landscape without, 'What seasonable weather we are having !' while we were sweltering in the heat under a copper sky, with the thermometer up to 98° in the shade of the awnings !

From the Equator, we had a splendid run to the Cape, taking altogether exactly sixty-five days clear for our passage from England.

During this interval I and my brother cadets had to attend 'school' every morning from half-past 9 o'clock to 11.30 in the captain's outer cabin under the poop, where the chaplain, who also filled the post of naval instructor, officiated as schoolmaster-in-chief, teaching us mathematics and the theory of navigation, as well as seeing that we kept up our logs, which Captain Farmer himself inspected once a week, to make certain that the chaplain, on his part, attended to his duty.

We got on very well with the Rev. Mr Smythe, who had all his longshore starchiness knocked out of him by his long bout of sea-sickness, the poor man having been confined to his bunk and completely prostrate with the fell malady from the hour that we weighed anchor at Plymouth until we 'brought up' at Madeira. I should not, perhaps, have made use of this term, as it savours of tautology, the unfortunate chaplain having been industriously occupied in doing little else save 'bringing up' all the time: especially when we were pitching and rolling in the Bay of Biscay!

Every day, too, at a quarter of an hour before noon, we had to muster on the poop, where, under the tutelage of the master, Mr Quadrant, we watched for the dip of the sun ; and, as soon as the master reported that it was twelve o'clock to the captain, who told him 'to make it so,' and Eight Bells was struck on the ship's bell forwards, we would adjourn to the gunroom below.

There we all worked out the 'reckoning,' showing our respective calculations or 'fudgings' as the case might be, to Mr Quadrant ; when if these 'passed muster,' we entered the result in our log books, along with other observations and facts connected with the daily routine of the ship and her progress towards her destination.

To ascertain this, in addition to taking the sun at noon and noting the attitude of certain stars at night, the log was hove every hour ; and each of us learnt in turn to fix the pin in the 'dead man,' as the log-ship is styled—the triangular piece of wood, with a long line attached, by which the speed of the ship is ascertained.

The first piece of this cord is termed the 'stray line,' and is generally of the same length as the ship, so as to allow for the eddy and wash of the wake astern ; and, at the end of this stray line, a piece of bunting is inserted in the coil, from which a length of forty-seven feet three inches is measured off and a disc of leather put on the line to mark the termination of the first knot, or nautical mile. Two knots are put at the end of another length of forty-seven feet three inches ; three knots at a third, and so on, until as much of the line has been thus measured and marked off at equal distances as will test the utmost sailing capacity of the ship—a single knot being placed midway, also, between each of these divisions, to denote the half knots.

Two sand-glasses are used in connection with the log line, as the old quartermaster, who was our instructor in this branch of our nautical education, explained, the one called 'the long glass,' which runs out in twenty-eight seconds, while the other is a fourteen-second glass, which is generally adopted at sea when the ship is going over five knots with a fair wind.

The first mentioned is only used in light breezes; and, as Bob Ricketts showed us by careful manipulation, reeling off bights of the line and keeping the slack loosely in his hands, the thing to be particular about is to heave the log-ship over the side clear of the ship, and see the glass turned as soon as the

bunting mark is reached, denoting that all the 'waste'
has run out.

Then, whatever mark you can distinguish on the
line nearest to your hand at the expiration of the
allotted twenty-eight or fourteen seconds, when the
man holding the glass sings out 'Stop!' as the last
grain of sand empties itself out of the bulb, that
will be the speed of the ship.

The division of knots on the log-line bear the same
proportion to a mile, as the twenty-eight or fourteen
seconds of the glass does to an hour of time; so, if
the four-knot mark be to hand, and the 'long' glass
be used, she is going four knots, or nautical miles,
per hour. It will be eight knots if the 'short glass'
be the standard of measurement; the time the line
has taken being only half the former, and the number
of the knots having to be doubled to keep the proportion between the length of line and the space
of time equal.

It did not take me long to master what the old
quartermaster had to teach me on this point; but
some of the other cadets were awfully stupid at first,
I must say, particularly that brute Andrews, in
spite of his bumptiousness and conceit.

He gave old Ricketts a lot of trouble before he
remembered to put in the pin prior to pitching the
log-ship overboard; though without this it could not
float upright, and was as good as useless to gauge
our speed.

The ass could not be made to understand this, and
omitted putting in the pin time after time so persist-
ently, that Ricketts had to tell the commander that
he 'could make nothing out of him.'

In addition to these details of 'boardship life, we
were also instructed in practical seamanship by one
of the boatswain's mates.

He was an old hand who had been at sea so long

that he seemed to smell of salt water and tar; while his face was like a piece of pickled beef covered with a quantity of hair that resembled spunyarn more than anything else, being as stiff and wiry as an untwisted rope.

Old Oakum, however, was a thorough sailor, every inch of him, and he taught me much more than I had learned on board the *Illustrious*, not only in 'knotting and splicing' and other things.

Under this worthy's guidance I practised the 'goose step' of going aloft, as it might be described by a drill sergeant, the mizzenmast being placed at our disposal every fine afternoon, and it was pretty nearly good weather all the time of our passage southwards, to learn the art of reefing and furling sails and to send down or cross upper yards; so that we became in the end almost as expert as our tutor, the old salt one day telling Tommy Mills and myself that we took in a royal 'as good and better as any two able seamen could a done it, blow me!'

It was not 'all work and no play,' either, for we had plenty of fun and skylarking down in the gun-room; making the oldsters there, like Mr Stormcock and the assistant-paymaster, Mr Fortescue Jones, frequently wish they, or rather that we, had never been born to come to sea to torment them.

The very duty of the ship itself was an endless source of occupation and amusement to us, the commander keeping the men 'at it' continually from sunrise to sunset, until he had so licked us all into shape that we were the smartest ship's company afloat, I think; for the discipline was such that the old *Candahar* might have been four years in commission instead of the brief three months that had elapsed from our hoisting the pen'ant to our casting anchor in Simon's Bay, a port to the eastward of the 'Stormy Cape,' where our men-of-war usually moor.

Here, we remained for ten days to refit, setting up our lower rigging, which had got very slack through the heat of the Tropics, and taking in fresh provisions and water, besides all of us having a run ashore to shake the reefs out of our legs.

All the men, too, were allowed leave by watches each day of our stay, and few took advantage of the licence to misbehave themselves although temptation enough was thrown in their way by the hospitable inhabitants.

Amongst these few, I am sorry to say, Corporal Macan distinguished himself, falling a victim to his 'ould complaint,' by coming aboard on the second day after our arrival in a state of glorious intoxication, despite his solemn promise to Dr Nettleby, through whom the commander had given him permission to land, that he 'wouldn't touch a dhrop ov the craythur, not if Ould Nick axed him !'

Larkyns, who was in charge of the launch, in which the culprit was brought back helpless to the ship in the afternoon, noticing his condition when he tried to go up the side, ordered him to report himself to the sergeant of marines ; but, Mr Macan, who was valiant in his cups, waxed indignant at this and flatly refused to obey the command, saying that he would not mind going before the commander, or the first lieutenant, or even meeting the doctor himself, though he was loth to see him for the moment with his broken promise staring him in the face ; but as for going and reporting himself to the sergeant he should not, no, not he.

'An' is it to rayport mesilf to that omahdaun ye're afther axin me, sor?' he said scornfully, tossing his head and leering out of his little pig eyes in the most comical way. 'Faix, I'd rayther not, wid your favour, sor. I wouldn't demane mesilf by spakin' to the loikes ov Sarjent Linstock, sor !'

The upshot was that poor Macan was put under arrest and confined in the cells that night; and when brought before the captain the next day for insubordination and drunkenness, as he had no excuse to offer he was disrated, losing his rank of corporal, with all its perquisites and privileges!

On the doctor taxing him with breaking his pledged word, however, in an after interview that worthy had with the delinquent, he vehemently protested his innocence of that charge at all events.

'I tould yez, sor, I wouldn't touch a dhrop ov the craythur, maynin' whisky, sure,' he said, with a miserable attempt at a grin; for he felt very much humiliated at losing his stripes, Macan sober being quite a different man to Macan drunk. 'An' faix I niver bruk me wurrud at all, at all, I'll swear, sor.'

'How can you have the face to deny it, man?' cried the doctor, angrily. 'Why, I saw the state you were in myself when you came aboard the other night!'

'That mebbe, sor,' replied the undaunted Irishman, with a little of his old bravado; 'but it warn't the ould complaint, I till ye, sor.'

'What was it, then, that made you drunk, you rascal?' rejoined the doctor, with a twinkle in his eye, knowing his man, 'for, drunk you were—ay, as drunk as Chloe?'

'Faix, sor,' said Macan, noting instantly the doctor's change of mood, and grinning all over his face in consequence, 'it wor the Cape shmoke that did it. Sure, it obfusticated me, sor, entirely!'

CHAPTER XXIV

WE JOIN THE ADMIRAL AT SINGAPORE

'CAPE smoke?' said I, inquiringly, to Mr Stormcock, who happened to come up the hatchway on to the main deck as the doctor was thus cross-examining the ex-corporal of marines outside the sick bay, where poor Macan was now doing 'sentry go' after his reduction to the ranks, to make his humiliation the more complete. 'What is that? It can't be real smoke, I suppose!'

The master's mate laughed.

'Smoke, eh, youngster?' he repeated in his ironical way, being the driest old stick we had in the gun-room and certainly, according to Larkyns, a judge of considerable experience of the article under discussion. 'Bless you, it's the most rotgut stuff any fellow ever put in his inside, and only a Dutchman could have invented it! I can tell you it's a liquor that's best left alone. Take my advice, Vernon, and don't you have anything to do with it!'

'I won't,' I replied. 'Have you ever tasted it, Mr Stormcock?'

He looked at me hard, thinking at first that I meant to chaff him; but seeing that I asked the question in perfect good faith, without any intention of alluding to his reported 'little weakness,' he proceeded to answer me, truthfully enough.

'By jingo! youngster, I can tell you, I speak from

my own knowledge,' he said, as he turned away to go forwards, 'I had too much of it once when I was at the Cape before and it gave me the shakes next morning so badly that my teeth rattled like a horse's jaws when chewing a hammer!'

This expression amused me very much, for I had never heard previously of a horse indulging in that species of diet; so, I went up on the quarter-deck to take my watch with a broad smile on my face, which attracted Mr Jellaby's notice at once, as he had a keen relish for a joke.

'Hullo, youngster, you're grinning like a Cheshire cat eating green cheese!' he exclaimed. 'I suppose you have heard the news, and that makes you so chirpy?'

This made me all agog in a moment, with the expectation of something very exciting coming, and I answered his question in the Irish fashion, by asking another with much eagerness.

'What news, sir? I haven't heard of any.'

'Why, the redcoats belonging to the garrison at Cape Town are going to give a grand ball in our honour, and of course all the gunroom officers as well as the wardroom fellows will be invited,' he replied. 'I daresay they'll be able to spare you from your important duties aboard for the occasion, and I'll try to smuggle you off myself if I can. By Jove, it will be a splendid hop, for the Cape Town girls are chawming, they tell me!'

I was not old enough yet, however, for this encomium of his on the young ladies of the colony to be any inducement to me, and, to tell the truth, was a little disappointed at hearing what his wonderful news was, imagining it to have been something very different.

'Oh!' I said, without any improved enthusiasm, such as he doubtless expected. 'Thank you, sir.'

'Well you *are* an ungrateful young cub!' he cried.

'Catch me putting myself out of the way again to give you a treat! One would think from your glum look that I was going to bring you up on the quarter-deck before the captain, instead of offering to take you to the ball!'

I felt quite sorry at having hurt his feelings, he looked so chagrined; but, before I could say anything in excuse for the apathetic way in which I had received his intelligence, Mr Bitpin, who had overheard the conversation, came to my rescue.

'Nonsense, Jellaby!' he said. 'What can a boy like that know about girls? Time enough for him to think of the petticoats when he's twenty years older; and then he'll be a fool if he runs after them as much as you do!'

'Ah, you're jealous, Bitpin, because you're not a lady's man!' retorted Mr Jellaby, recovering his good humour in a moment, as he always did, no matter how much he might be put out. 'If you were as great a favourite with them as I am, you'd sing a different song, I know.'

'As great a fiddlestick!' ejaculated the other with infinite scorn, having the reputation of being as much of a woman-hater as Diogenes. 'If I was as big an ass about those "chaw-ming girls" as you call them, I tell you what I would do—I'd go and hang myself!'

He said this so fervently, that, in spite of Mr Bitpin's burlesque of his manner of speaking, 'Joe' fairly roared with laughter, in which the gunnery lieutenant, who had just come up from below to see about something deficient in one of the upper deck guns, which had been reported to him by Mr Triggs during the morning's inspection, joined with much gusto.

Their merriment so enraged Mr Bitpin that he went down to the wardroom in the most wrathful mood, declaring that they were a couple of idiots and that the service was going to the devil through the Admiralty neglecting the claims of their best officers and promoting a lot of empty-headed coxcombs, who thought more of prancing about in a ballroom in patent leather pumps than of keeping their watch regularly and attending to their duties aboardship!

Notwithstanding all adverse comments, however, Mr Jellaby's news of the forthcoming ball proved true, for I heard it confirmed at the captain's table the same evening.

Captain Farmer was in the habit of inviting his officers in turn to dinner three times a week, the commander being a regular guest and one of the lieutenants and mates, with a couple of midshipmen and naval cadets being generally present on each occasion; while the doctor and chaplain, as also the purser and marine officers, only came occasionally to these gatherings, the conversation mostly dealing with professional matters in which those belonging to the executive were mainly interested and the other branches not much concerned.

It was for this reason, I suppose, the captain did not invite these latter officers more often than he could help!

During the progress of the courses this evening, the talk, as usual, was on service topics; but when the cloth had been removed and the toast of 'the Queen' honoured in the customary way, each of us youngsters being then allowed our one glass of wine to drink the health of Her Majesty, Captain Farmer introduced the subject of the garrison ball.

'I have here invitation cards for all of you, even including you, Master Vernon,' he said, handing them round and passing one over to me which was inscribed with my name in full; the 'sojer officers,' as Tommy called them, having managed through the purser or master-at-arms, or by some other means, to get hold of all our names correctly, both great and small. 'So, gentlemen, we must try and make as brave a show as we can in return for the compliment, the affair really being given in our honour. We need only keep an anchor watch, so nearly all of you may be spared, I think, for the night. You'll have to settle it with the commander as to who shall remain on board.'

This was soon settled, Mr Bitpin offering at once to do double duty for the nonce, as he did not care about dancing and besides wished leave for the two following days to go up country on a visit to a Caffre kraal; while Plumper, the fat mate, who had the toothache very badly, also volunteered to remain.

So did the master and purser and Mr M'Gilpin, the assistant-surgeon; the latter saying that he had no stomach for consorting with 'the meeletary,' they being 'a maist feckless set o' loons.'

As for the middies and us cadets, we had to draw lots to decide who should go and who stop behind; but, at the last moment, the commander gave permission for us all to go, save Andrews, who had been impertinent to the first lieutenant in the afternoon and was ordered to remain in the ship.

I was not sorry I went, after all, for it was a jolly affair and I enjoyed myself mightily, especially at the supper table, where the redcoats shone to perfection; this opinion of mine being shared, I believe, by most of my fellow youngsters, who cared more for the grand tuck out they had than all the dancing in the world.

I noticed, though, that Mr Jellaby kept up his reputation as a lady's man, waltzing and flirting all the evening with an awfully fat Dutch frau, who was broader of beam than comported with her short stature, and whom the susceptible lieutenant subsequently described as 'the most chawming woman' he had ever met in his life!

'Joe' got awfully chaffed about her by all of his

brother officers of the wardroom whose rank permitted them to take such a liberty with him; and, though we could take no share in their personal amenities, we youngsters grinned our approval of the various witty remarks and rejoinders that passed to and fro on our way back aboard the following day—the ball having lasted till long after daybreak the next morning, and Simon's Bay being all astir, with plenty of 'Simons,' black and white, astir ashore and afloat, as we rowed out to the ship, we having nearly outstayed our leave, the captain and commander preceding us aboard by a long spell.

We gave a return dance to the garrison folk and hospitable inhabitants generally the day before we sailed for the China Sea; when the old *Candahar* was decked out so gaily with bunting and evergreens, with which we were lavishly supplied from the shore, that the riggers of Portsmouth Dockyard would not have known her.

Her upper deck was a perfect parterre of flowers and foliage, intertwined with the flags of all nations, and enclosed under an awning, which latter had a canvas screen all round to keep out the prying eyes of the bluejackets on the forecastle.

Going round with Mr Fortescue Jones, the assistant-paymaster, whom I had taken a liking to in consequence of his having served under Sir Charles Napier, Dad's old captain and my own personal patron, he noticed this screen and he told me another anecdote of the old admiral, to add to my list.

'His flagship, the *Duke of Wellington*, was lying off Kiel or Copenhagen, I forget which exactly, and the officers were about to give a similar entertainment to ourselves as an acknowledgment of the kind treatment they had received from the inhabitants of the place. Like ours, the ship was decorated throughout regardless of expense, everyone subscribing to the fund, and a screen similar to what we had was being put up when the admiral coming down from the poop chanced to notice this.

' " Hullo ! " he cried.   " What's that for ? "

' " Why, sir," explained the commander, " it's to keep the men forrud from staring at the dancers."

' " The deuce it is ! " said the old fellow, taking an awful lot of snuff,' Mr Jones remarked, as if I were not acquainted with this habit of the veteran sailor. " By whose orders was it rigged up ? "

' " Orders, sir ? " replied the commander, a bit nonplussed.   " By mine, sir."

' " Then mine are for you to rig it down at once," cried the admiral, in a mighty fume, walking up and down and waving his arms about like a windmill backwards and forwards from his waistcoat pocket to his nose.   " I won't have any screens fitted up on board my ship to keep out my sailors from seeing what they have as good a right to see and enjoy as any of those with whom they have fought and bled. No sailors, no ball, or I'm a Russian !   You can put that in your pipe and smoke it, Mr Commander ! " '

' Did the ball come off, Mr Jones,' I inquired of the narrator, ' after all ? '

' No,' said he.   ' The fleet had to sail the very same day for which it was fixed.   I believe old Charley arranged that it should be so, on purpose to pay out the commander, who had set his heart on it ; for he was very hard on the men always, and the admiral could not stand that.'

' He was a good friend, always, to the sailors ? ' I remarked.   ' I have heard my father say so.'

Rather !   Why, he would do anything for them, regardless of his own comfort, and they in return would follow him anywhere, night or day, in the face of a thousand batteries.   He was, indeed, like a father to them,' continued the paymaster, who was fond of yarning about his old experiences with the admiral. 'I recollect after the bombardment of Bomarsund and the capture of a lot of prizes up the Baltic, we put into Kiel again, and the men wanted to draw advances to have a spree ashore, but the admiral told the purser to refuse them, and when they grumbled about it he gave them a "dressing down" from the poop, having them all piped aft by the bosun for the purpose. "Lads," says he, "I'll let you have ten shillings apiece, but not a farthing more to spend, now! I want you to save all your prize-money for your wives and sweethearts when you return to England, for I don't wish to have my eyes scratched out on Common Hard when I come out of the dockyard on landing, as I should, if I were fool enough to allow you to spend all your money out here instead of making you keep it, as I intend, till you get home!" He was a rare good old sort was the admiral, young Vernon!'

'So I should think,' I replied, 'from all I have heard.'

But there our chat ended, the Cape people just beginning to come off to 'cut their capers,' as Master Larkyns remarked to me, making me a target as usual for one of his fearful puns.

Our dance was as great a success, I think, as the garrison ball, judging by the approving comments of our guests, who kept it up till the middle watch had well nigh come to a close.

Mr Jellaby, I noticed, inconstant fellow that he was, payed attentions of the most marked character on this occasion, all the time the festivities lasted to a Cape damsel of the most slender figure, contrasting strongly with the stout lady who was his former flame and who had come off especially, so the wardroom officers said in their chaff, to renew her attack on the heart of the lieutenant.

Mr Jellaby, proved a recreant knight and the Dutch

lady had to content herself with the cavaliership of the youngest and most diminutive cadet on board, my chum, little Tommy Mills !

But Tommy's gallant championship of the deserted fair one and the lieutenant's fresh flirtation had to terminate, like everything else in this world ; and hardly had the last of our visitors quitted the ship than the hands were turned up to weigh anchor, the old *Candahar* sailing soon after daybreak and shaping a course southwards to pick up the westerly trade winds of the ' Roaring Forties.'

With studding sails, upper and lower, on each side, we bowled along gaily, the wind right astern all the way some two thousand miles odd or so, until we fetched the meridian of the Island of St Paul in the middle of the great southern ocean ; when, we hauled up to the north-east and steered for the Straits of Sunda, leading into the China Sea—finally joining the admiral in command of the station at Singapore. where we cast anchor again in the outer roads one broiling morning in March, just four months from the date of our leaving home.

CHAPTER XXV

'THE HEATHEN CHINEE'

'WHAT a rum place!' cried Larkyns, when the ship was safely moored and Captain Farmer had gone off in his gig to pay his respects to the admiral, whose flagship lay hard by, all of us then having time to look round and survey the strange and picturesque surroundings—semi - European, semi - Oriental, all tropical—of Singapore harbour, the capital of the Straits Settlements and great port of the Eastern Archipelago, amid which we now found ourselves. 'I'm blowed if it doesn't look like the pantomime of "Ali Baba and the Forty Thieves" at Drury Lane!'

'That's not at all a bad simile, youngster,' observed the commander, who was just coming down from the poop, after seeing everything snug and that the awnings had been spread over the decks, with wind-sails rigged up leading through the hatchways to introduce what air there was to the heated atmosphere below. 'Only, instead of forty, I should think there were forty thousand thieves amongst that crowd of Asiatics, with their serpent's eyes and slimy bodies! It looks like a water picnic, does it not?'

It was certainly a wonderful and varied scene that we gazed at over the hammock rail, the glaring sun overhead, the vividly blue sea stretching up to the white beach in front of the busy-looking town and the verdant hills beyond, with white villas nestling amid the green, like Madeira, and big, gru-gru palms and agaves, with other odd, broad-foliaged plants to tell that we were in more outlandish latitudes; while, skimming over the glassy blue water, that turned to an emerald green in its depths and was so transparent that the sandy bottom could be seen, with various molluscs crawling about amongst the algæ, were hundreds of boats of every description—from the trim-built man-o'-war's cutter down to the slipper-like sampan and aboriginal coracle of as queer construction as the catamaran of the Coromandel coast or the war canoe of the Sandwich Islands.

Other even queerer craft lay at anchor like ourselves, only further up the harbour, chief amongst them being Chinese junks of every size, from the huge, travelling tea-chest from Woosung or Amoy of three or four thousand tons burthen, down to the 'junklet' from the nearer provinces of the Celestial Empire of lesser proportions.

But, all were alike in form, veritable facsimiles of the picture of the *Great Harry* of the time of Henry the Eighth, which I remember seeing in an old book on history when I was cramming up for my examination and looked at every work I could come across in order to increase my store of knowledge.

These junks all had great, staring, goggle eyes painted on their bows on either side, John Chinaman believing that without these fanciful addenda his stagey-looking craft 'no see no piecee walk can do.

Their sails also were very funny, being huge mats, of trapezoidal shape, that resembled so many Venetian blinds.

These sails were hoisted on tall poles of eighty to hundred feet in height, without a joint, while their floating rattan cables completed their theatrical appearance, circling round their prows with the tide like snakes.

In addition to these were likewise any number of Malay prahus and ' prams ' from Borneo and Celebes and the Philippine Islands generally ; Arab dhows and ' grabs ' from the Persian Gulf; English-captained, Lascar-manned trading vessels from Calcutta and Madras ; fishing schooners from the Torres Straits and Sydney, laden with cargoes of sea-slugs, for Chinese consumption ; besides merchant ships from every port in Europe—although, I noticed that the British and American flags were decidedly in the ascendant.

All this heterogeneous collection of vessels, of every known nationality and rig, come hither at all seasons, but the Chinese junks mostly when the north-east monsoon sets in to blow them along with their favourite stern wind.

They resort here as to a common meeting ground or exchange mart, to swop their cargoes, the silks and teas and spices and precious gums of the East being bartered for the manufactures and merchandise of the West ; while the keen though sleepy-looking Dutch-men, Chinese, Jews, Parsees, Siamese, Englishmen and Yanks, who negotiate and this interchange of wares manage to conduct the bargaining in their various lingoes by the aid of a polyglot dialect of their own, chuckling over the dollars and cash and cowries as they rake them in with the impression that they are getting the best of the deal, when all the time, perhaps, they are being cheated themselves !

So Commander Nesbitt now told us, kindly parti-cularising the various points of interest to us two youngsters and explaining all we did not know, which meant pretty nearly everything, as he had served in these waters before ; while to Larkyns and myself ingapore and its migratory population, with their prominent characters and characteristics, were all new, as, indeed, they were to most of the fellows in the gunroom, exceping Mr Stormcock and Plumper, the fat senior mate, both of whom, like the commander, had previously been on the station and were acquainted of old with the place and its people.

But neither Larkyns nor myself need have been in any hurry to make our observations; for, we had ample opportunity of learning all we wished to know, and a good deal more, too, of Singapore and its surroundings, as we remained here over six weeks.

The *Candahar* had orders to await the coming of Admiral Hope from England by the overland mail, in succession to Admiral Sir Michael Seymour, whose period of service had expired before the former left London to take up his commission.

In order to understand the position of affairs leading up to the events I am now about to speak of, in which, possibly, I took a more prominent part than I might have chosen had I been given the option, I may mention that through the action mainly of the last-named officer, in capturing Canton and forcing his way almost up to the gates of Pekin, which seemed to bring the Imperial Ruler of the Universe and Emperor of the Sun, Moon and Stars to his senses, the series of intermittent wars between Great Britain and China, which had been waged at intervals since the year 1840, breaking out again after more than one temporary cessation of hostilities, like a smouldering fire ever and anon bursting into flame, had been, it was sanguinely believed by the authorities, brought to a permanent close by the Treaty of Tientsin, signed in 1858.

This treaty, however, which as Lord Elgin, our plenipotentiary, wrote home to warn the Government, had 'been extorted only from the fears' of the Chinese, was not to be ratified until the succeeding year, the date of our arrival on the scene ; where the Celestials hoped that they might by then have time to prepare themselves for a renewal of the struggle, although, of course, our wise men in office never thought of such a thing, implicitly giving faith to the assurances of the pigtailed mandarins that peace was as good as settled, and that friendly relations betwixt ourselves and the yellow-skinned descendants of the great Confucius would be resumed and their ports open to our trade at the time fixed—only, not till then !

How those blandly-smiling mandarins must have twinkled their little pig eyes and tossed their pigtails in gay abandon at the simplicity of the ‘ Outer Barbarians ’ whom they thus beguiled in the usual ‘ Heathen Chinee ’ fashion, as we subsequently discovered to our cost, although this is anticipating matters.

CHAPTER XXVI

TOWARDS the middle of April, to proceed with my regular yarn, within two months of the time fixed for the ratification of this paper treaty, our new chief arrived at Singapore; when, taking over the command from his predecessor, who at once started off in the homeward mail steamer, Admiral Hope sailed with the fleet to Shanghai—the *Candahar* forming part of the squadron that escorted our ambassador, Mr Bruce, to the mouth of the Peiho River, where he was appointed to meet the Chinese officials and with them journey on to Pekin, there to complete all the requisite formalities for the final execution of the treaty.

Reaching Shanghai without mishap and finding Mr Bruce ready to accompany us, although the mandarins had already interposed obstacles to delay his departure in order to evade the obligations they had entered into on behalf of their imperial master in the art of subterfuge and evasion, we proceeded on the 11th June to the Gulf of Pechili; anchoring under the lee of the Sha-liu-tien, or 'Wide-spreading-sand Islands,' some fifteen miles off the entrance to the Peiho.

The water here being too shoaly to allow the larger vessels of the fleet to approach near the shore, the admiral embarked aboard one of the smaller gunboats, thinking the coast clear and everything peaceful ; but on getting close to the mouth of the river, he discovered to his surprise that a series of formidable earthworks had been erected on both banks in place of the Taku Forts which Admiral Seymour had destroyed in the preceding year.

The river itself, also, had been rendered impassable by a series of booms and stakes, so arranged as to be protected by the fire of the batteries, whose numerous embrasures spoke to their containing a large number of guns ; while, to remove any doubts as to the hostile character of these preparations, the officer Admiral Hope sent to acquaint the authorities in charge of these fortifications of the arrival of our ambassador was refused permission to land.

On communicating this news to Mr Bruce, who was accompanied on his ambassadorial mission by Monsieur Bourbillon, the representative of the French Government,—a council of war was held on board the flagship ; when it was determined to force the passage of the river, so that the ambassadors should be able to go up to Pekin in accordance with the Emperor of China's express permission to that effect given under his sign manual.

The admiral therefore forwarded off at once a letter to the commandant in charge of the defences, telling him that unless the obstructions were removed within the next forty-eight hours, he, the admiral, would set to work to clear them away himself in the manner he thought best.

This was explicit enough ; and as no answer was received to this communication by sunset on the 24th, the limit of the ultimatum, Admiral Hope proceeded to prove himself as good as his word.

An unsuccessful attempt was made by the boats of the flagship the very same night to pull up some of the iron stakes driven into the bed of the river, that held the booms in their position across its mouth.

This failed through the tenacity of the mud, the effort of the bluejackets being discovered by the batteries, which fired on them, compelling them to desist and return to their ship ; but, this was a mere flash in the pan, the real attack being planned for the morrow.

In the meantime, the fleet had moved in from the Sha-liu-tien Islands to the anchorage opposite the entrance to the Peiho, where our ship and the *Chesapeake*, with some of the others remained out of range of the batteries, which we on our side, were unable to reach with our guns for any effective purposes.

The gunboats of lesser draught, however, proceeded to cross the bar of the river ; where also the boats of the bigger ships were subsequently despatched, filled with all the small-arms men and marines available to form a reserve force which was to attack the principal batteries in the flank after the gunboat had pounded them in front, as well as fill up casualties in the first line.

Every man on board the *Candahar* was on the alert on the morning of the memorable 24th June, I can tell you, when the boatswain's pipe went screeching through the ship at daylight, and the commander sang out the order to 'Man and arm boats.'

'I bet we don't have any fight at all!' grumbled Mr Stormcock, as he buckled on his sword and prepared to go in the launch with Mr Gilham, who was directed to command her, Larkyns, having to play second fiddle in the boat on this occasion. 'Those blessed Chinamen won't come up to the scratch as soon as they see we mean business.'

'Perhaps not,' said Mr Gilham. 'But, they were

precious sharp last night in detecting those fellows that went after the booms. I think they mean fighting this time, they're keeping so dark.'

'Well, I only hope they do, sir,' replied the master's mate, with a heavy sigh that evidently came from the bottom of his heart. 'For my part, I think they'll cut and run at the first shot, as they've always done before. I was out here, sir, in the Fatshan affair up the Canton River in '57, and I remember as we boarded the junks on one side, all of us racing after them up the creek, the yellow devils would jump out on the other, without standing up against us for an instant.'

While they were talking, I managed to scramble into the bows of the launch unobserved, nobody noticing me till we had left the ship and it was too late ; and, though Mr Gilham shook his fist at me and told me I was 'acting against orders,' he beckoned me to come aft, where Larkyns and Mr Stormcock made a place for me between them in the sternsheets, the rest of the boat being crammed with bluejackets and marines, the latter sitting down on the bottom boards between the thwarts and the knees of those pulling.

On pulling inshore we made fast to some junks which had been requisitioned and moored just inside the bar for the purpose, and here we remained while the gunboats went on to the assault ; Admiral Hope leading the advance in person and hoisting his flag on the little *Plover*, which showed the way to the rest, moving onward to the first obstruction in the river, a long row of iron piles linked together by eight-inch hawsers hove taut.

As we watched our comrades making this forward movement at last, the flood tide filled the turgid stream of the Peiho, flooding the reedy marshes on either side of its banks ; until, presently, a sheet of muddy water stretched up to the base of the forts, lapping their wide earthen escarpments.

These made no sign of defiance whatever, not a man being seen on the parapets, nor a gun peeping from their embrasures, which were hidden with mantlets.

Every heart beat high with excitement; and instead of fearing the worst, the worst we feared was a hollow victory!

The gunboats all took up their several positions, anchoring so as to command the forts and support those attacking the booms; and at two p.m., when the ebb began to flow and there was no danger of the stream carrying the vessels too close in, the *Opossum* was ordered by signal to pull up the first pile, which she did by the aid of tackles and steam power.

On the removal of this obstacle, the admiral passed through towards the second barrier, which was immediately under the concentric fire of the batteries on both banks of the river.

Here the question would be decided at length whether the Chinese meant fighting or not.

We had not long to wait for the decision.

Hardly had the bows of the *Plover* touched the boom than ' Bang ' went a single gun from the nearest earthwork.

This seemed like a signal; for, almost at the instant of its discharge, a terrific fire of shot and shell from forty pieces of cannon was hurled on the unfortunate *Plover* and her consort the *Opossum*, which followed her close up behind, both being immediately wreathed in smoke and flame and having their decks swept fore and aft by every discharge.

It was a regular ambuscade, a hornet's nest !

In less than twenty minutes, the two gunboats were so badly shattered as to be almost silenced ; though the plucky little *Plover* still remained in the van, with the admiral's signal still flying, ‘ Engage the enemy,’ with the red pennant under, which Mr Gilham told me meant ‘ as close as possible.’

She held out, too, in spite of her not having nine men of her original crew left efficient out of the party with which she commenced the action ; while Lieutenant Rason, who commanded her, was killed by being cut in two by a round shot.

The admiral himself was grievously wounded by the splinter of a shell in the thigh, and the rest of the officers swept down — a terrible amount of slaughter in so small a space.

Of course, we did not know all this till afterwards ; but we could see the poor little temporary flagship's battered state, as she swung all abroad across the sullen, dark-flowing river, now seemingly red with blood from the flashes of the guns, whose murderous roar rent the air each moment, sweeping down our comrades and laying them mangled and bleeding on the deck, every time we heard the sound.

Then, we noticed a signal for assistance thrown out from the solitary spar the *Plover* had yet standing ; and the *Lee* and *Haughty*, which were anchored below the first barrier and busily engaged with the batteries on the left bank, at once weighed and proceeded to the admiral's aid.

A few minutes later, Admiral Hope, though fainting from loss of blood, transferred his flag to the *Opossum*, which had not been so badly served out as the *Plover ;* but, no sooner had the square white flag, with its red St George's cross been seen flying on the second gunboat, than every gun in every battery was apparently directed on her, the admiral getting wounded a second time, while nearly every officer and man was shot down.

‘ By heavens, it's too cruel !’ cried Mr Stormcock, jumping up in the launch as the *Opossum* dropped down towards us on the ebb tide, away from the withering fire. 'Can't we do something to help them?'

CHAPTER XXVII

'BLOOD'S THICKER THAN WATER!'

'Ay!' replied Mr Gilham, who was equally impatient to go to the rescue of our poor comrades, and, if not able to help them, to fall beside them, the lieutenant speaking in a hoarse tone, with his face of that pattern which shows a desperate purpose, and biting his lip so that the blood came, to keep in his repressed feeling. 'But, not before the word's given for us to go forward. I wish to God this would come!'

It was terrible work for us, lying sheltered there under the lee of the junk to which we were moored, looking on inactive, listening to the whistle of the round shot hurtling in the air and hearing the heavy thud of the missiles as they crashed through the sides of the gunboats; for we pictured the devastation these missiles wrought inboard, with the shrieks of the wounded, the groans of the dying, and the hapless bodies of the dead strewing the decks.

It was more terrible far to us than for those participating in the grim tragedy with all its attendant horrors.

They were fighting and oblivious of everything save a mad longing to kill and slay; while we were doing —nothing!

Every one of us in the launch of the *Candahar* felt that; and yet, what could we do?

A limit, however, came at length to our endurance.

The *Plover* and *Opossum*, which had dropped out of the first line, drifted down nearer to us; and then, the captain in command of the reserve called for volunteers to re-man those staunch little vessels that had borne all the burden and heat of the battle so far, but were staunch, practically speaking, no longer, being almost floating wrecks, and their crews either wounded or dead.

No second call was needed, the men being all alert in an instant, the boats' crews vieing with each other as to which should supply the fresh hands required for the gunboats; although these would be going, as they well knew, into the very jaws of death.

Fortunately the launch was the nearest.

'Give way, men!' cried Mr Gilham, waving his sword over his head in a perfect delirium of joy at being at last no longer a mere spectator of the exciting scene. 'Now, we have a chance, lads; pull like devils lest it be taken from us!'

But, the lieutenant might have spared his breath, for the men's blood was up; and, with a bound, the heavily-laden launch dashed forwards as if she were a racing galley, distancing all her competitors, and being alongside the leading gunboat before the rest had got half way up, our start giving us an advantage, which even their lesser weight could not lessen.

In less than a minute, the lot of us scrambled on board the *Opossum*, bluejackets, marines, gunners and all.

We found the engineer and one solitary uninjured stoker below, the others having all been killed by a bursting shell.

These men, however, were still sticking manfully to their posts in the engine-room, notwithstanding that they must have been longing all the while to scuttle up on deck and 'have a shy' at the treacherous beggars who had caught us in such a villainous trap;

and at once piling on steam, the gunboat in which we were in, followed by the *Plover*, hurried up to the front again to relieve the *Lee* and *Haughty* which were now standing the brunt of the fire from the enemy's batteries, and looked decidedly as if they were getting the worst of it.

The *Lee*, indeed, had a hole knocked in her bows which a wheelbarrow could have been trundled into; while her consort had been hulled repeatedly below the water, and, being close in under the guns, these, as the tide fell, plunged their shot right through her bottom planking.

' Hot work, ain't it, youngster ? ' observed Mr Stormcock to me, presently, when we came under fire and I had the pleasant sensation of a jinghal ball passing close to my ear, cutting a bit out the collar of my jacket and making me wince, though I can honestly say I was not frightened at this, my first experience of being really in action. ' Keep moving about and there'll be less chance of your being picked off. A lively man who does his work without thinking of the shot, seldom gets touched. So I found it two years ago, at all events, when I was in the thick of it at Canton ! '

' That's thrue, sor,' put in Corporal Macan, who had lately regained his stripes after a long spell of good behaviour that atoned for his debauch at the Cape which lost him his rank ; the Irishman now being engaged in serving the bow gun of the gunboat with the utmost deliberation, taking steady aim with each shot which he pitched into the cavalier of the nearest battery and knocking the gun into ' smithereens ' at his third attempt, though, for every weapon of the enemy which we silenced they seemed to bring a hundred others to bear on us. ' Jist kape hopping about an' faith ye'll niver be hit, sure. Och, murther, what's that now ? '

As he jerked out the sudden exclamation, he certainly acted up to his advice ; for, he gave a hop that took him some ten feet in the air, ere he fell down on the deck, all covered with blood.

'Poor Macan!' said Mr Stormcock, bending over his prostrate form, and trying to lift him in vain. 'Well, he's done for at last, I'm afraid. We could have better spared a better man, perhaps!'

'He's dead, sir, sure enough,' corroborated one of the marines who had been assisting to work the big bow gun, the carriage of which had been smashed, on one side by a heavy chain shot, which must, we all thought, have settled the corporal at the same time. 'He'll never eat plum duff again, poor chap. He was a good one over his vittles, too, was the corporal, and likewise at his drink !'

'Faix, ye lie, ye divil,' cried the seemingly lifeless man, reviving at this moment and struggling to his feet. 'I'm not d'id at all, at all! D'ye think now I'm going to be kilt—by a Haythin Chaynee? Begorrah, whin I am kilt, may the saints in h'iven presairve me from it yit !—I hopes as how it'll be by a Roosian, or a Proosian, or a dacint Christian man of some sort or t'other, an' not, faix, by one of thim yaller-faced Johnnies over yander !'

We all laughed at this, it being quite a relief to find our old friend the corporal had not yet lost 'the number of his mess,' as he was the life and soul of the ship on the lower deck, drunk or sober !

He had, however, a narrow squeak of it; for a splinter had jogged his leg from the ankle to the knee, while the bollard on which he had been standing had been shot away under his feet.

This caused that wonderful jump of his which had surprised me so much, himself all the more, too, the heavy fall he had on the deck afterwards having knocked him senseless for the time and, indeed, bruised him very considerably.

Macan, though, had all an Irishman's pluck, and would not give in.

'Sure, sor, it's ownly a thrifle,' he urged, when told by Mr Stormcock to go below to Mr M'Gilpin, who was busy in the after cabin, attending to those of the wounded that the Chinese gunners, who aimed remarkably well, had not put altogether beyond the reach of surgical aid. 'I wudn't throuble the docthor wid it; an' faix, I want to pay thim Chaynee images fur smashin' me crockery! Bedad, an' I will, too, for I've got my hands left all right an' a straight oye, an', I'll have a slap at 'em ag'in, sure, by your leve, sor!'

'Carry on!' cried Mr Stormcock, who had been assisting to wedge up the gun so that it could be still fired, only the carriage having been injured by the shot. 'Make as good practice as you did before, Macan; and, then you'll soon be revenged on some of those beggars!'

'I will that, sor,' replied the corporal, bending down to the rear right of the sixty-four pounder, which had been slewed round in the direction of the battery abreast us, and taking careful aim. 'A ha'porth more illivation, Number 2. Well—muzzle left! Well—fire!'

Bang it went off, making the dirt fly from the embrasure opposite, while a cloud of smoke rose up, as if a magazine had been exploded; and so we continued, hammer and tongs, the atmosphere all sulphur and gunpowder, the deck slippery with gore, our ears deafened with the ceaseless discharges of the guns, till it really seemed 'as if Hell had broken loose!' as Mr Stormcock said.

It was the last sentence the master's mate ever uttered; for a bullet penetrated his brain the next instant, and he dropped down beside me stone dead, almost as soon as the words escaped his lips.

I hardly knew what occurred after that, I was so saddened by the loss of Mr Stormcock, whom I had always found a very good friend to me, for he had taught me a good deal ; and, notwithstanding that I had not taken to him at first, I had since learnt to have a most sincere regard for him, while he on his part, though so much older than myself, liked me, I believe, for he appeared fond of being in my company.

His death, however, only added one more to the long list of those who had already fallen ; while every moment some fresh casualty occurred.

The enemy's fire got hotter as the afternoon wore on and the fight proceeded, until everyone felt the task the admiral had attempted, with his comparatively weak force, in attacking such formidable defences, was doomed to failure ; although not a single man thought of abandoning the struggle or confessing, as was the case, that we were ' licked !'

But, it could not be much further prolonged ; for, at six o'clock, the *Kestrel* had been sunk, fighting her guns to the last, the *Lee* obliged to run on the mud to prevent her meeting a like fate; while the *Plover* and *Opossum*, which were still in the van, had been pretty well knocked out of shape.

The *Cormorant* was ahead of us all, with the sorely wounded admiral lying bleeding in his cot on her deck, our gallant chief persisting in watching the battle to its bitter end, in spite of being compelled from absolute exhaustion to give up the immediate command of the squadron to his senior officer, Captain Shadwell; though it was as much as the gunboat could do to keep her prominent position, in face of the terrible fire on her front and flanks.

To retreat, however, was impossible then, as there

was not water enough in the river for the vessels that still floated to recross the bar before midnight; besides which, if they attempted to move off while daylight lasted, they would be exposed to the risk of greater loss from the terrible fire from the batteries which was certain to be hailed on them.

Under the desperate circumstances of the case, therefore, it was determined by the senior officer, who acted in concert with the other captains present, that a bold stroke should be attempted to save the honour of the day, which was to try and carry the forts by assault—a 'forlorn hope' in every sense of the word!

No sooner was this desperate expedient resolved on than it was gallantly set about, the boats filled with the marines and small-arms men, who yet remained below the barrier at the river mouth being brought to the front—an operation in which we were generously aided by Commodore Tatnall, of the United States steam frigate the *Toeywan*, which had been lying off the Peiho for some time, out of the line of fire.

'Great Scott!' cried this noble-hearted American to his officers as he saw our poor fellows pulling up the heavily-laden launches and cutters against stream, under the withering fire of the batteries, with a sort of dogged resolution, determined to do or die, giving the boats a friendly tow to the nearest point of land and approaching as close as he could to the low, muddy shore on which the rising tide was beginning now to flow again, regardless of any ill consequences to himself or his ship; albeit he was supposed to be a neutral, the Government of the United States not having taken sides with us in the war. 'Blood's thicker than water, boys! Let us lend them a hand. Thunder, they are brother sailors and white men like ourselves!'

CHAPTER XXVIII

THE HARVEST OF DEATH!

NOR did the sympathy of the American commodore cease here; for the boats of the *Toeywan* helped to pick up many of our wounded fellows who were struggling in the water, while a lot of his men, coming alongside one of the gunboats, which had redoubled their fire in order to cover the landing of the assaulting party, climbed on board and 'lent a hand' to man the gun.

The stalwart 'down easters,' when called to order by their officer later on, when leaving this vessel to regain their own ship, excusing themselves for having taken so unneutral a part in the action, on the plea that seeing we were shorthanded and in a tight place, they had done it 'for fellowship sake!'

Most of our fellows were in the attacking column, though neither I nor Larkyns, nor, indeed, any of the other youngsters, were permitted to accompany them, but I can tell of my own knowledge with what wistful eyes we watched their progress from the deck of the little spitfire of a vessel that I was only on board of on sufferance, I having smuggled myself in with Larkyns, who was on duty as midshipman of the launch; for the gunboat had now returned to the barriers further up the river and began hammering again at the batteries,

in order to divert their attention from our field
column, after assisting to bring up a quota of the
force and waiting till they disembarked from the
boats.

Gallantly the little band, a compact mass of six
hundred men, pursued their way through the treacherous mud, night closing in as they struggled onward,
and the darkness only lit by the flashes of our guns
firing over the head of the column at the fortifications in their front ; the Chinese only replying to our
cannonade in a half-hearted fashion, as if they had
got weary of the job, leading us thus to believe that
the 'forlorn hope' had an easy task before it !

But, Larkyns and myself were both deceived, this
sudden quiet on the part of the enemy being really
a ruse ; for, hardly had the column reached firm
ground than the hitherto silent batteries all at once
burst into a sheet of flame, pouring shot and shell,
jinghal balls, rifle bullets, in fact every variety of
deadly missile known in war, on the heads of our
devoted men, at such close quarters, too, that not
one in three escaped the avalanche of destruction !

The Tartar garrison defending the place, we subsequently learnt, used bows and arrows and match-
locks, in addition to the best modern weapons, the
better to discomfit their foes ; 'those vile red devils
of barbarians,' as they called us, who had so rashly
ventured to tackle them at close quarters, thinking
to 'catch a weasel asleep.'

'Oh, Vernon, look, look !' cried Larkyns, as the
gloomy night with its overhanging pall of smoke
from the endless bombardment, which had been going
on ever since mid-day, was lit up by a crimson glow
that enabled us to see every detail of what took place
and even recognise the features of some of our officers.
'See how they are mowed down—not a man of them
will come back alive !'

Saying which, grown lad that he was of seventeen, and courageous and foolhardy to desperation, he burst into tears, the tension on his nerves from the excitement we had all gone through since the early hours of that ill-fated morning having completely unmanned him, making him for the moment a perfect baby!

But I was just as bad; and, to relieve our feelings, we helped the marine gunners, who were pounding away at the rascally Chinese, although we had presently to stay our fire, for fear of hitting friends as well as foes.

The end was not far off now, things shortly coming to a climax.

Half our men fell at the first discharge; but the remainder resolutely rushed on to the broad ditch in front of the bastion, and about a third of these got bravely through this obstruction, some fifty finally reaching the base of the works.

There were no scaling ladders, however, wherewith to climb the steep escarpments, no available reinforcements, for every man jack that could be spared from the gunboats was there, to fill the voids in the ranks which dwindled and dwindled each instant; and so at last, although the handful of heroes who succeeded in getting up to the foremost fort, advancing almost within sight, so to speak, of victory, might possibly have held their own where they were until morning, if they had been allowed to remain, being partly sheltered now by the salient angle of the fortification, our senior officer, perceiving the hopelessness of continuing any longer the unequal contest, ordered 'the retreat' to be sounded.

Then came the most harrowing scene of all.

If the Chinese fire had been hot before, its intensity was increased tenfold as soon as the bugle-call echoed out shrilly between the reports of the heavy guns and fusilade of the musketry, and the remnants of the gallant little band began to fall back on their boats, retiring in wonderful order despite the cruel pelting they received on all sides, not a wounded man being left behind whose life could be saved.

A wonder it was, though, as Larkyns said, that a single soul escaped; for the guns which were aimed at the poor, worn-out fellows as they waded out through the mud to their boats, were now turned on the latter as they got into these, scattering grape as they were massed together, and when the gunboat advanced to their rescue.

'Boom!' came the round shot hopping over them; and 'Bang!' and 'Rattle!' and 'Rattle!' and 'Bang!' they went on incessantly until all were out of range, the boats in tow resembling a funeral procession which, with its weird surroundings, seemed like Holbein's 'Dance of Death.'

It was such a ghastly picture, which those who saw it will never forget.

The lapping water had by this time overflowed the shelving banks of the river, which spread out far beyond its regular bounds into the reedy plains and marshes on either hand, the swollen stream bringing down, as the tide ebbed again towards midnight, the wreckage of the gunboats that had been sunk during the conflict.

Broken spars and the remnants of the destroyed booms floated along, impeding the progress of the craft that had escaped, and blocking the narrow channel where only sufficient depth could be obtained to admit of their passage out to sea; while the corpses of the slain that had fallen overboard floated by similarly on the turbid bosom of the Peiho.

All these baffled our poor fellows who were struggling for their lives when the boats upset, and endeavouring to swim to the steamers, which, on their part, were trying their hardest to get across the bar before it would be too late!

All the time, too, the Manchurian marksmen were busy taking pot-shots at some unhappy survivor wallowing in the mud under the forts, which were firing furiously without a moment's cessation, lighting up the hideous scene on which the dark heavens above, without a star to be seen, looked down in horror.

Of the eleven vessels we had engaged from first to last, three were sunk, four disabled, and three more so much damaged as to require considerable repair subsequently before being again fit for service; while out of a total of eleven hundred men who had started off so gaily in the morning to play their part in this tragic play, our casualties amounted to five hundred, so that not one half ever returned to swing in their respective hammocks again.

'By Jove we have got a thrashing!' said Commander Nesbitt, ruefully, next morning, when Dr Nettleby came to make his report as to the state of the wounded we had and there was a general counting up of losses. 'I didn't think John Chinaman had it in him to make such a stand!'

'Neither did I,' replied Captain Farmer, who was standing by on the poop, looking over the taffrail at the spot made memorable by last night's carnage, though the whilom muddy river appeared bright enough now with the sun shining down on its rippling surface, and no trace of the fight of yesterday visible save the masts of one and part of the hull of another of the sunken gunboats in the distance, and the grim forts staring down on them defiantly, apparently quite uninjured by the pounding they had received. 'They have certainly given us a licking, but they'll have a very heavy reckoning to pay for their temporary triumph by-and-by, Nesbitt, or I am very much mistaken! I suppose you recollect the old proverb, *Hodie mihi, cras tibi?*'

'Can't say I do, sir,' said the commander in answer, scratching his head reflectively as he raised his cap for the purpose, with the object apparently of quickening his memory by that means. 'I'm afraid I've forgotten all my Latin, sir, long since. What does it mean, eh?'

'"To-day it is my turn, to-morrow it may be yours,"' replied Captain Farmer, looking as grim as the Taku Fort as he translated the sentence for the other's benefit. 'The Emperor of China had best bear this in mind, for there'll be a pretty fine kick up, I tell you, when they come to hear of this business in England!'

'You are right there, sir,' agreed Commander Nesbitt. 'There will be a jolly row about it in the papers and in Parliament, I know! But it is none of our fault; we have done nothing to be ashamed of, for we've done our best!

'Ay, though defeated we're not disgraced,' said the captain, as he came down the poop ladder to go into his cabin. 'It's a sad affair, though, a sad affair. We've lost Bitpin and Stormcock and Morgan and that poor lad Jackson amongst the officers killed, besides those wounded, and I can't say yet how many men, but between thirty and forty, I fear!'

'Yes, sir, it is a bad job,' replied the commander, bending his head and looking grave for an instant, but the next moment a bright look came in his face and he shook his fist at the distant forts; 'but we'll pay you out yet, pigtails and all, for this day's work!'

'Let us hope so,' said the captain, as he crossed the quarter-deck and disappeared from view beneath the break of the poop, going into his own cabin to send in his report to our senior officer, Admiral Hope, who was subsequently invalided home, being so dangerously wounded as to be incapable of attending to any other business after forwarding his dispatches home. 'And, the sooner the better, Nesbitt—the sooner the better!'

Both officers judged the feeling of their countrymen well, but quite twelve months elapsed before all our preparations were completed for retaliating on the Chinese and proving to them, in that forcible mode which seemingly only appealed to their reason, that 'the worst piece of work they ever did in their lives was to tread on the tail of the British lion,' as Doctor Nettleby observed to Mr Jellaby in my hearing later on the same day.

CHAPTER XXIX

A GOOD 'DEAL'

IN the meantime, the fleet sailed away from the scene of action, after honourably burying the dead and destroying our sunken vessels; so that the Chinese, who had a weak habit at that time and in later years, too, of indulging in fiction when referring to their martial exploits, should not be able to boast of having captured our ships, the *Candahar* putting in at Hong Kong to refit later on, after visiting Shanghai again on leaving the Gulf of Pechili.

Here Larkyns, who had succeeded poor Mr Stormcock in his office as caterer of the gunroom mess, distinguished himself, quite unwittingly, in a financial operation which gained him the credit of being a very 'smart' fellow indeed in the sense in which our American cousins use the term; besides earning for himself the good opinion of all of us in the gunroom, whom he benefited by the exploit.

It happened in this wise.

Master Larkyns being ashore one day at Victoria, the chief town of Hong Kong, which is built up the side of a hill facing the harbour, noticing a lot of people collected round one of the merchant's stores, asked naturally, midshipman like, 'What the row was about?'

He was told an auction was going on; so, in he went to see the fun, taking much interest in the biddings.

Presently, a hogshead of claret was put up by the auctioneer, and, thinking this a good opportunity for laying in a stock for the mess, as we would be in commission probably in warm latitudes, for the next two or three years, when the wine would come in rather handy, Larkyns listened eagerly for the price and heard it offered at £12.

This seemed a big sum, but, if the worst came to the worst, and his messmates grumbled at his extravagance, he thought, he could pay for it out of his own pocket, he thought; and so, in his impetuous way, he bid £12, 10s., without waiting for anyone to make an offer, which no one doing, his sudden jump having paralysed the brokers present, to his great surprise and joy the wine was knocked down to him at the price he named.

By-and-by, however, his joy was changed to grief; for, the auctioneer asked him for a cheque or a reference, when he found out that, instead of buying a single hogshead of claret, as he believed to be the case on bidding for it, he had purchased a whole consignment of the wine, of which the single specimen offered had been a sample—the transaction involved the outlay of more than £1500, which of course he could never pay, although he had the £12, 10s. he had offered, and a few pounds more in his pocket as well.

Here was a pretty to-do; and, he was just wondering whether he should solve the Gordian knot by cutting and running, when, luckily, a man without a hat rushed in breathlessly from a neighbouring store, and coming up to the auctioneer, asked him if the wine was sold yet.

'You're a bit too late,' replied the master of the rostrum, pointing out Larkyns to his astonished gaze. 'I have just knocked it down to this gentleman.'

'Indeed!' exclaimed the stranger. 'At what?'

'£12, 10s.'

'Ah, that all?' cried the hatless individual; and, turning to Larkyns, he said with an entreating air, 'I'll give you an advance of ten shillings a hogshead if you let me have it.'

Our caterer was quite bewildered.

'I don't mind,' he said at last, looking from the auctioneer to the stranger and back again to his creditor, who stood waiting for the £1500 cheque. 'That is, if this gentleman here is satisfied.'

'Oh, that's all right,' said the auctioneer. 'I know Mr ——, and his word is as good as his bond. He'll give you the difference between your bid and his present offer, and you'll gain something by the deal.'

'By Jove!' cried Larkyns. 'I never thought of that, but I wanted some wine for the mess.'

'I daresay we can manage that,' said the buyer, evidently pleased with his bargain, though had he known of my friend's mistake in time before he made his offer he might not have been so generous. 'I'll tell you what I'll do, I will give you £50 to take over the consignment, and a cask of the wine into the bargain.'

This Master Larkyns readily agreed to, as may be well imagined; and the upshot of the affair was, that our mess funds were £50 richer by this visit of Larkyns to the auction rooms.

This enabled us to live 'like fighting cocks' while we remained in port; and when the wardroom officers chanced to pay us a visit, which I noticed they more frequently did now than formerly, we were able to offer them a glass of claret, which was rather a novelty in those days in the gunroom mess.

After refitting, we went for a cruise to the East Indies, where we found the new admiral who had come out to replace Admiral Hope; and, in the spring of the following year, having served for eighteen months as a naval cadet, I was promoted to the rank of midshipman, the captain and first lieutenant, having convinced themselves of my competency by asking me how I would manage to get a six-pounder to the top of a perpendicular hill, my answer to which question was that I would head it up in a cask and 'parbuckle' it up.

'Glass-eye' smiled rather quizzingly at this, requesting to know what sort of cask I would employ. I settled him at once, however, by saying that a claret cask would do; there having been a joke current of his coming to see how the gunroom was getting on about luncheon time, at the time our wine cellar had been so sumptuously replenished by Larkyns, who, by the way, got his step to acting mate the same month that I was made midshipman.

CHAPTER XXX

IN A BAMBOO CAGE

DURING the interval that had elapsed since our defeat in front of the Taku Forts, to proceed now to more stirring events, the English and French Governments had been organising a joint expedition against China; to demand an apology for the treatment their respective representatives had received, and insist on the stipulations of the historical Treaty of Tientsin being practically, and not merely formally, adhered to.

By the middle of the year 1860, the ten thousand men that comprised the English contingent, under the leadership of Sir Hope Grant, had assembled at Chusan, all ready for the campaign.

They were not joined here by the French under General Montauban, who mustered only seven thousand bayonets, until some weeks later, our allies being very dilatory in their movements.

On the 1st August, this imposing force, a joint army seventeen thousand strong, which was conveyed up the Gulf of Pechili in no less a number than a hundred and twenty transports, escorted by the French and English fleets, that totalled over ninety sail, landed at Pahtang, some ten miles to the north of the Peiho river. Here, their disembarkation was not interfered with, our old friends the Chinese expecting us to make another assault on the Taku

Forts, that had before repulsed us, which they had rendered much stronger in the months that had since elapsed.

But 'once bitten twice shy' was our motto; and, by making a march across country, we defeated a large army, mainly composed of Tartar cavalry, on the way, our redcoats, in company with the battalions of Monsieur Pantalou, made short work of the Chinese 'braves.'

The advance of the allies, indeed, was like a triumphal march; for we reached the rear of the Taku Forts on the night of the 20th August and took the formidable works by storm on the following morning, putting the defenders to flight and revenging our bloody defeat a year and two months after that tragic event.

The English and French forces then pursued their victorious march towards Tientsin, with the intention of penetrating to the capital of the emperor, should their just demands not be conceded without any further delay, as well as a heavy indemnity paid for the expense we had been put to by the evasions and treachery of the Manchurian monarch; but, I am not able to speak of my own knowledge of the further progress of the expedition after they had blown up the old forts and thrown open the entrance to the Peiho.

An adventure happened to me, which not only prevented me from sharing in the campaign, but very nearly put a stop to any possibility of my ever telling this yarn.

This adventure I will now relate.

As soon as the obstructions across the mouth of the river, which had previously foiled us, had been removed by working parties of sailors from the fleet, several gunboats went up to Tientsin by water to make provision for the arrival of the main body who were marching thither by land; and, amongst other officers of the *Candahar*, Ned Anstruther and I were detailed for this duty, proceeding to the port in question with a battery of artillery and military stores, which we had to see to the landing of near the close of the month.

Ned and I were glad of the outing, besides escaping from the routine of the ship, and when we got to Tientsin we strolled about having a look round at the queer-looking shops and shanties, the like of which we had never seen before.

Presently we got to some tea-gardens, where a funny old man, with a yellow hat and a pigtail the size of a small hawser, accosted us.

By signs he invited us to enter a rather nice-looking building, built just like one of those little pagodas resembling cardhouses that you see in the right-hand corner of a willow-pattern plate.

'What a rum old joker!' exclaimed Ned, as the old fellow came up to us. 'Chin, chin, Johnny, what you wantchee, no stoppee can do.'

I laughed at Ned's 'pijin English,' which the Chinaman evidently did not understand; but he bowed courteously and smiled very amiably, throwing open the door of the cardhouse in such a pressingly hospitable way all the while that I could not stand out any longer.

'Hang it all, Ned!' said I, 'let us go in. An old chap like that can't do us any harm; and, besides, we've got the cutter's crew within hail!'

'All right, old chap,' replied Ned, taking the old fellow's arm and leading the way in, while I followed him. 'Here goes.'

The moment, however, that we had entered the flimsy - looking building the door was quickly slammed-to behind us; while a gang of ruffians of the same kidney as the treacherous old scoundrel who had beguiled us, threw Ned and myself on the ground and gagged and pinioned us like a pair of trussed fowls, before we could call out or make a single movement in our own defence.

When they saw that we were properly secured, our uniforms were torn off our backs and a couple of blue cotton shirts, such as the Chinese coolies wear, pulled over our shoulders, as a sort of disguise.

An ugly old pith hat, of the shape of a mushroom, was then jammed down on the tops of our unfortunate heads; and we looked at one another in wonder as to what would come next.

We were not long in suspense.

The old chap, who was evidently a person of authority, shouted out some loud order or other, which sounded more like a pig grunting under a gate than any language I had previously heard spoken, there being a strong swinish flavour in the Chinese lingo, as about their fields, which Ned Anstruther and I had smelt coming along on our unlucky walk!

He had evidently given some order to the attendants; for, no sooner had he finished grunting than a couple of rum things somewhat like the palanquins I had seen when at Bombay, were brought in and put down in front of us.

They were, really, cages made of bamboo, and which only criminals are confined in, as I afterwards found out.

Into these, Ned and I were thrust separately, one in each.

We were then lifted up by the poles attached to our novel sort of conveyance, two men carrying mine and two more lifting Ned's 'trap'—I know I felt very much like what a mouse does when caught in one, for I was caged with a vengeance—they trotted off with us, through a back door, and then along a wide, country road, I knew not whither!

CHAPTER XXXI

WE could not talk together, for the very good reason that our mouths were gagged, nor could we see each other now, poor consolation as that would have been ; although possibly a friendly wink from Ned might have cheered me up a bit under the circumstances, the idea preying on my mind that it was owing to my fault in persuading him to enter into the treacherous ambuscade that we had been thus entrapped.

But whatever Anstruther's reflections might have been I had no means of knowing, as our bearers trotted onwards with his bamboo palanquin abreast of mine, both of our craft making good headway ; the artful, yellow - hatted old scoundrel who had so successfully planned our capture bringing up the rear of the procession and grunting away at a fine rate behind.

He was mounted on a diminutive pony, which he straddled in a clumsy fashion, his legs almost touching the ground ; while a parasol he held aloft in one hand nearly poked my eyes out when he came up every now and then alongside my cage, to see that I was there all right and had not wriggled out of my bonds since his last inspection.

If I could not speak, like the monkeys in the Zoological Gardens, I thought the more ; all sorts of curious fancies continually coming into my head as we were thus borne along.

For one thing, I was not in the least frightened about my fate; for, as the old chap had not killed us at the first start off, it occurred to me that he had merely taken us prisoners with the view of getting a heavy ransom for us by-and-by, being led to the belief that we might be important personages on account of his seeing us followed after we landed from the gunboat, by the cutter's crew.

Our stalwart bluejackets appeared to his little, rat eyes, no doubt, like the retinue of a mandarin with a peacock's feather in his tail at the least; and this impression had, probably, been confirmed by the fact of our being such young fellows, which was a proof of what 'big' men we would be when grown up!

Thinking this, I was in no ways alarmed.

On the contrary, I chuckled greatly when I recollected what a widely different value the captain or first lieutenant would attach to a couple of harum-scarum midshipmen to the estimation in which this wily old kidnapper evidently held us; glorying in the great sell awaiting him when he came in his bland innocence to exchange our poor carcases for hard cash!

This anticipation so pleased me, that I began to interest myself in the scenes through which we passed to our as yet unknown destination.

The one great drawback to my enjoyment of this amusement was that there was precious little to look at, the country being flat and dreary in the extreme, and consisting apparently of an endless plain, dotted here and there with heaps of earth, like mud-pies magnified, with the black Peiho serpentining through it in its snake-like curves.

Such are the surroundings of Tientsin, which means 'A heavenly spot!'

Burying places we met with at regular intervals, for we could easily tell what they were from the ends of the square box coffins peeping out of the soil that only half covered them, while the bones of the departed frequently covered the earthy track our conductors traversed, which it would have been a vile libel to have called a road.

Occasionally, we came near a collection of huts, with conical roofs resembling the form of the extinguisher usually employed in connection with a bedroom candlestick.

'Yellow hat,' however, would not allow the palanquin bearers to stop at any of these villages, as I supposed the huts represented, our procession not coming to a halt until late in the afternoon; when, on arriving at a place which, in addition to these huts had a pagoda or josshouse, the old rascal grunted a little louder than usual to our bearers and they set down our cages in front of a cardhouse of the same description as that at Tientsin where we had been so nicely 'taken in and done for,' as Macan would have expressed it in his Irish vernacular.

The gags were then dragged, in no very gentle way, from our mouths, and our hands and feet untied, and the leader of the party, in a more piglike squeak than ever, ordered us to come out of our very uncomfortable quarters.

We thought he meant this at least, from the violent gesticulations he made, waving his arms wildly and hopping about as if he were a parched pea on a griddle; for, of course, we could not make out his gibberish though he squealed and grunted at us at a fine rate!

'I suppose he means us to get out,' said Ned Anstruther, glad to be able to use his tongue again; 'but I can't, I'm so cramped.'

'Nor can I, old fellow,' I rejoined. 'I'm as stiff as a boiled lobster and couldn't move to salute the admiral if he came along.'

'I wish to goodness he would,' cried Ned. 'Ay, and with a file of marines at his back, too. Wouldn't I like to shoot this treacherous old scoundrel, ay, or string him up to the top of that pagoda there!'

'So would I too, Ned,' I replied heartily. 'But, I don't think the yellow rascal means us any harm ; at all events, not at present, old fellow. See, he's actually getting us something to eat, I think.'

'Some nasty mess or other, no doubt,' growled Ned, chafing one of his legs and then stretching it out. 'By Jove, though, I'm beginning to get some life in my limbs again, but these blessed cords they tied us with stopped my circulation. Here goes!'

So saying, he made an attempt to scramble up, and the old fellow, who had approached us with a big bowl of rice in both hands, put this down on the ground and gave my companion a lift, afterwards extending the same courtesy to myself.

We then stretched our cramped legs a bit; and, presently, sat down on the outside of our bamboo cages, instead of inside them, being comparatively free.

But, from the way in which the bearers who had carried us, and some other fellows with bows and arrows and broad-bladed knives in their belts, closed round us at the word of command from 'yellow hat,' we would have fared ill had we attempted just then to give him and his retainers 'leg-bail.'

We saw this at a glance ; so, making the best of a bad business, we commenced pegging into the rice the old fellow now handed us, which we did not find at all bad eating.

It was very well cooked, and besides had a bit of salt fish of some sort on the top of the bowl, which we smelt at intervals, being too small to bite, so as to make the main contents of the dish more appetising.

'Not bad,' commented Ned, after taking a preliminary mouthful of it for a taste, delving out the rice with his fingers, no spoon or fork being provided, and the chopsticks *à la Chinoise* furnished with the bowl being useless to us from our not being accustomed to their proper manipulation. 'Better served up, too, than we ever got on board!'

'Yes; I've tasted worse,' said I. 'They've cut us rather short with the fish, though, Ned. I think they might have served out enough for a fellow to put his teeth through.'

'Perhaps the old chap can't afford it, you know, Jack; and yet, he doesn't look badly off. That hat of his would fetch something in an old curio shop, and so would his breeches too. By Jove, they're big and baggy enough for a Dutchman twice his size.'

At this we both laughed, whereupon the old chap, thinking we did so in high appreciation of his viands, smiled and nodded, patting his fat stomach and saying in his guttural tones, 'Bono, Johnny, goot—goot!'

'By Jove!' exclaimed Ned, quite startled. 'You speak English?'

'Mi one piecee can do,' replied the other, with a broader smile that made him look quite venerable, the deceitful old wretch! 'No goodee number one chop!'

'Oh, you can speak it well enough,' replied Ned, as our friend said this in 'Pijin English,' implying that although he could manage a little of our language he was not a first-rater at it. 'What wantchee can do, my one two?'

Ned pointed at the same time towards me, and then indicated himself, requesting in this idiotic jargon to be informed of our fate.

'Yellow hat's' reply was not of a reassuring

character, although he uttered no word. What he did was, to draw the forefinger of his dirty hand across his throat in the most unpleasant manner.

Ned shuddered at this; and, I confess, so did I.

Seeing the effect his gesture had produced, the old chap, smiling affably, proceeded to justify the extreme course he had suggested.

'Yang—Keitze catchee one Chinaman, one piecee shootee chop chop,' he argued, on the retaliatory principle, which, of course, held good in war, although no comfort to us at the moment. 'Chinaman one piecee catchee Yang-kei-tze, mi takee Pekin.'

'And what will be done with us there?'

The old scoundrel answered this question in the same mode as before; his action being if possible even more expressive.

'I say, Ned, show him a dollar or two,' I said, not liking his humbly suggestive way of stating that we were going to be taken to Pekin and there beheaded —at least that was what I gathered from the conversation. 'Perhaps he'll be open to silver reason if we argue on the other side of the question?'

Ned pulled a handful of money out of his pocket, at the sight of which the old chap's little eyes glistened and he smiled more genially; but, he shook his head.

'No one piecee take can do,' he said sorrowfully, as if it went to his heart to refuse it. 'Talkee, talkee no bono, mi takee Pekin chop chop, Yang-kei-tze catchee one piecee by by.'

He then turned away to give some order to the men, and Ned seized the opportunity of his being out of earshot to speak to me.

'I think he's open to argument, Jack,' he said encouragingly, seeing I looked rather glum at the prospect before us now, although I had been so light-hearted before, not thinking things were going to turn out so badly as they now appeared. 'The old chap, as you can see for yourself, with all those soldiers about him, must keep up his reputation as a bloodthirsty foe to all foreigners; or else, he'd lose his billet as a mandarin and have that rum old tile of his taken from him! But, he tipped me a wink, Jack; didn't you see him? That means business, and tells me as plain as a pikestaff that he's open to be bribed to get us off by-and-by, although he is forced to take us first to Pekin. They want as many of us as they can catch, you know, to show to their blessed emperor as a proof of their having licked us again, and "wiped out" all the red devils—that's what Yang-kei-tze, means, "red devils," though it sounds very like Yankee! Ain't that so, old chappie, and don't you agree?'

He jingled the money which he still held in his hand, addressing his last remark to our friend 'yellow hat,' who had approached us again after conferring with his men; and, catching the sound, he nodded his head and gave Ned a perceptible wink, as if he thoroughly understood what he had said, and would be our friend—for a consideration!

The bearers then coming up, the old chap motioned us to take our places in the bamboo cages, although he did not offer to gag or bind us again; when, on our being seated, our travelling prisons were raised to the men's shoulders and we resumed our journey.

CHAPTER XXXII

ON THE ROAD TO PEKIN

As we got further up the countryside, we saw numbers of gardens full of peach trees, the fruit of which was plentiful enough, with an occasional poplar grove, the usual decoration of a cemetery; while the villages became more frequent, too, and more populous, one meeting us almost at every mile.

The people that we met, however, received us in a very puzzling fashion, coming round our cages to look at us, as if we were so many wild animals, and roaring with laughter at our appearance; even the very babies crowing with merriment on our being pointed out to them by their fond parents, much to Ned's disgust, although I joined in with their hilarity, it was really so hearty and catching!

That night we all slept together in one of the inns along the road, where, although the bed-place was fixed, it had plenty of moving tenants before our arrival; and, I'm sorry to say, we carried off a few of them when we went away in the morning, and suffered in consequence.

But beyond this little personal matter, which is a mere detail to anyone travelling in China, and the staring of the inhabitants, we did not suffer much inconvenience during our journey, the old fellow in charge of us giving us the best food he could get, in the shape of rice and eggs, the latter of which were sometimes in such a state of perfection that they deserved to have been promoted to the rank of poultry ; and, on the third day after leaving Tientsin, although the distance between the two places must be eighty or ninety miles, we saw the walls of Pekin in front of us.

So our guide, the old chap, told us, at least ; but, although the sight of this celestial city is asserted by the Chinese to 'strike awe' into the beholder on first sighting it, we should not have known we were gazing on such an imposing object as the capital of China undoubtedly is !

On closing up with the town, we passed a collection of tombs with stone tortoises carrying memorial tablets on their backs, and other signs of mourning, and a josshouse; and we soon after this entered Pekin by a granite causeway over a tumble-down bridge, passing for some distance along, the massive walls, which were some fifty feet in height and of equal thickness.

'Yellow hat' was evidently anxious to keep us as private as possible ; for, he hurried the bearers through the streets, which, though dirty, were wide, and the buildings on either side, with their roofs of glazed yellow tiles and fronts all carved and gilded, looked showy enough in the sunshine.

It was like a panorama, being thus carried through these strange streets, with the people stopping to look at us, but not behaving at all rudely, although our army must have been known to be marching on the capital ; and Ned and I absolutely enjoyed it, noting as we sailed past the temples and curio shops and pagodas and all, the constant stream of umbrella-bearing passers-by and the fact that nearly all the old men held birds in their hands tied on to sticks, looking just like those wooden monkeys which pedlars hawk about at home for the delectation of rustic juveniles.

'Yellow hat' told us subsequently, with reference to this curious picture of their domestic life, that it was the custom of the country so to take out their pet canaries and other little songsters for an airing, instead of lapdogs.

These they reserve for their pies and other choice dishes.

Ned and I seemed to pass through miles of real nightmares as we went along, the people and their surroundings having an air of unreality.

The only things about Pekin we thought genuine were the smells, which were something awful; as we learnt from bitter experience during our four weeks' captivity here, locked up in a cell with all the common criminals, and, I believe, all the vermin of the city.

Somehow or other, the old man had mysteriously disappeared after leaving us at a quiet inn in the Tartar quarter, where, as well as we could understand him, we were to remain until he had a chance of communicating with the approaching English force to have us ransomed.

'Chin, chin!' he said to Ned as he left us. 'Mi go one piecee and yo waittee; Fanqui comee one piecee by by.'

The next day, instead of his coming back again, a file of rough Tartars belonging to Prince Sankoliu-sin's army rushed into the room where we were, and throwing us roughly on the floor, proceeded to strip us of everything we had about us, leaving us only our shirts, which were rather ragged by this time and not in a condition to do our laundress credit!

We were, after this, cruelly tied with ropes that cut our wrists and ankles, and then dragged to prison, where we remained until one day we heard the booming of guns in the distance.

'Good heavens, Jack!' cried poor Ned, who was by this time the wreck of his former self, and whom nobody on board the ship certainly would have recognised, 'Those must be Armstrongs! I know the sound of them too well. Thank God, our comrades now are near at last to release us or revenge us!'

Later on, the same day, some Chinese soldiers entered, instead of the usual Tartar guard which we had seen since we had been in this hole; and these, putting chains round our necks, marched us off, as we thought, to execution.

'Good-bye, Ned, old fellow, if they separate us,' said I. 'Should you escape, please tell my old Dad about me, and the people at home.'

'Nonsense, Jack,' he replied, trying to laugh it off. 'If we die, we'll die together. But, I should like to pay out old "yellow hat" first. By Jove, I should like to see him now!'

Talk of—angels!

At that every moment, as we were passing through a narrow stone passage beneath the walls of the city, as we judged from their height, the very individual of whom Ned had been speaking the instant before appeared on the scene; and, all I can say is, that if we had thought him the reverse of an angel previous to his coming, we were, on the contrary, inclined to believe him to be the genuine article as soon as he told us his errand!

It was to release us, and take my poor emaciated and ragged comrade and myself to the English camp.

Then it was that we heard the news that had happened since our imprisonment.

Sir Hope Grant, with the French troops under Montauban, had fought their way up to Yuen-ming-Yuen, the Summer Palace of the emperor.

This place, I may mention, was subsequently burnt

to the ground by the English, after the French had
looted it and carried off more than a million's worth
of plunder, leaving only the husks of the spoil for our
gallant men, who had done all the hard work of the
campaign !

The Summer Palace was burnt, I should explain,
as a punishment for the cruel murder by the Chinese
of a number of our officers and men, as well as poor
Mr Boulby, the special correspondent of the *Times*,
all of whom had been taken prisoners and tortured to
death, though at the time they were under the protection of a flag of truce !

Our troops had pretty well paid out the Chinese
before this, however ; their infantry being annihilated
and the Tartar cavalry of Prince Sanko-liu-sin
'doubled up' by our dragoons.

This news 'yellow hat' told us on our way to the
English camp opposite to the Anting gate to the
north of the city, explaining that the reason we had
not seen him before was that he had gone away
trying to open communications with our friends, and
that he had made arrangements that no harm should
befall us in his absence.

'It didn't look much like it, though, half-an-hour
ago!' said I, on Ned's translating this to me, his
knowledge of Chinese, originally pretty good, having
increased considerably during our long detention
amongst our criminal companions of the prison.
'That ugly beggar next me seemed just about to
slice off your head like a carrot when he turned up.'

'Better late than never, old chap,' said Ned, with a
grin. 'He mightn't have turned up at all!'

The next moment, we passed a couple of men of
the Royals who were doing out-post duty; and, ere
we could realise the fact almost, we were amongst
friends and comrades once more !

This was on the 10th October, on which day Sir

Hope Grant sent a demand to the Chinese authorities that unless the Anting gate was surrendered by the 13th, or in three days' time, the city would be bombarded.

The morning of the 13th came, but the Chinese were still unyielding ; so, the guns in front of the fortifications were sponged out and run back ready for loading, with the gunners standing by awaiting the order to fire.

Every heart beat high with expectation, and it looked as if we were going to have a last fight of it ; when, just on the minute of the hour fixed for the ultimatum to expire, the gates were thrown open and the defences of the city surrendered to the English army.

Another minute, and the Union Jack was floating over the walls of Pekin.

The rest is a matter of history.

CHAPTER XXXIII

'HULLO, Bamboo Jack!' cried Larkyns, as I came up the side of our old ship again after a tedious voyage down the Peiho in one of the gunboats, accompanied by Ned Anstruther, my comrade not merely in arms but in captivity. 'Chin, chin, my hearty, I'm delighted to see you and Ned safe and sound, after all your wanderings and wonderful adventures, which a little bird, not caged, though, has told us of! Come below, now, to the gunroom, old chap, and have "one piecee chow chow," and spin us a yarn about it all yourself. It seems like old times seeing your ugly old phiz once more, by Jove!'

All the other fellows, too, appeared quite as pleased to see us both back, except that surly brute Andrews, who looked as if he wished the Chinese had made puppy pies of Ned and myself.

Truth to say, I was jolly glad myself to be on board again with my messmates, amid the old familiar scenes and surroundings.

Indeed, when swinging in my hammock the first night after my return, I fancied all that occurred was but a dream—so it seemed to my heated imagination —and that I had never left the *Candahar* for a day, nor passed through such exciting experiences!

T

A week or so later, after all the details of our treaty with the Chinese Government had been settled, and Lord Elgin departed from Pekin on his way to Europe on the conclusion of his highly successful mission, we likewise weighed anchor before the Gulf of Pechili should be closed by the ice and our egress therefrom barred for the winter months; and then, bidding a long farewell to the poetically-named but 'beastly hole of a place,' as Mr Jellaby called it, the 'Bay of the Wide-spreading-sand Islands,' we sailed for Hong Kong.

Here we arrived at the end of November, the north-east monsoon being all in our favour, and the current along the coast as well; both these favouring causes making the old *Candahar* travel as if 'Old Nick' was after her.

None of us were sorry to be amongst an English-speaking community once more, with its attendant advantage of our being able to procure most of the comforts and luxuries of civilised life, for our commissariat was in the most deplorable condition.

My friend Larkyns, able caterer of the mess as he had hitherto proved himself to be from the date of his deposing poor Mr Stormcock up to our going to the Peiho, was at his wits' end to replenish our sadly-depleted larder, which brought on the head of the unfortunate Dobbs every day at dinner more abuse than even the long-suffering steward could well bear.

The fact was, really, fish and rice were the only articles of food to be obtained to diversify our stock fare of pickled pork and salt horse from the neighbour-ing inhabitants of this northern portion of the domain of the Ruler of the Universe, and Emperor of the Sun, Moon and Stars; for our French allies had so bullied and plundered all the Celestials in the immediate vicinity on the seaboard that those dwelling in the interior, where provisions of all sorts was quite plentiful, were too frightened of the ferocious and light-fingered Gauls to care to come forward with their goods—although, we invariably paid for all we had from the natives in good, sound dollars, the reverse of the practice of Messieurs Achille and Jules of the Chasseurs á Pied who generally reimbursed 'ces pauvres bêtes des Chinois' for what they unceremoniously appropriated, with true Parisian deviltry, 'in kind' of the most unkindly description!

Under these circumstances, the gourmands of the gunroom were most unfeignedly delighted at abandoning such an inhospitable region as that of 'The Widespreading-sand Island,' where they had to starve in the midst of plenty; so likewise was I, the only thing which I had to thank our sojourn off the province of Shan-tung for being the nickname Larkyns gave me in his sportive fancy on my return on board from Pekin after my imprisonment.

This was, certainly, nothing to be proud of; and yet, such is the incongruity of things, the sobriquet stuck to me from that day to this, following me about from ship to ship while I have been on active service.

Some fellow, whom I had never previously seen in my life, perhaps, or knew from Adam, accosts me immediately on hearing my proper patronymic, with a sudden lighting up of face and hand outstretched as if I were an old friend. 'Oh, yes; why, I've heard of you before, I think, old chap! Ain't you Bamboo Jack, eh?'

This, of course, is extremely gratifying, illustrating the truth of the adage, which my poor old Dad used to quote to me frequently enough, that 'More people know Tom Fool than Tom Fool knows!'

We all of us enjoyed our long stay at Hong Kong, accordingly, the *Candahar* having a thorough ove.-haul and refit with the rest of the fleet, now that the campaign was over; for, the residents were accordingly hospitable and kind to us, including the principal merchants of the place and the government officials, as well as the military stationed at Kowloon on the mainland opposite, where there was a large camp—all of them keeping open house, where we were welcomed at all hours, dinners, balls, picnics and all sorts of festivities being the order of the day while we remained in Victoria Bay.

Our ship, however, nearly left her bones behind her here during a terrific typhoon that sprang up of a sudden, on the eve of our departure; when all the junks and fishing-boats in the harbour were wrecked, besides several trading vessels and most of the flimsier of the buildings ashore demolished.

We dragged our anchors in the very height of the storm, although we were moored securely with both bowers down ; and, it was only by good seamanship and the active exertions of all hands that we escaped, cutting our cables and putting to sea for safety, so as to let the old barquey brave it out on her own element, which she gallantly did.

When we were all ataunto again, we sailed for Bombay, whither the admiral had preceded us; and from thence, after a grand entertainment at the celebrated Biculla Club, we were despatched on detached service, spending the summer months in cruising up the Persian Gulf and about the Indian Ocean hunting up pirates and Arab slave dhows, in pursuit of which we ran down the East African coast as far as the Mozambique Channel.

We captured a lot of slavers, laden with cargoes of poor wretches that, but for our release of them, would have spent the remainder of their days in picking cloves at Pemba, or serving the Egyptians like the Israelites of old ; and, giving a look in at Zanzibar, we handed over our prizes, for each of which we had a bounty of so much per head on the slaves captured, besides the value of the dhows we did not destroy.   We then returned to Bombay whence we were ordered back to the China station, making our old port, Hong Kong, again at the beginning of spring in the following year.

From here, in company with the admiral and most of our fleet in the eastern seas at that time, we paid a visit to each of the Treaty Ports, which, mainly through the efforts of England, had been thrown open to the commerce of the world, and by which not only has the Manchester cotton spinner and Birmingham hardware dealer profited, but the empire of China herself and her people.

CHAPTER XXXIV

HOMEWARD BOUND

IT was getting on for the expiration of the fourth year of our commission, when we had finished this tour and we paid a last visit to Hong Kong, before going on to Singapore to await our relief from England.

Here, having been over three years a midshipman and being specially recommended for promotion by Captain Farmer, there being three captains in port to constitute our examining board, according to the Admiralty regulations, I passed for lieutenant; whereupon, I was given an acting commission as mate until my return home, when, on getting my certificates in gunnery and steam at the Naval College, I would be entitled to my epaulets—the which, I may here state, I ultimately obtained in due course.

At Singapore, we sweltered from the month of April, when our relief was due, up to June without her even putting in an appearance; and, we were all beginning to believe she had gone down to 'Davy Jones's locker' and that we were never going to be relieved at all, when one fine morning, as our hearts were getting sick within us, the ship was sighted in the offing.

I don't think I can ever forget the excitement and

enthusiasm aroused on board as the news became known, and on her coming up with the sea breeze at breakfast-time everybody seemed to go mad with joy, the officers shaking hands with each other all round and the men crowding the rigging and cheering the *Daphne* as she passed up to her anchorage inside of us.

That very same afternoon, being all ready and waiting, we sailed from Singapore for the Cape, 'homeward bound.'

What a night that was down below in the gunroom.

Although it was not Saturday evening, when our weekly sing-song was usually celebrated, youngsters and oldsters alike united with a common impulse to have a general hullabaloo, their efforts resulting in such a row as never had been heard, I believe, on board the old *Candahar* before, and, I am equally positive, has not been equalled since, even after she became a harbour ship and was reduced to her present condition of 'Receiving Hulk.'

I can fancy I see the scene now before me as I write these last lines of my yarn.

There were Larkyns and Ned Anstruther, both of whom, like myself, had passed through the chrysalis stage of midshipmen and came within the category of oldsters, the one with a banjo, and the other handling a broken-down concertina, very wheezy about the gills; with little Tommy Mills, who was only a 'midshipmite' still, in every sense of the word, accompanying them with a rattling refrain from a pair of ivory castanets which he had purchased for a paper dollar in a curio shop at Canton.

All the rest of the fellows were shouting out at the pitch of their voices, as only middies and mates and

such-like fry can shout, the chorus of the old sailors'
song :—

> 'We'll rant and we'll roar like true British sailors,
> We'll rant and we'll roar all on the salt seas,
> Until we strike soundings in the Channel of Old England ;
> From Ushant to Scilly 'tis thirty-five leagues !

Those on the deck above, however, did not wait
until we had arrived 'in soundings'; for, just as the
song was being repeated by acclamation for the
third time, the chorus getting louder and louder
after each repetition, Sergeant Macan, as he now
was, having gained his extra stripes soon after his
reinstatement as corporal for his gallantry in the
assault on the Taku Forts, appeared at the door
of the gunroom in his old fashion, being yet re-
tained by express permission as Dr Nettleby's
factotum.

'Plaize, yer 'onner,' said he, addressing Larkyns,
who was still caterer of the mess and the senior
in rank of those present, as he was twanging
away at his banjo with infinite zest, 'the docthor
sez if ye can't be aisy he axes ye to be as aisy as
ye can.'

An uproarious shout was all the answer he
got; and, grinning from ear to ear, he retreated,
only to be succeeded by the master-at-arms,
who came down to put out the lights by the
commander's orders, when those who had not
to go on night duty turned in and peace was
restored.

Sailing with the south-west monsoon, we did not
have so speedy a passage homeward as we did
when outward bound, but we made way southward
as well as we could, close hauled, and reached the
Cape two months after passing through Java
Heads.

At Simon's Bay we refitted ship and took in fresh supplies; and while we remained getting these latter on board several old friends came to see us from Cape Town.

Amongst these was no other than Don Ferdinando Olivarez, who told us he had given up the sea as a profession.

He still adventured on the deep, however, despite his memorable experiences of its perils; for, he said, he had to voyage about a good deal from port to port in the prosecution of his new avocation as the agent for a large firm of wine exporters at Cadiz, where he lived when at home, being now married.

At Captain Farmer's request, Don Olivarez took passage with us to Madeira; and while on board with us made himself, if possible, better liked than before.

All of us parted with him with regret when he left us at Funchal, where we put in to land him and correct an error in our chronometers, which had gone wrong from an accident resulting from a violent thunderstorm we fell in with when crossing the Equator for the last time, in which the ship got struck by the lightning, when the captain's cabin, where the chronometers were kept, was seriously damaged by the electric fluid.

From Madeira to England we had fair winds and fine weather, crossing the Bay of Biscay, which had given us so much trouble going out, with all our kites flying and the wind well in the quarter, which made all the old hands say that the 'Portsmouth girls had got hold of our tow-rope.'

Talking of the men, Master 'Downy,' the ex-gravedigger, although he had been scraped into something of a sailor in appearance in the time he had been afloat, now nearly five years, in which period, by the way, he had accumulated enough prize money to more than discharge the debts he had left behind on quitting his country, could never be taught to be smart in his movements, always going about the deck as if he were engaged at a funeral.

One day, a wag on the forecastle, as we heard through the marine sentry, took a good rise out of this slow-going individual.

' Hi, Downy!' said he, seeing him creeping forward, with his eyes bent down, counting the planks, apparently. 'Chips, the carpenter's mate, wants to see you, sonny.'

'See me?' repeated the other, wonderingly. 'What does he want to see me for?'

'Why,' said the other, 'he wants to measure you for your coffin. He says you're more'n half dead already, cos you crawls about like a cripple. Only you're so bloomin' lazy, you'd die out and out at once and be chucked overboard comfortable like!'

Downy did not make any reply to this, which was an acknowledgment of his having the worst of it, as he was generally credited with possessing the gift of the gab and not easily silenced.

Another queer old stick came to the sick bay complaining of being ill, notwithstanding that he looked hale and hearty.

'What's the matter with you?' asked Dr Nettleby, in his sharp, incisive manner, which had not grown any milder from his sojourn in the China Sea and an attack of liver complaint. 'You seem all right, my man.'

' I've got overhand knots in my gaffs, sir.'

'What on earth do you mean?' cried the doctor, puzzled by the name of this new disease.

'Overhand knots in your gaffs—why, you must be drunk!'

'No, sir, I ain't,' replied the old sailor, soberly enough, holding out his hands, which were twisted about, the fingers resembling the strands of a rope overlaying each other, and the knuckles distorted out of shape. 'My spars, sir, refuses duty.'

He had very aptly described his complaint, although it might not be similarly designated in any medical dictionary.

The poor fellow was suffering from rheumatism!

CHAPTER XXXV

'PAID OFF!'

BUT it is time to bring this long yarn of mine to a close.

It was a fine, bright day, in the early part of October, that we hove the ship to for soundings, our observations then showing us that we were near Scilly and closing the land; so, on getting sand and shells at five-and-thirty fathoms, which proved that we were well within the Chops of the Channel, we squared away our mainyard before a brisk sou'-west breeze and made for the Lizard, which we sighted at Four Bells in the forenoon watch.

We then bore up Channel direct, and, the wind holding fair, we passed St Catharine's Point next morning; saluting the port admiral on our rounding Bembridge Ledge and anchoring at Spithead somewhere about midday.

'By jingo!' cried Mr Jellaby, who was now our first lieutenant, having gained a step by the promotion of our former chief officer, 'glass-eye'; though most of the old officers who had sailed with me from England paid off in the ship with us, there having been few changes in our complement, whether through death, disease or desertion, beyond the losses we had experienced in our unsuccessful attack on the Taku Forts, and from the subsequent sickness we had aboard when we were up the Gulf of Pechili in the hot season. 'How jolly glad I shall be to see the general's daughters again, young Vernon; what chawming gurls they were, to be sure! I do hope they're not all married!'

'Indeed, sir?' said I, interrogatively. 'I hope they're not, I'm sure, for your sake, if not for their own. But, I'm not thinking, now of any young ladies, sir. I'm looking forward to seeing my dear old Dad again, and my mother and sister.'

'Ah, that's what you say now, my boy,' he retorted, with his genial laugh. 'But, when your whiskers are grown, like mine, you'll be thinking of some other fellow's sister, I bet.'

His surmise might have been correct; though all I need add on this point is that my old friend 'Joe' is now an admiral, with grown-up daughters of his own, and from his austere manner no one would ever dream of his susceptible nature and flirtive disposition in the days of which I speak.

Not so Larkyns, who is the same sprightly, merry fellow as of old, albeit his hair is streaked with grey, and the crowsfeet winkle in the corners of his eyes when he laughs, as he is ever doing.

But, my dear old Dad, who came on board the ship to see me while she was at Spithead, without waiting for her to go into harbour, he, like 'Poor Tom Bowling' of the song, has now 'gone aloft;' my mother following him, within an early date of his departure to that bourne whence no traveller returns.

Gone where I hope to meet them both by-and-by; for, I can honestly say, that, beyond trying to do my duty when wearing Her Majesty's uniform, I have considered myself always as serving 'Under the Pen'ant' of even a higher power, and hope, perhaps, to earn a crown like that which I know my poor father strove for ever, when I come also to my last anchorage.

Ay, even as our dead laureate has sung in his deathless verse :—

> ' For tho' from out our bourne of Time and Place
>   The flood may bear me far,
>   I hope to see my Pilot face to face
>   When I have crost the bar.'

THE END

Colston & Coy., Limited, Printers, Edinburgh.